THE STONE THIEVES

AND THE HONOURABLE
ORDER OF INVENTORS

~ AUGMENTED EDITION ~

Eddy Telviot

FOREWORD BY TERRI TATCHELL

CONCEPT ART COMMISIONED
BY NEILL BLOMKAMP

WWW.FABULOUSATOMS.COM

ISBN: 9798427954976

Social Media

For my wonderful friends and family.
Thank you.

Concilio et Labore

When They come, it will not be in mighty vessels.
No host shall darken the skies,
for They shall not descend from the heavens.
Cities will not crumble or burn,
when all the voices fall silent.
There will be no destruction. No war.
Not even a whimper shall be heard.
For They shall come swiftly, from the shadows.
Of single mind and purpose, the Darkest of Tides,
Cleansing us from this refuge, finally and for all time.

FOREWORD
BY TERRI TATCHELL

By now, you've figured out that some moments in life, you get to keep forever. Generally, these moments involve beginnings or endings. Special ones. Ones that affect or alter your life experience either positively or negatively. I find it interesting that we can only recognize these moments in hindsight. I wonder, if you knew you were embarking on one of these life-altering positive beginnings – would you want to know? If the answer is yes, stick with me for a few more paragraphs, and I'll share what my experience has been. If not, turn the page to the story's beginning, pretend we've never met and enjoy the journey ahead on our own terms!

Okay – you "want to knowers" are with me! And if you could see me now, you would see I am grinning ear to ear, rubbing my hands together in anticipation. Eager anticipation. Because I know that you are at one of those "keep-forever" moments as you open this book. You are at the beginning of a story journey that I believe will define a decade, span mediums and inspire generations to come. The characters, ideas and world which lies ahead will thrill you, surprise you, comfort you, challenge you and above all, expand your concept of what truth is. And the best part? It's going to be fun!

Bold claims for sure, but I've read this book from cover to cover more than once. I've listened to the audiobook and imagined the adaptation. I know this book. But more than that, I've been privy to what comes next. And trust me when I say there is no one but the creator that can envision that. It is mind-blowing. And he's done it all for us.

I am honoured to be writing this intro and spent a while considering what would best serve you, the reader. There was the inclination to delve into just how smart and well-researched it is. How the science is real while seeming fantastical all at once. There were the characters. The inventions. The historical, literary and scientific references. The heartbreak, the coming-of-age angst and of course, the twists and turns you won't see coming. But ultimately, I decided that it is in your best interest to jump in without knowing where you are going. I haven't given anything specific up, and a few pages in, you'll see for yourself. This is unquestionably one of those special beginnings that you will get to keep forever.

Happy reading,
Terri

Terri Tatchell is an Oscar-nominated screenwriter and author
of the Endangered and Misunderstood books series

In an old car on a litter-strewn street sat the most remarkable man who had ever lived.

Through the dirty windscreen, he stared at a Royal Mail post box. Like everything else in this neighbourhood it was worn out, its flaking skin of old flyers barely covering tacky graffiti. The flap was bolted shut; the post box closed for business.

Or so it seemed.

The car door groaned, strained and stuck. But with a bump of his elbow the warped panel popped free. A carnival of debris sought to entangle the man's legs, yet his eyes never left the red post box, his fingers worrying at the edges of two neatly addressed envelopes.

From his pocket, he drew a magnet. A very special magnet comprised of pieces that had been scattered across the globe.

The man placed the magnet carefully on the side of the post box and twisted it forty-five degrees, then ninety degrees counter-clockwise. He moved his hand exactly five inches up and rotated it again. Then he pushed the magnet horizontally, snagging the posters; another twist, a well-rehearsed slide, and the post box came to life.

The battered red top rose an inch, revealing a band of polished metal. In the centre were three dials: day, month and year. It was set to the first of January 1654.

Beside the dials, carefully etched into the metal, was a coat of arms with the words '*Nullius in verba*' inscribed below. It was the crest of The Royal Society.

'*On the word of no one,*' the man whispered.

He could not help but stare longer than he should.

After all these years…the Time Box. The most fabled of Christopher Wren's Hidden Inventions. It was real! An incredible invention hidden in plain sight.

He fumbled at the tumblers, not noticing the faint kiss of a mechanical spider guarding the dials. The lid rose another inch, revealing an envelope-shaped slot.

It all came down to this. There could be no margin for error.

The kiss left on his finger became a tingle, then a burn. Then angry, oozing blisters. Darkness crept across his vision and his legs gave way as the poison took hold. How could he have been so careless? What clue had he missed?

No margin for error.

He forced his arm forward and the corners of the neatly addressed envelopes caught in the slot, only slightly, but enough to cause his grip to fail. The letters teetered in the opening for an agonising eternity, before a feeble gust of salvation finished the job and pushed them into the past.

Sated, the lid slid down and the Time Box resumed its impassive watch, oblivious to the passing of this most remarkable man.

Scan the QR code with your camera to see the Concept Art for each chapter in the book:

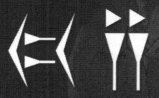

Part I

'Any sufficiently advanced technology is indistinguishable from magic.'

Arthur C. Clarke

Why me?

The thought gnawed at Sam as he slumped at his school desk. It was a day they all dreaded: parents spouting the joys of their profession in front of the entire class.

He rubbed his eyes. At least his father had been promoted and was no longer just a Patent Clerk, though Jasper was still quick to point out that Einstein had once been.

Jasper Van Sandt looked nervous, his hands fidgeting in the lap of his faded tweed suit as Sally Jacobs' mother droned on about insurance. Despite a classroom of rapt faces, not one student would recall five words from her speech, all of them were instead focused on the glamour and gossip surrounding her brief appearance on The Apprentice.

'Any questions?' Mrs Jacobs purred.

Twelve hands shot into the air.

'About selling insurance,' the teacher clarified.

There was a rustle of retreating cotton.

'Yes, Adam?' Mrs Walsh bit off each word. Sighs and cross-eyed expressions spread, heads lolling back. Adam Pinnyswood was dull. He put the 'd' in ditch water and he was also a pretentious know-it-all.

Sam drifted off as the Pinnyswood inquiry began, his voice becoming a distant murmur.

Despite being tall and athletic, with an infectious smile and quick wit, Sam was new to St Vincent's and treated like an outsider. Born in England, but raised in southern Africa, his parents were far from affluent and his scholarship to the private school was an affront to many elitist sensibilities.

He glanced over at Victoria. She was the other outsider in their year, though her mother was some hot shot in a big tech company, so she was considered a fitting addition.

Must be nice to feel like you belong...

She caught his forlorn gaze and winked back.

'Mr Van Sandt?' The teacher invited his father to take the floor.

Jasper tripped as he approached the lectern and Sam's gut tightened.

'Um, thank you, Mrs...' Surreptitiously, he checked his sweaty palm. 'Walsh,' he deciphered the letters.

The teacher smiled awkwardly, then nodded towards the class.

'Right. Hello everyone, I'm Jasper – Sam's father – and I work for the Patent Office in London. It's my job to oversee the team responsible for cataloguing and storing all patent applications.'

Sam heard someone yawn – loudly – at the back of the room, prompting a titter of laughter. Mrs Walsh fixed the perpetrator with a stern gaze.

Mr Van Sandt continued, 'Every year, we receive thousands of applications, from inventors, scientists and businesses all over the country.

They send all manner of weird and wonderful ideas. My department processes them and ensures none are misplaced. Or forgotten! Now, you may wonder why all this is important—'

'No!' Came the reply from behind a concealing hand, and this time the laughter was loud and unrepentant.

'That's enough!' Mrs Walsh declared. 'Who wants to spend their afternoons trimming the faculty lawn with blunt nail scissors?'

Mr Van Sandt abandoned his notes and stepped out from behind the lectern.

'Everything you want, every road you take and decision you make, will be in pursuit of a particular arrangement of atoms.'

The room fell silent. Sam noticed a few of the children exchange confused glances, but the silence held.

'Everything you are, everything you see, everything that has been or ever will be, no matter how magical or mundane, is nothing more than an arrangement of atoms. We're all just atoms. The one thing that defines us, however, is their arrangement. A fabulous arrangement of atoms promises unlimited potential.

Two girls, heads bent, returned to their phones.

Pulling a device from his pocket, Jasper flicked a switch. 'This arrangement, for example...' The girls jumped when Mr Van Sandt's voice blared from their respective speakers, 'allows you to commandeer the broadcast capability of any active electronic device within a twenty-foot radius.'

Mrs Walsh confiscated the phones. The offenders blushed. Sam and the rest of the class snickered.

Jasper held up a small silver stick with a neon purple tip. 'Can anyone guess what this is?'

A boy near the front shrugged. 'Looks like a match.'

'First prize! But what makes it special?'

He scraped it across the lectern, producing a trail of greenish blue sparks. The class were enchanted by the chemical fire. This time, there was awed silence.

Jasper banished the flame and relit the match to demonstrate its capabilities. All eyes were now firmly on him.

Sam's hand strayed to the faded scars on his forearm. He was not a fan of fire.

'Strike-a-lot matches: Just one of a thousand prototypes that never made it to production because the patent was quashed by billionaires or greedy conglomerates. There's a host of brilliant ideas – truly spectacular arrangements of atoms – dying a dusty death... Except of course, during a time of war.'

He waited. The hook was baited.

'What does that mean?' Big Col the rugby captain tried not to seem too interested.

Sam watched, as his father leaned forward.

'It means,' Jasper began in a hushed tone, 'that when Britain is at war, the Government will use any patent or power to protect the sovereignty of the Crown. Remember that the electric car was invented sixty years ago. There could be light bulbs that never burn out, hover shoes, jet packs – yet they remain untouched scribbles on my shelf. But in wartime, all bets are off.'

A boy at the back sat up. 'What about weapons? Guns, bombs, lasers!?'

'Flying cars?'

'Robots!'

The existence of such unimaginable wonders fed their dormant imaginations and for the first time in ages, excitement seized the room.

'A Time Machine!'

'Bottomless bags?'

'Atomic batteries!'

The list mushroomed, in both scope and extravagance, every student jostling for their flight of fancy to be heard.

Sam could not help grinning at his father.

Mr Van Sandt leaned back and tapped his nose in a knowing manner. 'Official Secrets Act, I'm afraid,' he delivered with aplomb. 'I'm sworn to silence by the King himself.' His voice dropped to a whisper. 'But there are secrets in my archives so fabulous, so incredible, they could change the world forever…' he paused, every ear held '…if they ever got out.'

An awed '*Woah*' and the odd expletive followed. Mrs Walsh, ignoring the latter, stepped forward and began to clap.

'Thank you, Mr Van Sandt, for that very surprising insight into the world of the Patent Office.' The students followed her lead, the whole class in awe of Sam's father. Could the tide have just turned in his popularity stakes?

'Questions?' The teacher asked.

It took ten minutes for the din to subside.

Sam closed the front door of the old gatehouse.

Arthur's Rest had been in his family for generations. It was a tall, narrow stone building with a stout, studded door and high-pitched roof. Beneath the swept eaves and ornate gables, climbing roses and ivy wound their way around narrow leaded windows and carved stone mullions. Sam's bedroom was in the octagonal turret which overlooked the vast grounds of the Witheringham Estate and their own modest, quintessential walled English garden.

He shrugged his bag onto the hall table and caught the edge of a neatly addressed envelope. The letter slid to the floor unnoticed and disappeared beneath the thick mahogany dresser.

'I'm home!'

'In the kitchen.' His mother's reply was followed by shrieks of delight.

'Sammy, Sammy!'

The twins roared into view covered from pigtail to plimsoll in sugar, flour and dough and caught him in the lounge. They leapt upon their older brother.

'We bakin'!'

'You're *kidding*!' He spread his arms and gawped at them theatrically.

Tugging at his shirt, the little girls ushered him toward their heinous laboratory in the kitchen. Surrounded by rolling pins, pastry cutters and deformed offerings to the cookie Gods, his mother smiled warmly. Dusting her hands on her apron, she leant over to kiss him.

'Judging by the lack of bruising, I'm assuming your father didn't completely ruin you?'

Sam grinned. 'He gave the '*fabulous atoms*' speech, whipped out a few toys and somehow had them eating out the palm of his hand!'

The rest of the day had been surreal. By home time, the entire school had heard about his father being a mad scientist who used a flame-thrower and fired a prototype laser at the headteacher.

The twins, oblivious to the conversation, were hiding under the table and feeding dough to the dog who was nearing a sugar-induced seizure.

'Girls, no more for Chloe,' their mother warned. 'If she pops, there'll be an awful mess and you'll have to clean her up!'

The front door slammed, and Sam was barrelled aside when the diabolical duo leapt up again. 'Dada, Dada!'

Jasper and Angie listened to their son re-live his day whilst they ate.

The twins were swapping spoonsful of green jelly and thick yellow custard. Very little, however, was finding its way into either mouth.

'... and I've even been invited to go to the cinema on Saturday, in Leicester Square. Big Col's dad invested in a production company and has tickets to a world première – all the stars will be there!'

'Fantastic,' Angie said, 'but your father or I will drop you off and collect you. You're not running around London on your own.'

Sam's face fell. 'But I'm fifteen!'

'Barely! I'm – we're – very happy that the boys are finally including you, but you're not going on your own. Maybe your father can go into the office and catch up on some work?'

Jasper raised a finger to object. However, further debate was interrupted by Chloe, who stood up, retched and parted company with several pounds of cookie dough. The girls (convinced that the dog had, in fact, duly popped) screamed and fled.

Saturday, rather disappointingly, took all week to arrive.

Sam had fended off several earnest visitors from school with the news that his father had been summoned away on 'business', but this revelation had only fed the rumour mill, expanding both curiosity and Sam's burgeoning popularity.

'Ready?' Jasper called.

Sam finished the message he was sending, slammed his feet into his trainers and gave his blonde hair the tenth check before heading down the stairs three at a time.

The train ride into London was cramped; it always was.

Sam sighed. Loudly. For the umpteenth time in the half-hour journey.

'Spit it out,' his father said.

'Do we *have* to go to your office? It's so boring. Can't we do something else please?'

'It'll be fun.'

Sam wasn't convinced.

He was already impatient and uncomfortable in the hot sardine-can-carriage. A man with an offensive body odour stood too close, and the smell of garlic made him gag. The man gave Sam a withering look and shuffled away slightly.

Jasper made a face at him and Sam shrugged. Turning, he noticed a very cute girl through a new gap in the packed bodies. Perhaps this trip would present other opportunities. His mood lifted considerably when their eyes met and the girl smiled at him.

Now if he could only ditch his dad…

Chapter 1

'This is a bad idea.'

Remus scanned the room. 'You don't say?'

Far below the busy streets of London, away from the noise and bustle of The Mall, two men contemplated an ill deed.

A Theft.

A Robbery.

There was simply no euphemistic way of looking at it.

'Remind me again why we're doing this?' Eindhoven crouched beside his partner-in-crime. He fiddled with a cigar-sized cylinder. The logo on the side of the weapon was an amalgamation of the letters 'H' and 'R'. *Harbinger Robotics*: a name that had, until recently, been held in the lowest regard.

'Uh... For fame? Fortune? Glory? Our names in a thousand ballads?'

'Hmm. You do realise we're turncoats?

Remus snorted. 'We chose our path. I know what – or rather who – is really on your mind. I still don't trust this *Ms* Keller, and she couldn't care less about our welfare.'

'Still,' Eindhoven mused, 'I wonder if there's a Mr Keller?'

'If there was, I'd put good money on her having eaten him before the honeymoon. You'd do well to steer clear.'

Eindhoven huffed and rocked on his haunches. The easy part had been getting inside the building. In the background, the hum of the fluorescent lights seemed to grow louder. 'If Baid finds us down here, we'll be praying for a thousand Black Widows.'

Remus swallowed at the name but said nothing.

'Ready?' Eindhoven braced his foot against the wall.

Remus did the same. 'As I'll ever be. *Nullius in verba!*' He caught the sour expression. 'Too soon?'

'Too soon!'

The two men dashed from the shadows, bent low as they crossed the large chamber. The room belonged to an archive, and a secret one at that. One they had sworn to protect with all the other archives, for there were quite a few: clandestine structures, hiding in plain sight, concealing unimaginable treasures and terrors.

Eindhoven felt a stab of guilt. *Jasper and his precious bloody atoms!*

This particular archive was vast. There were countless floors each housing a seemingly endless number of rooms filled with high shelves and cabinets, faded wooden drawers, skeletal metal racks, boxes, files, folders – even old Tupperware. Finding something in here must be impossible.

Arriving at the first set of cabinets, Remus began opening and closing doors and drawers, rummaging through the depths.

'Nothing!'

Eindhoven laughed. 'You didn't seriously think it would be that easy?'

'Well, I've little to go on. I've never stolen anything before.'

Eindhoven gave him a pithy look.

'And the more I think about it,' Remus continued 'the more I think we should just…'

'It's too late for that now. So, let's just crack on, as I, for one, would like to see another sunrise.'

From the shadows, a dark-skinned man with intricately scarred cheeks watched the pair.

Baid shook his head. There would be no tomorrow for these traitors.

S am and Jasper arrived at Charing Cross station and made their way through the crowds toward the Strand, dodging umbrellas, backpacks and the odd toddler on a Gruffalo case.

They crossed over to The Mall, before climbing the steps toward the Duke of York column.

'*The Royal Society*,' Sam read out when they stopped at a black palisade gate beside a large cream building. 'I thought you worked at the Patent office?'

'This is where the real work is done,' came the evasive reply from his father as he led Sam down some steps to an unremarkable door. It had no buzzer, wore no grandeur. It was just a plain, sturdy panelled door. A tarnished silver plaque was set above a post flap on the wall next to it.

'*Fabulous Atoms*' it read.

Sam pointed. 'You didn't?'

'Hmm? The sign? Oh, I couldn't resist. It's a free service to help people register a patent. Inventors are a lazy lot, especially when it comes to paperwork.' Jasper slid his hand into the letterbox and Sam heard the mechanical whir of a scanner. Buzz. Click. The door opened, and in they went.

Sam's shirt was stuck to his back and the cool air was a relief.

A spiral staircase led down to a lobby of highly polished white tiles. At the far end was a single door, and beside it sat a guard. He wore a crisp grey uniform and a very shiny pair of shoes. In his lap rested a dog-eared copy of '*Perpetual Motion: Getting the ball rolling*'. He had a calm, pleasant face, small bushy moustache and equally bushy brows. Setting down his book, the man rose to greet them.

'Good afternoon, Mr Van Sandt, right on time, I see. And this must be Samuel.' The guard smiled, extending his hand. 'I'm Harold.'

Turning, he tapped a nondescript panel on the wall beside his chair, which became a holographic screen. 'Where to?'

'Level Sixteen, please, Harold. Just need to collect a few things for Monday. The audit is nearly upon us!'

'Oh, aye? Bet Flic is in a right old state. Sixteen, you say,' Harold rotated a three-dimensional schematic. The image expanded until Sam could make out floor plans. Stepping aside, the guard allowed Jasper to enter a code.

Sam jumped when the metal door lit up and slid open.

'Mind you don't wander off down there – we's still lookin for the last person that did!' Harold winked when the door slid closed, the whiskers of his moustache twitching.

* * *

'Well, this is a fine mess you've gotten us into!' Remus spat.

'Me?' Eindhoven blustered, snatching a glance around the corner.

'It certainly wasn't *my* idea to break into The Royal Society archives and steal some sodding scroll for a woman who fluttered her eyelashes at me! Let alone one who works for Harbinger!'

'You seem to have conveniently forgotten the money!'

'That's because there are no shops in the graveyard, you moron!' Remus fumed.

Further debate was interrupted when a searing blast slammed into the wall, and sent the pair crashing to the floor.

Coughing, Remus scrambled up, pulling his stunned compatriot with him. 'How the hell did Baid know we're down here?'

'You *know* how!' Eindhoven choked. 'Still, we're not dead yet.'

Remus touched a wet patch spreading across his side. 'Easy for you to say.'

Eindhoven swore. 'Come on. This way.'

* * *

The lobby lift door slid open again as soon as it had closed, and Sam expected to see Harold fussing with the button. Instead, they stood before a gloomy chamber filled with row upon row of shelves.

'How…?'

Jasper stepped past his dithering son and triggered the light sensors. 'Speedlifts!'

'How far down or up did we go?'

'We're about two hundred metres below The Society lobby.'

'What?' Sam hurried to keep up. 'We travelled two hundred metres in a second? That's impossible!'

Jasper favoured his son with an expansive grin. 'Boring old office, indeed! Down here,' he spread his arms, '*impossible* is one word that's seldom used. Now where is Theoretical Genetics? I swear it moves every time I... Oh, I give up. Flic!' He turned and shouted.

There was a minute's silence, and then Sam heard a faint humming before a bright object shot over his shoulder.

'Yes, Mr Van Sandt?' a female voice asked.

'Ah, there you are, Flic. I'm looking for the Electrochemical Sap patent.'

'You've gone past it, as usual.'

Sam stared open mouthed. Hovering before them, about the size of a football, was a robot: smooth and shiny with a band of neon blue light around its middle. The air beneath the robot shimmered.

Jasper noticed his son's jaw dragging on the floor. 'Sorry, Sam, this is Flic, our Cybernetic Curator.'

'But wha… what is it?'

'It?' The blue bled to red and the floating custodian rounded on him. It had two cameras for eyes and a speaker grill mouth.

'*I* am a highly intelligent, self-aware cybernetic organism. One who has catalogued every document on all two hundred and seventy-two levels of the London office, right down to the mjöð soaked napkin upon which Gustaf Felvovin scribbled the recipe for self-levitating hydrogel!' A telescopic arm unfolded and poked Sam in the forehead.

'*It,* indeed!' Flic whizzed away, muttering.

'*Mjöð?*' Sam rubbed his forehead and looked at his father.

Jasper laughed. 'Viking beer. Quite an acquired taste. And no, is the answer to your next question!' He pointed after the robot. 'Farnsworth's Learning and Interactive Cybernetic Curator: Flic for short. Felicity Farnsworth was the curator here for over sixty years and on the day of her retirement, presented us with her replacement.

'Apparently, the old genius passed her time studying the patents in Advanced Robotics and Synthetic Neurological Cybertronics. Flic was the result and her design formed the basis for all our Cybernetic Assistants. I think Felicity programmed more than a little of her own personality into Flic though, for she gets a little touchy at this time of year.'

'How come?'

'It's the audit soon and Felicity used to take it very personally if our Index scored below ninety eight percent in catalogue accuracy.

'Now, we must get a move on if you're going to make this movie.'

* * *

Remus slid to the floor. 'It's no use.'

The wound was fatal. The wet patch was no longer a patch and he was losing feeling in his arms and legs. 'That man's not human. We've scoured every floor of this place – there's no scroll and nowhere to hide.'

'Come on,' Eindhoven tugged at him, but Remus was spent.

'Get out of here.' His friend's eyes were rolling. 'Take the Speedlift and head for the lobby. You can use Harold's computer to find your bloody scroll. Here,' he handed Eindhoven one of Ms Keller's devices.

Putrid cow. This was all her fault.

'You'll need it. Now go!'

* * *

Sam wandered past tall, densely packed shelves crammed with every manner of manuscript, and labelled by neat and patient hands, until they found the robot near the top shelf, her pincer moving from spine to spine.

'Digesting Root Beetles, Dynamite Tubers, Elastic Vines, Electrochemical Sap – here we are!'

'Brilliant, thanks Flic! Back to the Speedlift, if you don't mind. Sam's got a big afternoon planned.'

'Hmm!' Her neon nimbus had changed to a sulky green by the time they reached the lift.

'Thanks again, Flic,' Jasper said. 'See you Monday.'

The robot banked and disappeared, the rows of chamber lights pinging off behind her.

Again, no sooner had the door closed than it slid open, and they were back in the white tiled lobby. Though it was not at all how they had left it.

The charred pages of *Perpetual Motion* were scattered to all corners. The blackened, smoking cover lay beside the empty chair. The air reeked.

Sam stared at an ugly smear on the pristine floor, a clotted crimson streak that stretched across the room. At its end lay a crumpled body, limbs bent at unnatural angles.

Placing a hand across his son's chest, Jasper peered out of the lift, then hurried over to the wall and pressed a panic button. The lights bled to red and an alarm began to wail. He turned to Sam.

'Stay! There!' then ran over to the fallen man.

The lift door slid closed and Sam was left in the dim, pulsing steel box. He blinked. It took a moment to realise he was alone. No buttons, no apparent way out. A wave of claustrophobia gripped him, and Sam banged the door.

'Help!' he shouted, kicking and beating on it. 'Dad! Dad! Get me out of here!'

The door opened. His relief, however, was short lived.

He was back on Level Sixteen.

Here, too, red floor lights beat in time with the alarm. Sam peered into the gloom. He could make out shapes, but they did not look like shelves. Sam shuffled forward, arms and fingers searching.

'Flic?'

Nothing.

His foot struck something hard and he stopped, cursing. Bending to rub his toes, he fished out his phone for a light.

The something hard was a large metal foot. Joined to an ankle, then a knee.

A giant metal robot out of a 1950's movie, all right angles, welded joints and exposed bolts. Serrated rubber pincers, capable of crushing him whole, hung at its side. The head was a kite shaped block of iron and the quatrefoil eyes glowed demonically.

A noise caused Sam to turn just in time to avoid a beam of light that burst past him and sliced into the steel centurion. He stumbled away from the robot amidst a shower of sparks as another flash followed the first. Then he tripped, dropping his phone. Heart pounding, Sam swore and scrambled away.

There was a humming, followed by a rush of wind and he was flung across the room, landing hard, and rolling before being lifted and slammed onto the ground once more. The force drove the wind from him, and bright spots skittered across Sam's vision. Gasping, clawing at the musty air, he lay with his cheek pressed against the rough floor, ears ringing.

He heard a click, the flicking of a switch, and suddenly the air around Sam turned warm and sticky, like glue. He struggled but whatever had him, held fast. The muffled sound of footsteps drew nearer.

'Busy down here, considering it's the weekend. And such splendid weather, too,' a man's voice remarked. It was deep and heavily accented. 'I certainly didn't expect the archives to be so busy, being such a well-kept secret. Do you know how hard Level Two Seven Three was to find? Yet here *you* are.' The voice paused, then sighed with genuine regret. Raising his hand, he pointed a cigar shaped device at the boy, its tip glowing. 'Still, dead men and all that... Goodbye.'

From the shadows sped a blur of metal and angry red light. Flic rammed into the stranger at speed and the viscous air around Sam evaporated.

'Not allowed! Never allowed in here!' she shrieked. 'Who are you? Show me your face!' The stranger regained his balance and rolled away. Coming to his feet, the man struck out at Flic with a retractable staff. It glanced off her side. He then narrowly avoided her next charge and staggered against Sam. The two became entangled. Something came away in Sam's hand, but the man didn't notice, his attention firmly on his airborne assailant.

Seconds before Flic reached him the man clapped his hand over a panel on his chest. The device made a whirring sound and pulsed between his fingers. He turned on his heel as the device emitted a bright flash.

'No!' Flic screamed. 'That too is forbidden. Forbidden!'

But the man was no longer there.

The Speedlift opened and three behemoths bustled into the room, flashlights in their hands.

Sam slumped, his every bone and muscle on fire. In his hand, however, he held a strange prize: a long tube wound in cloth. One end was peeled back and he could make out the faded wooden spindles of a scroll.

'You have it!' Flic swooped down, steam venting from a crack in her side. One of her camera eyes had been smashed and was leaking green fluid. Farnsworth's design had not anticipated volatile aerial incursions.

'Well done, boy. Well done, indeed.' She took the item in her pincers and, spluttering inky smoke, disappeared into the maze of dusty relics.

'You all right, son?' One of the men knelt in front of Sam. He wore a long black and purple coat with a steel vambrace around each wrist. Both hands were gloved, but his palms glowed and crackled with energy.

'I think so.' Despite the ringing in his ears, Sam was unable to take his eye from the man's hands.

'You'd better come with us. Mr D'Angelo will want to see you. Your father's already in his office.' He laughed when Sam winced as he tried to stand. 'Cheer up, it's not every day you face a rogue Paladin and survive! Baid caught up with his mate a few floors up and that chap, let me tell you, wasn't so lucky.'

Sam had no idea what or who he was talking about. The man clapped him on the back with a force that rattled Sam's teeth, before they headed towards the lift, flashlights scouring the room.

Eindhoven flinched, expecting the crazed robot to crash into his back. But the device on his chest had transported him to safety.

'Clever.'

He appeared to be in an office near the top of a tall building; a neat, minimalist room with a solitary mahogany desk. The only remarkable décor was two rows of tribal masks on the walls beside the double doors. Some were small and round, beautifully carved and highly polished. Others were elongated and rough, scarred creations with hollow eyes and snarling lips.

The front of the office was glass and the view was spectacular. To the west, the sun was sinking into a cherry sea, casting the mask collection in a menacing crimson hue. Far below, the busy streets of a city were already blinking neon.

To the east, an imposing, flat-topped mountain dominated the horizon, draped in a cloth of marshmallow cloud.

'Welcome to Africa, Mr Eindhoven.' The doors opened, admitting a slim woman carrying a briefcase. 'No Mr Palatine?'

The final image of his childhood friend slumped against the wall would haunt Eindhoven forever, but regret would serve no purpose right now. 'Ms Keller,' he nodded.

She had changed since they parted company in London, her casual tourist garb replaced with a tailored suit and painfully high heels. Making her way behind the desk, she took a seat, motioning him to do the same.

'I trust everything went according to plan?' Ms Keller opened the case, turning the gaping square toward him. It was empty. Hungry.

Eindhoven crossed his ankles and looked out the window, 'It's quite a revelation, being on the other side of the fence.' He reached inside his jacket and placed the first of the devices she had given them on the table. It looked like a water pistol, made of smoky plastic with a cone shaped barrel. 'The Mangler made short work of poor Harold. And this – I forget its name – the Hot Spot, was it?' he placed a cigar shaped device beside the gun '…was not without its uses. 'But the Turner,' he tapped his chest, 'now this came in handy.' He paused. 'One can't help but wonder what is worth so much effort?'

Ms Keller's lips formed a firm line. 'We've a great many assets at our disposal. Harbinger is unparalleled in technological innovation. And now, thanks to you, we have even greater insight into the Mods of your Cadres, so in return, we've allowed you to sample a few of our... toys. Amazing what you can achieve without petty rules and meaningless constraints, wouldn't you agree?' She could not help but dig at the dogma of his former employer as her fingertips found a button beneath her desk. 'Now, the scroll?'

Too late to turn back now. Eindhoven had enjoyed little glory or reward in recent years and Harbinger's offer was welcome. The Ex-Paladin reached for the scroll at his side, and was hit by a wave of cold panic when he found an empty pocket. He checked the other, but it, too, was bare.

Eindhoven swore. 'Why, that little…'

Ms Keller watched the colour drain from the man's face. Fighting the disappointment that his failure brought, she chose instead to cherish the faint silver lining. Her fingertip traced the hidden button once more, and then she pressed it, ever so slowly.

Eindhoven looked down in surprise when the Turner on his chest sprang to life. 'Wait…'

But it was too late. A needle shot from the back of the housing, administering an agent into his bloodstream.

'Are you familiar with the tale of King Ferdinand of Naples, Mr Eindhoven?' Ms Keller picked at a stray piece of cotton.

Unsurprisingly, the paralysed man did not reply.

'I'll take that as a 'no'.

Ferdinand, or Ferrante, ruled Naples in the late fifteenth century. He was an exceptional and ruthless politician, infamously so, for he dealt with his enemies in a most gruesome manner. Once he had helped them shrug loose their mortal coil, he had them embalmed, dressed and put on display in his own macabre museum. The only visitors he allowed were those he suspected of disloyalty, to show them the fate that awaited all who crossed him. It proved a most successful object lesson for improving devotion.'

She paused.

'Morbid as it is,' her voice dropped, 'I was fascinated by the tale. So much so, that I shamelessly plagiarised the idea. You've been injected with a neat little concoction the ladies in the lab refer to as LS_2, or the Living Statue serum. Its chemistry is fascinating, but I won't bore you with the details. Essentially, it puts your body into a state of suspended animation. With one evil little twist: You can still see, still hear and remain quite conscious. You are a living statue. One that will have a place of honour in my own museum; which, I'm not too proud to say, has yet to be graced by a Paladin.'

Ms Keller smiled, spreading her hands. 'So, welcome! You're going to make a fine addition and quite the talking point for my next tour.'

She snapped the empty case shut. 'Harbinger does not accept, condone nor reward failure, Mr Eindhoven, and I must now find another way to acquire that which you've so spectacularly failed to deliver.'

Ms Keller took the case and left the room; flicking off the light, as she closed the door, the rhythmic click-clack of her heels growing fainter.

Eindhoven struggled. From the wall, hollow eyes and gaping mouths mocked him. He watched the sun dip and set, perhaps for the last time. *So much for that sunrise.*

His mind shied away from the fate that now awaited him. Sentenced to an endless nightmare in some twisted mannequin freak show. To be leered and laughed at by this evil woman.

Remus had been right. *Too late for regret.*

Inky blue-black sullied the blushing sky, a great hand plucking the first stars from hiding. High above the bustling bay, far from the continual beep-beep of the taxis and lively music booming from the bars, the traitorous Turner flashed and came to life once more.

When the moon rose on silver rails, the office was empty.

Chapter 3

It was a tight fit.

The guards sandwiched Sam into the lift. A steer-sized hoof crushed his toes. 'Sorry.'

Sam barely noticed. His head was spinning.

What the actual hell had just happened?

Thankfully, the door opened straight away and Sam hobbled onto the deep vermilion carpet of a windowed hall. Opposite the lift, a round table and chairs nestled beside an imposing set of double doors with well-polished brass handles.

The lift closed, leaving Sam with a guard who motioned for the boy to take a seat, then knocked on the doors before entering.

Sam spied a bowl of toffees and helped himself to a crinkly wrapper, feeling grateful for the sugar-hit as he walked over to the closest window, curious to see what level of the archive they had reached. The view left him confused.

It was one of rolling hills and grass seas; a wide river wound sluggishly through them from distant snow-capped peaks, and a herd of horses traversed the prairie. When he leaned closer, Sam could even feel the sun radiating through the glass. This wasn't St James' Park!

'What the—?'

A deep rumble caused him to turn to the opposite window, through which ruffled palms and honey sands held white crested waves at bay. Sam touched the pane. It was damp from the spray.

In the distance, dark clouds drew closer to the beach. Lightning tore across the nebulous horizon, followed by another growl of thunder, and the toffee bowl rattled skittishly.

Sam took a step back, unable to wrap any understanding around where he might be. It couldn't be London, and definitely wasn't underground. The herd was now close enough to make out the prancing antics of the foals.

The grand doors opened and Sam jumped.

There was a crunch when the guard stepped on the wrapper.

'Been at the toffees, have we? Come on then, sweet tooth.'

A second thunderclap caused the guard to wrinkle his nose. 'So much for surfing after work.'

'Sam!' Jasper rushed over, patting his son's chest and stomach.

'I'm fine, Dad,' he said, pushing the hands away.

'Of course you are, my boy,' declared a tall, silhouetted figure standing before a long window spanning a large room.

'Have you ever seen a ghost cat, Samuel? *Panthera uncia,* the snow leopard. A truly magnificent creature.'

He turned to face them. The man's eyes were piercing and his cheeks bore the ruddy glow of a frosty morning. 'Come see for yourself.'

Sam looked to his father, who nodded. He felt the chill before he saw the snow, his breath steaming when he drew near the window. The landscape beyond lay in deepest winter, icy tendrils and heavy drifts rested against the glass.

'There.' The man pointed toward the far end of a clearing. Sam squinted against the glare but could see nothing among the rocks and ice. Then he caught sight of the ghostly predator.

The snow leopard's long tail swayed as it padded across the crisp ground a few meters from them. Its chest was white, but the rest of its fur was mottled smoky grey to tan, with dark rosettes adorning it from head to tail.

'Magnificent,' the man sighed. 'Though soon it will be extinct.' They watched the creature stalk across the clearing, sniff the air, then disappear behind a tree, oblivious to its audience.

'Where are we?' Sam blurted. This was all too much to take in. 'How are there windows of different places in the same room? Are they real or electronic? And how are they hot and cold, or wet. . . ' He faltered.

'Sammy! So many questions! But first, introductions; I'm Salvador D'Angelo, your father's... supervisor.'

'Just Sam,' he corrected. Never Sammy. He rubbed the scars on his forearm, suppressing memories of the only person aside from the twins to call him that. Introductions were all very well, but no one had answered his questions.

Their host plucked the stopper from a decanter. 'That'll be all for now, Owen,' Salvador informed the guard waiting by the door as he filled a tulip-shaped glass.

'Cognac, Jasper?' The bottle hovered over a second glass.

'No, thank you.'

He gave Sam a sly look. 'How about you?'

'Uh, a Coke if you have one? Please.'

'With a drop of the good stuff? For the shock?'

'Just the Coke, thank you.' Jasper headed off any temptation.

Sam paused to marvel at Mr D'Angelo's office, which resembled a well-loved study. Deep, comfortable chairs, a dark wooden desk and multiple shelves that strained under the weight of books and ornaments of every shape, size and cultural persuasion. The remaining walls were draped in maps and paintings.

He turned to study its architect. Salvador D'Angelo was a tall man, straight of back and broad shouldered. His dark hair was neatly cropped, with a smattering of grey dotting his temples. He was not wearing glasses, although Sam saw some balanced upon the mass of papers strewn across the desk. One of them, he noticed, was an open scroll, and he leaned in curiously.

Upon the faded parchment he could make out a careful rendering of a temple with a subterranean chamber. Runes and strange markings decorated the drawing.

Mr D'Angelo casually rolled the scroll closed as he picked up his glasses.

'Persephone, what's the time, please?'

'Which time zone, sir?'

'London.'

'Four forty-five.'

Sam looked around. He spied a shiny silver-blue teardrop torso hovering behind a lamp.

'How rude of me,' Salvador apologised. 'That's Persephone, my C.A.'

Sam tried not to look blank.

'Cybernetic Assistant. A descendant, if you will, of Farnsworth's Curator model; whom I believe you met earlier? Now with a few improvements.' The robot's nimbus brightened at the praise.

'Right then, the windows.' He swirled his glass. 'They're called Far Sight windows. Think of them as very powerful telescopes that allow you to not only see but experience every sensation of your chosen vista from the safety and convenience of...' he spread his arms showman-like, a slosh of cognac escaping, 'your own home. Far more impressive than a television, you must agree?'

Sam nodded.

'Now tell me all about your afternoon, I hear you had some fun and games on Level Sixteen?'

'Two Seven Three.' Sam corrected

Salvador's smile never quite reached his grey eyes as he looked at the boy. 'There is no Level Two Seven Three.'

'Well, that's what *he* said.' Sam's voice broke at the memory of the attack, of the searing light and the suffocating pain.

'*He*, who is he?'

'We didn't get around to introductions, it was the man who disappeared. He said we were on Level Two Seven Three.'

Mr D'Angelo said nothing.

'And the guard?' Sam continued. It would be hard to forget the twisted body on the blood-stained floor. Another memory to bury.

'Harold? He slipped on the stairs and dropped his soup. Out cold when your father found him. I just don't understand why people can't use the canteen, after all the money I've spent on it ...' Salvador muttered.

Sam knew he was being fobbed off. Mr D'Angelo had too quick an answer for everything.

'Now if you don't mind, young man, I'd like a quick word with your father. You can wait for him outside.'

'You're not going to fire him?'

Mr D'Angelo laughed. 'Heavens, no.

'Persephone, why don't you change the windows in the lobby, show young Sam Tokyo at night?'

The robot glided forward. 'Certainly, sir. May I also suggest the Easter Islands: it will be sunrise there soon?'

'Splendid.' Mr D'Angelo extended his hand. 'A pleasure to meet you, Sam, and I'm sorry if we caused you any alarm. I hear you've an exciting evening planned, so I won't keep you any longer.' And ushered him into the hall.

'I'm so sorry,' Jasper began when Salvador had closed the door, but he was waved to silence.

'How were you to know we'd have saboteurs running around today?' Salvador sat down, and began picking at the worn leather chair. 'Bloody Harbinger! I thought we were past all this...

'What does the boy know?'

'Sam? About us? Nothing. After what happened in Zimbabwe, we've tried to let him enjoy his childhood. I know other parents drip feed the truth to their children, but he's been through enough already.'

Salvador swirled the brandy. 'I may have a solution to that. Bring Sam to the college at the end of his school term.'

'What? Why?'

'The Council has been debating a new project for some time, an apprenticeship of sorts. It may prove the perfect introduction for your son. We're becoming too reliant upon the gadgets and gizmos. Need to start training younger students in the old ways. Go back to basics.

'The boy seems bright, athletic and has certainly showed some stomach today. He could be a perfect candidate to help us shake things up.'

Jasper spluttered. 'It was more like dumb luck. He's barely fifteen. I was nineteen when I went through my Induction, and I scarcely coped. What about his regular schooling?'

'This will only last for the summer and is nothing like a full Induction. It's important to assess their skills early. We're not all cut out to be Paladins. But he may be.' Salvador managed to hide his smile as he saw Jasper flinch. Vanity was his favourite sin.

Jasper paused. 'You think he has that potential?'

'Who knows? But if today's anything to go by....'

Jasper chewed his lip, childhood dreams of fame and glory rising with narcotic charm.

'Then it's settled. But in the meantime, we need to find out what our "guests" were up to and if anything was taken. Keep me posted.'

* * *

Heat. Oppressive, burning heat. Sam rolled over, away from it.

Screaming.

Someone was shouting his name. A disturbance sent to interrupt his pleasant dream.

Smoke. Caustic fumes, filling his lungs. Choking him. Sam coughed and his eyes shot open.

'Sammy!' His twin sister was shaking him, her eyes wide.

'Soph,' he coughed again, 'what's wrong? What's going on?'

'I don't know,' she cried. 'I heard shouting. Everything's burning. Sammy, I'm scared!' Sooty tears were streaming down her face.

There was smoke everywhere. Sliding under the door, puffing past the ill-fitting window frame, even seeping through the thatched roof.

Sam felt sick. He remembered the burnt colour of the African sky the day before. Dark, angry clouds that smothered the horizon. His father had assured them they were safe, that the Research Station was of no interest to the rebels; yet most of the labourers had left days ago, carrying everything they could manage.

There was more shouting. Harsh voices. His mother was screaming their names.

Sam grabbed his sister, pulling the blankets from their bed and draping one over her.

'Soph, we need to get out. Put your hand over your mouth and stay under the blanket!' He wrapped a blanket around himself before giving the door a tug. The handle was hot and he snatched his hand back, cursing. He tried again using the corner of the blanket. Behind him, Sophie's sobs grew louder.

A wall of heat from the corridor burst in.

'Come on!' He shielded his sister, heading for their parents' bedroom.

'Mummy!' he shouted. Five years old and so very frightened. '*DADDYYYYY*!'

There was an awful splitting sound as the roof gave way. Sam pulled Sophie past, propelling her toward safety.

A beam fell between them, spewing molten thatch.

'Sophie!' He screamed, losing sight of her. 'Quick, open their door, get inside!'

'Sammy!' Her voice was desperate. Scared and alone.

They had never been apart. They'd shared a womb and everything since. He leapt forward, swatting the pyre.

Strong arms swept him up and away from the flames. 'Come, we need to get out.' The man's voice was muffled, a wet rag over his mouth.

'No!' Sam writhed, kicking free, clawing at the smoking wreckage separating him from the other half of his heart. The blanket caught and a fresh crest of flames devoured his arm.

Sam screamed. The man found him again, relentless, pulling him back.

'Sammy!' He heard his sister's voice for the last time. 'Don't leave me!'

Sam sat up in bed, drenched in sweat. Heart pounding.

There was no smoke. No fire. Only the most bitter of memories.

His head hurt. Usually, it was just his heart.

His tongue had died and begun rotting in his mouth.

'I hate you, beer,' he cursed.

Bleary eyed, he squinted at the clock. It was a little after three. He flopped back, whimpering.

The movie premiere had been a welcome distraction. As had Sam's first adventure into alcohol, but he had predictably overdone it.

'There's no way!' His mother's voice drifted up the stairs. 'I don't care, he's only fourteen—'

'Fifteen!' both he and his father retorted from different rooms.

'Only just! And I want to know more! An apprenticeship is it? You can't just throw him in the deep end. Do you even remember *your* induction?'

There was a sullen silence. 'It's just for the summer. D'Angelo said he has Paladin potential!'

His mother swore. 'Are you honestly that gullible? You're allowing your own childhood fantasies to obscure the fact you're talking about putting our son through an ordeal that most adult candidates struggle with. Even if it's a watered-down version, I'm just not having it, Jasper...' A door slammed and their voices became incomprehensible.

Sam knew he should be curious, and probably even concerned about what he'd just heard, but his gut was still bubbling like a volcano and it took all his concentration not to vomit. He needed water but couldn't move. He shut his eyes to stop the room spinning.

A voice drifted into his head, as another smoke-infested bout of sleep rose to claim him.

Still, dead men and all that. Goodbye.

Chapter 4

It was the last day of term. The beginning of a summer of freedom; and it flew by with very little work being done.

Sam watched the children flow past him in chattering packs, exchanging plans to explore far-flung destinations and enjoy sun-drenched sojourns abroad.

His new group of friends were no different. Mullins was heading to Ibiza. Again. Flynn Oliver's family were 'doing' South America, the adventure of a lifetime, and no one seemed able to top that.

'We're just going back to India again!' Sanjay looked crestfallen.

'What about you, Van Sandt?' Big Col asked. 'Off to Africa? Lions, tigers and all that.'

'Tigers are endemic to central Asia,' Adam Pinnyswood piped up from beyond the group's periphery.

Big Col flicked a crust of sandwich in his direction.

Sam shrugged. 'Don't know yet. Dad's been M.I.A all week. Something kicked off at the office and he's barely been home since.'

All eyes were on him in an instant.

'Go on, then!' Mullins prodded him. 'Spill the beans, you git!'

'Robbery.' Sam could not help himself. 'Armed.'

'No. Way!'

'Yup. Can't say any more than that, I'm afraid.'

Big Col punched him in the shoulder. 'You nob. Details now!'

'Well, all I know is that they broke in, killed a guard and made off with something Top Secret.'

Sam tried not to think of the twisted body on the blood-stained floor.

'Wooah…'

'Yup, serious stuff.'

The minute hand had at last marched past fifty-nine and the bell rang, releasing them from the oppressive yoke of learning for six glorious weeks.

The goodbyes were varied. Some emphatic, others fleeting. A few girls fought tears. Adam Pinnyswood cried openly.

Victoria was off to France with her uncle. 'I'll miss you.' She pressed close to Sam, her green eyes smiling, full of mischief.

'Of course, you will, I'm quite the catch.' That earned him a dig in the ribs, then a fleeting kiss before she turned tail. For a moment the weight of old and new events lifted and he grinned at her retreating form.

Summer! He looked up at a rare blue expanse. It lacked the golden depth of an African sky, but then there was no sickly black smoke either. Sam's scars throbbed. His heart began to pound and his vision blurred. *Sammy, don't leave me!*

A hooter beeped, and he looked down, blinking. The twins waved wildly from the car and Chloe yipped from the boot, snot and saliva splattering all the windows.

He smiled, forcing his worries away, and decided it was going to be a great summer.

The barbeque popped indecisively, then roared into action.

Standing as far from the flames as possible, Sam waved the tongs, his eyes watering. No matter where he stood, the smoke blew *right* into his face.

This was his father's job and no way to treat his trauma! Sodding fire.

It was early evening and, for once, rain had not soured a Saturday. The flames raced across the coal bags and another sneaky puff of smoke caught him unawares. Coughing, Sam retreated, swearing at length. His mother's phone rang and Chloe barked.

'Quiet!' the twins scolded, mimicking their mother as they ran around the garden.

His father was at work. Again. Sam was certain he was avoiding him. Hardly what Sam needed, after everything that had happened.

He had tried to talk to his mother about it, but was told to put his imagination to better use and instead entertain his sisters with the stories of floating robots and funny windows.

'Your father's on the way.' Angie Van Sandt leant out of the window, phone pressed against her chest. 'So, don't put the meat on yet.'

'Goodie, goodie!' The twins raced onto the patio. Chloe chased them, snapping at their heels and sending them into fits of mock panic. They dashed across the lawn and dived into the Wendy house. Chloe leapt up at them, barking plaintively.

'Becky, Amy,' Sam said, 'don't tease her, it's not nice.'

'Girls, come wash your hands,' their mother called.

Chloe knew what that meant and deserted her quarry, racing inside to continue her never-ending quest for food.

After sizzling steak, juicy chops, sausage, corn and jacket potatoes, all smothered in garlic butter, they were all well and truly stuffed.

Sam burped. 'Excuse me,' he managed before a hiccup quickly followed. The twins giggled.

'Come on, girls, help Mummy with your plates, please.' Angie wiped the ice cream from their fingers before handing each a dish.

'How was the audit?' Sam asked his father, who had arrived only a little late for the meal.

Jasper looked surprised. 'Good. Very good, in fact. 98% for the third year in a row. Finished this morning. Takes a while to get through two hundred and seventy-two floors.'

'Seventy-three.'

'Pardon?'

'Nothing.' Sam muttered, wondering how long his parents would continue to act as though he was stupid.

His father rested his fork. 'Look, I know we've not had a chance to talk yet, about what happened—'

'How's Harold?'

Jasper looked away.

Sam couldn't let the opportunity go. 'Spilt soup? I guess the book he was reading spontaneously combusted in his lap?'

Silence.

How typical!

'Why'd you even take me there, if you're going to treat me like a child?

'I thought you worked in some dreary basement, stamping *Approved* or *Denied* on boring patents. But no, there's Speedlifts, magic windows, and a flying robot with an inferiority complex – oh, and did I mention the dead body? Never mind the maniac who attacked me on a level of your 'office' that you and your smarmy boss say doesn't even bloody *exist*!' Sam was standing now, shouting at his father, all his suppressed fear and anxiety boiling to the surface.

His mother bundled the gaping twins inside and closed the door.

'I'm sorry,' Jasper said, staring at the chipped stone paving. 'I just wanted you to be proud of me. I saw the way you looked when I got up in front of your class. You were embarrassed, Sam. Ashamed that I wasn't a rich executive or hot shot lawyer, but there's so much you don't know...' His voice trailed off and he shook his head. 'I thought a few fancy inventions and a bit of mystery might change things. I had no intention of throwing you into all... that.

'But tomorrow,' he looked up, 'tomorrow will start to explain things. Your mother doesn't approve and I must admit I'm less than thrilled by the prospect, but now you know that there's something to know, well,' he ventured a half smile, 'you can't put the crap back in the cat, can you?'

Sam managed a half laugh. His father was rarely crude. The tension between them lessened. 'Sorry. I just felt like I was going to explode and there's no one I can talk to about this. Even Mum thinks I'm nuts.'

'That's okay, she's used to it, living with me!'

'I do have a question for you.' Sam was determined to get at least one answer from his father.

Jasper looked wary. 'What?' he asked, gathering the remaining plates.

'That robot, Flic, said it was self-aware. Artificial Intelligence?'

'That's right.'

'You've seen the movies, isn't that a bad idea, won't they get tired of taking orders and turn on us? Judgement Day and all that?'

Jasper laughed. 'If you knew how many times I've heard that. Our A.I. aren't slaves, Sam. They're helpers. We don't order them to do anything. They're designed with a role in mind and performing that duty is elective.

'Take Flic, for example, the job we do at the archives is one that serves the greater good and that's what any intelligent life form wants – peace, harmony, the protection of knowledge. Flic doesn't simply do a job a human is too lazy to do; she does the job many humans would be needed to do. She's quicker, better and far more efficient. Just ask her!'

Sam forced a weak smile.

'It's a symbiotic relationship.' His father assured him.

'Hmm.' Sam could see the logic but remained dubious about the potential of an army of flying robots. He could not help but wonder what other secrets his father was keeping from him.

Sundays at *Arthur's Rest* were usually lazy days. Sam could enjoy a little longer in bed, woken by the scent of cinnamon and coffee creeping up the stairs. It was the day of the Sunday papers, endless cartoons, online gaming, rich leftovers for Chloe and a brief reprieve for Sam from his parents. It had something for everyone.

This Sunday was different. It would be a day of answers. Sam was already up and dressed.

Jasper popped his head around the bathroom door. He was dressed in jeans and a checked shirt, a thick jacket hung over his arm.

'Bring your winter coat.'

Sam peered through the window at the sun-drenched lawn. There was not a cloud in the sky.

'You're kidding? It's going to be twenty-five. I'm in shorts and sliders all the way.'

His father looked vexed. 'Trainers or boots would be better. And make sure it's a warm jacket.'

Four bulky guards now lurked in the white tiled lobby. Harold, it seemed, was yet to recover. 'I guess it's hard to bounce back from a bout of being dead,' Sam muttered, eyeing the men.

If his father heard the barb, he ignored it.

Two of the guards flanked the lift and the others stood on either side of the room. They wore long black and purple coats with a small silver badge on the collar, gloved hands folded over their stomachs.

'Well, well,' sneered one of the guards near the lift as Sam and his father approached. 'Van Sandt! Been a while. How's the leg?'

Jasper's hand instinctively strayed to his right thigh.

'It's fine, Greeves. I see you're still battling the functional end of a razor. Did you finally get kicked out of Prague? There can't be many stations left that will have you.'

The man mountain chuckled, a nasty humourless rasp. 'After your buddy Eindhoven went rogue, the Council assigned the grownups to guard your dusty hovel.' He looked around with disdain. 'Trust me, I'm no more pleased by it than you are.'

Jasper's face was ashen. 'It was Eindhoven? But he nearly killed Sam!'

'Ha! You didn't know!' Greeves gloated. 'Priceless! Your finger was always fumbling for the pulse, Van Sandt. Wasn't he best man at your wedding? Classic!' His gaze drifted to Sam.

Greeves did not have what one could call a pleasant face. His nose was bulbous and misshapen, a purple hue to its tip and edges. His eyes were too close together and the massive jaw that jutted from his skull was covered in coarse stubble, trying to hide a long scar that stretched from chin to ear.

'This your boy?'

Sam could feel sweat trickle down his spine.

'Got more to him than you do, Van Sandt. Must get that from his mother. How is the lovely Angelique? Talk about punching above your weight!'

The guard closest to Sam left his post at this point.

'Wher'to, Jasper?' The man's accent had the musical twang of the Caribbean. Standing shoulder-to-shoulder with Greeves, he was of equal size, with dark skin and thick dreadlocks.

Sam noticed his eyes were a striking hazel, flecked with dots of green and grey.

'The College, please, Abiwe.'

Greeves let out a scoff. 'The Invisible College? Why?' He indicated Sam with a curt nod. 'He's not old enough, what business you got there?'

'Tha's enough, man!' Abiwe snapped. He turned to Jasper when the lift door opened. 'I'm afraid, giv'n the current situation, you 'ave to go tru Shen Pi.'

Jasper nodded. 'We've brought jackets.'

'Jus' jackets? The password is "Sandcastle". Som egghead's idea of a joke, I tink.'

'Sandcastle.' Jasper nodded. 'Greeves.'

The man said nothing, however Sam noticed his middle finger made heavy work of scratching his neck when they passed.

'You may want to put that on now.' Sam's father pointed at his jacket.

A second later, the lift door slid open and an arctic blast of air rushed in carrying thick snow, whipping and swirling around them.

Sam stood dumbstruck staring out at the high white mountains before them, whilst his father zipped his coat up to his chin and stuffed his arms into deep pockets.

'Come on.' Frost was already forming on his glasses. 'Stay behind me and – whatever you do – don't turn around!'

Despite the brief blast of snowy air, none appeared to be falling on the mountain, which glistened under the starry sky. Ignoring the only piece of advice he had been given, Sam turned around and nearly suffered a heart attack.

There was no lift behind him.

No door.

In fact, there was nothing behind him. Well, not for several thousand feet at least, for two strides away, the ground vanished into darkness.

He panicked and lurched into his father's back, sending the pair tumbling to the ground.

'Sam!' came the muffled remonstration; Jasper's head and shoulders were buried in the snow.

'Are you lost, stranger?' a voice asked.

Sam looked up at a dark shape looming over them, blotting out the stars. One became several shapes, fur-hooded men now stood between them and safety.

The newcomers held long staffs with heavily-studded points touching the snow. Curved blades swung from their hips and a long strip of cloth was wound around each face.

'The Guardians of Shen Pi,' his father said, as if it would mean something to Sam. Jasper tried to rise.

Seven swords slid from their scabbards, flashing in the moonlight.

'Please, do not move again.'

Sam's stomach tightened, the tips of several blades less than an inch from his face.

'We, The Few— Wait, that's not it... Sandcastle!' Jasper shouted, hunched over on sodden ground. 'Sandcastle, damn it, Jen Si!'

The swords slid into their sheaths and Sam was lifted to his feet.

'My apologies, Mr Van Sandt.' Jen Si's voice could have come from any of the hoods. 'But I'm sure you appreciate the necessity for caution.'

'I do, I do.'

All but one of the guards retreated, joining a row of men who formed an ominous corridor leading toward the summit. As they passed, Sam was surprised to see that every other man was, in fact, a statue. Each stony sentinel carried a burning torch or a short bow, their arrows knocked and ready to be drawn, others held supple throwing spears. The real warriors were so still it was hard to tell man from carving.

In every direction, the horizon bristled with snow-capped peaks. The wind whipped across the lip of the summit in swirling charges. As it rose toward the peak, the outcrop widened to create an avenue, leading to a stone fortress set into the mountain.

Taking a torch from the nearest statue, the man called Jen Si led them toward the stronghold. It was no fairy-tale castle, rather a squat, solid series of interlinked buildings, slathered in snow and ice. It was foreboding.

Sam could just make out a pair of carved dragons guarding the entrance, weathered claws extended, their faces sculpted into a perpetual snarl. Beyond them, the dark maw of the forecastle awaited. Two battered wooden doors stood off their hinges, thick drifts piled against them.

Sam felt yet more questions amassing. 'Where are we? And just how the hell did we get *here*?'

'Speedlift, of course. Shen Pi is a monastery in the Himalayas.'

Sam's socks were sodden and squelched with every step. His feet were starting to freeze. It was all getting too much. 'Dad, my head is about to explode! What is The Invisible College?

'We're going to head office, the birthplace of The Royal Society and so much more before it. But to get there, we have to come here first.'

'Oh.' Sam replied. His toes were almost numb and the thin air was making him feel lightheaded. This adventure was rapidly losing its appeal.

They passed the wrecked doors and walked into still shadows. Sharp slivers of ice hung from the ceiling of a long tunnel, catching the light of the torch. A series of narrow slits were spaced at regular intervals along the walls.

'For archers,' his father supplied as he noticed Sam's interest. 'This is the only way in or out. In the olden days, guards would have sat behind these walls, armed with crossbows and throwing spears.'

Sam peered into the small voids, imagining malevolent eyes staring back.

'What happened to the doors?'

'They've always been that way,' Jen Si said. 'They're bait to lure attackers into this tunnel. There's a hidden door that rolls into place, preventing any retreat.'

Sam swallowed but said nothing.

The corridor narrowed and the proximity of the walls was oppressive by the time they arrived at an intact door of stained timbers. It was steel bound and heavily studded. Sam noticed the walls on either side of it were also perforated, although these holes were at floor level.

'And what are those ones for?'

'Oil. Vats of pitch could be poured down them making it very difficult for any enemy that made it this far to maintain a stable footing.' He raised the torch, revealing blackened stone around the door. 'It's also flammable.'

Sam felt a rush of warm air when the door swung in and Jen Si led his visitors into the heart of the monastery.

Ms Keller was no longer amused.

Progress had been too slow and failure rife. The stench of it frustrated her. Three of her four pawns had been removed from the board, the late (and far from great) Mr Eindhoven, being the most recent. She now had but one tiny seed from which to harvest success. And it was proving a hard nut to crack.

Flattery, bribery, blackmail and extortion, she had applied all without success. It was time to go back to basics. Good old-fashioned fear.

The person opposite her was enduring a great deal of that right now, and had suffered for several hours. Fear, she imagined, would be a welcome relief from pain.

'Of course, if you continue to refuse, we will never harm you again. In fact, we'll even keep you alive when you'd otherwise wither. Your family, however, will always suffer. And you will watch. Taking in every detail, creating beautiful, enduring memories to cherish during the long life I will make sure you live. Am I making myself clear?'

Her victim was slow to reply, sweat drenched and shuddering from the Capsaicin gas, from relentless and untold agony. Burning from the inside out. She used it as an encouragement in the interludes between their little chats, to keep the mind focused.

'Yes.' It was barely a whisper.

'Good.' She smiled. 'I trust we've reached an accord?'

The figure nodded, head slumping.

'Excellent.' Ms Keller rose, smoothing the front of her crimson silk blouse, nails painted a perfect jet black. 'You have a month. Two at the most. After that, well, I'm sure you can imagine.'

She turned and left the room, heels clicking a steely march.

Chapter 5

QUESTIONS AND ANSWERS

S am waited in a cosy round hall.
At its centre was a large fire pit surrounded by piles of deep cushions and fur throws. It was from one such divan that Sam pointed his bare feet at the radiated warmth. The rest of him was as far away as possible from the fire.

Steam rose from his socks and shoes draped over the iron bar around the hearth. A large crusty cooking pot dangled over the coals, waiting to feed the monastic masses.

The walls around him were covered with faded tapestries. Sam squinted at scenes of majestic palaces and cherry blossom gardens, wrathful deities and raging battles.

'Food?' Jen Si offered.

'Thank you.' Sam peered into the cloudy depths of his bowl. Chunks of meat and vegetables wallowing in a thick, greasy stock, a generous wedge of bread bobbing against the sides like a little gravy-coated island.

By the time Sam had licked the last morsel of stew from his fingers, his socks were dry and toasty. His shoes, though a little damp, were dry enough, and with a burp he fell in behind his father, following their host from the hall.

The décor of the monastery was sparse and, in most cases, barely functional. They passed dark, dreary chambers furnished only with thin mattresses and tattered blankets, and praying rooms with faded idols and stubby incense sticks. Finally, they reached a steep staircase near the rear of the complex. As they climbed, tiny portals in the wall provided Sam with a breath-taking view of the moonlit mountains.

Their ascent ended at a small landing, where a lone door rattled against its latch. Strong gusts of wind whistled around the tower and the door flapped open, revealing the torches of the guards far below. Confused, Sam realised there was no room on the other side. Why had they come to the top of the tower, if there was nowhere to go?

Neither his father nor Jen Si seemed perturbed by this fact. Their guide produced a small stone amulet on a string before sitting down on the last step. Murmuring what sounded like a prayer, he pressed the carving between his palms.

Sam looked up at his father who was chewing a fingernail.

Jen Si finished the incantation, stood up and placed the amulet around Jasper's neck. Before Sam could draw breath, his father surged forward, giving the door a firm push, and stepped into the dark night sky, pulling his panic-stricken son behind him.

Instead of falling into an abyss, Sam's foot encountered carpet. The scream died in his throat and he fell to his knees.

- 35 -

Jasper turned and smiled down at his son, sweat glistening on his brow. 'There's a lot to be said for the modern age. The old way of doing things required a lot of faith.' He helped the boy stand.

A flying robot barely missed Sam's head.

'Sorry,' the saucer shaped body slowed slightly before humming off, 'didn't realise that door was still in use...'

Sam staggered back against it. The monastery and mountain had vanished. There was no rushing wind, no tower or wobbly door.

Jasper avoided another airborne messenger. 'We're here! The Invisible College! And you can finally have all your answers. Well, some at least; I imagine what you'll see here will only lead to a great deal more questions!' He removed the amulet then placed it in a box on a three-legged table beside the door and began fussing with his collar.

Sam reached for the box to examine the amulet, but it was empty. He closed the lid, and opened it again. Still empty.

'Of course it is.' He gave up and turned his attention to the College.

They were standing at the foot of an enormous curved staircase that wound around a large classical stone statue of a man. On either side of the hall, a row of metal doors swished open and closed. People hurried in and out of them carrying papers and books, the odd bulky scroll or long tube tucked under their arm. Some paced in pairs or clustered in tight groups, heads bent in conversation.

Sam gawped at robots of all shapes, sizes and colours which buzzed, bobbed and weaved between the crowds, their soft neon lights pulsing hypnotically.

They hummed up and down the colossal statue, an old man in a toga and sandals.

'Herredrion,' Jasper supplied. 'The first of our Order, first of "The Few".'

'The who? What Order?' Sam was trying to soak up every detail, 'I thought you worked for the Patent Office, or The Royal Society? God, Dad, I'm so confused!'

'You're right, I do, but they're both a part of something far older and larger, serving a much wider purpose.' Jasper gazed up at the idol.

Sam waited. 'Which is...?'

'To protect humanity from itself.'

'I don't understand?'

'I'll let Ruben explain it. Come on.' With a neat side-step, Jasper avoided a group of women in green uniforms and headed for the stairs.

Floor after floor, Sam tried to peer down the corridors as they ascended. Each level of the atrium was a hive of activity. He was fascinated by the array of weird and wonderful robots, not to mention several unidentifiable creations roaming the halls.

He hurried to catch his father, his attention having been snared by something that looked suspiciously like a floating carpet, two levels down. 'So where exactly are we now?'

'You mean where is the College?'

'Yes.'

His father shrugged. 'Everywhere. This hall is simply a meeting of corridors, a bit like an anthill, except every room is located somewhere else; the thresholds are portals, much like the Speedlifts. You can access a thousand rooms from here, spread all over the world. It's truly amazing, hence the name.

'There are many Far Sight windows, as well, of course, like those in Mr D'Angelo's office. And,' he indicated the cloudless sky far above them, 'a rumour has it that the atrium ceiling is the largest Far Sight window ever built.'

Sam suddenly felt a tad claustrophobic. 'That's not the real sky?'

Jasper left the staircase at the penultimate level, and stopped in front of two gothic doors. 'Here we are, the Old Library.'

On the opposite side of the atrium a set of shiny new doors stood open, admitting a constant flow of traffic.

'That's the new library.' Jasper explained.

The staircase made one final curving ascent to a landing behind the head of the statue. Sam could now make out the man's long, bristling beard, fierce eyes and bushy brows. His forehead was furrowed and in his arms, he also carried a bundle of scrolls.

The boy peered up at two guards in purple and black coats who stood either side of the banister.

'What's up there?' Sam stretched onto his toes.

'That's the Chamber of the Council.'

'Let me guess – through another magic door behind the statue's head?'

'Yup!' The old library doors gave a protesting groan.

'Now in here you'll find Ruben. He's going to answer some of your questions,' Jasper lowered his voice, 'tends to go on a bit though, so be …' he made a pincer movement with fingers and thumb, 'concise. I'll be back later. Enjoy!'

The Old Library was indeed old. The floor was a mirage of faded chequered tiles. Two crescent desks near the door were piled high with papers, dusty green glass lamps illuminating the laden counters. Row upon row of columns supported a vaulted honeycombed ceiling. A huge, discoloured map covered the wall to Sam's right. A globe, taller than the average person, rested in a cradle below it, rotating slowly. As he drew closer, Sam was amazed to see tiny clouds floating above the three-dimensional landscape, turquoise seas and blue-black oceans rippling in the light of its own little sun.

'That's one of my favourite pastimes.' A rusty voice took him by surprise. 'I've spent hours watching typhoons and hurricanes ravage this poor little orb. Even saw a volcano erupt once.

'It's the only hologram I allow in here. A real-time projection of the Earth, collecting data from every satellite in orbit.'

Sam turned to find a short man regarding him, his hands clasped over a stout tummy, fingers wiggling. Wire spectacles balanced on the end of his button nose.

'Ruben?'

'That I am. Da Vinci. And a direct descendant! Though our family tended this library long before Leonardo put us on the map. Ha, map!' He pointed at the faded one on the wall, with a chuckle. 'Very bright chap. Of course, most of his truly inspiring works never saw the light of day. All squirrelled away in here, or the archives. You've been there? Well, there's no fancy Farnsworth thingamajig flying around and making a mess in here. Oh no! Had one, briefly. Archimedes, they called it. Gone now. There's loads over there though,' he flapped his arm in the direction of the new library. 'Full of gadgets and gizmos. But in here,' he beamed at his dusty empire, 'we do things the old-fashioned way. If you want the important information, you'll find it in here.' He paused, smiling.

Sam looked at the man, not sure if he'd finished or if Ruben expected applause. Perhaps he was just drawing breath to continue.

He continued. 'To business then! The others are waiting. Come, come.' Picking up a thick book, the librarian huffed and puffed up a stout spiral staircase to an alcove set between the columns, where several mismatched leather chairs were arranged around a coffee table; discoloured lamps of various shapes and sizes were also dotted around the landing.

Sam noticed that three of the seats were already occupied.

'Please.' Ruben pointed him toward an empty chair.

To Sam's left sat a tall boy with short hair and muscled arms. He was easily as large as Big Col, without the mischievous look. He regarded Sam's arrival impassively, arms folded.

Beside him, an old squat red armchair appeared to have almost swallowed its occupant. In it sat a much smaller boy with pale skin and mousy hair. His hands were folded in his lap and he sat bolt upright, blinking. He did venture a smile and Sam winked back.

To Sam's right a girl sat with her back to him, her long legs draped over the arm of the chair as she stared up at the ceiling. Her long hair was blonde and she had skin the colour of honey.

'Right.' Ruben took a seat and called their attention, resting a tome across his generous thighs. His feet did not reach the floor.

'Forget everything you think you know. This requirement has changed the lives of countless young men and women over the centuries, and the instruction forms the opening speech of every Induction. So, fitting, I thought, to begin with these words today. You will now find that the impossible is, in most cases, possible, and that things you never thought probable, do exist. Accept that and you're halfway to understanding our world.' He beamed at them excitedly. 'Who knows the history of the Order of The Few?'

Sam was relieved when the small boy with the mousy hair quickly raised his hand.

Ruben's day was complete. 'Excellent! Giuseppe, is it?'

'I prefer Joe.'

Sam thought the boy could be Italian.

'Of course, of course. And do you know, Veronique? Fedor?' He looked at the others, but both shook their heads. 'Sam?'

'Um, I thought that's why we're here.'

Veronique smirked and Fedor gave a snort.

'Yes, yes,' Ruben waved his hands, 'just wanted to see where I needed to start.'

'How about at the beginning?' Fedor suggested. Russian, Sam guessed from his accent.

The poor librarian was not used to dealing with moody teens and appeared crestfallen by their reaction. Sam watched him fuss with the book in his lap, picking at the cover.

Joe tossed Ruben a lifeline. 'My grandfather told me that the Order started long before the Crusades.'

'Yes, yes. Very good. Herredrion was, in fact, a philosopher and inventor in the time of Homer, a thousand years before the birth of Christ. He's said to have come from across the seas and the first account we could find of him, outside our own records, of course, was at the downfall of Troy. Such was his humble nature, he kept no account of himself, for he lived to serve a simple purpose: to preserve and protect knowledge. He carried with him a book, and gathered all manner of secrets in it. Mathematics, astronomy, chemistry, engineering, he sought to catalogue and preserve them all in the hope that they could be used to uplift and better our world.'

'Must have been a big book,' Fedor said.

'Well, the majority were recorded on scrolls,' Ruben admitted. 'He saved the most important finds for his book. But these were troubled times and word soon spread of this mystical book that held, it was said, the secret to life itself. He gathered many followers, but those who wished to wrest these secrets from him also sought Herredrion and he was forced to flee. The faithful few who followed him into exile swore to protect the book, and so the Order of The Few was born. Over time it developed other names, branches and divisions. Some eminent, such as The Rosicrucian and The Royal Society, others...' he paused, curbing his tongue, 'were darker and more secretive.' He scratched the arm of his chair with his fingernail. 'Do you know what makes the Order so special?'

'Service is hereditary and exclusive,' Joe said. 'Only the descendants of Herredrion's Few can serve.'

'Close. Only direct descendants can serve in the field. However, the world soon became a much larger place and we were forced to make use of outsiders in a controlled manner. The work they do is compartmentalised. The Cadres, however, are all of the Blood.'

Sam was becoming intrigued by this bedtime story. 'Cadres?'

'Teams who serve in the field. Each Cadre has four members: Readers are the academics with a capacity to store vast amounts of knowledge,

Charlatans are the team chameleons. They spy, cheat and steal; brilliant at retrieving information. Juggernauts provide the muscle, of course. And finally, each Cadre has a Paladin, a "Glory Hound".' He smiled. 'They lead the Cadre, and are the strategists, possessing guile and cunning – and diplomacy when needs must.'

The boys were grinning. This was interesting.

Veronique spoke for the first time. 'Sounds a little sexist?' Like Joe, her accent was light, and Sam thought he detected a French lilt.

Ruben looked shocked. 'Not at all, my dear. Most Cadres have a female Reader, Charlatan or Paladin. I even think there have been a few female Juggernauts, though not many, mind. We cast no favour upon sex, creed, or colour, I can assure you. All of the Blood are equal.'

She nodded. Her blue eyes strayed to Sam and he looked away quickly.

'Where was I?' Ruben paused. 'Oh, yes. The Order was started with the purpose of protecting Herredrion's book. He witnessed what humanity had become capable of at the fall of Troy, and knew that more power would only goad us into far worse. So, The Few began collecting and hiding any advancement which, in the wrong hands, had the potential to unleash destruction and chaos. As their treasure grew, so did their power, and The Invisible College was built. The Cadres evolved from necessity and over the centuries, The Order grew to encompass every continent.

'We monitored all the great inventors, such as Sir Christopher Wren, Tesla, Faraday, Edison, Curie, Einstein – they were the real cause for concern, and we even inducted a few into the Order. Or "The Honourable Order of Inventors", as Wren liked to call it. Most came to understand that just because something could be invented, did not mean it should. Unfortunately, ethics and social responsibility often take a back seat in moments of genius.

'Of course, we're not always successful. Things have slipped through: gunpowder, the cannon, the gun, mustard gas, Agent Orange, the atomic bomb – dare I say, the Internet. But, for each of those cataclysms, we were able to prevent hundreds of others, and so our purpose has remained to protect humanity and the world around us.'

'What other things?' Sam was now itching with curiosity.

Ruben rubbed his chin. 'Well, you have the Forbidden Inventions. There's invisibility, shrinking and time travel. We use some of the less risky secrets ourselves, of course. As you have, too. Every Speedlift and door in the College is a wormhole. We can bend time and space to bring two places together, punch through and *voila*, a portal! And the Elixir of Youth formed the basis for our CarboSilicone technology. But the Forbidden inventions are too dangerous, and there are some which will never even be opened, simply catalogued and sealed in the depths of Herredrion's Belly for all time.'

'Wow!' Joe was impressed, and also intrigued by the mystery of the Forbidden. 'But what's Herredrion's Belly?'

'It's a nickname for the archive inside our founder's statue. It can only be reached through the Council Chamber and is heavily guarded.'

'So why are we here?' Fedor asked. 'My brothers are Juggernauts, as is my father. They left home at eighteen, not fifteen.'

'Quite right.' Ruben wiggled and adjusted his glasses. 'Each household of the Blood is required to dedicate at least one child to the Order. When they reach the age of eighteen, the candidate is brought to the College to go through an Induction, to see if they are fit for field service. If they fail, they join our support functions, otherwise, they are assigned a discipline and begin their field training. Only after that does their Cadre service begin.'

Joe looked worried. 'But I'm only fourteen...'

'Yeah,' Sam lamented. 'This sounds like fun, but I've got friends and school, then Uni. I doubt my parents would even sign off on a gap year, let alone secret agent training.'

'You're here because you have been chosen, Sam,' the familiar voice of Mr D'Angelo came from behind them. 'As have you all. And your parents have agreed to your participation.'

He was standing at the top of the stairs and approached them as he spoke. 'You've heard some of the glory, the things we've achieved in the name of greater good.' he prowled around the island of chairs. ' *"We Few, we happy Few, we band of brothers; For he to-day that sheds his blood with me, shall be my brother..."* Do you know Shakespeare? With the light, must come the dark. You see, Herredrion's legacy did not stay in Ancient Greece and, just like the tales of Jason's Fleece or Pandora's Box, the legend of the Book of Power grew. It was not long after, in a dark place, that another group was formed – the Harbingers. Except they were not the philanthropic sort and they were many. These were greedy, malicious people, who would stop at nothing for power.

'Over the centuries, they wormed their way into the company of mighty monarchs, whispering tales of a treasure that would raise the ruler upon high. Exalt him above all others.

'They encouraged the Greeks to lay waste to Troy, urged Hannibal to cross the Alps and convinced the emperors of Rome to tear Europe apart; Genghis Khan's conquest of Asia. Alexander the Great, even the Christian Crusades – all have searched for Herredrion's book. The Spanish Inquisition, the British and Dutch, even the Vikings scoured the globe for it.

'None were more single-minded than the Nazis, who plunged the world into two wars in their quest for power. But in the shadows, as always, a far more menacing power pulled their strings.'

'Ruben mentioned the Forbidden Inventions, those we have confiscated, but there are also the Hidden Inventions, inventors we didn't reach in time or who refused to accept our cautious logic. Entire Cadres are dedicated to scouring the world for these secrets and their creators, for if they fall into other hands the outcomes would be catastrophic.' He stopped behind Sam and placed his hands on the boy's shoulders.

'And so, we prevail. Operating from the shadows, we continue to serve Herredrion's somewhat idealistic purpose and adapt it to the modern age. For times are indeed changing.' He resumed pacing around the circle. 'In the past hundred years, we have made more technological progress than in the previous thousand. Projects like the Fabulous Atoms initiative have allowed us to find and control many dangers. And it's proven very successful, even more so with the rapid expansion of the Internet.

'We own and operate some of the largest global technology companies and can actively influence the development of society, releasing helpful advancements and managing the dangerous ones. The Global Village has not always been a boon for it transformed the playing field instantly. Now anyone can create a virus or an electromagnetic weapon that could send us back to the Dark Ages. And so, we've concentrated on steering global politics to challenge cybercrime and clandestine terrorist groups.

'But in doing so, we've created a double-edged sword. We've focused on technology and become overly reliant upon it; and if we lost the ability to power these new wonders, we'd be helpless. So, we've designed a contingency plan, a different type of apprenticeship to create a new breed of field personnel, who will learn the skills of the Old Order before they tackle A.I., Earth Song networks, CarboSilicone implants, Far Sight cameras and Inertia Dampening Armour.

'You four have been selected to take early training in Psychokinesis, Bugei Juhappan, Ethnobotany—' He stopped behind Ruben. Four confused faces were staring at him. Salvador hated explanations. 'You know nothing of the old skills?'

'No, sorry,' Sam apologised. The others nodded in agreement.

'What do they teach you in school these days? I'm surprised you still learn Latin.'

No one had the heart to tell him they didn't.

He drew a deep breath, 'Psychokinesis – from the Greek word *psyche,* meaning mind or soul, and *kinesis* meaning movement – is the ability to control and, in certain cases, bend the world around you.'

'Like at Shen Pi,' Sam blurted.

'Exactly. The monks are experts.'

'*Bugei Juhappan,*' Salvador continued, 'is a Japanese term that refers to the eighteen skills studied by *Bushi*: swordsmanship, archery, unarmed combat, espionage, strategy, to name but a few.

'And lastly, Ethnobotany: the study of plants and their qualities, which gives one the opportunity to create cocktails for every situation.

These are the types of skills missing from the modern Cadres. So, the Council selected four promising youngsters,' he looked at each of them, 'to complete a summer apprenticeship. You've been given the chance to become the first of a new generation.'

They all beamed back at him.

Vanity, he smiled, was still his favourite sin.

'There is, however, an important condition. If you fail to pass the course, your family will not be able to remain in The Order, there is too much at stake.

Joe's eyes were wide and Fedor's frown had intensified; only Veronique kept complete composure.

'So, at the end of the six weeks, providing you passed,' he spread his arms wide, 'your skills will be put to the test against a modern Cadre at the annual CruciBowl tournament, held at The Inventors Fair!'

Sam had never head of either event and his worried expression mirrored the others. Things had escalated quickly.

'Nothing too dangerous, I promise,' Mr D'Angelo assured them.

The potential recruits looked unconvinced and he chewed his lip thoughtfully. 'Perhaps I shall arrange for you to meet a few of the teams before The Inventors Fair. Your names will be on every tongue and all this before your Induction. You'll be famous!'

A million questions and concerns were on Sam's mind, but he managed a smile.

Pride! Mr D'Angelo suppressed a self-congratulatory grin. As sins went, it came a close second.

'Einstein once said, "*The most beautiful thing we can experience is the mysterious, the source of all true art and science. He to whom the emotion is a stranger, who can no longer pause to wonder and stand rapt in awe, is as good as dead; his eyes are closed. To know that what is impenetrable to us really exists. This knowledge, this feeling, is the centre of true.*"' He stood back from the chair he had been leaning against. 'Will you take that journey, will you become one of The Few?'

Lost for words, Sam and the others simply nodded.

'Excellent! Ruben will inundate you with reading material and we'll see you back here on Monday.'

Chapter 6

S am lay on his bed, staring at the ceiling.
  What a day!

He looked over at the pile of books on his desk. *The Art of War*, by Sun Tzu, was on top. Below that, the faded green spine of a heftier book showed the title *Meditation and Psychokinesis: Practical Application* scrawled in flaking silver leaf. The Ethnobotany book at the bottom of the pile was even larger.

He had got some answers today, but as his father had predicted, they had only led to a load more questions. His mind was alight with excitement, confusion and doubt. The summer was going to prove very interesting.

* * *

Joe turned the last page of *Meditation and Psychokinesis*. He'd found it fascinating and had devoured it in hours.

The young Italian was a quick study and could recall every word, line and sentence he had ever read – verbatim. Which was no small amount of information considering that he had been reading a book a day before most children had learned to walk.

Of the assigned books, only, *The Art of War* lay untouched. Joe had read it when he was eight and thought Joseph Marie Amiot's French translation to be closest to Sun Tzu's original text. His obsession with reading was part compulsion and part shield. His books protected him from the outside world and today he felt like he needed more protection than ever.

If you fail, your family will not be able to remain in The Order...

With a grunt, he heaved the Ethnobotany digest onto his lap and once more allowed his curiosity to wash away the sense of foreboding.

Hours later, his mother nudged open the door to his father's study, carrying a tray. She set it down on the bed in a small clearing amidst the sea of books, and then tugged the curtains open, allowing the afternoon in. The view of Lake Como was stunning, and she could not help but sigh at the bright sails bobbing on the water, wishing her son were outside and not locked away in the book-lined mausoleum which had become his bedroom.

She sat on the chair beside Joe's bed, moving a strand of hair from under the frame of her son's glasses. 'Nonno says you had a good day?'

'Si! Very interesting. Huge library! *And* there is another one. I hope to see it soon, too.'

His mother gave a sad smile. 'Your father was the same. He spent more than half his life in this room, nose buried in a book. I had to leave notes between the pages, to remind him to eat.' She paused. 'He would be very proud of you.'

'I've read all his books now.' Joe patted a crimson cover beside his pillow, *Prestupleniye i Nakazaniye*. 'This was the last one.'

'Russian?'

'*Crime and Punishment*, by Dostoevsky. I can see why Papà liked it. It explains that your conscience can be far stricter than any physical punishment.'

'Oh, Joe. You're too *young* to be wallowing in such serious things. You should be outside! Playing, chasing girls, getting into trouble. We live in one of the most beautiful places on earth and you'd never know, for all the time you spend up here.'

'You want me to get into trouble?'

'I just don't want life to pass you by while you read about other people's. Now tell me all about your day whilst you eat, and then you must agree to go outside for a while.'

Working the tray onto his lap, Joe began his account slowly.

Lake Como was beyond compare.

The water shimmered and the fairy tale shoreline of neat lawns, sculpted trees and graceful buildings were bathed in gold. Many of the world's most elite families called it home, and Joe's ancestors had lived there for countless centuries. It was the centre of his small universe. He stood on the balcony, looking out at the lake, the patio and garden lit by hundreds of tiny lanterns, flickering in the breeze.

'Well, well, I see the Little Lord has left his tower.'

A familiar face grinned up at him from a hammock.

'Very funny, Bella.' He stuck out his tongue. 'I didn't know you were here.'

The girl stretched. 'Just popped in to bring some wine we found in the cellar, but that was over an hour ago. Would your Lordship care to go to the lake?'

Joe felt anxious whenever Isabella was about. 'Okay.' He managed to not squeak.

He paused before a mirror on the landing and gave his hair a quick check. Cleaning his glasses, he scurried through the kitchen and into the garden, his heart fit to thump through his chest.

Bella was a year his senior. She went to an all-girls school in Switzerland and now they only saw each other during holidays but, when they were children, they had been inseparable. Playing in the grounds, swimming in the lake and always scheming ways to wrest delights from the cook.

That was before his father died.

That summer Bella had returned from school a young woman and things had never been the same between them. He looked at her differently now, her long dark hair, olive skin and sparkling eyes, the same cheeky grin but more interesting lips...

Stop it! She's your oldest friend, only now she's beautiful and you're still just...you!

'Took your time,' she teased. 'Come on then, let's get some air into those dusty lungs!'

The gravel path crunched underfoot. The evening was warm and the first stars bright. Bella flopped down on the grass, resting on her elbows. 'Aren't they amazing?'

'I guess. Did you know the closest star to us, after the Sun, is Alpha Centauri? It's only 4.3 light years, which doesn't sound like a lot, but that is over 41.7 trillion kilometres…'

Bella laughed, a golden sound. 'I bet you have the girls lining up at the gates, Joe.'

'I…'

She patted the grass. 'Zip it, smarty pants, and sit down before you strain something.'

He frowned, but complied, leaving a respectable gap between them. 'How was school?'

'Boring, but I'm off to Ibiza next week. You?'

If only you knew. 'Not sure,' he lied. 'Nonno wants to go to Bali.'

'Cool – awesome beaches!' She rolled over onto her stomach and was now next to him, looking up with her big brown eyes.

He was sweating buckets.

'You know, it's been so long since I've seen you without glasses.' She drew herself up, inches from his face, fingers reaching for the frames. His world became blurry.

'You're growing into quite the handsome young man, aren't you, little Lord Joe?'

'You know I don't like being called that. Can I have my glasses back, please?'

'*Si, si*!' She held them just out of his reach. 'But I want something first.'

He swallowed. 'What?'

'A kiss, you fool.' And with that Bella leaned forward, the smell of her perfume filling his senses.

Joe closed his eyes, heart hammering. He could not believe this was happening. There was a rustle of cotton. He opened his eyes. Her blurry form was gone. And so were his glasses.

She laughed. 'You didn't think it would be that easy, did you?'

'Bells, I can't see!'

'Love is blind,' she teased. 'Didn't you know?'

He took a few steps in the direction of her voice.

'Over here,' the next call came from behind him.

'This isn't funny, Bells.' That awful feeling of helpless anxiety was rising in his stomach.

'Don't be such a baby,' she called from his left side. 'Besides, some things are worth fighting for, no?'

Joe bit his lip, fighting back a hot retort. The sheen of his infatuation with *Signorina* Giordano was wearing off. He turned toward the hazy shape that should be the house.

'Oh, come on, Joe,' Bella called. The disarming scent of her perfume washed over him. 'Here,' she slipped his frames in place. 'Is it so bad to let someone else be in control just for a moment?' She was disappointed and Joe suddenly felt guilty.

'ISABELLA! We're leaving.'

'I…' he began, but she had already started toward the house.

'Have a good summer,' she called over her shoulder. Then turning to look at him, she blew a kiss. 'Better luck next time.'

* * *

Fedor was the strong, silent type. Not by choice. It was just easier to be that way.

His gene pool swam with brawn, oozed it, in fact, leaving little space for intelligence to manifest, and yet Fedor had been blessed with both. Blessed, however, was a subjective description. He would argue that he was cursed.

Fedor bent to pick up his books and caught a boot to the rear.

'You don't need books.' His father scowled. 'You're a fighter, not a poet!'

'Not all books are about poetry.'

The next kick caught him on the leg and he winced.

'You see! Already you're trying to be smart with me!'

Fedor's mother slapped her husband with the tea towel. 'Leave him be, Alexis!'

'There were no books when I did my training. Lots of punch bags, vomit and blood! Hard floors and stinky sawdust to land on – if you were lucky. Who's this Ruben, anyway?'

'The Librarian, Papa. These are his books. Mr D'Angelo told him to give them to us.'

His father's brow knotted. 'Well, that's his business. But whilst you're under this roof, you follow my rules.

'Now get changed and bring the wood in, unless your mother can use those to feed the stove?'

Fedor shepherded the books away from the cast iron maw.

His bedroom was at the back of the old stone farmhouse. Thick walls, heavy larch beams and warped windows impregnated with dust. The squat building nestled among a copse of spindly pines, overlooking the valleys to the south. To the north, the horizon bristled with thick forests. As children, he and his brothers had built forts and waged wars from their imaginary strongholds in the woods, between their chores, trapping game and practicing Sambo in the barn.

His brothers were gone now. Dimitri had left last year and Karl two years before that. They were both excellent fighters, Sambo champions, with not one original thought between them. Perfect, in their father's eyes.

Fedor was better than both of them. What he lacked in size, he made up for in strategy, adapting his father's holds and submissions with great success; a feat that had both troubled and angered Alexis. Now, at nearly sixteen, Fedor made short work of his brothers when they returned home for Defender of the Fatherland Day, and that served to incense his father even more.

Fedor shrugged off and neatly folded his town clothes before trudging out into the yard. Prising the axe from the wood-pile, he whistled to the pair of Laika hunting dogs rolling in the dust beside the kitchen door. Misha and Mikhail darted past him, snapping at each other in their hurry to take the lead. They barked a lot, much to his father's disgust, and Alexis could often be heard bellowing at them from within the house. But they were brilliant hunters, and both affectionate and loyal to Fedor.

The clearing where Fedor liked to chop wood was about a ten-minute walk from the house and he had chosen it for that very reason. The weight of the day fell away with every step he took.

He had known of the Order ever since Karl had returned from his Induction. Until then, Fedor believed he had joined the army. His father and brothers were Juggernauts. Good ones. They often returned from assignments battered or bruised, but were none the worse for wear; and he enjoyed the stories they told around the fire late into the night, limbs soaking in steaming baths of salt, bellies full of vodka.

Mr D'Angelo's speech carried grave consequences for Fedor. If he failed the apprenticeship, his family would lose *everything* – and they would blame him.

Slowing to a plod, the dogs out of sight, he did not notice that a silence had settled upon the forest. Even the wind had died, retreating through the undergrowth and carrying away the faint scent of unclean fur and fetid breath that should have warned him about the bear.

The demon rose from the undergrowth in a shower of branches. Long claws stretched toward the boy, slavering jaws parting inches from his face. Fedor staggered back and tripped. The fall saved him from a vicious swipe. The ground shook as the bear lost its balance and landed on all fours, squashing Fedor beneath its matted gut. The boy lay frozen, his mind racing in terror.

He had dropped the axe but dared not move a muscle. The animal shifted its weight; a low growl reverberating near the boy's head, and Fedor knew his final moments were upon him.

Two streaks burst from the undergrowth, snapping and snarling. Misha and Mikhail launched themselves at the massive creature smothering their master. Darting back and forth the dogs drew the bear's attention from one to the other. Misha managed to tear the soft underside of its foreleg, whilst Mikhail snapped at its nose.

The bear reared in response, offering Fedor a chance to escape, but not before stepping on the boy's ankle. Ignoring the pain, he rolled away until his shoulder encountered the handle of the axe. Snatching it, he turned and swung with all his might. The weapon whistled through the air and sank into a tree.

The dogs had now placed themselves between him and the bear, hackles raised, growling. The bear's black eyes were wide and saliva dripped from its jaws. Its fur was dark and wet where the dogs had nipped at it, but the rage and hunger that had driven the animal to attack eclipsed its pain.

Frantically working the axe loose, Fedor raised it over his head and hurled it at the monster towering before them, then turned and ran.

Discretion is the better part of valour! 'Dogs, *COME!*'

The pain from his ankle was white hot, but far better than sharp claws raking across his back. He plunged through the forest, hands raised to shield his face from the wooden fingers trying to tear at him. Then the ground gave way and he fell, tumbling over and over.

Fedor stopped with a crunch.

Darkness.

* * *

Veronique marvelled at the sight of Paris at night.

It was a magnificent city, but the true Parisian atmosphere could be found away from the crowded streets, in Montmartre and Montparnasse. They were her favourite places, filled with artistic charm and colourful characters. And tonight they held the promise of even greater magical delights, for it was *Bal masqué* – her family's annual masquerade ball.

Her silk and chiffon gown rustled, as she made her way to the dressing table. 'Who shall we be tonight?' she asked the face in the mirror.

To the world, she was simply Veronique. However, when she chose to hide from it, the girl in the mirror was rarely the same person twice. The prim persona of that dutiful daughter was pushed into the shadows and the face she saw in the mirror could do anything, be anyone. She had played every conceivable role, and tonight she would be Nikki.

She lifted a crimson mask with gold lining and a bright red plume from Ruben's pile of books, dismissing their call.

Mañana, as the Spanish would say.

She waved the red mask and puckered her lips. '*Nikki, the Temptress*?

'Or *Nikki, the Noble*?' The black and silver mask complimented her golden skin. Tilting her chin upward, she sucked in her cheeks and put on her best pout.

'*Nikki, the Fool*?' Crossing her eyes behind the visage of the jester, the bells jingled mournfully when she set it down.

'Ah, the mysterious *Papillon*.' The butterfly mask was beautiful. A gift from her grandmother, it was made from jade and gold leaf, with gentle curves and tiny sequins. '*Parfaite!*' She smiled at the mirror. 'Perfect, darling,' she repeated in her aristocratic drawl, rummaging through her make up box.

Veronique loved acting. As a child, her dressing up box would have put the Théâtre des Bouffes-Parisiens to shame. From silk kimonos and richly plumed Native American headdresses to glitzy 1920s fashion and trendy Sixties outfits, face paints, false teeth, wigs, glasses and gaudy jewellery – Nikki's armoury was endless.

Her obsession did not end there, for she was fascinated by people's accents and inflections, and could mimic them all within minutes of meeting someone. Lisps and stutters, giggles, laughs and snorts, she kept them all. In fact, her skill became so precise that she had earned the nickname *Le petit perroquet*, the little parrot.

Every time she sat at her dressing table, she asked her reflection the same pressing question, but tonight presented her with a new opportunity. For tonight Nikki could stand where usually only Veronique was permitted. And tonight she would be *Nikki, the Southern Belle*.

The Beauchamp *Bal masqué* was hosted at their lavish townhouse. An evening of meticulous décor, sumptuous cuisine and sophisticated spirits. No expense was spared and the event was a staple fixture on the social calendar for both celebrity and royalty.

Veronique stood at the banister surveying the lavish hall below. *Les diamants de la couronne* drifted through the open terrace doors; the musicians gathered near the fountain. Guests wafted across the floor in glamorous costumes, feigning sincerity at every meeting. She could see long-nosed Venetian masks, colourful Mardi Gras costumes, jesters, make up and feathers, there was not a bare face to be seen. Champagne corks popped and the nectar of privilege flowed.

Veronique found it anonymous, impersonal and flamboyant. She descended the stairs and scooped up a drink.

'*Bonsoir*,' a tall man in a black and gold Venetian mask greeted her, brandishing a fluted glass.

Veronique unleased Nikki's southern charm. 'What's that now?'

'*Pardon*. You're not French?'

'Heavens, no.' She tittered, waving her hand. 'Well, distantly, perhaps. I'm from Savannah, Georgia – in the United States. Of America.'

'Yes, I know where it is.' She could hear the slight scoff in his tone. This was too easy. 'And what brings you to this fine party, *Mademoiselle*...?'

Veronique waited the perfect length of time.

'Oh, you mean my name?' She laughed again, slapping the man's chest. 'Why didn't you just say so, silly. It's Anastasia. Anastasia Swanson. And you are?'

'Gerard Bordier.' He took her hand, kissing her fingers. 'Welcome to Paris.'

Her uncle did not recognise her.

'I see you're drinking fruit juice, *ma chèrie*, you must try the champagne, it's what we French are famous for. Amongst other things...' He had yet to release Veronique's hand, or notice that his wife was watching the exchange from across the room.

'Well, I'm afraid bubbles go straight to my head, sir, and I certainly don't want to be making a spectacle of myself amongst all these fine folk.'

'Nonsense!' He swiped two glasses from a passing tray. 'I'll not hear of it. Let's find somewhere a little quieter and you can tell me all about your… Savannah, was it?'

'Gerard!' Veronique's aunt stood at his shoulder, hands on hips, her naturally stern demeanour even more formidable beneath her Faustian mask. 'I hope you're not trying to get our little *perroquet* drunk?'

'Bianca, this is *Mademoiselle* Swanson, from America, I've yet to see Veronique and I can assure you I wouldn't…'

'*Mon Dieu*!' She turned her attention to the young woman. 'You look lovely, my dear. Mother will be delighted to see you've chosen her mask. Have you seen her?'

Nikki vanished.

'No, not yet,' Veronique replied. 'I love your costume too, Aunt Bianca. Very feisty!'

Gerard's jaw dropped. 'Veronique!' His cheeks had darkened beneath his long-nosed mask. 'Why, you…'

'Oh hush, Gerard!' his wife snapped, whisking her niece away.

* * *

Jenny MacLeod sat outside Mr D'Angelo's office, chewing a toffee and admiring a glorious, albeit smog-stained sunrise from the top of the Empire State Building. The other window displayed a damp, grey Machu Picchu.

It had been a long time since her last holiday and three glorious weeks of sailing the sun-drenched islands of Fiji were now but hours away. She had thought it a certainty before her summons to see the Boss. On a Sunday.

Jenny was an ambitious Trainer. She was responsible for seven of the top ten Cadres, and had successfully introduced Krav Maga to their martial arts syllabus. She was known to be smart, competitive and driven. But now she was tired. *So* tired! Her head flopped back. Just a few more hours now...

The door to the office opened and Owen's bull neck swung into view. 'Come on in, Jen.'

Inside, Persephone was humming along the bookshelf near the door.

'Hi, Seph.'

'Miss MacLeod.'

Salvador was wading through reams of text on a holographic screen. 'One minute, my dear,' he murmured.

Jenny waited, staring at the peaceful mountains through the long window, the succulent green grass rippling hypnotically in the breeze. So tired.

With a faint click, the holographic projector shut down, and Salvador turned to her. 'Thank you for coming in at such short notice, Jennifer, I understand you're getting ready to go on leave?'

Sunday name. This did not bode well. 'Yes.'

'Anywhere nice?'

'Fiji.'

'Wonderful place. Rebecca and I were in Vanua Levu for the Millennium.'

Jenny only had a very hazy memory of her own Millennium celebrations. She smiled in response and he continued.

'I've got some good news and some bad news for you.' Salvador laced his fingers and pursed his lips. 'The good news is that your apprenticeship project has been approved. The bad news, I'm afraid, is that it must begin tomorrow.'

Jenny's stomach tightened. The project he was referring to had been as much his idea as hers. In fact, she was fairly certain he had 'let her have' the incredibly bold idea, as it had never quite felt her own.

'I know this disrupts your holiday plans, but such an important project cannot be entrusted to anyone else, so I must insist that you delay your trip.'

She forced a smile and tried not to sound stiff. 'That's fantastic news, sir. What finally changed the Council's minds?'

'Gabriel made the final decision. Your reputation has reached considerable heights, he was very impressed.'

Gabriel Laurent was the Head of the Council and Jenny could not help but smile.

Vanity. Oh, how Salvador loved vanity.

'The Council has decided that an apprenticeship to recruit and train field operatives several years before their formal Induction age, is a good one. They agree that it could imprint key skills, set them apart from the modern Cadres, and increase their effectiveness in the field.'

'Wait, *before* their Induction? But that would make them kids. I wasn't suggesting that—'

'Fourteen or fifteen: Old enough to handle the physical requirements. We've got six weeks, and you'll need to push them to their limits. If we succeed, it'll be the start of a new era. And who better to break the mould than the young woman who's single-handedly re-inventing our approach to training? You'll be famous, Jennifer!'

She blushed.

It was almost too easy.

Chapter 7

Fedor awoke in pain.

His head hurt. His ankle throbbed. It felt like his entire body was bruised, but it did not *feel* as if he had been eaten...which was an immediate plus. He could hear panting and hoped it was the dogs.

He opened his eyes. The sun was setting upon the very tips of the trees. Below, the richness of the forest had bleached into the monotones of twilight and the crickets were strumming in the undergrowth. He was lying at the bottom of the dry riverbed, and Misha and Mikhail crouched nearby, their backs to him, ears pricked as they sniffed at the woods. He raised his hand to his head and his fingers came away bright red.

Great.

The movement caught the dogs' attention and they leapt up, fussing over him. 'All right, dogs. I'm all right. Good dogs. *Gooood* dogs.' He closed his eyes and mouth, whilst they smothered him in canine kisses.

When Fedor finally pushed himself off the ground, his vision swam, a wave of nausea rising. 'Urgh.' His father was going to have a field day with this.

'You could've been killed!' his mother fumed, raising his ankle onto her lap. She peeled away his boot. The joint had swollen into his footwear and the two were reluctant to part.

Thankfully, his father had not been home when he returned, but his mother's reaction was almost as bad. Where her fury came from concern, his father's would have born of annoyance, or disappointment. Probably both.

Alyona deposited a bottle of vodka in front of her son before pouring boiling water into a basin and fetching her first aid bag. It was far from the first time one of her boys had come home battered and bruised, though never before from wrestling a bear.

'Drink. But only a sip!'

Fedor was only too happy to comply.

'What was it doing so close to the house?' She stripped away his sock. The ankle was purple but the skin was not broken and he could wiggle all his toes. Just.

'The bins are sealed, the dogs eat indoors and we're nowhere near winter, I just can't understand it.'

Fedor's hand strayed toward the vodka. For medicinal support, of course.

'Oh no, that's enough of that! Now bend forward, let me see your thick head.'

He closed his eyes, the warm water from the sponge running down his neck.

'It's quite a bump.' She felt around the lump. 'But only a small cut. You'll be fine.'

Misha was sniffing his swollen ankle and licking it, whimpering. He was too tired to flinch and the warm caress of her tongue was soothing.

'You do realise your father will expect you to fetch the axe in the morning?'

'*Da.*'

'And I suppose you still need to pack for this trip?'

'Uuuurgh!' His head was beating like a thousand drums and the last thing he felt like now was packing, let alone going on this stupid training camp.

Her demeanour softened and Alyona kissed her son's forehead. 'I tell you what, you hobble over there and light the fire. I'll bring a footbath to soak that ankle and then I'll pack your bag. You can check it over in the morning. *Da?*'

'*Spasibo*, Mama,' he whimpered. Feeling very sorry for himself, he heaved his large frame out of the chair and shuffled into the lounge, Misha and Mikhail never leaving his side.

'Good dogs.'

It had been a long day.

* * *

Joe sighed. Long, hard and with feeling. It had been a trying evening all round. First Bella, and now his mother – who had scattered half of his wardrobe around the room and currently held a massive, stuffed toiletry bag under her arm.

'I don't need all this.' He rolled his eyes when a third plaid sleeveless cardigan was added to the pile. 'Nonno says it'll be just like Summer Camp. A few pairs of shorts, some shirts, a jacket and hiking boots.'

'How does *he* know?' She held up two pairs of beige corduroy trousers. 'What about your allergies? Your medicine? Not to mention a spare pair of glasses! Have you packed a swimming costume? You'll need sunscreen, SP50, at least!'

Joe flopped onto the bed, head in his hands.

It was true, they had not been given a list. In fact, Ruben had been pretty vague on details. A six week course with a free weekend midway and a trip to the mysterious Inventors Fair at the end. They needed parental consent, basic necessities and their wits.

Wits, Joe had in abundance. *Check!*

'How about an umbrella?' from deep within the wardrobe.

Patience, on the other hand, he did not.

He swore.

Quietly.

* * *

Veronique studied the books she had dismissed only hours ago. In the hall below, the ball continued in muffled reverie.

'*Nikki, Monte Cristo,*' she sighed.

Her father had tracked her down, probably with Aunt Bianca's help, and marched her upstairs at midnight. 'Your selection is a great honour, Veronique, and you will do your family proud,' he had told her. 'It's time to put away this childishness.' He indicated the costumes draped about the room and slammed the door.

He was the reason she had created Nikki, her complex alter ego who could enjoy life without the pressure of carrying the family honour. It was not Nikki's fault that Veronique's father had no son. Nikki did not feel guilt. Nikki was free.

Sitting crossed legged on her bed with the books beside her, all finery forgotten, she picked up the worn deck of Tarot cards and flipped the top one over.

The Wheel of Fortune.

The cards never offered an exact answer, the Wheel had many potential meanings. She flipped over the next card.

The World.

A trend was forming. The end of a cycle of life and a pause before the next.

There was one last card to turn. Her fingers trembled.

The Magician.

This felt a little more positive: she must embrace her talents and tap into her potential.

Veronique flopped back onto the pillows and stared at the ceiling rose. She did not notice one final card slip from the deck and slide to the floor, coming to rest on the pile of masks beside her bed; the most well-known and misunderstood card in the Tarot, the skeletal figure of Death.

* * *

Sam couldn't sleep. He lay in his bed, hands folded behind his head, feet shuffling.

He had packed. A bulging bag awaited destinations unknown. The twins had hampered the process, taking great delight in removing clothes the second they were folded and stowed.

'You're sure you want to go?' his mother had asked. 'You don't have to. Not yet.' Angelique was not ready to lose another child.

Sam's teenage bravado had crushed any misgivings he might have had. 'Of course! Dad says it will be Summer Camp on steroids!'

His mother had not been impressed with that analogy.

'Besides,' Sam had gushed, 'there's so much I want to know, a whole world that no one knows about – that I didn't know existed! And it's somewhere that we – *I* – actually belong! I'm one of The Few!'

'Well, just remember, not everything that glistens is gold. Oh, and there is a letter on your desk for you. Who is writing to you nowadays, isn't everything "DMs" for you lot?'

In his excitement Sam had forgotten about the neatly addressed envelope and it still lay unopened.

He glanced over at the red display of the alarm clock. It was *01:17*.

He tried to clear his head, listening to the rise and fall of his chest, to his father's occasional snore drifting across the hall through two closed doors, but his thoughts returned to the same words.

If you fail, your family will not be able to remain in The Order…

Sam would not fail. This was his chance to find something real in the turmoil that had been his life since the fire.

Tomorrow was going to be a big day.

'You can leave your things here,' Ruben told them. 'Coats, too. And you won't be needing *those*!' He removed the bulky camera and safari binoculars from around Joe's neck. 'Jennifer MacLeod will be looking after you for the next six weeks. She's one of our best Trainers and is eager to meet you. This way, please.'

After a twist and several turns through row upon row of bookshelves, the tour ended before an old wooden door near the back of the library. It was beautifully carved with an intricate storyboard, but Sam was given no time to study the carefully worked relief as Ruben tugged it open. 'Come along now, through here.'

Fedor stepped aside to allow Veronique through.

'*Merci*,' she smiled, squinting into the dark. The Russian boy followed, ducking under the doorframe. Joe was hanging back, unsure, so Sam gave him a nudge and smile of encouragement.

He caught Ruben's eye. 'You're not coming?'

'Heavens, no! I'm agoraphobic. Never leave the library if I can help it. I need an umbrella just to venture into the hall.' He tittered nervously.

Sam nodded, not sharing the joke. 'Stick together,' was the last instruction he heard before he followed Joe into the gloom.

Chapter 8

The floor crunched under Sam's feet.

Fedor, Veronique and Joe stood nearby in the flickering shadows.

He turned, but the doorway, Ruben, and his library were nowhere to be seen.

Why am I not surprised?

'Where are we?' Joe's voice trilled.

They seemed to have entered a large cave. The air was cold and dank. Several long, dark rivets were embedded in the floor. The walls, roughly cut, were lined with metal rings, from which wooden torches hissed and spat. Above them Sam could make out a series of dimly lit ledges, one on top of the other, running around the chamber and stretching up toward the ceiling. He craned his neck to see how far they reached, and as his eyes adjusted to the dark, he was shocked to see gigantic arms and clawing hands reaching down towards them, a gaping mouth opened wide in an endless roar. Sam pointed until they all stood staring up at the hideous ceiling carving. Three similar figures adorned the walls.

Veronique screwed up her face. Today, it would seem, she was to be *Nikki the Spelunker*.

Further reverie was cut short by a harsh grating sound. The floor shook and Sam stumbled. Stone plugs rose from beneath the rivets, sealing them off. The sculpture above them began to groan, making the deep gurgling sound of a blocked tap, until a stream of liquid erupted from its mouth.

'What the hell is going on?' Veronique cried, dashing for cover.

Backs pressed against the wall, they stared at the deluge.

'A drain,' Fedor shouted. 'Those holes in the floor. Must've been a drain.'

Joe blinked. 'He's right. And unless that stops,' he indicated the statue, 'or the drain opens, this cave is going to fill up—'

'And we drown,' Fedor finished.

Sam saw Joe was shaking. 'What the hell kind of library is this?'

They stared at the deepening pool in disbelief.

'A test,' Veronique blurted. 'It must be some kind of twisted test.' Her hair was matted and mud splattered. They all cut similar sodden figures, cowering against the wall.

'*Nikki the Drowned Rat*!'

Sam grabbed a torch. If this was a test, then they'd damn well rise to it! 'Look around. If you're right, there will be a clue or some instructions somewhere. If we can get up there,' he pointed to the ledges, 'we can buy ourselves some time.'

Fedor handed a torch to Veronique who began to scour the walls for clues. The last went to Joe. He needed two hands to hold it.

'Over here,' Joe called a few minutes later. 'There's something under here, but it's caked in this sh…' He hit the wall. The old plaster sent up dust, but remained in place.

'Water,' Sam said. 'We need to get it wet.'

'Shirts?' Fedor suggested.

'Yes!'

The pair turned and ran over to the rising pool, ripping off their t-shirts. Veronique pretended to look away when the bare-chested boys ran back.

Slapping the material against the wall, they began to scrub. 'It's working!' Joe whooped, the crude plaster coming away in his hands. 'Keep going! More here. Here!'

Veronique began to claw at the mud, too, manicured nails forgotten. The tide was now pooling around their ankles.

They soon exposed a mural. Joe traced the relief, lips moving as he translated the instructions. 'There's someone pulling a lever, closing the drains. That looks like a reservoir above the cave. It empties here… from the mouth of the statue.'

Veronique stabbed at the picture of the gigantic reservoir. 'It's bigger than this cave!'

'We have to get that drain open,' Sam shouted.

'Or stop the water.' Fedor said.

'You're both right,' Joe agreed. 'Look. This figure is placing something into the side of the statue. That seems to stop the water and opens the drain.'

Sam peered over the boy's shoulder. 'But what?'

'There.' Veronique patted a smudged section. 'They're climbing onto those ledges. But how do we get up there? They're so high.'

'Well,' Sam paused, 'what if we wait for the water to rise and float up?' Fedor nodded.

'Um, guys…' Joe sounded worried as he cleaned another section of the mural. 'I don't think we can do that. Look!'

The next image showed serpents attacking the figures in the water.

'Oh my God!' Veronique cried. 'What the *hell* are those?'

Sam turned. 'Let's not stick around to find out.'

'There's nothing else here!' Joe rubbed at the wall. 'That's it, what're we gonna do?'

'Not panic,' Fedor replied.

Sam noticed the bruises on the boy's face and wondered what had happened to him in the hours since they had parted company.

'Come on then.' He wrung out his ruined shirt. 'Let's get a move on.'

The ledge was so high above the cavern floor that neither Sam nor Fedor could brush the bottom of it.

'Well, that's not going to work,' Sam panted, hands on knees.

Fedor squatted. 'Get on my shoulders.'

They wobbled their way toward the lip of the ledge but were still just too short. Sam swore when Fedor staggered and fell, dumping them both into the water.

'Sorry. It's my ankle. Had a run in with a bear yesterday.'

They all stared.

'You what now?' Joe gawped.

'I'll tell you about it later.'

'I've an idea,' Veronique said. 'What about making a human pyramid?'

Sam looked embarrassed. 'I didn't think of that.'

Veronique smiled and patted him on the cheek. 'Well then, you're lucky you have me. Now on your knees, my minions!'

As the tallest, Sam and Fedor were at the bottom of the pile, noses in the water, eyes wide as they kept watch for serpents. Joe clambered on top.

With two nimble leaps, Veronique crested the pyramid and reached for the ledge. *Nikki, the Acrobat!*

Her heart sank; it was still not high enough. Then she noticed that the stone lip appeared lower to the right. Clambering down, she dragged the boys out of the water and reformed the pyramid.

The image of the Magician card on her bed came to mind. Embrace your skills. Tap into your full potential. You will be tested. *Today, I am Nikki, the Victorious!* Veronique looked up, bent her knees and launched herself toward the ledge.

Everything slowed down as she jumped, the din of the waterfall becoming a muffled drone. Hands outstretched, legs pedalling, she propelled her body toward the outcrop.

Contact!

With considerable kicking and wiggling, Nikki the Acrobat dragged herself up and onto the ledge. Rolling onto her back, she lay gasping for breath. Everything hurt.

It took a moment for her to catch her breath, so she didn't hear the sound of the hatches in the walls opening. Long, dark shapes glided into the water.

Joe's high-pitched scream startled her. 'Something just brushed my leg!'

'Mine, too!' Sam shouted and the boys began to splash about.

'*Veronique*!' three voices screamed. 'Hurry up!'

A knotted rope lay coiled a few feet away and Veronique scrambled toward it. Her stomach twisted when she realised it was not anchored to anything. There were two rounded stones at the lip of the ledge, spaced a few feet apart, but they were not large enough to use. Veronique was out of time. Nikki took over.

She wrapped the rope around her waist and braced her feet on the stones, throwing the length over the side. 'Send Joe up first!'

The rope jerked, nearly pulling her over. She leaned back and let out a cry, the rough twine fighting her grip and tearing her hands. The pain was almost unbearable.

'I want to go home!'

Veronique heard sobs between gasps and a tuft of mousy hair appeared. 'Hurry!'

Joe wriggled onto the ledge and they quickly shared the line between them.

'Now Sam!'

The rope snapped taut and the pair grimaced. Thankfully, he did not take long to crest the ledge and took over from Veronique as she rushed toward the edge to find Fedor.

'GO, GO, GO!'

Fedor had his back to the wall, distracted by movement in the water on every side.

'Look out!' Joe shouted.

There was a tremendous splash on the far side of the cave and the boy started. Another followed and the snakes began to drift toward the disturbance.

It was all the invitation Fedor needed, surging for the rope.

'It worked!' Joe laughed, kneeling beside Veronique. He flung a final projectile into the seething mass. 'I hate snakes, filthy beasts!' he laughed manically. Noticing her look, he shrugged. 'I laugh when I'm nervous...'

'*Spasibo*!' Fedor splatted down on the ledge beside them, panting as the others explored the area.

'Over here.' Joe had found a small alcove.

With a groan, the Russian got to his feet.

'What is it?' Sam asked.

They all stared at Joe and, startled by the fast-rising water behind them, he stuttered. 'It looks like a brainteaser,' he gushed. 'A tile puzzle. You have to slide eight slates around nine spaces until you complete the picture. It must be a clue to what we do next.'

Fedor was in a black mood after his narrow escape. 'Just smash it up and put it back together.'

Sam shook his head. 'Doubt we can cheat. Try to figure it out, we'll look for a way up.'

Joe was already fiddling with the pieces. 'We need a key to help with the pattern.'

'I'll look,' Veronique said. *Nikki, the Explorer!*

Not far below, the waters churned.

'Found something!' Veronique called, indicating the pile of stones near the rope. 'They're Roman numerals.' She turned one over. There was a pattern underneath. 'I put them in order, but there are three missing.'

Joe seemed cross at first, then paled. 'Oh no,' he looked toward the ledge and then back at the pile of stones. 'I didn't realise, I just threw them....'

'Well, there's nothing we can do about that now,' Sam said. 'Can you solve it without them?'

'It'll take more time.' The boy said, uncertain.

The water was now a few feet from the base of their refuge.

'Better hurry then,' Fedor muttered, 'time is running out.'

Joe dashed back to the puzzle.

The water was soon lapping at the ledge.

'Try that one.' Veronique had been standing over Joe's shoulder 'helping' for some time. The boy sighed but moved the tile.

'I've got it!'

'You're welcome,' Veronique looked annoyed.

'No, I've realised what I've been doing wrong.' His fingers raced around the board in a different direction. There was a 'click' and the stone behind the puzzle rolled away. Inside, was a stout lever beside a small stone disc.

'Well done!' Veronique patted Joe on the back. The boy picked up the coin-shaped stone, turning it over. Fedor gave the lever a firm tug and a rope ladder unfurled from the gloom.

The second ledge was larger than the first.

Its floor was divided into a board of squares, each marked by a carving. Sam placed the ball of his foot on the closest square. It sank under his weight. He withdrew his foot, relieved when the slab returned to its original position. Maybe they could run across it.

'Seems safe enough.'

'Wait,' Fedor said. 'There must be a catch.'

Veronique pointed to another mural on the wall, too far away to read. The only way to reach it was across the unstable chess board.

'I hope that's not the key.' Joe laughed, his anxiety returning.

'Why put the puzzle in the way? Why not put it over here?' Sam shook his head.

Fedor bent to examine the stones. 'We are meant to work it out. Those two stones are the same. So are those.'

'One of us has to get across.' Sam stepped forward. 'I'll go.'

'No,' Joe said, still feeling outdone by the first puzzle. 'Let me try to figure it out.'

Veronique started pulling up the rope ladder. 'Here. If anything happens, hold on tight!'

Joe laughed again. 'Okay. Got to start somewhere.' Taking a deep breath, he stepped onto the chequered floor, choosing one of Fedor's stones. It sank down an inch or two but, thankfully, no more. He looked for the same marking and took another step giving the others a reassuring thumbs up when nothing happened.

The next stone, a new design, was not so forgiving. This time, the square sank onto a button.

Click.

Water began to gush from the mouths of three other statues.

Joe spun about, swearing.

'Keep going,' they shouted over the pounding waterfall.

Three more careful steps saw Joe clear of the squares.

The mural showed a birds-eye view of the ledge and the board; Fedor was right, most stones had a twin. There were, however, four that were not paired. One of these could trigger the way out, or shut off the water. Or speed up their deaths if he was wrong.

Turning back to the board he made his way over to the closest odd symbol and gingerly stood on the square. It sank and he felt it click. Gripping the rope ladder, he awaited his fate.

Nothing happened.

Still alive. Result! He started to move but tripped and accidently landed on the square next to him. This time, the stone fell away.

Joe threw his arms out, dropping the ladder and pedalling backward. The others rushed forward, but he steadied himself and held up his hands.

Think!

Four markings, four people. He made the connection and formed a theory. They had to each make their way to a singularly marked stone, using the paired stones as a pathway. When all four were down, the puzzle would be solved.

'I've got it,' he shouted over the noise of the waterfall. 'I hope!' he added under his breath.

Veronique went first, nodding to the boys, when the button beneath her stone clicked into place. Sam followed, and Fedor wasted no time making his way to the final stone.

Beside the mural, a hatch popped open to reveal a narrow staircase and a second stone coin.

The third ledge was perilously small. Four sturdy levers protruded from the wall. All were in a 'down' position.

'Right,' Joe said studying them closely to distract himself from vertigo. 'This looks simple enough.' He bent to lift the first lever.

'Wait!' Fedor shouted. 'Let's grab hold of something first.'

Sam saw Joe's cheeks darken.

'Good thinking,' he agreed. 'Keep hold of each other, too.'

Using all his strength, Joe managed to lift the lever. High above them, a knotted rope unfurled several feet from a winch in the wall.

When he let go, however, the lever crashed to the floor and the whole ledge moved slightly, retracting into the wall.

'WHOAH!'

'The rope's gone!' Veronique cried, pointing upward.

'We have to try keep the levers up,' Sam said.

Joe shook his head. 'They're too heavy.'

'Four people, four levers,' Fedor noted. 'It has to be done at the same time.'

Veronique did not look convinced. 'If you're wrong, we could fall.'

Sam shrugged. 'And if we don't get off this ledge soon, we'll be swimming with the snakes.'

'We have to try,' Fedor agreed. 'Veronique, will you be able to lift one?'

'*I* can't hold it!' Joe looked pained. He was not built for this. Books were his bag, not brawn. He fought off nervous laughter.

Sam's brow furrowed. 'Fedor and I will each lift a lever. You two can keep them up with your shoulders whilst we tackle the last two.'

Fedor nodded. 'Good plan.'

With a grunt, the boys worked until the final pair clicked into place and the winch unravelled the rope completely. The end was dangling just out of their reach.

'It's too far out,' Joe cried.

'We're going to have to jump for it,' Sam edged backward, the water centimetres away. With a deep breath, he dashed forward and like a monkey leaping for a vine, arched his body toward the dangling length, grasping it and swinging wildly out over the flooded cavern and through the waterfall.

Veronique was next and came very close to missing the pendulum entirely, before hurrying, hand over fist, toward safety.

'Now you,' Fedor pressed himself against the wall to let Joe past.

'OMG…' the boy stammered. The end of the rope was now in the snake-infested water.

'Now,' Fedor snapped, 'or we're both in deep water. Literally!'

'I…' Joe fussed, rubbing his sore hands. 'I can't!'

'Yes, you can,' Fedor forced a smile. '*GO!*' He gave the boy a clap on the back. Joe bolted. He jumped too soon and soared across the empty space, certain to fall short. Fortunately, Sam gave the rope a sharp flick and sent it spinning toward Joe's outstretched arms.

'Quickly!' Veronique called down.

Scaly bodies were rising out of the water toward him, but Joe was frozen stiff, clinging to the rope.

There was nothing for it. Fedor was going to have to jump and hope he did not send them both hurtling into the murky depths.

His swollen ankle protested at the first lunge, but he put the pain from his mind, focusing on Joe and the spot of rope above him. He had to reach it.

The jump was good. Fedor grabbed the rope and wrapped his legs around Joe. He could hear the boy crying. Hands white, jaw clenched, his eyes clamped shut.

'This isn't happening, this isn't happening…'

'Joe,' Fedor bent toward him, 'Giuseppe, I've got you. Come on, we can do this. Together.'

Joe opened one red-rimmed eye.

'Come on.' Fedor pulled himself up, letting his legs dangle so that the youngster could move. 'Let's get out of here.'

Joe sniffed, then laughed involuntarily. He unclenched his fists and edged slowly toward Sam and Veronique who waited above him, arms outstretched.

'Was there another coin?' Joe collapsed on the ledge, snot running freely.

Sam held it up. 'Yup, got it! That's three.'

'I can't do this anymore,' Joe moaned, holding his aching arms and Veronique nodded. The ordeal was taking its toll.

Nikki, the Weary.

Sam was furious at the peril they had been placed in but now was not the time for anger. 'We must be close to the end,' he said, trying to sound positive. 'Nearly out of here – wherever the hell "here" is!'

Fedor was pacing, looking for clues.

'There,' Joe pointed, still on his back. They followed the line of his shaking finger. Suspended from the ceiling on a thin cord, a final stone coin spun slowly. It was too far over the water to grab.

Sam swore. 'How on earth are we going to reach that?'

'Maybe we could use the rope?' Veronique sounded vague.

Fedor shook his head. 'The slightest movement could send it into the drink and I don't fancy going after it.'

Sam stared at the elusive disc.

Joe broke the silence. 'What's been the main theme in all these puzzles? Us! Working together! How could four people reach that coin?'

Veronique snapped her fingers. 'Monkey chain!'

Nikki, the Genius!

'Hashtag winning!' Joe applauded weakly.

Fedor rolled his eyes and turned to the wall. A dusty iron ring was barely visible. 'There!' Grabbing it, he stretched out to Sam who took his wrist and extended his arm to Joe.

'No,' Veronique said. 'I'm stronger. She slipped her cool hand around Sam's wrist. They were now at the edge, the water closing in.

'Don't. Look. Down,' Sam heard Veronique whisper to Joe, when she took his arm. Joe leaned out, accepting his inevitable death, certain he would slip into the murky waters. He stretched onto his toes, his fingers waggling. Sam watched him make every attempt to lengthen his body. Ever so slowly, the boy edged toward the coin swaying seductively in front of him. So close now, so close…

One moment the tips of his fingers brushed the coin and the next, he was plummeting toward the blackness.

Joe hit the water with a tremendous splash. He kicked his arms and legs, fighting to get to the surface before slimy coils could drag him to a suffocating doom. He breached the pool just below the statue's mouth, which spat unrepentantly upon him. The others were on what was left of the last ledge, shouting and reaching toward him.

Sharp teeth sank into his leg and Joe screamed. A long, muscular body bashed against his back and he kicked at it, thrashing in the water. Another buffeted him from the other side. He kicked and clawed. The outstretched hands were so close, just a few more kicks...

Then they vanished, as a long body wrapped around his leg and dragged him under.

Joe was overcome with terror. Water filled his mouth and throat as he screamed. He hadn't even begun to live; all the books and studying had been for nothing. Bella flashed through his mind. He should have kissed her…

Strong hands gripped his. Something struck the coil around his thigh and suddenly he was free and rising toward the surface.

A firm arm was dragging him to safety. More hands found him and Joe felt himself lifted from the water, worried faces peering down as he wretched. Familiar faces.

'Joe!' someone shouted.

Was that his name? His head rolled from one face to the other. How did he know them? He lifted a clenched fist, and then opened it to reveal a small stone coin pressed into his palm.

Then he fainted.

'You got it!' Veronique shrieked. 'Joe, Joe!' She shook him but the boy was out cold, blood oozing from a nasty bite on his leg.

Sam dropped his head to Joe's chest and listened.

'He's breathing. He's okay, I think. But he won't be for long. We need to get out of here. Guys, any ideas?'

Fedor pointed to a set of rings buried in the ceiling. 'They lead to the top of the statue.'

'Monkey bars.' Veronique stood up. 'I can do this.' She held out her hands for the coins. 'Just lift me up.'

Nikki, the Acrobat!

Fedor looked at her and then at Sam, who was still kneeling beside Joe, soaked to the bone. His bravery had impressed the young Russian. Sam had hit the water seconds after Joe had slipped beneath the surface, with no regard for his own safety. He waited for a response.

Sam handed Veronique the coins. '*Allez!*'

Fedor lifted her toward the first ring. Gripping it, she hung there, sizing up the distance. Then with a flick of her hips, Veronique began to swing backwards and forwards. She let go with a faint cry and lunged forward.

Just two rings separated her from the statue, close enough to make out slots in its neck and she swung again.

One to go.

Her arms had begun to ache and cramp threatened to paralyse her raw fingers, but taking a deep breath, Veronique made the final lunge.

Her fingers gripped the statue and she slipped.

'NO!' she heard the boys cry above the din.

'Not like this,' she moaned, plummeting toward gaping jaws.

Cold stone brushed her palm and Veronique snapped her fingers closed, halting her descent on the statue's ear.

She laughed; she could not help it. Joe's nervous malady appeared infectious.

'Are you okay?' came the shout from the ledge.

'*Oui*,' she whispered to herself. 'Yes!' This time, a shout.

Summoning her last ounce of strength, she worked herself upright. The slots were within reach. With great care, Veronique drew the first coin from her pocket.

She heard it rattle and roll into the statue, tripping some mechanism within. The column of cascading water slowed.

'It's working!' she shouted over her shoulder.

The torrent of water waned further with the second coin, and the third saw the deadly torrent subside to a trickle, and then, to their relief, it stopped.

'You've done it!' came the cheer from the boys. 'The last one should open the drain.'

As Veronique worked the final token free of her pocket, it caught on a stud in the denim and slipped from her fingers. She watched in horror as it spun away.

'NOOO!'

With her legs locked in place, Veronique quickly fell backward like a trapeze artist, throwing herself into the path of the falling coin. The desperate act paid off, and she snatched it moments before it disappeared into the water.

Nikki, the Magnificent!

Sam slumped to his knees. 'I don't know how much more of this I can take!'

'Nor me,' Fedor muttered. 'You okay?' he shouted to Veronique, who still hung upside down.

'No!'

'Fair enough...'

She clambered back to her perch and, with a defiant whoop, slammed the final coin into place.

There was a gurgling, sucking sound, followed by a surge of bubbles, and finally the dreaded water began to recede.

'Quick!' Fedor shouted. 'You need to get back before the water gets too low, otherwise if you fall...'

Veronique wiggled around to face the row of metal rings.

* * *

Salvador D'Angelo let out a sigh when the girl landed in Fedor's arms. The large Far Sight window in his office was tuned into the cave feed, captured by Levi Orbs, small camouflaged floating cameras. The gripping real-time action was streaming to both Mr D'Angelo's office and to the quarters of their very concerned Trainer, Jenny MacLeod, who had been completely against the trial by water.

Salvador turned to smile at his guest and refill their glasses. The Head of the Council had already made his opinion quite clear, and now regarded his host's presentation shrewdly.

'You're a gifted Operations Director,' Gabriel had told him earlier that afternoon, 'and you'll get all the credit if this "apprenticeship" pays dividends, but it'll also sit squarely with you, should anyone be hurt or killed.'

They watched as Jenny and Jen Si rushed to help the battered youngsters. Fedor and Sam lifted Joe and together the group made their way out through a door at the top of the chamber.

The feed ended and the window returned to the peaceful view of a Swiss mountain top.

Salvador could hardly conceal his smugness. 'An impressive performance.'

'Indeed.' Gabriel seldom wasted his words. 'They show promise. I'll keep an eye on their progress.' He rose and walked towards the door. As he did, a dark-skinned man with scarred cheeks emerged from the shadows and followed him from the room.

The door clicked shut and Salvador swore. 'Where did *he* come from?'

'I didn't see him come in, sir. He's a bloody ghost,' Owen said from his post by the door.

'More like the Grim Reaper.' Salvador snorted. Baid had always protected the Head of the Council and his reputation was legendary, but his presence left a chill in the air.

'I thought Sam did well, sir?'

'They all did, didn't they? Wasn't Fedor a surprise? He may have the family muscles, but there's a lot more going on upstairs. This could be an intriguing summer, Owen, my boy. Very intriguing indeed.'

Part II

'There are more things in heaven and earth,
Horatio, than are dreamt of in your philosophy.'

William Shakespeare, 'Hamlet'

The four shattered teens lay sprawled beside Shen Pi's crackling fire pit. 'How are the legs?' Jenny asked Fedor and Joe, watching Joe squirm to get comfortable in his nest of cushions. The brimming cup of sweet tea sloshed over his hand and he swore.

'It's throbbing.' He shook the liquid off.

Joe looked around, hoping to find an orphan book within reach.

There were none.

'Do you have any books?'

Jenny looked confused. 'I, er, no. The pain will soon go, Jen Si is a wonder with balms. Got a cure for anything.'

Sam got the impression Joe did not really 'do' conversation.

The young Italian stared at the flames, blowing on the tea before taking a tentative slurp. The damage to his leg had proved minor: two six-inch rows of punctures, which had been cleaned and dressed by quick, practised hands while he bemoaned his impending demise.

Jenny told them that the cave was known as 'The Deep End' and was a training-ground designed by Shen Pi's warrior monks. It had been used to test the teamwork and resourcefulness of (far older!) recruits for centuries.

'Most attempts border on disaster,' the lecture began when her charges emerged, ruddy faced and relaxed from the steaming baths. Dressed in soft woollens and snug fur boots, they had been shown to the main hall and given bowls of honeyed oats and fresh tea before settling by the fire.

'I've seen more coins lost than I can count, and as many legs, arms and ankles broken; infighting, snake fighting, hissy fits and even one sit-in. How most make it out alive, I still don't know. And that's after a lot of hard training! I'm sorry you were put through it – but what you achieved today was truly remarkable!'

The compliment drew fleeting smiles, though Joe was not so easily won over. 'So, what's next?' he muttered. 'Run a lion to ground with our bare hands, perhaps wrest the Kraken from the pocket of Davey Jones?'

Fedor looked up. 'Davey who?'

Veronique laughed, a light, cheery sound brightening their sombre mood. 'You don't watch many movies, do you?' she teased with a flawless American twang.

Fedor looked embarrassed. 'No. My father believes spare time should be "invested in improving oneself". What's with the accent?'

She shrugged. 'Old habit. I've always loved pretending,' she replied with Jenny's Scottish lilt.

'What a coincidence,' Joe muttered. 'I like pretending that I'm not here.'

'Hey,' Sam turned to Fedor. 'Didn't you say something about a bear?!'

Joe sat upright, sloshing his tea again. In the absence of any reading material, a good story could prove a suitable substitute. 'That's right, you did! Spill it,' he mopped himself, 'no pun intended.'

Fedor rolled his stiff ankle. The monks had slathered his joint with a sticky salve that made it feel ten times better. 'I wouldn't want to bore you with—'

He was cut off by shouts and remonstrance before waving them to silence.

Awe was the general sentiment felt when Fedor had finished his account.

'You should find out where it lives,' Joe gave a hard look, 'slip into its cave,' his eyes narrowed and he leaned forward, 'then eat all the porridge and sleep in its bed!'

Everyone laughed but Fedor, who grunted. Joe turned his dulled attentions to Jenny, who was glad to see the group were bonding. She hated to admit it but Mr D'Angelo had been right, in some cases stress and danger were the quickest ways to build trust.

'You haven't answered my question.'

All eyes were upon her. 'You're quite right. Before we go into what comes next, let's cover what you know so far. Sam?'

The boy blinked. 'Huh?'

'*Pardon*,' Veronique corrected, then blushed. 'Sorry, manner-obsessed parents!'

Sam felt put on the spot, and like so many teenage boys, instantly hid behind humour. 'Well,' he began, 'I can't speak for the others, but a few weeks ago, I thought my Dad was a boring geek who worked in the Patents Office. When in fact he works for this secret organisation that keeps the good, the bad and the ugly of the inventing world off the streets and safely under lock and key.'

Jenny frowned but let him continue.

'The mysterious "Few" are divided into field and non-field personnel and spread all over the globe. But that's not a problem, 'cos they've kept all the best stuff for themselves and can pop about by simply walking through a magic door.'

'It's not quite that simple.' Jenny decided to move on. 'Anyone else? Fedor?'

'Well, I know that Induction lasts for a year, during which you're assessed for field training. If you pass, Cadre training is a further two years. After that, you enter active service.'

'What if you're not suitable for the field?' Joe fidgeted and Sam guessed the memory of dark, swirling waters and teeth was still very fresh.

'Operations,' Veronique supplied. 'A support role with a four-year internship – Tactical, Research and Development, Training,' she looked at Jenny, 'or something like that. My mother's in Ops.'

Their Trainer nodded. 'Those are the basics, which lead us on to why you're here. We've developed a new training programme for younger recruits. Our aim is to create stronger, more well rounded Cadres who are less reliant upon technology. If we succeed, then next summer you'll return and the lessons will continue. The following year, you'll be Inducted along with everyone else, but with a new range of skills already under your belt. Some may argue, an unfair advantage—'

Sam cut in, voicing what they were all thinking. 'And if we fail? D'Angelo said our families would be kicked out of The Order. That's a lot of pressure for something we didn't ask to be part of!'

The others nodded and Fedor looked away, clearly troubled.

'He said *what*?' Jenny looked genuinely surprised. 'Well, we won't fail,' she assured them. 'I won't let you. Neither will Jen Si. You're going to learn ancient arts and secret skills,' she gave them a mischievous grin, 'it will be a wild ride. By the end of this summer, you're going to be lean, mean, mysterious teens!'

'Isn't that a song?' Sam quipped half-heartedly, but her reaction was reassuring and he didn't quite feel as alone in all this as he had.

'What if we're already mean?' Joe puffed out his chest, flexing his thin arms.

Fedor scoffed. 'I think you mean lean!'

'Then I'll make you meaner.' Jenny laughed. They all did.

'Does this mean we'd be a Cadre?' Sam asked.

Jenny pursed her lips. 'I hadn't really thought about that. I guess it does. 'The Deep End' tests your suitability, and you passed.'

'Do we get a name?' Veronique's voice mimicked Joe.

Nikki, The First has a nice ring to it.

'I guess you do. Any suggestions?'

They all shouted at once, their proposals ranging from funny to absurd, several laced with not-so-subtle innuendo.

'Boys!' Jenny and Veronique exclaimed. Tears were rolling down Sam's cheeks at his toilet humour.

'What was the name of the first Cadre?' Joe asked.

Veronique rubbed her hands. '*Ooh*, yes, I like that.'

Jenny squinted into the fire. 'You know, I'm not sure. Nessy, can you help?'

Sam looked around, confused.

'Of course.' Jenny shook her head with disgust. 'The Stone Thieves; how could I forget that!'

'Er, hello?' Joe raised his eyebrows. 'Who's your invisible friend?'

Jenny patted her ear. 'Nessy, my A.I.'

'In your head?' Sam asked, wondering how far their AI technology extended.

Jenny reached into her pocket and drew out a slim device.

'This is an Episteme – Stem for short. It's the standard issue Personal Digital Assistant that connects us to the Earth Song network and the Cube, our Artificial Intelligence server farm. Each field agent is assigned an A.I. profile that they name once activated. It learns about you and develops a personality to best complement your character. My A.I. is called Nessy.'

'As in Loch Ness?'

'Exactly.'

'Because she's Scottish, and not some reclusive creature you can never find?'

They laughed.

'But how'd you talk to it?' Veronique had managed to pick up Sam's African twang already. 'Is it in your head or your pocket?'

Jenny winked. 'It's magic.'

'Oh, c'mon!'

Their Trainer laughed. 'It's a CarboSilicone implant,' Jenny tapped her cheek. 'A small injection of Nanodes form an organic microphone and receiver in your cheekbone, sort of like a hands-free kit. The stem is a dumb terminal, as cortical implants remove the need for a screen and voice activation means no keyboard.'

'OMG!' Joe, back straight, was brimming with curiosity. 'You have stable, working Nano technology?'

'*We* do,' Jenny corrected. She saw Sam's mouth open as his brain caught up. 'But enough about technology – did we like the name?'

'The Stone Thieves.' Veronique made rosebud lips and put on her snootiest English aristocrat accent.

Nikki, Queen of Thieves. She liked that.

'Seems apt, considering the day's activities,' Fedor cast his vote.

'Very!' Joe agreed. 'Sam?'

Sam nodded. 'Sure.'

'*Oui*!' Veronique cast her vote, too.

Jenny nodded. 'The Stone Thieves, it is.'

'And what's next…?' Joe was like a dog with a bone and Sam smiled.

'It will be a lot more fun than this morning, I promise!'

They slouched around the fire for a few more hours, chatting freely.

'So, who's loved up?' Sam asked.

Joe thought of Bella and sighed. 'No opportunity: boys' school,' he declared, dodging the issue.

'Same here,' Fedor shrugged.

'Veronique?' Sam couldn't believe for a minute that she was single.

Veronique tapped her nose. 'A lady doesn't kiss and tell!'

In blasts of frosty air, the monks came and went behind them, swapping their empty bowls for sturdy weapons.

Sam watched his new companions as they chatted. He liked them. Joe had a quick, dry wit, laced with sarcasm. Fedor appeared to be equally large of frame and intelligence but did his best to hide it. Though sparing, his comments were factual and insightful, rarely wasting a word.

As a teenage boy, Veronique was a complete mystery to Sam. There was no denying she was smart and attractive, he had caught himself staring at her across the fire several times. She chatted and laughed, asked loads of questions, but gave little away.

His thoughts drifted to Victoria. Yesterday he'd sent her an email (his parents had yet to allow him access to anything resembling social media) to let her know he was going on a surprise outdoor summer camp and that he'd be out of touch for a few weeks. It was only a slight lie. She hadn't replied by the time he left and he suppressed a pang of jealousy, wondering what she was doing, and with whom. His fingers stroked his scar.

Veronique laughed at another of Joe's jokes lifting Sam's eyes from the flames. She caught his gaze and smiled back.

* * *

Fedor listened to the banter. They were all nice enough.

He liked the Italian boy, though he believed he would benefit from some hard labour and rough living. Joe's hands were soft and pink, with no calluses or scars. Fedor doubted they had ever spent hours cutting wood in the biting snow.

The English boy had a bit more about him. He was strong and confident but didn't seem arrogant. His accent had a slight twang to it which Fedor could not place – Australian, maybe?

The French girl was also strong, but she giggled and asked lots of questions, flicking her silky hair and batting long eyelashes. But what was with all the accents and who was this Nikki person? She had, thankfully, grown tired of interrogating him. Fedor had not been around many girls and was the product of his father's renowned social skills.

Despite being stiff and sore, Fedor had enjoyed the challenge of the cave. He was used to being mentally and physically tested, and always alone; working in a team had been both foreign and exciting.

He probed his ankle, rolling it from side to side. The pain and swelling were receding and Fedor was optimistic that he'd be back to full strength in no time.

Nikki The Pauper stood in the centre of a barren room, looking at her accommodation with dismay. Her bags had been placed beside something with a thin mattress that could not possibly be described as a bed. A table with a small lantern and round three-legged stool stood next to it.

'Mine's the same.' Sam's head poked around the door. 'Talk about the bare necessities!'

'It's horrid, darling,' she groaned, now a disenchanted movie star. 'So drab and cold. Where are the creature comforts?'

'I'll go see if I can find the manager,' Sam laughed and disappeared.

If this is what her tarot cards had meant by adjusting to change, then she was getting a new deck.

'Who shall I be tonight?' she sighed. There was not even a mirror to quiz.

'*Nikki, the Peasant,*' she moaned to no one.

A small sob escaped Joe's lips. In the dark room, far away from his books and everything he knew, he felt lonelier than ever.

The dusty covers were pulled up to his chin. Treacherous tears seeped down his temples and into his ears. His leg hurt, though it was his pride that had taken the brunt of the beating during the test. Sat around the fire laughing and joking, he'd not been able to dwell on the day. Now, however, alone in the cold bed, he was gripped by homesickness and doubt.

He couldn't get through it. He was not 'athletic'. He needed glasses and sometimes had trouble breathing. Not to mention his allergies. How could he be put in this ridiculous situation?

His melancholy deepened and soon his nose was running too from the musty bedclothes. It simply would not do. In the morning, he would find that Jennifer lady and inform her that he would be returning home at once. Back to his room. To his father's old study.

His father...

Joe's pique deepened. What would his father have said if he returned beaten, tail tucked between his legs?

In truth, he had no idea. He remembered very little of the man. But he doubted he'd have been proud. Nonno would certainly not be.

Joe clenched his teeth. He sniffed and wiped his eyes, flipping his lean pillow to banish the tear-soaked patches. He would not be beaten. This was a monastery – they must have books, even a library, perhaps. His mood brightened with the thought and he wriggled further under the covers. He was rewarded with a stab of pain from his wounded leg, and let loose a long, colourful and cathartic string of expletives.

It had just been one of those days.

Ninety-seven, ninety-eight, ninety niiiine... one hundred!

Fedor rolled onto his back when he finished the last press up. Not just any press up, diamond press-ups, the most difficult sort. His father insisted they did at least a hundred each day, and twice as many sit-ups. His breathing returned to normal and he began the crunches, counting them in his head.

His room was small and functional, devoid of any distractions or frivolous décor. He liked it. The bed was on the short side, so he'd pulled the straw mattress onto the floor.

Fedor eased into a series of stretches, before sliding into the splits. Wetting the small cloth beside the water bowl, he gave himself a quick wash, before settling onto the futon and lighting the lamp on the floor next to him. He reached for and opened the first book with hungry eyes, safe in the knowledge that his father could not come in at any moment and tear it from him.

He immersed himself in *'The Art of War'*, by Sun Tzu for hours.

No phone. No email. Sam felt isolated.

He flicked off his shoes and flopped onto the flimsy bed, breaking it.

'Naturally,' he sighed at the crack, closing his eyes and shaking his head.

Books were all that he had to distract and help him, three books and four relative strangers.

He scratched his scar. It was safer to do this with strangers. He wasn't responsible for them, and they seemed to be able to take care of themselves. Well, most of them. He wondered what Sophie would have made of it all.

I miss you so much…

He immediately blocked such thoughts and forced his mind to drift to Victoria, imagining instead what she was up to. Sam had tried not to become too attached to her, but it had not worked. It made no difference now; he could not contact her even if he wanted to. He could only hope she was waiting for him.

'Is this the start you had in mind?' Jen Si asked Jenny once their wards were in bed.

She sighed and tousled her hair. It had been a stressful day. 'Well, it's certainly not the way I'd have eased them in, but when has D'Angelo ever done things by halves? Still, Harbinger is at our door, so we need to throw everything we have at it. It could certainly tip the balance if we pull it off.'

The monk frowned. 'No pressure then.'

They were roused by a gong before dawn.

The thin mattress, coarse blanket and straw pillow had given Sam little in the way of comfort during the night, so he felt far from rested.

Someone knocked briskly on each door before the metallic echoes had subsided, leaving behind steaming mugs of green tea. Dressed in woollens, the teenagers shuffled sleepily back to the fire, greeting bowls of honeyed oats with gaping yawns.

Only Fedor was fresh-faced. He devoured his breakfast in minutes before helping himself to seconds and then thirds.

Joe was nursing red eyes behind his glasses. He studied the energetic Russian with suspicion. 'How are you so sprightly at this hour?'

'A forty-five-minute workout before the gong.'

Still draped in her paper-thin blanket, Veronique choked on her porridge and collapsed into a coughing fit.

After breakfast, Jenny showed them to a small room in the east wing of the monastery. The walls were covered in long tapestries and wax encrusted candle-holders (spaced a safe distance apart).

Sam saw flimsy wooden birdcages hanging from the rafters; tiny metal wind chimes tinkled in the breeze from the open window. Statues, deities, stuffed creatures and trinkets covered the floor and shelves, a small patch left in the centre of the room for cushioned seating and a smouldering coal pan.

'Welcome.' Jen Si smiled warmly. 'Please, sit.'

Over the next few hours, the monk lectured them in the basic principles and teachings of the three vehicles of Buddhism. Sam was relieved when the pace picked up, moving on to meditation and the less publicised, yet more mysterious skills it could enable.

'Buddhists pursue meditation as part of the path toward Enlightenment and Nirvana. But with the right teaching, meditation can also be used to control the body, to ignore pain and withstand extreme heat or cold.'

Sam's stomach growled loudly and he raised an apologetic hand. 'Can it do anything for hunger?'

Jen Si ignored the quip. 'Using "*g Tum-mo*" meditation, you can raise the temperature of your fingers and toes by as much as twenty degrees. Some of our brothers have spent entire nights on our rocky ledges during winter in temperatures well below zero degrees. Wearing only cotton shawls, they could stay motionless until dawn.'

Sam's boredom and hunger vanished. The class shuffled closer.

'Under careful instruction a monk can even achieve Astral travel: the separation of the spirit body, allowing the conscious mind to travel beyond the confines of the flesh. The pinnacle of this discipline is psychokinesis and teleportation. Moving matter and ultimately, yourself, with the power of the mind.'

'Woah!' Sam whispered.

The monk nodded. 'Thoughts can be focused to fold time and space, creating a passage for the physical body. The Order uses a similar technology to accommodate our vast numbers of travellers, but in the time before machines, only the strongest minds could achieve this form of travel. It is known as Folding.'

'And you're going to teach us to do it?' Joe was giddy with excitement, his glasses glistening in the amber rays of the afternoon sun as he fidgeted.

'No,' Jen Si laughed. 'I'm afraid not. It takes a lifetime of study and meditation to achieve the pure and focused state of mind needed. No, I am going to teach you how to cheat!' He held up a cluster of carved stones, each tied to a long cord.

'What are they?' Veronique asked.

'*Krusa*. Stepping Stones. They are remnants of a relic Herredrion discovered; a series of paving stones ending at a broken archway. He believed they had been used to create a doorway to another place. Perhaps even another world. These fragments are all that's left.'

'An ancient Speedlift!' Joe gushed.

Jen Si smiled. 'Better. Speedlifts can only open on places where doors have been constructed. The Krusa can take you anywhere you can imagine!'

Sam gazed at the familiar talisman.

Joe was champing at the bit. 'How do we use them?'

'Slow down.' Jen Si patted his arm. 'First, you need a calm mind.'

Joe took a deep breath. 'Okay. Ready!'

They all laughed.

Hours later, the amusement had worn off. Meditation was harder than it looked!

'The Krusa can boost your ability to create a Fold. To use the stones, you need to be able to focus completely then extend your consciousness to where you want to go. Start by shutting your eyes.' The monk let out a long, metered breath. 'Now, let your mind wander. Focus only on your breathing.

'In . . .' he paused, ' . . . and out.'

In his hungry state it did not take much for Sam's mind to wander. He tried to follow the instructions and concentrate on the rise and fall of his chest.

'Clear your mind of all thought. I want you to picture a flame. I want you to push every thought that comes into your head into that flame until nothing exists but the fire. In and out,' he continued. 'Nothing but the flame.'

Sam shuddered. It had to be fire. He dared to open an eye. Joe's face was screwed up, clearly battling with it, too. Veronique's eyes were closed, her face a mask of boredom. Only Fedor seemed to be succeeding, his shoulders relaxed and his face calm.

Sam closed his eyes and redoubled his efforts.

'In and out, in and out.'

His imaginary flame flickered. He focused on it, on the colour, the leaping movement, watching it dance before him. *'Sammy, don't leave me!'* He shuddered again and tried to banish the memory.

Victoria's face popped into his head, the scent of her sweet shampoo. *Nope! Not helping.*

Veronique was next to appear, her smile, the graceful curve of her neck. Sam cursed and gritted his teeth. Why were girls all he could think about?

His breathing began to settle and, after a while, he no longer had to concentrate on keeping the regular tempo. He felt himself becoming lighter, more relaxed. The flame seemed to brighten and he watched in wonder. Nothing existed but the flame amidst an endless sea of quiet darkness.

'Sammy, don't leave me!'

'Very good.' Jen Si's words were a welcome relief. The boy's eyes snapped open. The candles had all but burnt out.

Joe looked dark and petulant.

'No luck?' the monk asked.

'Nope.' He snatched off his glasses and ran the hem of his top over the lenses.

'That'll be all for today. Try again before bed. Perhaps you will stay a while longer, Joe?'

'Um, sure.'

The monk lit a vanilla and sandalwood candle when the others had left. 'Why do you think you battled with the exercise?' he asked Joe.

'I don't know. I tried to concentrate on the flame but there are just too many things in my head. Every time I manage to put one from my mind, two more replace it. I feel like Perseus, chopping at the Hydra.'

'Do you have a happy thought?'

'Huh?'

'A memory or idea that calms you.'

Joe pursed his lips. 'My room. It used to be my father's study. It's full of his books, maps, memories. The smell reminds me of him. It's all I have left.'

The monk settled down. 'Let's use that. Close your eyes and think of that scent. Picture the room. Imagine you are standing outside the door. Craft every detail of the door. Imagine I was going to paint it and need to know every feature, the grain of the wood, the shape of handle, the style of hinges. Then reach forward and take the handle. Imagine how it would feel in your hand. Open the door. Sniff the air, let the smell fill you – wash everything else away. Magnify every detail, the floor, the walls, the windows. Shelves, books, maps. Fill your mind with every sensation you can link to it until you are there, standing in the centre of the room... Are you there?'

'Yes,' Joe murmured, his tone almost sleepy.

'Good.'

The boy was holding the Krusa and Jen Si placed his hand over it. 'Now picture how it looked when you left it. Fill in every detail that makes the space yours. Pull yourself towards it.

'Imagine stepping into the room, feel the floor under your feet, hear the world beyond. Reach out and touch it, pull yourself into that memory.'

Joe's mind was filled with his room. The sun was streaming in, the sounds of the lake sneaking between the long flowing curtains that rustled in the breeze. His father's desk, piled high with books. His bed, rumpled and unmade. Wood and leather, musty pages and a hint of cherry carried up from the orchard. He felt the breeze now stirring the hairs on his arms, cool against his skin. He heard the muffled roar of a motorboat on the lake, followed by the excited screams of children.

'Open your eyes, Giuseppe.'

Sunlight blinded him and Joe lifted his free hand to shield his eyes. The sounds, the smells – they were all real. He reached down and felt the familiar bedclothes, heard the chime of the grandfather clock in the hall beyond the door. His vision adjusted. Before him, at the edge of his bed, sat the monk.

They were no longer in the monastery.

'How?'

'We just needed to calm your mind. The Stepping Stone did the rest. Well, with a little help,' he admitted.

Joe gaped. He opened his hand and looked at the innocuous stone.

'There are more things in heaven and earth, Horatio, than are dreamt of in your philosophy.'

'Pardon?'

Joe looked around his room. 'It's Shakespeare. Whilst I don't think this is quite what Hamlet had in mind, it seemed somewhat fitting.'

Jen Si heard voices drifting up the stairs. 'Best we get back.'

'Couldn't I just grab a few—' Joe stretched toward a tantalising pile of books.

Jen Si tightened his grip, holding the boy back. 'Just close your eyes and relax.'

Joe looked around longingly, savouring every detail of the office, then the temperature plummeted and Jen Si lifted his hand from the boy's shoulder. They were back.

But Joe had returned victorious.

'You're kidding!' Sam exclaimed, patting him warmly on the back. 'Well done, you!'

Joe had found the others in the Dojo, Fedor poring over the arsenal of practice weapons hungrily.

'Simply amazing, sugar!' Veronique slipped into her Southern Belle. 'Do you think you could do it on your own?'

Joe nodded. 'Oh yeah, it's quite easy once you know how. Not!'

They laughed. Fedor came over, eyes bright. 'The instructor says he'll show me how to use some of the weapons tomorrow morning. What are you lot looking so pleased about?'

Joe filled him in.

'Wow! Good for you.' He gave the boy's shoulder a meaty swat. 'Now let's get some supper, I'm starving.'

'A good day then?' Jenny asked at the dining table, having been subjected to an even more embellished account of Joe's adventure.

The boy's legs jiggled under the table, causing the bench he shared with Veronique to shake.

'*JOE!*' she snapped for the tenth time, tea sloshing over her hands.

'Sorry.'

'That bit about the monks spending the whole night on a rocky ledge seems a bit hard to believe,' Sam frowned.

'How about a demonstration, then?'

They turned to see Jen Si standing in the doorway.

Sam blushed. 'I didn't mean any disrespect, Jen Si, it's just—'

'It's natural to doubt what you cannot see or explain. Come with me.'

'Nice going, big mouth,' Joe muttered.

Sam spluttered at the irony.

They fell upon a selection of heavy boots, furs, mittens, cosy deerstalker hats and long scarves. Jen Si watched them struggle into every ounce of clothing they could find. 'Ready?'

Four fur lined heads bobbed.

The monk heaved the great door open on a blast of icy air. Wearing only his sandals and a thin cotton robe, he trudged down the tunnel and onto the frozen mountain.

Sam gasped. Hundreds upon thousands of tiny, twinkling stars were set against the deepest blue. There was not a cloud in the sky and the perfect snow crunched underfoot.

Ahead, the line of statues and guards waited. Not a single figure stirred as they made their way toward the cliff.

'Your mind is the most powerful weapon you'll ever possess,' Jen Si shouted over the rising wind. 'If you can control it, you can learn to control everything around you.' His breath frosted with every word, but he did not shiver. Taking off his sandals Jen Si stepped into a drift, his legs disappearing to his knees.

To their amazement, the monk then sat down and closed his eyes.

Joe looked at Sam.

Sam looked at Fedor.

Veronique looked at Joe.

'No way!' Sam's voice was muffled beneath his thick wrapping.

A tendril of steam began to rise from the hole the monk had made. After several minutes, Jen Si's body was not only free of snow and ice, but so was the ground around him. Clothes dry, eyes closed and legs crossed, he sat with his hands folded neatly in his lap.

'Imcweadible!' Joe was almost unintelligible through the excessive layers of wool.

Sam bent to examine the monk. He peeled a mitten off and touched his shoulder. It was as warm as a kettle.

Jen Si's eyes shot open and Sam fell back, landing in a snowdrift.

The others burst out laughing as Sam wriggled. Fedor grabbed a flailing limb and dragged him to his feet.

'Hard to believe now?' the monk asked.

'No, sir,' Sam said. 'Pretty damn amazing.'

'*Si!*' Joe bustled between them. 'That was the coolest thing I've ever seen.'

'Warmest.' Fedor grunted.

Joe laughed. 'The hottest!'

Veronique did not want to spoil the moment, but she was losing the feeling in her toes. 'Could we go in now?'

'Jen Si?' Joe was hot on the monk's heels. 'You wouldn't happen to have any books I could read?'

Sam could not help but chuckle as he hurried to catch up.

Their first week passed in a blur. Awake at dawn, they ate and attended early morning meditation sessions. Hours of memory exercises followed: they were allowed brief glimpses of pictures, then asked to recreate the scenes, recalling every tiny detail until Sam's mind ached.

Afternoons saw them in the Dojo, weaving and gliding through the endless stretches of Tai Chi Chaun, exercises designed to focus the harmonies of their Chakra.

'Our what?' Sam asked Ling Pi, the martial arts teacher.

'Oooh, I know this,' Joe bobbed. 'Have you not read your books? The Chakra are energy centres along the spine located at major branching points of the nervous system. They begin at the base of the spine and run upward to the skull creating seven focal points which are believed to be energy centres of the body.'

They had all fought the urge to kick Joe in the rear when Ling Pi turned and nodded with approval.

Their evenings were spent relaxing around the fire and playing Tribes. The monks had thrust the game upon Joe, in the vain hope that it might stem the relentless requests for more books.

The board had two sides. The first side was designed for two players and had thirty-six squares arranged in a chess-like grid. The reverse was arranged as a much larger board and could accommodate four players.

There were quite a few Tribes to choose from. Most of the sets were chipped and faded, paint and weapons missing. There were Samurai, resplendent in ornate armour and fierce, colourful masks. Stealthy Ninja, favoured by Sam, garbed in black and fierce-looking. The most cared for pieces, were the mighty Mongol warriors of the Khan.

Each player started with a lone tribesman at one corner of the board. Taking turns, they could add other tribesmen to the adjacent squares and eventually conquer the squares of their opponents. The object of the game was to fill the board with your tribe, and it ended when no further moves could be made.

Veronique provided hilarious commentary in the accents of each tribe, whilst Sam dodged, parried and succumbed to seemingly endless attacks. The game was not as easy as it looked.

Clandestine alliances, double-crossing, triple-crossing, sophistry, and all manner of dirty tactics made the rivalry unpredictable and hugely enjoyable. Screams of anguish, delight and frustration – and the odd temper tantrum – were not uncommon.

Enthusiasm for the game renewed when Jenny suggested substituting the pieces for chocolate coins and had deposited a large bag of colourful delights on the table. They corrupted everyone but Joe who, as a chess prodigy, took his strategy very seriously and became extremely annoyed when his tribesmen were eaten.

On one such night of games, they received the first of Mr D'Angelo's visitors...

Chapter 10

Joe was winning, much to everyone's disgust, for he was far from gracious in victory.

Fedor swore and pushed away from the table. The fire was burning low and he stalked over to hurl a few logs at it.

Behind him, humming '*Another One Bites the Dust*', Joe restored the Tribes board. 'Next?'

'I'll have a go,' a new female voice announced.

Joe looked up in surprise when a slender woman sat down and fished around in the box, snapping up Sam's ninja figurines.

'Er, I don't mean to be rude, but who are you?' Joe asked.

'I'm Selina.'

They waited, but no further details were forthcoming. Selina did, however, place her piece on the board. 'Game on, short stuff,' she said with a smile and leaned back in her chair.

Joe huffed, adjusting his glasses. Sam grinned at Veronique. They sat up and even Fedor edged closer.

'So, I assume you all know what a Reader is?' Selina asked, deploying another of her assassins. She had straight dark hair, cropped into a bob. Her fringe fell across her face as she bent over the board. She wore simple, functional clothing. Cargo trousers, knee-length boots and a fur lined tan jacket.

'*The Readers are the academics; quick students with a capacity to store vast amounts of knowledge.*' Joe recited Ruben's words verbatim.

Selina looked up. Sam saw grey-green eyes beneath her smoky lids, and a small scar across her right eyebrow. The stud piercing in her nose gave her an edgy look. She was probably around the same age as Jenny, and he wondered why she was there. They had seen no one else but their trainer and the monks all week.

'Well, yes,' Selina replied, 'but there's a bit more to the job than that.' She added another warrior, drawing Joe's attention back to the board.

'Are you part of a Cadre?' Veronique asked.

Sam's eyes widened as the penny dropped. 'Did D'Angelo send you?'

'Maybe.'

Joe wriggled. 'Oh, come on. Are you a Reader? Which Cadre are you from?'

'*War Mind*,' she laughed, 'and yes, I'm a Reader.' She chewed her lip before adding another piece. 'You're not bad at this.'

Joe beamed. However, his delight was short lived when his first Samurai was escorted back to the barracks.

Sam heard Fedor give a satisfied grunt.

'OMG!' Joe whined. 'Whose side are you on?

The decision was unanimous. 'Hers!'

'Oh, very nice!' he pretended to reach over his shoulder. 'Would anyone like their axe back?'

Sam could tell Veronique was intrigued by their mysterious visitor. The girl was watching the woman with an intense expression on her face. 'Please, go on,' she urged her.

Selina gave Veronique a sideways glance. 'What would you like to know?'

Joe dived in before anyone else could draw breath. 'Are you on a mission now?'

'I am.'

'Please say it's to beat him at Tribes,' implored Fedor.

They all snickered. Except Joe, who simply began humming the *Mission Impossible* theme tune.

'Where's the rest of your Cadre?' Sam asked.

Selina kept a watchful eye on the board. 'Meeting with Jen Si, we've hit a bit of a snag.'

'What kind of snag?' Veronique asked.

The woman straightened. 'We've been following a group of Dark Mod traders, trying to locate their supplier. We were getting close, but then they upped and vanished. It reeks of Harbinger, but we've no proof yet.'

'Mr D'Angelo mentioned them. Who are they?'

'Harbinger Robotics,' Selina made a sour face. 'They'll stop at nothing to get their hands on as much of our tech as possible, especially the Dark Mods. But we give as good as we get.'

Sam leaned forward, 'What's a Dark Mod?'

'They're Blacklisted Mods. The really nasty ones like Black Widow Bite, Scorpion Sting, Blue Ring Octopus and the demonic Gympie-gympie Mod. All illegal to supply or use.'

There was an awkward silence and Veronique finally spoke for the group. 'Um, what's a Mod?'

'Oh dear, you lot *are* green!' Another of Joe's pieces left the board and a strangled cry came from across the table. 'Mod is the slang term given to Transient Genetic Modifications. A scientist named Dominic Creed pioneered a procedure using CarboSilicone and Retro viruses to infect humans with controlled expressions of animal genes. Cadres use these Mods in the field, to give us special abilities.'

The blank looks remained and Selina struggled not to roll her eyes. 'You know what genes are? The stuff in your body that's basically the instruction manual for how you're going to grow?'

They nodded.

'Good. Well, imagine you could isolate the gene that allows an owl to see in the dark or a moth to hear the tiniest sound and could safely inject that into a person. Not permanently effective, but for a short period of time. That temporary modification to their genome is called a Mod.'

The news was met by snorts and scepticism.

She sighed. 'You're gonna make me show you, aren't you?' Selina sat back and opened one of the pockets in her trousers, pulling out a few coloured pens. 'These are Mod pens. Each one contains a different Mod. Right, let's see what I've got... Eagle Eyes takes too long and I'm definitely saving this Snake mod.' She flicked through the collection. 'Here, this will do.'

She had a quick look around. 'Right, we keep this to ourselves, Okay? This was meant to be a meet and greet, not a show and tell.'

Veronique and the boys nodded. 'Deal!' Joe had given up the game and could barely contain himself.

Sam watched as Selina rolled up her sleeve and pressed the nib of the pen against her forearm. There was a slight hiss when she pressed the clip, injecting the chemical concoction.

'Mods take up a lot of energy and can take a while to kick in, depending on how complicated the change is. This one is pretty quick and easy.' She held her hands up for inspection.

The group leaned forward, staring intently.

'There!' Veronique gasped, pointing at Selina's index finger. Her skin had begun to shimmer and what looked like small blisters were forming. 'What is it?'

The bumps spread across her fingertips until they formed a series of ridges. 'Gecko Fingers!' Selina waggled her new climbing apparatus at them. 'Suck on those, Spider-man.'

'Oh my God.' Sam said what they were all thinking.

'How are we getting on in here?' Jenny asked, coming into the room.

Selina flipped her hands over and the group quickly turned their attention back to the Tribes board.

'Terrible!' Joe moaned. 'She's beating me!'

Fedor nodded. 'Best day ever.'

Veronique laughed nervously, trying not to make eye contact with their mentor.

Sometime later, after a relentless barrage of questions, Selina left to find her team. Thankfully, Jenny did not notice when she lifted a hand to wave and an entire clan of ninjas stuck to it. She shoved it behind her back and disappeared.

Joe waved, sadly. 'We're gonna miss you guys.'

In the days that followed, and under Jen Si's careful supervision, Veronique and Fedor each attempted their first Fold.

Veronique had chosen her family's box in the *Bouffes-Parisiens* theatre. Her earliest, most magical memories were of standing tiptoe at the balcony, enthralled by the tales below. They had fuelled her penchant for theatrics.

For Fedor it had been the clearing near their house, his refuge from his father, his brothers and constant feelings of inadequacy. He homed in on the damp, woody smell of the log pile and the weathered tree trunk, reaching for the safe, comforting picture in his mind.

Sam had battled with this part. So many places were tainted. *Arthur's Rest* had never felt the same since they had returned to England without Sophie and he had no desire to think about nor go back to Africa.

'Sammy, don't leave me!'

He backed away from that memory, rubbing his scar. *No, thanks.*

He wasn't sure he had a safe place. Mr D'Angelo's office was still fresh in his memory, so he focused on that. Its rows of crowded shelves and cluttered walls, the comfy leather armchairs, the amazing Far Sight window, the clinking sound of the crystal brandy decanter, the oaken smell of the sideboard. Salvador's desk brimming with books, and Sam focused on their titles, even remembering the strange scroll with the odd-looking temple marking, which the Director had been so quick to put away. But it wasn't working. He didn't move.

Then he thought of a better place. A place where every sight and smell had been ingrained in his memory. The corners of his mouth twitched and he began remembering. 'Ready.'

He felt the monk's warm touch, then the surge as he pushed his own energy into the Stepping Stone. The floor he sat on became cold and hard, the faint buzz of fluorescent lighting echoed around them.

Sam opened his eyes and grinned. Beside him, in the gloom, a familiar chunky metal foot draped in heat-seared plastic greeted him. He gave it a quick rap with his knuckles. It was real.

Jen Si looked around. 'Where are we?'

'Officially, nowhere.' Sam shrugged. 'Level Two Seven Three doesn't exist.'

'What! We shouldn't be here!' Jen Si stood up. The movement triggered a newly installed motion alarm and the lights began to pulse. To make matters worse, a siren on the ceiling began to screech.

The monk looked down at Sam with disappointment. 'This isn't what I had in mind.'

'Sorry.' Sam suddenly felt bad. 'But this is the best I could do.'

'Well, you'd better try again.' The monk sat down and placed his hand over Sam's. 'Now hurry! I don't fancy explaining this to Baid.'

'Who?' Sam remembered hearing that name before.

'Never mind. Just get on with it!'

Sam closed his eyes, the siren piercing his concentration. Hundreds of images flashed before him and he fought to grasp one. His school. His bedroom. The river where he had fished with his father as a child, why had he not picked that? Mr D'Angelo's office swam into view again and his attention was drawn to the temple scroll on the desk.

What was that place? He felt Jen Si's hand warming up and the Stepping Stone tingling in his sweaty palm.

'Wait!' Images were flashing before him in a maddening kaleidoscope of memories. In the distance he heard the faint sound of the Speedlift doors opening, followed by the pounding of heavy feet. He tried to shake his head, clear his thoughts.

The monk's energy surged through him and the Krusa sprang to life.

Sam heard muffled shouts and felt something bump into him. It broke his contact with Jen Si and he toppled over.

He opened his eyes. The siren had stopped.

Thank God!

The lights had also ceased flashing. In fact, they had gone out altogether.

Strange. Sam put his hands on the floor to push himself up but instead of cool, smooth tile, his palms found cold, gritty stone.

He sat bolt upright; eyes wide in the gloom. Wherever he was, it smelled old, musty and damp. He closed his fingers around the Krusa but it was not there. Panic gripped him. Patting the ground blindly, he started praying.

Nothing.

Sam swore. 'Great. Failed at the first hurdle.'

This was not good. His heart pounded. He looked around, eyes adjusting to the almost non-existent light. He wondered for a moment whether he was back in the cursed Deep End, but the smell was different. The air tasted foul. Stale.

He sat panting, trying to calm down, and noticed the faintest crack of light in the darkness to his left.

He shuffled forward. The stone floor stayed even though Sam could feel the edges of the slabs every so often, smooth thin lines between the flush settings.

His feet soon encountered something hard and he stopped. It must be a wall. He spread his legs wider and edged along in the direction of the glow.

It was the tiniest of fissures in the mortar. When his fingers traced the joint, the sliver of light faded.

Sam tried to peer into the tiny crevice but could make out very little. The air, however, was cooler and fresher around it.

He pushed at the wall. It was solid.

He moved back and kicked at the barrier with his foot. Nothing. Drawing back, he kicked again, hard. This time, he felt movement and some plaster crumbled away.

Sam redoubled his efforts and booted the wall repeatedly. More mortar broke off and just when the cramp in his thigh threatened to bring the excavation to an end, the stones toppled outwards.

Sam scrambled forward through the hole.

It was lighter here. In front of him a set of steps led down into more darkness. Two statues holding what appeared to be spears flanked the top of the staircase, their long, muscular backs turned to him. A shaft in the ceiling lit the chamber. It cast its spotlight on a large stone table covered in centuries of dust.

Sam moved away from the hole, leaving a trail on the dusty floor. The shadows at the edges of the narrow room were filled with objects of varying sizes, including archaic-looking tools and weapons. He could make out markings on the walls, paintings, perhaps.

The object in the centre of the room caught his attention when he realised it wasn't a table. Looming out of the darkness, reminiscent of the bow of an ancient ship, was a sarcophagus.

Sam moved toward it. The sides were carved with intricate battle scenes and mighty hordes. The lid was a spectacular three-dimensional relief of, presumably, the coffin's host. An imposing figure with thick arms folded over a long spear, its tip resting on the warrior's lips.

An object on its chest caught Sam's eye. He reached out. It was light, smooth, and several inches long.

'Sam!' The boy jumped, stuffing the object into his pocket.

Jen Si emerged from the gloom and Sam swore. 'You scared seven hells out of me!'

'Sorry,' the monk muttered. 'But where the hell are we?'

'I have *NO* idea! You must know, you're here too?'

'Folding leaves a signature and once I'd explained my presence to the archive guards I was able to follow you. Thanks for that, by the way.'

'Sorry. Do you have the Krusa? I can't find it.'

'It broke.'

Sam could not see the monk's face clearly, but could tell from his tone that he was not happy. The boy suddenly felt two feet tall. 'Oh God! I'm sorry, Jen Si, I had no idea this would happen.'

'It's not your fault.' But his tone conveyed little warmth or reassurance. 'It may yet be fixed, but I'll not know till we get back, which I think we should now do. Who knows what sacred resting place we are defiling?' He beckoned in the gloom.

Sam looked around one last time, torn between his guilt and a strong desire to explore the mysterious catacomb.

Just as he turned away, his eye caught sight of the only writing on the sarcophagus. He committed the runes to memory and followed Jen Si back through the hole.

Chapter 11

Jen Si left Sam in his bedroom and, muttering into his A.I., hurried off to report the incident.

Sam followed the monk to the door, catching only a few of his words before the other teenagers appeared in the hall demanding their own account of what had happened.

He'd caught deep concern in the monk's voice, and fear that Sam might have become trapped in the chamber. He hoped he'd heard wrong.

What is it?' Veronique asked when Sam produced the mysterious object, after swearing them to secrecy, and threw it on the bed. The four youngsters crammed in, to get a better look.

It was a tube with smooth carvings along its length, perforated with a row of indentations, and was light in both colour and weight.

'Could be ivory, horn, or maybe bone.' Joe turned it over. 'Nonno has a Colonial chess set carved from whalebone and the pieces feel very similar to this. But these…' he poked the holes in the stem, 'I wonder what they're for?' He lifted the bone, peering down the shaft. 'Oh duh. It's a flute. Look!'

Wiping it with his sleeve, he pressed the fine end of the shaft between his lips and gave the pipe a cautious blow, creating a low, but melodic sound. He covered one of the holes and the pitch changed.

Excited, Sam forgot his manners and grabbed the find, placing it in his own mouth.

'Hey, tha—' Joe began. He was cut off by the tune Sam drew from the carved bone instrument, a piercing screech that violated every fibre of his being.

Sam spat the flute out. 'Urgh!'

Joe's mouth hung open, he seemed to be staring into space. Veronique was peering intently at her fingernails. She was not moving either. Nor was Fedor, peering at Veronique out of the corner of his eye, veiled fascination frozen onto his face.

'What the…?' Sam looked down. Had the flute done this?

'Guys?' He poked Fedor. Nothing. Sam clicked his fingers in front of the boy's eyes but he did not so much as blink.

Sam groaned, flopping back, head in his hands. His day was going from total turd to downright disastrous. He looked at the pipe trying to remember which holes he had covered and gave it a cautious toot.

Nothing. He swore and tried again, desperately trying to recall the combination.

After several more failed attempts, he let out a frustrated shout and fought the urge to throw the contraption against the wall.

'No! No, no, noooo!' Sam pleaded with his frozen friends and whatever unseen powers held them. This could not happen, he was just starting to lower his guard, daring to let them in.

Panicking was useless. He cleared his head, trying again to remember the placement of his fingers. Eyes closed, he slid his fingertips along the stem, feeling the depressions. He settled the last finger in place and lifted the flute.

The same awful sound pierced his ears.

'—at's not fair!' Joe finished. 'Didn't your mother teach you to share? Well, go on then, give it a toot?'

Sam looked at Veronique who glanced up at him. He looked over at Fedor who had averted his sideways glance. 'Go on then.'

Sam looked down, engraining the combination into his memory before taking his fingers off every hole. He blew and the whistle produced a light-hearted trill.

Joe beamed. 'Cool, huh?'

'Very.' Sam forced a smile. They had no idea what had just happened. Maybe nothing had – for them. He should not let himself become attached to people. One way or another, they would all leave him.

He suddenly felt uncomfortable and isolated, and very certain that this mysterious instrument was meant to stay buried with the ancient warrior.

'It's a simple precaution,' Jenny assured them later, lifting the syringe gun.

Sam watched Joe back away. 'I really don't like needles.'

'Don't be silly.' With a flick of her finger, the needle shot in and out of his shoulder.

'*OW!*'

She aimed her weapon at the others. 'See, nothing to it! Every trainee is injected with Tracker Nodes,' Jenny explained, picking up a small scanner. 'The Nanodes are programmed to attach themselves to free base pairs within your genetic code, creating a unique signature that Earth Song can pinpoint anywhere in the world. So, you'll never get lost and we can always find you!'

Sam suspected that his recent 'adventure' was the catalyst for this precaution.

Jenny ran the scanner over each of them until it beeped and flashed green.

'Done. Your genetic signature has been uploaded to the Cube.'

Joe rubbed his bruised arm. '*Trés* Orwellian!'

'I want *you* for the US Army. Enlist now!' Veronique spoofed Uncle Sam.

Jenny laughed. 'Come on, we've got a treat for you. A week in this cold, drab place is about as much as I can take. Besides, you can only learn so much from books and lessons. I find practical application gets better results.'

'Move, meat bags!' Uncle Sam instructed when their mentor had set off down the hall.

Jen Si waited for them in the training room. He was tending a caged nightingale that serenaded him from its ornate wooden home.

Sam thought he looked drawn and tired. Ling Pi, had overseen their meditation sessions for the last few days.

'Here you go.' He dropped a familiar stone carving into Sam's hand. 'Try not to break it again.'

'Thank you. I'll take better care of it this time, I promise.'

The monk took out the digital frames containing the pictures they'd been forced to memorise in previous lessons and handed them to the group. The devices were set to a tropical beach with crystal blue waters, arching palms trees and a thatched wooden pagoda, its purple flags flapping from its upturned eaves. Sam even noticed sun loungers.

'You've completed the first part of your meditation training. Now a test, to sink or swim.'

Sam's stomach dropped. 'I thought we already did that,' He cut in. The others nodded.

Jen Si raised an eyebrow. 'What doesn't kill you...

'This is a live feed.' To illustrate his point, Jenny strode into view and gave them an exaggerated wave before stripping down to her bikini and flopping onto the sand.

'Study this scene, commit every detail to memory...'

'Don't think that'll be a problem.' Sam muttered to Fedor, grinning. Veronique caught the comment and rolled her eyes. Sam blushed.

'Then, when you're ready, Fold to the sun lounger on the pagoda.' He turned back to his nightingale, giving the students a few moments to focus.

Joe, are you ready?'

'I c... can't!' he stammered. 'Not without your help.'

'Yes, you can. I'm right here.'

'*This* is why Jenny injected us! In case we end up sticking out of a busy road or lying across a railway track somewhere. What if I Fold to the bottom of the ocean?'

Jen Si remained calm. 'Have you ever been to the bottom of the ocean, Joe?'

'No, but Sam had never been to that bloody tomb before and look what happened to him! I've been on plenty of busy roads and the odd railway track!'

'Well then, I'd suggest you don't think about them and try to concentrate on the beach.'

Sam could see how upset Joe was. He took a deep breath. 'I'll go first,' he offered. 'Will that help?'

Joe nodded; eyes wide.

'As you wish,' the monk said.

Sam's stomach was filled with rocks, but there was no going back now. He steadied himself and focused on the chair, the weave of the fabric, the colour of the cloth, imagining how it would feel beneath him. He pictured the wind rustling through the fronds of the palm trees, the rhythmical rush and retreat of the water on the sand. The taste of the salty air. He felt the wooden arms of the lounger under his hands, visualising how the canvas would sink under his weight.

Pulling at the image, he tightened his grip of the Stepping Stone and channelled every fibre of his being into pushing himself onto the chair.

The wood creaked. A whoop caused him to swivel. Jenny was jumping up and down clapping her hands above her head and beaming proudly.

'You did it! Well done! Wave at the camera!'

Sam rose from the chair, shaking, but gave two thumbs up. Grinning, he ripped off his shirt and ran into the surf.

Jen Si smiled. 'See, nothing to it!'

There were over three hundred islands in Fiji and they had this one all to themselves.

Jenny handed each of her young team a small pink pill.

Joe looked wary. 'More tracking devices?'

'No. Tan-a-lot tablets. Chemical sun block.' Jenny popped one into her mouth. 'Factor 50, good for 48 hours. You've passed the first part of your training – time to celebrate!'

'This is more like it,' Sam said, sipping a cold drink and watching the sun set.

'I'll say,' Joe agreed.

'I was meant to be spending the summer here,' Jenny lamented into her drink. 'But someone had to make sure you lot didn't get into any trouble.'

Joe waggled his injured leg.

'My shift hadn't started,' she shrugged. 'Well, we're here now, even if it's only a flying visit. And who knows, if you carry on working as hard as you have this week, maybe we can come back for another little break?'

'YEAH!'

'This is my first time at the beach,' Fedor admitted, arms around his knees, staring across the crimson waters.

'You're kidding?' Sam said.

'Nope. My father's not one for holidays.'

Veronique patted his arm, causing him to jump.

'Calm down,' she laughed, mimicking his accent. 'I wasn't going to steal it.'

'Sorry,' Fedor said. 'We're not a very tactile family. Unless we're fighting.'

Joe scrambled up and leapt on the boy. 'Sounds like Fedor needs a group hug!'

Sam whooped and joined the fray.

Veronique surveyed the wrestling for a few respectable moments, then dived onto the pile of arms and legs, shrieking with laughter.

Jenny swirled her drink, fighting the urge to join in.

As night fell properly, Sam walked away from the bonfire on the beach, his fingers toying with the flute in his sand-encrusted pocket.

When he was a safe distance from the others, he drew it out. The pale object glowed in the bright moonlight. He placed his fingers across the holes, wondering what other secrets the notes held. He had been too scared to use it again but, as the shock wore off, he found himself thinking about the flute constantly.

I'm turning into bloody Gollum.

Like the Krusa stones, he couldn't fathom the way that it worked. Judging by the age of the tomb, it had been hundreds, if not thousands of years since it had been laid to rest with its occupant. Sam wondered who the man was and what other secrets lay dormant in the crypt.

This was all beginning to get too much. He should tell a grown-up. His parents were the obvious choice, but they'd already kept so much from him and he still didn't understand why. Jen Si or Jenny would probably just confiscate it and Sam wasn't ready to lose his find yet. Who could he trust to help him unravel its mysteries and keep them a secret...?

A thought occurred to him. It was a long shot. He could get into even more trouble, or worse still, be expelled, but he had to try.

Sam snatched a look toward the fire. Jenny was engrossed in a book and the others were huddled over a Tribes board.

He sat down in the sand and crossed his legs. *Now or never!* He closed his hand around the Stepping Stone and pushed.

'Flic?' He hoped this plan was not going to backfire.

'Flic?' he called again, a little louder.

Moments later, a faint whirring reached his ears and a glowing blue nimbus hovered into view.

'Sam! What are you doing here? Is your father with you? There is no record of you on the Visitors Log.'

'No, I'm here alone. Flic, I need your help.'

'My help? How can you be here on your own, the Archives are off limits to—'?

'Please, Flic, I don't have much time. Will you help me?'

Her nimbus softened and the shutters of her camera eyes narrowed. 'This is most irregular.'

Sam told the robotic curator his disastrous first attempt at Folding, the tomb and the mysterious flute. 'I thought with your extensive knowledge, there was no one more able to tell me what it is.'

The compliment played to Flic's vanity and her nimbus pulsed.

'Well, from what you've described,' she buzzed closer to look at the flute, 'it sounds like an elementary sound weapon. The Harmonics and Non-Lethal Acoustic Weapons section is inundated with patents and speculation as to the use of harmonic frequencies to achieve all manner of results. Through subsonic or infrasonic wavelengths, one can cause pain or generate severe nausea. The human body does not react well to extremely low frequency noises. They can cause loss of balance and a subsonic shock wave could even cause tissue damage. It stands to reason that frequencies could exist that may inhibit or impair synaptic functions – the nervous system — achieving the paralysis you've described. This flute could be the result of some such primitive discovery...'

Sam stared at the robot blankly. 'So, it could cause harm?'

'In theory, yes.'

'How come I wasn't affected by it?'

'Perhaps the shape of the flute is such that it directs the sound wave away from the user? You said you felt some discomfort, but not the full effect. Perhaps if you play a few notes for me, I can record and analyse the spectrum and come up with some other chords? I'll also take a physical sample and see if we can find out what it's made from.'

He was hesitant to use it again, but his desire to know more about the mysterious object overcame his fears. Sam focused on the finger-placement. When they were done, he remembered another detail. 'Oh – do you know anything about runes?' Sam asked.

'Of course.'

'Could you translate some, please?'

'Show me and I will locate the source,' Flic buzzed over to a nearby stack, picking up a clipboard and pen and Sam sketched the rune.

'I'd better get back. Thanks again! Oh, and Flic, can we keep this between us for now? Just till we figure it out.'

Flic finished the scan and her nimbus flickered showing a conflict between protocol and programming.

'For now.'

'Wonderful!' Sam beamed. 'You're the best, thank you! I'll come back when I can.'

Fedor watched Sam reappear on the sun lounger. He walked over to the pagoda. 'Good trip?'

Sam leapt into the air and swore. 'Don't sneak up on me like that, you'll give me heart failure!'

'Then neither of us should be sneaking around.'

Sam looked embarrassed. 'It's not what you think.'

'How do you know what I think?'

'Well, it's not what it looks like then.'

'What does it look like?'

'Like I blatantly ignored Jen Si and used the Krusa the minute his back was turned.'

'You're right,' Fedor said. 'That's exactly what it looks like.' He loomed over Sam, dark eyes boring into him. 'If you fail, we *all* fail, and my family is not getting kicked out of The Order because of you or me.'

'You're right, I'm sorry. I just needed some help.'

'Help with what?'

'With the flute,' Sam sighed. 'I think it's dangerous.'

Fedor backed away. 'Dangerous, how?'

'Let's just say I've discovered that blowing it in a certain way has some rather unusual effects on the people around me and I wanted to try and find out more before it hurts someone.'

'What sort of effects?'

'It froze the three of you, that first evening, still as statues. No recollection afterwards, either. It scared the life out of me. Have you ever heard of anything like that before?'

'Well, no. Not until now. But then nothing we've seen or done recently has been normal. I think you should give us the benefit of the doubt. We may not understand it, but you don't need to do this by yourself.' Fedor realised how ironic that advice was, coming from someone like him.

'You're right,' Sam said feeling slightly ashamed of keeping the secret. 'I guess this is going to take some getting used to, isn't it?'

Fedor nodded. 'Come on. How about we go back to the fire and you help me beat bookworm and the parrot at Tribes? They think they're invincible and it's really getting on my nerves.'

Sam could not help but laugh.

* * *

'I thought the terms of our arrangement were clear?' Ms Keller regarded the person opposite her.

'They are. It's just taking more time.'

She rolled her head from side to side, staring at the ceiling. 'Time,' she drawled. 'You need more time? Do you know what happened to the last person who disappointed me?'

The individual in the chair stared at her, unperturbed.

'If you want to kill me, kill me, just don't torture me with amateur theatrics.'

Ms Keller was growing impatient. 'Well then, perhaps I will explain it to your children, given that you're so... immune to my persuasion.'

The look she received in return was nothing short of poisonous and she chuckled. 'Oh, is that compliance?'

'It is.'

'Good. When can I expect to be in possession of the scroll?'

'It's still not that simple. The Council sent the scroll to Shen Pi and the monks have hidden it. Not even the Council knows its location. So, you see, we're at a potential impasse.'

'How unfortunate. For you. With whom shall I start? Your daughter? Perhaps your little son?'

'I said a potential impasse, not dead end.'

'Careful with your choice of words, then.'

'Skinning cats, my dear,' drawled her guest. Never had the word 'dear' conveyed less warmth or affection. 'There's always another way. Success in this case, however, relies on certain events running their course.'

Ms Keller was intrigued. Perhaps this fool could pull it off. A pity she had already decided to dispose of her pawns.

Never leave an enemy behind you... Her father's words had stuck. Words were all that remained of the great Victor Keller now.

'Tell me more,' she smiled.

All things come to she who waits.

Chapter 12

After sharing his secrets, and a blissful night in a hammock, Sam felt much happier.

The other teens had awoken with similar positive energy. It was amazing what a bit of sun and sea air could do for the disposition. A bracing early morning dip, a hearty breakfast and they would be ready for another long day lazing in the sun.

Jen Si had other plans.

'Oh no,' Joe muttered, when he spied their mentor making his way along the beach. 'I think the holiday is over.'

The monk looked strangely normal in a pair of jeans and a polo shirt. He held up a postcard. 'Who fancies breakfast in Tokyo? Get ready. You'll find clean clothes in the pagoda. Don't be long.' With that, he vanished, the postcard wafting to the sand.

Veronique stooped to pick it up. She turned it over. 'It looks like a booth in an American-style diner. *"The best breakfast in Tokyo. Wish you were here! Jenny xoxo".'*

'Well, now we know where she disappeared to,' Joe sulked.

They rummaged through the pile of clothes and trainers, then Veronique retreated into the undergrowth whilst the boys tried to match tops to torsos.

'Nice!' Sam laughed at Fedor. His jeans were too short and the largest top looked as though it were sprayed on. The Russian moved his arms and was rewarded with a ripping sound.

He swore.

Joe was admiring himself in a faded 'Born to surf' t-shirt when Veronique reappeared wearing shorts and a black vest top, a teal jersey tied around her waist.

Nikki, the Tourist!

'Hardly high fashion, darling, but...' she eyed the boys, 'it could be worse.'

They found four backpacks each holding a wallet, raincoat, pad and pen, digital pocket translator, and a torch.

'No phone,' Sam sighed. 'That would be too much to ask.'

'Love the cash though,' Veronique fanned herself with a fistful of dollars.

Sam shrugged on a pack. 'All set? I'll go first, then Joe, Veronique and Fedor.' They nodded, deferring to him without question.

'I don't see any passports, so avoid anyone who might start asking you questions. It could be a little hard to explain how you got there without one. Worst case, plead ignorance and shrug a lot. Okay?'

They shrugged.

'Very funny!'

'*No lo sé, hombre,*' Veronique beamed.

Sam closed his eyes and slowed his breathing. Taking hold of his Stepping Stone, he created a Fold.

'Ah!' Jenny winked above a candy-striped straw. 'Fancy meeting you here!'

Sucking the last dregs from a tall milkshake, she handed him another postcard. She could not help feeling proud. They were making fantastic progress. Whether it was D'Angelo's idea or not, Sam and his friends were well on their way to proving that the Council's faith in her was well placed.

'I've taken the liberty of ordering and paid the bill. Feel free to join me when you're done!' With a final slurp, she left.

Sam realised the booth had been well chosen. No one in the busy diner could see the teenagers popping from the proverbial woodwork.

'How'd we not end up on top of each other?' Veronique asked when the waiter had retreated, leaving their table brimming with hot food and drink.

Joe stuffed a sausage into his mouth, then pointed his fork at Veronique. 'No two objects can occupy the same space. Did none of you losers read the books?' He started cutting his slice of toast, tutting.

Veronique eyed the syrup pancakes. 'That's why we have you, *mon petit chou*!'

'Who you calling a cabbage?'

Fedor plucked the next postcard from Sam. '"*The view from Coit Tower*".'

'San Francisco?' Joe's lips were now yellow with yolk. 'Would be nice to see a bit of Tokyo first.'

'Nope. We're procrastinating.' Sam downed his drink. 'Fedor, you keep watch and let's try stick to the order this time, people!'

'Yes, boss!' Joe muttered. Once the boy had vanished.

The view of San Francisco from Telegraph Hill was spectacular.

Veronique sighed. 'I wish I had a camera!'

'I wish they'd not confiscated mine.' Joe commiserated.

'What's that pointy building?' she asked.

Joe didn't even need to look up. 'It's the Transamerica Pyramid. Always gets totalled in disaster movies along with the Chrysler building. Oh, and speaking of New York…' He waved a postcard at them.

Fedor would never admit it but these first weeks had been the most enjoyable time of his life; the monastery, Fiji, Tokyo and now America. He had seen all these incredible places already. He hated to think it would all soon end. Still, at least he would see Misha and Mikhail again. He did miss them.

Veronique favoured them with her Upper East Side drawl. 'Fifth Avenue, baby!'

Joe promptly extinguished all hope of a shopping trip. '"*St George Ferry Terminal – Staten Island*," baby!'

'Pah!' she snatched the card. 'Where's the fun in that?'

It was raining in New York.

'And that's why they packed the raincoats.' Veronique's mood was less than jovial as she watched the deluge lashing against the windows of the terminal. They had Folded to the only quiet corner, where Jenny sat reading The Times. It was now a little after five in the afternoon and the hall was awash with commuters.

'Not so sunny here, sorry! Let's get the ferry across to Manhattan – I'm sure it's just a shower.'

As she predicted, the rain passed, so they braved the open-topped city bus, huddling together on damp seats to enjoy the sights. Times Square, Rockefeller Plaza, Radio City Music Hall and then on to Veronique's beloved Fifth Avenue. Not to mention the majestic Empire State Building, presiding over the skyline.

'I can't believe it only took one year and forty-five days to build.' Sam was gob smacked by the facts the tour guide rattled off. Craning his neck, he tried to see the top. 'How many floors did he say?'

'One hundred and two.' Joe already knew the answer. 'It's hardly surprising, with three and a half thousand workers on it. The Great Depression certainly 'motivated' people.'

'Imagine working up there, walking the girders.' Sam had a wild look.

'Not for me,' Joe said. 'I'm afraid of heights.'

Sam laughed. 'I don't mean to sound funny, but is there anything you're not afraid of?'

Joe scratched his nose with his middle finger. 'Only one.'

Fedor was not listening. He was both amazed and overwhelmed by the city. He had never been to one.

The buildings stood so close together, blotting out the sky. There were people everywhere. Hundreds. Thousands! All pushing and shouting. Cars, buses, taxis, trucks, hooting, weaving and jostling on the crammed roads. He felt a little overwhelmed and sat back in his seat.

'Hotdogs!' Joe shouted, the sound and smell of sizzling onions wafting up from the street below. 'We've got to have a New York hotdog, come on!' He shot down the stairs before anyone could object.

Food! Now that thought *did* appeal to Fedor.

Veronique was a bit bored, but tried not to show it.

She'd been to New York many times; she came at least once a year, either Christmas shopping with her mother and aunt after Thanksgiving or sometimes earlier for the parade and floats.

It was not until sunset that she felt the city come alive. New York was even more magical by night. Endless bright lights, colourful laser shows and great swivelling spotlights bouncing off smog.

The crowds were more relaxed than the pavement prowlers of the day. And they were certainly louder, jostling their way between the theatres, restaurants and bars, shouting and laughing.

The teenagers crossed the road near the Plaza and followed Jenny into Central Park.

Rope lights swung between the trees and the paths were bathed in warm pools of lamplight. Men on stilts juggled an array of neon skittles. They wore colourful trousers and extravagant silk shirts, which shimmered when they moved. Makeup had transformed them into animals: one a lion, the other a tiger.

They gave way, allowing the group to pass between them, an arc of skittles over their heads. Fedor ducked. The jugglers laughed and smiled.

Next they saw acrobats, and Veronique moved to the front, most interested. They flipped and jumped, contorting their bodies in all manner of ways, but the girl was not that impressed.

A woman in Mardi Gras regalia brought up the rear of the procession. An oriental parasol rested on her shoulder and she waved a slender cane in the air, conducting two meticulously groomed poodles who danced around her on their hind legs.

Joe raised an eyebrow. 'Is there a carnival we don't know about, or is this just normal for New York?'

Veronique cupped her ear. 'There's music – you're right – it's *Cirque*!'

Sure enough, over the next rise, Central Park had been overrun by magic. Magicians, jugglers, acrobats and clowns, fire-eaters, belly dancers, fortune tellers and stuntmen, all crowded around a massive Big Top. Lions roared, chimps screeched and elephants trumpeted from inside.

The air was laced with the sugary tang of candyfloss and hot buttered popcorn. Red-faced children staggered under the weight of multi-coloured lollipops as clowns fashioned dogs, cats, and swords from coloured balloons and older children tried their luck at the coconut shy.

Sam heard pellet guns pop and the occasional tin toppled. Shady fortune tellers with painted faces prowled the crowds, plying their mysterious trade.

Flames were belched by painted devils, to the tune of startled gasps, as sword eaters raised long blades above their heads, causing Sam to wince when they devoured them.

'This is *incredible*!' Joe breathed, heading toward the caged lions.

'Not so fast.' Jenny caught his backpack and pointed to the Big Top. 'That way.'

A large man blocked the entrance to the red and white candy stripe tent. He had a barrel chest and a mass of curly dark hair with a grey streak running through it. His beard was neatly cropped and only slightly flecked by age.

He looked down at Joe and raised an eyebrow. 'Yes?' he asked the boy with a broad Scottish accent.

Joe thrust out his chin. 'Table for five, my good man, and there's a little something in it for you if it's near a window.'

'Very funny. The show doesn't start for another hour, go play in the ball pool.'

'They're with me, Reaper,' Jenny said, squeezing past Fedor.

The man's expression didn't change. 'And do you or your unfortunate looking offspring have a ticket, Miss Four-by-four?'

'No, but I have a photo of me standing above you on the wrestling podium and I'm more than happy to show it to them and demonstrate how that happened.'

The man snorted. 'Every dog, Jenny. You never beat me at the caber toss though.' He tugged the heavy canvas open, then stuck his foot out.

She rolled her eyes and stepped over it.

'Who was that?' Veronique asked, once they were inside.

'Alistair Crane, the Juggernaut for Pandora's Box,' Jenny replied. 'The Cadre we're here to meet.'

'Why did you call him Reaper? Is he deadly?' said Joe.

Jenny laughed. 'He'd certainly like to think so. He cut off a few toes messing around with a scythe when we were kids.'

'Oh,' Veronique chuckled, 'how unfortunate.'

'Big mouth!' Sam heard Reaper shout through the canvas and Jenny laughed.

A short, wiry woman sat at the edge of the sawdust arena, wrapping her hands and wrists in support bandages.

'Ah, you're here! Come on down,' she stood and beckoned them into the ring. They picked their way through the debris of show snacks to the centre of the tent.

'Hi,' she smiled. 'I'm Pip.'

Jenny did the introductions.

'The Stone Thieves, eh?' Pip pursed her lips. 'I like it. We're the sixty-third Cadre to carry the Pandora's Box sigil.'

'You met Reaper. Patrick, our Paladin, and Brychan, our Reader, are getting ready for the next show. As I'm sure you've guessed,' she spread her arms, 'we travel as a troop of acrobats.'

'What's a sigil?' Sam had not heard the term before.

'It's your clan crest – a bit like a coat of arms.' Pip rolled up her sleeve and showed them an intricate tattoo on her forearm.

'You're a Charlatan?' Veronique asked, when they were done admiring the artwork.

Pip nodded.

'And one of the best,' Jenny admitted.

'So you spy, cheat and steal?' Joe recalled.

Pip laughed. 'And those are just the nice things people say about us! Our job is to blend in, to see everything, hear everything – gather the intelligence that could give our team the upper hand or a quick escape.'

Veronique was enthralled. To her the role sounded amazing. 'They must rely on you a lot.'

'Well, they'd never admit it,' Pip wrinkled her nose, 'but they'd be lost without me and my Mods.'

Sam realised that there had been little mention of Mods since their evening with the mysterious Selina.

'What sort of Mods?' Joe asked.

'Well, we try to use Mods that enhance our natural capabilities. You met Reaper; he favours the Silverback Mod, which gives him the strength of a great ape. He's used it so many times he even has a silver streak now.

'I'm quick and nimble, so I tend to use Bird or Marsupial Mods, to help me jump and climb.'

Sam frowned. 'Marsupial Mods?'

'Kangaroos, mate. Ya know – hop, hop?' Joe made an awful attempt at an Australian accent.

Veronique shuddered. 'Leave it to the professionals, *mon petit chou*.'

'Stop calling me that!'

Jenny sighed. 'Maybe a demonstration, Pip?'

'Sure, I took Bird Bone about twenty minutes ago, so by now my skeleton is full of air pockets, making me much lighter and able to do this.' Pip ran for a few steps and soared into the air. She completed a series of twists, turns and somersaults before landing so gently that the sawdust didn't even stir.

'Woah!' Fedor gasped. 'That could be very useful.'

Pip grinned. 'You've not seen anything yet.' She rocked forward onto her toes, bent her legs, uncoiled and shot upward like an arrow towards the trapeze in the roof of the tent. Making contact with the bar, she used her momentum to swing back and forth in long, plunging arcs.

Veronique could feel her heart pounding. How she longed to be that graceful. Then she noticed that Pip's arc did not bring her close enough to the platforms on either side of the tent. Perhaps she would jump it, but it looked too far. 'Er, how's she going to get down?'

Jenny shrugged.

On cue, in the highest recesses of the tent, Pip suddenly let go of the swing.

The world slowed down as they watched her fall.

'Help her!' Joe screamed.

Veronique, hands over her mouth, felt a cold sweat grip her.

Sam and Fedor both swore. Even with her lighter skeleton, Pip began to plummet toward them. She wore no harness and there was no safety net. Her fate seemed inevitable.

The Charlatan drew in her arms and legs, and then suddenly extended them into a star formation, opening her wing suit. She swept over the teenagers, causing them to duck, and soared back into the roof of the tent. Round and around she glided, rolling and weaving like a fighter jet.

'Flying Fox suit,' Jenny laughed.

With a final theatrical loop and barrel roll, Pip landed safely in the centre of the ring.

'Tada!'

Veronique was sold. She had found her calling. She rushed over to the woman, a million questions racing through her mind.

Joe turned to the boys. 'How the hell are we meant to learn or compete with that? We're going to get annihilated at this CruciBowl thing!'

Sam patted him on the shoulder. 'I'll admit, they have some pretty neat tricks, but I'm sure we'll have some good ones of our own by the end of the summer, so don't worry.' But secretly he was just as worried about the mysterious CruciBowl match and the stakes involved. They all were.

Outside the Big Top, the carnival was in full swing.

'Right, fun's over,' Jenny announced, when they had said goodbye to Pip and Reaper.

The news was greeted by scowls.

'Oh, dry your eyes! At least you're out of the monastery. Jen Si wanted you to complete a much more convoluted task here, but I would like to keep it light, so you must simply find three more of these.' She drew a small brooch from her pocket and put it on her palm to show them. 'It's the MacLeod family crest. Find all three tokens and you'll find the destination for tonight. I've made it really simple – so please don't tell Jen Si. Think outside the box and it won't take long. Good luck!'

Sam watched her melt into the crowd.

'Needle in a haystack, anyone?' Joe huffed.

Veronique looked around. 'Let's split up. My little cabbage can keep me company, you two are big enough and ugly enough to fend for yourselves. Meet back here in an hour?'

Joe scowled at the moniker.

Sam agreed. 'Sounds good. Fedor, happy?'

The Russian nodded. He was hungry.

'*Allez, mon petit chou.*' Veronique linked arms with Joe. 'Walkies!'

'Please stop calling me that!'

Fedor was still feeling overwhelmed.

People pressed him from all sides. Bumped him. Spilt things on him. A group of children had laughed at his ill-fitting shirt and he was forced to put on his raincoat to avoid further ridicule. He had tried to enjoy it, indulging himself on the Strength Test, and was now encumbered with a giant pink teddy.

He scanned the crowd. This was not easy. Make believe was rife. He'd tried looking up close at the chests of the passers-by, searching for the pin, but the approach had only brought scoffs and raised eyebrows, and he had been forced to resort to less overt surveillance.

A bear and his handler crossed his path. The bear reared and roared at the gathering crowd, much to their fear and delight. Fedor paled, turning away.

This could not get any worse.

In hindsight, pairing with Joe had not been Veronique's smartest move, for there was not one ounce of willpower between them.

They flitted from stall to stall and, within five minutes, had painted faces, animal balloons and candyfloss encrusted lips.

Nikki, the Clown!

'Oh, look at the monkeys!' Veronique pulled Joe towards a ring toss. 'I want one!'

'Then give it a go or buy one. I've the hand-eye coordination of a drunk turtle.'

She pointed to a gorilla on the top shelf. It had a familiar crest pinned to its chest.

Joe swore.

'Language!' Veronique chided. 'Well, if you're not prepared to have a go, I will.' She puffed out her chest and went Texan. 'Step aside, short stuff!'

Joe muttered something unflattering but gave way.

Not one of her rings made it as far as the first peg. In fact, two did not even make it back into the stall.

Now Veronique swore.

Joe chuckled.

'Put a sock in it!' She handed over another five dollars.

This time one ring did hit something. Unfortunately, it was the man in the tombola store next door.

'Sorry!' she bit her lip. The man rubbed the back of his head and returned the heavy wooden ring.

'Maybe this isn't your game, sugar lips?' the bemused attendant chuckled.

'One more go!' She handed over their last five dollars, wondering whether they could get a refund on the face painting.

The first hit the man in the *other* neighbouring stall.

The second barely missed the man in her stall.

The third took an unsuspecting prize squarely between the eyes and the fourth ring got lodged in the roof of the tent.

Veronique took a step back and swung the last with murderous intent.

'Wait!' The stall owner surrendered. 'I'll give you the toy! Just don't throw another ring, lady! Please!'

'Magnifique!' Veronique pointed at the black gorilla. 'That one, please!'

Veronique, cuddling the gorilla, looked very proud of herself. 'One down.'

Joe could not speak; he was still laughing too hard.

Sam was enjoying the sights.

He had never been to a circus with animals and could not help wondering what the twins would make of it. So far, he'd seen the lion act, a troupe of trapeze artists in an outside arena and several magicians performing mind-boggling tricks.

None of them, sadly, were sporting a crest.

He caught the eye of a pretty girl and asked the time. It was 9.20pm.

A clown blew an air horn right next to him and Sam jumped, much to the amusement of the children who were following the prankster. He could not help laughing, despite his pounding chest.

'Fortunes told.' The invitation came from a stooped woman in a shawl. Her long curly hair all but hid her face and she spread pale arms before her, jingling a mass of silver bracelets and charms as she moved. She caught Sam's eye and veered toward him.

'How 'bout you, handsome?'

Sam opened his mouth to decline, but noticed a crest hanging on one of her many charms. 'Sure, how much?'

'Your first born.' She wiggled her fingers suggestively.

'Er…'

The woman laughed. 'I'm just kidding, sugar. It's ten bucks.'

She settled onto a hay bale, smoothing her silk skirt and patting the straw.

Sam rifled through his money stash, examining each note like the proverbial tourist. The woman smiled then stuffed the note into her cleavage.

'Hands,' she demanded, holding out her own slender fingers. Her grip was cool but firm. 'Relax, honey.' The woman flipped his hands over in hers and began to examine his palms. 'Now, let's see…'

She became silent, tracing the lines of his hands, first one and then the other.

'Well, Sam,' she began.

'Woah!' How'd you—?' He tried to pull away, but his hands were held fast and the examination continued.

'What kind of Fortune Teller would I be, if I couldn't even guess your name?' She looked up and winked. Her hair fell away and Sam was surprised to see how young she was. Astonishing grey eyes twinkled beneath layers of sooty kohl and thick mascara.

'My name is Aura. Now don't interrupt me again, or I'll have to start over, and 'll charge you another ten bucks.'

Sam fell silent. Jenny must have told her his name. She arranged this.

'I see darkness.' Aura's voice changed. 'It's cold. Very old. A sacred place. You shouldn't be here. You've taken something… It shouldn't have left that place. Nothing should. There is a great evil in the shadows, evil that must never again be woken…'

Sam's heart was in his throat. Did she mean the flute? Neither Jen Si nor Jenny knew he'd taken it. Unless Flic had told them? The others would not have…

'There is a letter that never existed. It has found you, but you have not found it.' Aura paused, troubled. 'Now I see a beautiful girl. Eyes of emerald.' Her voice softened. 'You love her.'

Sam beamed. This was more like it. Victoria had green eyes. Love though…?

'She will break your heart,' Aura took a deep breath, 'and betray you. There is another,' the woman sounded ominous, trying to make out figures in the dark, 'But she will die.' Her voice dropped to a regretful whisper.

Sam gulped. So far, this had been a depressing use of his money.

'You will face a difficult decision. I see two doors. Both lead to danger, but one leads to a god...'

God? Sam raised an eyebrow at the unexpected spiritual twist.

Silence.

'Which door is it?'

Aura looked up; eyes groggy, unfocused.

'Huh?'

'You said there were two doors. One leading to God.'

'What? I haven't said a thing, sugar. Now don't interrupt me or we'll have to start again and that will be another ten bucks!'

'Sam!'

He looked up. Two children with painted faces, balloons and a toy gorilla were rushing toward him. This night was getting stranger by the second.

Then he recognised the 'children'. 'Oh my good God!' He could not believe his eyes, 'You're meant to be looking for clues, not improving your looks or stealing from toddlers.' They were now close enough for him to smell their candyfloss breath. 'Seriously?'

Veronique waved him to silence. 'We've found one! Unlike someone else, sitting on his rear watching the world go by.'

'Hey, I'm—' Sam turned to the fortune-teller for support but there was no one there.

'Where'd she go?'

'Who?'

'The woman. The fortune-teller. She was right here.'

The monkey and the tiger exchanged looks.

'Er, there was no one there, Sam. You were just sitting by yourself. Maybe she left before we got here?' Joe glanced meaningfully at Veronique.

'Never mind that now. Here.' She waved the stuffed gorilla in front of his face.

Sam felt as though the world had turned to treacle. What had just happened?

Joe was clicking his fingers in front of his face.

'Hmm?' Sam muttered.

'Snap out of it. Look, the gorilla has the crest on it. It's a clue!'

'Uh.' Sam blinked, pulling himself together. 'Well done.' He stood up. 'I've come up dry.' He had failed to get the crest charm from the woman's bracelet, or even check it.

I see a beautiful girl with emerald green eyes.

'What's the time?'

You love her.

Veronique accosted another passer-by. 'Nine thirty.'

She will break your heart.

'Let's find Fedor, hopefully he's had more luck than I did.'

She will betray you.

Joe looked around. 'Which way is it?'

There will be another.

Sam glanced up at the Big Top to get his bearings. 'That way.' He pointed.

She will die.

Chapter 13

Fedor's evening had been anything but fortunate.

'Excuse me…' Another person rudely pushed past him. But the startled woman took one look at the scowling young man in a flimsy raincoat and tight-fitting shirt, brandishing a teddy bear and veered away, ignoring him.

Fedor swore. Colourfully: in Russian and at great length. It was most satisfying.

'My, oh my. Someone's not in a party mood.'

He turned to find a woman staring at him. She carried a sweets tray looped over her shoulders, her eyebrows arched.

'You speak Russian?'

She nodded.

Fedor had the good grace to blush. 'I'm sorry, I didn't think anyone would understand me.'

The woman smiled. 'You'd be surprised, most of the vendors here are from Little Odessa.'

Fedor looked blank.

'Brighton Beach?'

Still nothing.

'You're not from around here, are you?'

He shook his head. 'Do you have the time, please?'

The woman took the weight of the tray with one arm and twisted her wrist.

'Nine twenty-five.'

'Thank you,' Fedor said, turning away.

'Hey,' the woman called after him. 'Here. On the house!' She tossed a bag of fizzy cola bottles his way. 'Maybe that'll sweeten your mood?'

Fedor looked at the bag of sweets, surprised by the gift. Tucking them into his pocket, and feeling a bit better, he once again braved the crowd.

'Van Sandt?!'

Sam blinked in surprise. Stopping, he stared around.

'It *is* you!'

'Col!' Sam was dumbstruck at the sight of the burly rugby captain.

'What the hell are you doing here?' they asked in unison then burst out laughing.

'I—' Sam began.

'We—' Colin stopped, when they did it again.

'C'mon, Col!' A girl was pulling at his sleeve oblivious to the exchange 'We're going to lose her!' Her voice was drowned by the noise of the carnival and she did not look back, her attention fixed on someone in the crowd.

'But it's—' Colin tried to get the girl's attention.

'Sam!' Joe called out as he tried to keep up with Veronique, who was already disappearing in the throng. The boy stood still, unsure whom he should follow.

Sam turned to his school friend and shrugged.

'Go! We'll find you later.' Big Col waved him off with a grin.

'Cool.' Sam was relieved at being spared an awkward explanation.

'Who's that?' Joe asked, when he and Sam caught up with Veronique.

'Guy from school.' Sam shook his head. 'That's so weird.' He caught a glimpse of another familiar face and pointed to Fedor. 'Look, there's Chatterbox.'

The group found a quiet spot to swap stories.

'So, we only have one of the three crests we need.' Sam felt deflated.

Joe was staring at the Russian and his bear.

'Hold the phone.' He grabbed the pink teddy and flipped it over. Embroidered on its furry rear, was the MacLeod family crest! 'Now that's just lazy.'

Fedor shook his head. 'I can't believe I didn't notice that. Sorry, guys.'

'Don't apologise.' Sam's mood brightened a little. 'At least you've not returned empty handed. We're still one short, though, thanks to me.' The thought of the fortune-teller still troubled him.

Fedor's stomach rumbled. He dug in his pocket for the bag of sweets.

'Oooh! Cola bottles,' Veronique licked her candyfloss encrusted lips.

Sam laughed when Fedor tossed her the bag with a sigh.

'Much obliged,' she said, fussing with the ribbon tie.

The boys began examining the stuffed toys, pressing, prodding and squeezing them, flicking the plastic eyes of their helpless captives.

'Er, gentleman,' Veronique cooed.

She was waggling Fedor's bag of sweets at them.

'Not now, V,' Sam huffed. 'You have them.'

'Ahem!' she coughed, waving the bag closer.

Hanging from the curly purple ribbon that held the clear bag closed, was a small, plastic crest.

Joe clapped his hands. 'That's three!' Jenny was right, she really had made it easy.

Fedor felt something hard in the arm of the bear and ripped the appendage off with more aggression than the situation called for, a cloud of stuffing launching into the air.

'Mummy!' Sam saw a little girl pointing in horror, as Fedor dug around in the severed limb. 'What's that man doing to the Teddy!' The mother fixed Fedor with a murderous look, ushering her daughter away.

Fedor found a small plastic tube. There was a piece of paper curled up inside.

'It says *Carla*.' He handed the others the scrap.

Sam had found another lump in the back of the gorilla and was picking at the stitches. Fedor snatched the toy and tore it open. Another scream signalled the traumatised youngster was still within sight.

'*Magical.*'

'Aha!' Veronique had tipped the sweets into her lap. Licking her sugar-coated fingers, she read the final clue aloud. '*Madame.*'

They all mouthed the words.

'Magical Madame Carla?' Joe ventured.

'Excuse me.' Sam accosted a nearby clown. 'Where will we find Magical Madame Carla?'

The clown hiked a thumb over his shoulder. 'Past the rides. Nasty old Carnie caravan, you can't miss it.'

'Thanks! Well then, let's not keep the mysterious Madame C waiting!'

They kept to single file, slipstreaming behind Fedor. The noise of the circus changed as they searched, the roar of animals giving way to electronic music, robotic cackles and jubilant screeches. The Big Wheel shimmered above the merriment, surrounded by flashing merry-go-rounds, stomach-churning cups and the ever-popular Haunted Mansion.

Joe's eyes lit up and he slowed down earning a foot in the rear.

A group of scruffy circus children blocked their path. Shouting and swearing, they traded kicks and insults. Most patrons refused to make eye contact with them, muttering in distaste.

Fedor ploughed straight through.

A gangly upstart squared up to him, but a deft shove coupled with a foot behind the boy's ankle sent him crashing to the ground. Two others took his place and soon found themselves in a heap beside their companion. Sam watched the rest of the group step aside, sniggering at their hapless comrades.

At the corner of the fairground where the coloured lights dimmed and the cacophony of sound faded, was a wooden caravan. Capturing the essence of a long-forgotten time, it would have once been a spectacle to behold with its spindle wheels, ornate gables and finely worked trim. Now, however, the paint was chipped and faded, the wooden shutters hung askew and the wheels were warped.

Sam eyed the rotting staircase leading to the door. Above it in looping swirling letters the sign read *Magical Madame Carla*.

'This must be it.' he said, turning to the others.

Veronique pushed him forward. 'Go on, then. Age before beauty.'

Sam placed a foot on the first step. It groaned but held, as did the next. Reaching up, he tapped his knuckles on the mottled blue and purple door.

Nothing.

He turned and looked back, shrugging.

Joe was jiggling and Fedor put a hand on his shoulder. 'Do you need the toilet, or is it excitement?'

The boy cocked his head thinking. 'Little of both.'

Sam drew back after knocking, but the door clicked and swung open, emitting a cloud of scented smoke. He choked on the incense.

'Come in, come in,' a voice called.

The door creaked as he stepped inside, the others following closely at his heels.

The interior of Madame Carla's caravan was indeed magical.

In the centre of the small room a squat round table draped with a beaded cloth hosted the obligatory crystal ball clasped in a bronze hand. Mismatched rugs covered the floor; their thick and colourful weaves faded to patchy, mottled hues. Sam marvelled at the array of chimes and dream catchers that swung from the rafters. The walls were lined with shelves and trunks, rows of books, and piles of trinkets.

'Ah, at last!' Their host ushered them into the confined space with great, sweeping motions. 'Old Carla thought you would leave her waiting all night,' she chided. 'Sit, please.'

They complied, Joe suppressing a wave of claustrophobia.

'So, you're our hope for the future, are you?' Carla held them with a piercing gaze, her fierce grey eyes serious beneath her dramatic gypsy make-up. She wore layers of flowing silk and a thick crocheted shawl was draped over her thin shoulders. Her fingers, ears and arms jangled with gaudy golden jewellery.

'Strange auras,' the old woman muttered. 'Troubled paths. Many twists and turns, Old Carla sees. Brave, you must be, very brave. And true. True to one another.'

'Is she pretending to be Yoda?' Joe whispered. 'Definitely AFK, more like.'

Sam muffled a laugh.

The gypsy ignored them and looked at Veronique. 'You follow the cards. Don't follow them too closely, for the hand that holds them is not always your own.' She paused, chewing her bottom lip, looking at something in the distance.

'You're all here to learn from Old Carla.' She straightened with a flourish sending her orchestra of jewellery into a jangling concerto. 'To learn of paths and doors. Gateways both near and far.'

They peered at one another out of the corners of their eyes.

'The stones you wear,' she reached forward to flip the Krusa from under Joe's shirt, holding it between her leathery fingers, 'are keys. Not only to the mind, but also to many doors.' Joe looked down, leaning away from her. The gypsy's hygiene left a lot to be desired.

'You need to learn how to recognise them,' her chipped lilac nails clacked against the stone.

'Why do we need doors,' Sam asked, 'can't we just Fold?'

'Been everywhere, have we? Know the Sumerian Temple, do you? Been to the Mountain Kingdom? Seen the shimmering streets of the Aztec City? Fold there, you can?'

Sam shook his head.

'Then doorways you will need! You must place all of the stones before the Gate of the Gods.' Her serious expression changed and she smiled, exposing chipped teeth. 'So, Old Carla will show you.'

The gypsy scattered a handful of small bone tiles on the table, all etched with an archaic script. 'Seven runes, there are. Seven signs to mark the way to places both near and far.'

Veronique, drawn to the mysterious old woman and her sing-song manner, moved closer.

Joe also peered at the table. 'Where will these markings be?'

'The frame is the border. The border holds the key. Look to the frame, for it will be plain for all to see.'

'Urgh.' Fedor could not help himself. Their host either did not hear, or chose to ignore the derision.

Joe probed deeper. 'Are there only seven destinations?'

The gypsy fixed the boy with another toothy smile. 'Seven there are and seven there will be, but only six are plain to see.'

'Meaning one is hidden?'

'Not all doors should have a key.'

Sam was getting frustrated. 'What opens the doors?'

She looked at him, irritated by the interruptions. 'Clear the mind and find your peace. The keys will do the rest.'

'It has to be the Krusa! Let's give it a go!' Joe's enthusiasm was now a good two steps ahead of his common sense.

Old Carla clapped her hands and swung around, drawing back a curtain to reveal an engraved wooden arch set against the far wall of the caravan.

Sam let out a low whistle. The craftsmanship was impressive.

Every inch had been worked and refined with meticulous precision, creating a flowing, winding sculpture that wrapped the empty space with regal grace. In the centre of the arch, the flowing lines culminated in a rune, and the wood had a lustre that almost shone in the gloom.

Veronique was in awe. 'Do they all look like this?'

'Doors come in all shapes and sizes.' Madame Carla's gaze caressed the arch. 'But no two are the same.'

'Where does this one go?' Fedor asked.

The gypsy winked. 'Now that is for Old Carla to know, and for you to find out.' She grabbed Joe's wrist. 'Clear the mind and find your peace. The key will do the rest.'

He looked at Sam, who shrugged and nodded toward the door. Joe got up and approached the arch. Closing his eyes, he reached into his shirt. The Krusa tingled. With a deep breath, he stepped forward.

The moment his foot passed through the arch, Sam saw the air shimmer and his friend disappear.

The old gypsy clapped her hands with delight and caressed the side of the carving. 'Now you.' She wiggled her fingers at Veronique.

Nikki, the Explorer!

Moments later, she, too, was gone and Sam was left with Fedor.

'Very good! Not without skill.' Magical Madame Carla said. 'Your turn, my large friend.' She shooed Fedor from his seat. He ducked when his head encountered the nest of chimes in the rafters.

'Do not despair,' Sam heard her tell him quietly. 'So proud he is of you. More than you will ever know.'

Fedor looked down at the old woman, shocked.

'Go on.' She offered no further explanation.

He dug his hand into his pocket. It was empty. He turned to Sam, his face pale.

'What?'

'It's gone. The Krusa. It's not in my pocket.'

Sam swore.

'What was it doing in your pocket? It's meant to be around your thick neck!'

'This stupid shirt! It was so tight, it was digging in, so I put it in my…' His face darkened. 'That thieving little bastard!' He swore and turned for the door, fists clenched.

'Um, we'll be right back,' Sam apologised to Magical Madame Carla.

'Duck!' she shouted after him.

'*What?*' Sam muttered, shaking his head, as he leapt down the stairs and almost slipped on the dewy grass. His friend was heading toward the rides.

Then Sam realised what had happened. One of the circus kids must have pick-pocketed the Krusa during the scuffle.

Sam broke into a run. 'He'll kill them. *FEDOR!*'

Fedor knew who he was looking for. Fixing on his quarry, he charged. Never had a pack of juvenile miscreants disbanded with such haste.

His target broke away from the group and the Russian bolted after him.

Sam swore, as he watched the pair disappear between the rides.

The thief was swift and nimble, but Fedor was at his heels, jaw set, face like thunder. They leapt onto a carousel, winding between faded plastic ponies and their bright-eyed riders. The boy snatched a glance over his shoulder before leaping and rolling under a tent. Fedor followed and almost got a foot in the mouth, for his quarry was waiting on the other side and stamped at his skull when it appeared. His Sambo training saved him. Fedor caught the foot and twisted it, forcing the boy to buckle when he cranked the ankle further. Swearing, the little savage kicked free.

The chase continued through the tent past the animal cages, provoking roars and snarls in their flight.

The boy burst from the tent and grabbed a torch from a Fire Eater. Turning, he thrust the business end at Fedor, who dropped and delivered a savage kick, catching the boy on the thigh. He staggered backwards, still brandishing the torch.

'Hey, what the *hell* do you kids think you're doing?' the Fire Eater demanded. 'Give me that!' He snatched back his abused prop, aiming a cuff at the boy's head.

The boy ducked, not taking his eyes from Fedor, then darted away again with the Russian in tow.

Sam skidded into the back of the Fire Eater, sending them both sprawling. The torch landed on a hay bale that immediately went up in flames.

Sam untangled himself. 'Sorry!' he shouted, leaving the man swatting the flames with his coat.

They had reached the other end of the fairground now and the crowds were thinning. The thief, free of the masses, broke into a sprint, heading into the park and the safety of darkness.

Sam was now only a few seconds behind them. 'Fedor!' he shouted, chest burning. 'Wait!' This could end *so* badly.

The thief appeared to be circling back toward the circus, snatching glances over his shoulder as he wound between the trees. For the first time, they lost sight of him. Something caught Fedor squarely in the chest and he fell heavily.

'Duck!' Madame Carla's peculiar instruction echoed in Sam's mind and he dropped to the ground. The baseball bat glanced off his shoulder and sent him spinning to the floor.

They had run right into a trap.

Two boys armed with baseball bats flanked the thief, who stood over Fedor, hands on hips and gasping for breath. The Russian lay crumpled on the ground with his arms around his chest. One of them kicked him in the back, laughing.

'I can't believe this ugly necklace is worth the trouble.' The largest of the thugs began swinging his baseball bat, taking aim at Fedor's head.

'Do it, Mikey,' they egged him on. 'Nut him!'

'Yeah, come on Mike – batter up! No one will know, crack him good.'

Mikey grinned, lifting his arms.

Fedor was dimly aware of the bat looming above him. Unable to defend himself, he squeezed his eyes shut. *I'm sorry, Pappa.*

The blow never came.

Mikey towered above Fedor; bat raised. The thief stood back, eyes glistening, holding the Krusa in his fist. The other boy's mouth hung open as he drew breath for a cheer, bat against his ankle.

Sam lay on his back, panting. His bruised shoulder was on fire. The bone flute was pressed to his lips.

Sammy, don't leave me! This time, he could save someone.

For a few peaceful moments, he stared at the tatters of carefree cloud, then swore. Another few seconds and, well, the possibilities did not bear thinking about.

He rolled to his feet and stared at the frozen figures, then pulled away their bats and hit the thief's hand, causing his stiffened fingers to open and the Krusa to fall.

Sam grabbed Fedor's ankles and pulled. 'You weigh a flipping ton!' He stopped and chewed his lip. Putting the bats down, he went to work.

When he was done, Sam stood back and blew the bone whistle. The thief let out a cry and fell to his knees, clutching his hand. Mikey swung nothing, at nothing and toppled over, falling on top of the third boy who suddenly found himself on the ground. All three were in their underwear.

'What the f—!' Mikey choked.

'Dude, get the hell off me!' the other boy shouted, wriggling away. 'Where are your pants? Where are mine? What the hell is going on!'

'You ladies want some privacy?' Sam enquired; the baseball bats crossed over his shoulders. He couldn't help feeling a bit cocky.

Mikey and his friend stopped squirming and looked up.

'I'm going to count to five,' Sam said with open hostility. 'And if you two are still here cuddling, I'm going to start swingin'. Sound familiar?' He made it to three before they disappeared around the nearest tree.

'And as for you,' Sam dug his shoe spitefully into the ribs of the thief, still nursing his broken hand, 'I'd be gone before my friend regains his wits. He's liable to split you like a wish bone.' He drew a line with the tip of the bat. 'Nuts to neck.'

The boy looked over to where Fedor had begun stirring and ran after his friends.

Sam heaved a sigh of relief. Fedor was safe. He had saved him. 'You okay?

Fedor grunted, probing his chest.

'Nothing's broken,' he wheezed. 'Teach me to go running blindly around corners.'

'We all make mistakes. Luckily, we made this one together.' He offered Fedor a hand. 'I don't know about you, but I've done enough sightseeing for one day. Let's get back to the door.'

By the time they staggered up the rotting wooden steps, the rides were slowing and the crowds thinning.

The door was ajar.

Books, trinkets and broken chimes lay scattered around. Trunks were overturned and shelves broken. The gypsy's table was on its side, the crystal ball damaged, viscous fluid seeping between the floorboards.

Sam swore.

'Madame Carla?' Unsurprisingly, there was no reply.

The curtain that had covered the mysterious wooden arch was torn and scorched, the portal appeared unharmed.

'What do you think?' Fedor muttered.

'We have to use it.' Sam handed Fedor his Krusa. 'You first.' He flipped one of the bats and offered the grip. 'Just in case.'

Baid watched the sandy-haired boy follow his friend through the ancient portal. Rising from the shadows, he continued to examine the wreckage.

The caravan was in a state of turmoil when he had arrived, a final flash of light streaking under the door as he mounted the steps. Inside, the incense-laden air was charged with static, smouldering scorch marks in the wood giving off an unpleasant scent. Singed feathers and scraps of burnt paper still floated to the floor.

Neither the gypsy nor her assailants were anywhere to be seen. He made a quick pass around the room, before walking back to the door.

'Get me Gabriel, Pandora.' He peered into the darkness beyond the fairground.

'One moment, please,' his A.I. said.

A few seconds later, the call connected.

'Baid?'

'Yes. I'm here. Someone found Carla. Probably Harbinger looking for Aura. They're both gone.'

There was a long pause. 'Is the Door intact?'

'Yes, two of D'Angelo's kids just used it.'

'Did they? They shouldn't have been there in the first place.' He paused. 'I need to speak to Salvador; he's not keeping these children very safe. Make sure no one else comes or goes. I'll send The Silent Knight to retrieve the door. It's no longer safe there. Head back when they're done.'

'Will do.'

Baid did not notice the emerald eyes peering up at him from between the floorboards.

Chapter 14

S am stumbled through the door and into a dark, humid room lit by flickering torches. The bulky silhouette of Fedor loomed before him, one arm clutching his ribs.

'Where've you been?' Joe's voice startled them. He waited behind Fedor in the low light with Veronique and Jenny.

There were looks of shock when Sam described the ruin of Carla's caravan and their adventure in the woods. He glossed over how the flute had managed to save the day.

'Just bruised.' Jenny prodded Fedor's ribcage looking relieved. 'Now I need to find out what happened to Madame Carla. Please excuse me.' She left them alone in the room.

'So, where are we?' Sam asked the others, as he looked around the unadorned chamber.

We're in *Peru!*' Joe's excitement was palpable. 'It seems to be an Inca temple! We've just had a quick look around, but I'd love to explore it further.'

Veronique snorted. 'You should've seen his face when Jenny told us to watch out for booby traps. Scuttled to her side and hasn't left the room since. You're no Dr Jones, are you, *mon petit chou*?'

'I do wish you'd stop calling me that,' the intrepid explorer sulked.

'You're right, Madame Carla has disappeared.' Jenny returned looking worried. 'We don't know any more than that.' She paused. 'We'll sleep here tonight. It's too late to be heading into the jungle. You'll find sleeping bags and fresh clothes in those packs. No shower, I'm afraid.'

'Shower in a can?' Joe suggested, producing some deodorant and giving it a shake. 'Though I think this is your pack.' He handed Veronique the can of wild orchid body mist.

'Oh, I don't know,' she smiled, 'it's got you written all over it!'

Their evening meal proved a most surprising feast.

'Now *that* is the perfect invention,' Sam managed, around a mouthful of pizza. After the events of the day, comfort food was most welcome.

'So how *exactly* does it work?' Joe could no longer contain his questions about Jenny's amazing bag, the surprising source of their marvellous feast.

'Joe, you promised,' Veronique chided. 'No looking the gift bag in the flap!'

'Oh, I know, I know, but it's just too incredible!'

They had been told to order anything they wanted for supper and their sceptical requests ranged from pizza to ice cream. Thirty minutes later, Jenny opened the flap of an empty cloth bag and to Sam's amazement, produced a steaming pizza box. Then another. Two bottles of cola followed and, finally, a tub of ice cream emerged.

'OMG! Are you Mary Poppins?' Joe was wide eyed, his mouth watering.

Sam drew breath to speak, but Fedor cut him off. 'I know who she is, before you start.'

A thought occurred to Joe. 'Any books in there?'

They all laughed.

'Why doesn't the ice cream melt?' Veronique was equally perplexed.

Jenny grinned. 'It's Nevamelt.'

'Neva-who?' Sam asked.

'Nevamelt. Awesome patent. Prevents chocolate and ice cream from melting.'

'You're kidding?'

'Nope.' Jenny winked. 'We keep all the best ones for ourselves.'

She patted the bag, 'It's called a Rummager, or Rufus Mandle's Portal Satchel to be precise. It allows the one-way transportation of inanimate objects – so nothing living. Very handy for food, supplies, clothing etc. Each bag is linked to a shelf in the Quartermaster's Stores, where teams of support staff receive orders from the Field and stock the right shelf. It goes wrong every now and then though.' She grimaced. 'I once put in a rush order for anti-venom during a training mission in Australia and got two pairs of ski socks and a woolly hat.'

Sam was impressed. 'Anything else up your sleeve?'

'Oh no,' Jenny chuckled. 'I'm not getting drawn into that. As I said before, plenty of time for technology and gadgets during your Induction.'

Veronique dabbed the corners of her mouth with a paper napkin. 'So, why are we in this spooky temple?'

'Plants!' Jenny quelled a burp. 'And where better to study them than in the Amazon?'

Joe looked worried. 'The Amazon? As in the home of anacondas, poisonous frogs, piranha, panthers and caimans? Not to mention malaria, yellow fever and dengue fever – which, I might add, cannot be vaccinated against. I'm not going.'

'You forgot the candiru,' Fedor added.

Joe paled. 'That's a myth.'

'I know what I need for Christmas,' Sam moped, feeling stupid, 'a bloody encyclopaedia.'

'So last century, and you've already got one,' Veronique hitched her thumb at the quivering boy.

'So, what's a candiru?' Sam asked.

Joe swallowed. 'The Toothpick fish. A parasitic freshwater catfish. They supposedly swim up your—' He looked at the females, laughed nervously, and pointed at his groin. 'Up there.'

'What?' Veronique looked shocked.

'I know!' Joe's voice rose to almost the same octave. 'That's what I'm telling you. I'll be AFK for that trip!'

'Calm yourselves,' Jenny sighed. 'We're going to the Gardens of Inti and there are no anacondas, piranhas or panthers there, I can assure you.'

'What about candiru?'

'Only small ones,' she assured Joe.

'*What?*'

Sam chuckled. 'She's winding you up.'

Joe scowled.

'The injection I gave you at Shen Pi covers malaria amongst other things. Besides, they use Tengar pollen in the Garden.'

'Which is?' Joe appeared somewhat mollified.

'I'll let Miguel explain. He's the Curator.'

'What are the Gardens of Inti?'

'Well,' Jenny leaned against her pack, 'that's actually quite an interesting story, bit of a history lesson though, you'll be too tired —'

'No, no,' they cut her off. 'Please, tell us.'

'Sure you won't be bored?'

'Well, there's no guarantee.' Sam winked.

Veronique cuffed him.

'Okay then. Let's see. You know about the Conquistadors, I take it?'

They nodded.

'Well, in the late fifteenth century, Europe was afire with talk of the New World. Many expeditions set off to conquer its rumoured cities of gold and with one of them went a man named Fernando Ortega. The Order had tasked him with cataloguing and preserving any significant finds.

'Ortega joined a group of Spaniards and Inca renegades, led by Francisco Pizarro, who ultimately conquered the Inca Empire. During this time, Ortega and his men worked in secret with the Incas to hide and safeguard many of their treasures in a hidden valley called the Garden of Inti.'

'Who's Inti?' Veronique interrupted.

'The Sun God,' Joe shushed her. 'Read a book would you. Please, Jenny, go on'.

Sam noticed the dark look Veronique shot him.

'Fernando Ortega fell in love and married an Inca princess and stayed in Peru. Their descendants have tended the Garden ever since. Over the last hundred years, as colonisation and over-population reached devastating heights, the Garden has become the last outpost for many flora.'

'And the fauna?' Joe interrupted and Veronique huffed.

'A good question. The Ark, our game preserve in the Mountain Kingdom of Lesotho, performs a similar function to the Garden. Apart from marine life, every species discovered over the past four hundred years can be found there.'

Joe looked sceptical. 'What, even a dodo?'

'And the quagga,' she countered.

'Quagga?' Fedor had never heard the name.

'Oh, my God – I actually know this one!' Sam was amazed. 'They're a type of zebra, used to live in southern Africa. We learned about them in school.'

Jenny wrapped up the impromptu lesson before it led to even more questions. 'It's been a long and very eventful day and tomorrow promises more of the same.'

There were a few grumbles, but they were half-hearted. Ensconced in his sleeping bag, Sam was soon dead to the world.

They left the temple before dawn, and entered a world shrouded in a heavy mist.

Unable to see more than a few feet ahead, Sam followed the others in single file, eyes fixed on the person in front, Jenny leading. All around him, the high-pitched whoops and chatter of exotic birds echoed off the trees, punctuated by chirps and squeaks, as insects and small animals scurried through the undergrowth.

Joe's nervous laughed carried through the gloom.

The jungle hemmed them in, low hanging vines and snaking roots seeking to entangle with every step.

'Remember not to touch the Lanelia vines,' Jenny had warned before they left. Sam had no idea which one was Lanelia or why they shouldn't touch it. Judging by the way the others avoided every scrap of vegetation, he was sure they didn't either.

'Stop!' came the sharp command from up front, bringing them to a skidding halt. Joe's head sank into Fedor's backpack with a muffled 'Oooph'.

'No free rides.' Fedor quipped.

Moments later, Jenny's hand appeared from the gloom, a ghostly apparition guiding them forward one by one. Not five feet from the path the ground dropped away into a precipice.

The mist vanished, parting like a heavy curtain. Behind them, the fog still clung to the jungle. Below them, in complete contrast and bathed in glorious sunlight, Sam saw a lush green valley, walled by more cloud-covered mountains.

A river wound through densely packed forests, cultivated fields and neat orchards. Plants of every size, shape, colour and texture dotted the landscape, accessible only – it would seem – by the steep path cut from the hillside.

'Keep one hand on the guide rope at all times,' Jenny warned, 'and eyes firmly on the track – it's a long way down and there will be plenty of time for sightseeing later.'

Despite the advice, Veronique could not help snatching glances at the valley. She had always loved plants and flowers. Her parents' vineyard was one of her favourite places and she had spent countless summers playing in the maze of sweet-smelling vines. Deep in reverie she stumbled, sending a shower of rubble over the edge and causing Joe to shriek. Knuckles white she clutched the rope and endured a nauseating wave of vertigo.

Fedor glanced over his shoulder. Veronique was still there. He turned back to the path.

He had not slept well and was stiff and sore. Things seemed to be going from bad to worse on the injury front. His father would have turned the air blue if he knew how easily Fedor had let the Red Mist lead him into trouble. That said, were it not for Sam and that flute of his, Fedor would not be here to worry about his father. He looked at the sandy haired boy and contemplated the debt he owed him.

Sam's thoughts were as far from Fedor as they could be. He'd been concentrating on descending the path without skidding into Jenny, his gaze fixed on her trim form solely for safety, but it now assessed her differently. The jungle heat made her clothes cling to her body, and sweat ran from the nape of her neck right down to...

'Ahem!' he heard a cough and looked up. Jenny was regarding him over her shoulder, eyebrow cocked.

'Your eyes should be on the path, young man.'

Sam blushed, cheeks burning. 'I, er...' he stammered.

He was spared further embarrassment as their Trainer sighed and carried on without waiting for an apology.

'ROTFLMAO,' Joe hooted from the rear. 'Busted!'

Sam glanced over his shoulder to find Veronique watching him with pursed lips. A smirk tugged at the corners of Fedor's mouth. He lifted his free arm and gave them a one-fingered salute before turning back to the track.

After what seemed like hours of shuffling and several close calls, their feet finally reached the valley floor.

Joe, responsible for most of the near misses, kissed the earth. 'I'll never leave you again!'

'Thank God that's over!' Sam gasped, slumping down beside him.

'Really?' Veronique quipped with a Scottish lilt. 'I thought you were enjoying the view?'

Sam flushed and avoided looking at Jenny who was conversing with someone, one hand at her ear.

'How's the chest?' he asked Fedor.

'Sore.' The boy stretched from side to side.

'Did you take any painkillers this morning?' Veronique asked.

He shook his head. 'I didn't like the effect they had on me.'

'Effect?' Joe laughed, rolling over. 'You mean that terrifying moment when you almost laughed.'

'Shall we press on?' Jenny came over. 'Miguel will meet us near the village.'

'More walking?' Joe groaned. 'These shoes are giving me a blister!'

'We could always float down the river,' she offered. 'Nice and cool, very relaxing. I'm pretty sure there are none of those nasty little fish you mentioned.'

Joe was up in a flash, pointing toward the trees. 'This way, is it?'

The well-travelled path to the centre of the valley took them past grain fields and runs of colourful flowers. Further on, the fields gave way to dappled orchards, brimming with fruit and succulent berries. The path ended at a perpendicular road that appeared to be running around the jungle in a wide circle.

Sam looked left and right down the dusty track. 'Where now?'

'Up!' Jenny pointed to footholds in the trunk of a monstrous Kapok tree. They followed her finger to a platform from which a series of rope and wood pathways branched off into the canopy.

'Not more heights!' Veronique sighed.

Fedor did not look pleased either. Walking with a bruised sternum and sore ribs was one thing, climbing was another.

'That's the only way?' he asked, rubbing his chest.

'Afraid so. Sure you don't want those painkillers?' Jenny offered.

Veronique answered for him. 'Yes, he does, thank you.' She stepped forward before he could object and waited whilst Jenny rummaged around in her pack.

'Open wide,' the girl said, fixing him with a determined look.

'I'd do it, pal,' Sam laughed. 'Otherwise she'll be on your back all day.'

'Literally,' Veronique nodded, holding out the two red and white capsules.

Nikki Nightingale!

Fedor grunted and took the pills.

'Now swallow,' his self-appointed nurse instructed, hands on hips.

He complied, opening his mouth to show they were gone.

'There's a good boy.' She patted him as one would an obedient puppy. 'Was that so hard? Now you and my little *chou* can make happy chit chat all afternoon.' She spun on her heel and pranced off, looking very pleased with herself.

'They always get their way.' Sam patted him on the shoulder. 'The trick is giving them the easy wins so that you can *try* to stand your ground on the big ones.'

Fedor grunted. 'How come you know so much about women?'

Sam smiled. 'TV!'

The equatorial sun reached its zenith and was beating down on the group with considerable force as they arrived on the platform.

'*Hola*, Jenny!' Miguel Ortega greeted them in a deep, booming voice, which Sam thought could probably carry across the entire jungle.

'It's good to see you again, *chica*.' Miguel hugged Jenny, patting her back.

'Likewise, Miguel. I see The Gardens are flourishing under their new curator. Is your father enjoying his retirement?'

Miguel barked a laugh. 'He's bored stiff. Last I heard, he and my mother were lying on the beach in Buenos Aires, waiting for their cruise to leave. After all those years in his little valley, he's aching to see the world, not lie on a beach!'

'Miguel and I were in the same Induction year,' Jenny explained as she introduced Sam, Fedor, Veronique and Joe.

Miguel shook their hands in turn.

'*Hola, Señor,*' Joe showed off.

'*Hola, amigo,*' Miguel smiled, fanning his face with his hat. 'Let's get out of this heat. You must be famished?'

'I could eat,' Fedor shrugged, perking up.

'He's cured!' Joe laughed. 'Now, tell me, Miguel, how comprehensive is your library?'

The sprawling village of Inti was attached to the trunks of the jungle monoliths, huts of all shapes and sizes clung like thatched limpets.

Miguel's ancestral home was wrapped around a mighty Kapok tree. Spanning several floors, it was completed with a rooftop balcony above the canopy.

The visitors breathed in the sight with awe. Steep cliffs and dense vegetation hemmed the valley and clouds hugged the mountains. The basin was awash with vibrant colour and succulent greenery.

A table had been laid for them under a thatched gazebo, plates of fresh fruit, cheese, cuts of meat and dark chunky bread piled onto curved bark plates. Pitchers of cool water and fruit cocktail glistened invitingly.

Sam felt the pressures of the last few days starting to melt away. Maybe, in this magical place, they could find a little respite?

Chapter 15

'Ruben!' Sam was surprised to see the diminutive librarian seated at the table. 'What are you doing here, I thought you said you were, what was it… aglaploblic?'

Joe barked a laugh. 'Agoraphobic.'

Fedor was still a trifle relaxed from his pain killers. 'What's that?'

Ruben shuddered. Despite being seated beneath the gazebo, he also held an umbrella above his head. 'Fear of open spaces.'

'I see,' Fedor said.

Miguel motioned to the table. 'Please, sit.'

Fedor, however, was not done. 'And who is he?'

Sam looked around. There was no one else there.

After a long pause, a man stepped from the branches at the edge of the platform.

The teenagers stared. He was huge! Not only tall but with a thick neck and shoulders so broad, he made Atlas look like a long-distance runner. He bristled with muscle. A scar traversed the man's face from his square jaw, over one milky eye and across the crown of his shaved head.

Jen Si appeared just as shocked as the others. 'How did you know he was there?'

The Russian boy grabbed a fistful of grapes and shoved them into his mouth. 'I could smell him.'

'Crocodile Dundeeski,' Joe laughed.

'Never mind,' Sam said, when Fedor's forehead furrowed. 'I'll explain later.' He turned to Ruben. 'But seriously, who is that guy?'

'Allegarus Nazareth. My chaperone for the day.'

Sam lowered his voice. 'Is he real? He's massive!'

'Try standing next to him! Yes, yes, he's quite real.' Ruben laughed at his own expense. 'Still, I wanted to see how you're getting on. I felt just terrible after dropping you into The Deep End. You still have your books, don't you?' He fidgeted with his collar. 'In a good state of repair, not all battered and—' he choked off, unable to say any more.

The conversation continued as they took shelter from the midday sun. Jen Si scowled when Sam told him of their ordeal in Central Park and Ruben appeared quite shaken.

'We could've done with your man there.' Sam hiked his thumb over his shoulder.

'The First are in short supply, I'm afraid. In fact, I was very surprised to hear one of them was accompanying me.'

'He's one of the First?' Joe's eyes widened.

'Who are the First?' Sam, once again, seemed to lack the basic information everyone else had.

'They're the guardians of the Council,' Joe supplied. 'Though I don't know exactly where the name comes from.'

Ruben jumped in, eager to share his considerable knowledge. 'I can help with that.' Jen Si gave him a guarded look but Ruben didn't notice and continued on. 'They are the oldest part of our order.

'Long before the Cadres were created, when Herredrion still wandered the old world by himself, he came to an ancient place filled with tradition, a crucible of culture and radical thought. The king's son, Al'Ubaid, had fallen in battle, wounded by a tainted arrow. So virulent was the toxin, it ate his tissue to the bone. The king summoned all manner of healers from every corner of the known world, promising riches and wealth beyond imagining to the man or woman who could restore his heir.

'Vaidyas from the far east, wise men from the dry lands and witch doctors from the dense jungles to the south, all visited the prince's bedside, administering a multitude of remedies. Leaches, flesh eating beetles, blood sacrifices and all manner of dark rites were used to halt the inevitable march of death.

'None prevailed.

'Herredrion, drawn by this gathering of mystics and healers, also visited the temple. In his account of their meeting, he claims he did nothing more than examine the prince but during this time –whether it was the result of the cocktail of remedies or the poison having run its course – Al'Ubaid began to improve and Herredrion was heralded as his saviour. Months later, when Herredrion was ready to resume his wandering, a restored Al'Ubaid swore himself into service and became his guardian.'

'Cool,' Sam said.

Ruben smiled. 'It gets better.'

Fedor, Veronique and Joe were leaning forward, engrossed.

Sam noticed Jen Si now glared at Ruben, but the librarian was in full flow.

'Many years later, when Herredrion had established the Order and left his faithful Few to continue his work, Al'Ubaid was still the fresh-faced youth who had left his father's kingdom. The prince showed no signs of aging, nor had he suffered so much as a cough or sniffle in all that time. He assumed the role of guardian to the head of the first Council and trained an elite band of warriors to watch over the other members. They became known as the First.' Ruben paused, eyes shining with excitement. The group was hanging on his every word. 'And their descendants still report to him to this day.'

The table was silent.

'What?' Veronique scoffed. 'You're saying he's *still* alive?'

Fedor raised a cynical eyebrow.

'He can't be.' Joe gasped.

'No way,' Sam agreed. He looked at Jen Si, who remained silent.

Ruben continued. 'Who knows what free radicals are? Joe?'

'Um…' He pillaged his brain. 'They're the result of oxidation in the body. Highly reactive compounds that start chain reactions that deteriorate molecules.'

'Textbook answer, thank you. When free radicals act against a body's cells they can cause abnormalities, but the normal reaction is aging. To prevent or reduce this damage, our bodies use a complex defence system of antioxidants, vitamins, minerals and enzymes found in our food.'

Sam was not connecting the dots. 'But how's he still alive?'

'Well,' Ruben leaned forward, 'the venom that poisoned the prince when combined with the multitude of remedies introduced into his system created a unique super antioxidant. His body was able to produce an antibody that hunts free radicals, thus preventing him from aging. He's by no means immortal – he can break and bleed – but, in terms of aging naturally, Al'Ubaid, or Baid as he is now known, is a unique and fantastic freak of nature.'

The boys were impressed.

'How terrible for him.' Veronique sat back, looking sad.

Joe gaped at her with amazement. 'What?'

'He must feel so lonely. Everyone he has ever known or loved grows old and dies while he lives on.'

Jen Si barked a laugh. 'I wouldn't shed any tears for Baid. He's the most unemotional person I've ever met.

'Now, if you're suitably refreshed,' the monk swiftly changed the subject, 'we'll get down to business. Miguel has been kind enough to offer us the use of his facilities and has agreed to teach you a little more about what he does in the Garden, including the uses for some of his more special plants. We'll also be continuing with your other studies, however, so the morning meditation will be held here at sunup.'

The teenagers groaned in unison.

'That's the spirit!' Jen Si said. 'In fact, I have just the thing to get you going. Miguel, let's show your guests to their accommodation.'

'That sounds ominous,' Joe muttered.

'If it's all the same,' Ruben interrupted, 'I'm going to take my leave. I've had quite enough excitement for one day. Allegarus?' he called.

'Good luck!' Ruben smiled, sliding down from his chair with a concerted effort not to look up at the sky. Allegarus picked up another umbrella from beside the table and flicked it open. Stooping, they shuffled toward the stairs.

'Now there's a sight.' Jenny smiled at Allegarus, bent double, his charge tugging his sky shields lower, muttering all the while.

'You're kidding,' Sam laughed.

They were looking at an impressive house nestled in the branches of another tree some fifty metres away. Between their platform and the tree house was no rope bridge, only a large gap.

The monk pointed. 'Your new home.'

'Just one question, my good man' Joe asked. Veronique's penchant for theatrics was rubbing off on him. 'Small matter really. How exactly do we get to it?'

'Simple,' the monk smiled. 'You Fold.'

Veronique sighed loudly. All she wanted was a hot bath and a soft bed.

'It's time for you to learn Line-of-sight-transport. LOST for short. Same principle as long distance Folding, except instead of studying and memorising a picture, you observe your destination. Like so.'

He disappeared, reappearing at the door of the tree house.

'Get lost yourself, you smug son of a...' Sam heard Joe mutter.

'Tell me about it,' he agreed.

'And if we get it wrong?' Veronique asked. 'A metre short and you're in thin air!'

Fedor nodded. The painkillers had worn off and his perennial scowl had returned.

'I don't want to become the most intelligent splat on the forest floor,' Joe flapped.

Sam was peering over the side. 'Chill, people; look. There are nets around the tree. Just try to miss the branches!'

Joe rolled his eyes. 'FML!'

Sam tried his luck first. Five minutes later they were all flapping around in the nets, cursing and pulling each other to safety.

'Well, that was fun!' Veronique fumed when Sam helped her onto a lichen-encrusted branch. 'We could've been killed!'

Fedor had almost succeeded. Folding to within an arm's reach of the platform, he had managed to cling on for a moment before he tumbled into the nets. Joe then fell onto his comrade, knocking the wind from his already bruised sternum.

'No time for cuddling,' Sam called to the pile of arms and legs. 'Need a hand?'

Fedor shouted something back in Russian. It did not sound remotely cordial.

'I'll take that as a "Da".' Sam shrugged at Veronique, then clambered down.

Jen Si was seated at the table, waiting. He opened his mouth to congratulate the group as they wandered into the tree house, before he noticed the grazes, twigs and leaves, adorning his pupils. 'Ah! Too much, too soon?'

Sam winced when Fedor cracked his neck and replied. 'Yes.'

'I'll get Miguel to put the bridge back for now and we can work on this again tomorrow – maybe on the ground this time.'

'Yippee.' Veronique's tone dripped with sarcasm. She spotted the bathroom and stormed past, slamming the door behind her.

'I'll come and fetch you for dinner.' Jen Si rose and disappeared.

Fedor flopped onto the sofa. 'I need vodka!'

Despite being in the middle of the jungle, the cottage tree house was equipped with hot water, a toilet and a well-stocked fridge.

They found their packs in their rooms – the boys were sharing while Veronique had a small chamber to herself.

She had emerged from the bathroom a new person. The boys had followed suit and the teenagers were soon sitting in the lounge, refreshed and chatting away.

'All is forgiven?' the monk asked Veronique when he returned.

'That depends,' she said, eyes narrowing as she looked past him. The bridge was back. 'I guess you've bought yourself some time, Mr Monk.'

Dinner was served on the Ortegas' deck.

'Welcome,' Miguel said, getting up from the candlelit table. 'This is my wife, Orma,' he said, introducing a slender lady seated beside him. She smiled warmly, her tanned features lit up by a flash of white teeth and the colourful flower in her hair.

'*Hola* children! I hope you're hungry? We have prepared a *Pachamanca* for you'

'Meat?' Fedor asked, never one to waste a word.

Orma chuckled. 'Yes, there is meat. *Pachamanca* is a traditional Peruvian dish baked in a *huatia* – an earth oven. Served with potato, habas, and cassava – it's very, very tasty.'

Fedor nodded his approval.

'You'll have to excuse our comrade,' Joe butchered a Russian accent and Veronique shook her head sadly at his attempt. 'He is ruled by his stomach.'

'Miguel tells me you've come from New York?' Orma placed her hand on Veronique's arm. 'How does it compare to Paris?'

Veronique stifled a sob.

'OMG, don't open that wound,' Joe moaned. 'She was so close to Fifth Avenue, she could almost smell the glitter.'

Veronique cut her eyes at him. 'Glitter, Darling, is *so* last year.'

'Oh, dear!' Orma made a face.

'I know,' Veronique muttered.

Nikki, the Fashion Pariah!

The girls continued to talk whilst the starters were served.

'Miguel,' Joe nearly lost a mouthful of avocado between his words, 'Jenny mentioned Tengar pollen, I was wondering what that was?'

Miguel's eyes brightened. 'Ah, yes. Tengar is a chemical present in certain pollens and nectars native to this valley. It's been found to cause sterility in certain insects and helps reduce pestilence. We synthesised it using cross pollination and recombinant DNA techniques to target certain species such as mosquitoes.'

'Don't mosquitoes suck blood?' Sam asked.

'The females are blood suckers.' Miguel winked. 'Like many insects of their type, they feed on nectar, but the females are also capable of hematophagy.'

'Brilliant!' Joe applauded. 'So, no malaria?'

'Well, never say never. We've all seen Jurassic Park, but we've had no cases in the Garden for over fifteen years.'

Sam was confused. 'How come you've not used this to cure malaria in Africa?'

'It's not that simple, Sam. Mosquitoes are an important link in the balance of an ecosystem. As I said, they feed primarily on nectar. The female ingests blood to obtain protein and iron for reproduction, but they still pollinate a wide variety of plants and provide food for other creatures. If you were to remove them from the food chain, the knock-on effect would be disastrous. We can't play God. There are strong ethical guidelines around the use of this type of technology. Most of the plants in our valley are not native to Peru, and, therefore, our ecosystem is artificial and carefully controlled. Outside this valley, however, there is a very fragile balance upon which man already impacts far more than he should.'

'But malaria is one of the biggest killers in Africa.' Sam could not see the logic in this at all.

'Rest assured, we have not abandoned humanity.' Miguel soothed. '*Plasmodium falciparum*, the protozoan parasite that causes malaria in humans, is the focal point for many monitored studies. As harsh as it sounds though, Sam, disease is a necessary part of life, a way for nature to keep balance and prevent an ecosystem from breaching its Carrying Capacity. Humans, whether they like to believe it or not, are still part of nature and must respect her power. If we cured every disease our population would soon explode and we'd exhaust this planet before we realised it was too late to save.'

Sam looked sheepish. 'I guess I didn't think of it like that.'

'That's okay. You're here to learn. As Newton said, *"To every action there is an equal and opposite reaction"* and nowhere is that more true than in nature. Without plants, everything on this planet would die. It should be our collective duty to preserve all life, but instead we Few must protect humanity from itself. For the most evolved species on the planet, we behave more like a virus than any intelligent form of life. We reproduce until we destroy our habitat, then we spread to another and do it again.

'The Gardens are dedicated to preservation. If the worst should happen, we would be able to reintroduce almost every floral species on the planet from the stores and greenhouses in our valley. And through this endeavour, we've made some startling discoveries.'

'Lanelia,' Fedor said.

'Exactly!'

Sam jumped when Miguel slapped the table. 'The vines Jenny told us to look out for?' he asked.

'Yes, like Tengar, they're endemic to this valley,' Miguel announced proudly. 'When my ancestor, Tupac Yupanqui, brought these mountains under Inca control hundreds of years ago, there was just one area from which his scouting parties never returned; a haunted place of fog and mist, where Inti, the Sun God, held no power. They called it the doorway to *Ukhu Pacha*, the underworld, where Zupay, the god of Death and ruler of *Ukhu Pacha*, waited in the shadows.'

All conversation quietened as everyone became absorbed by Miguel's tale.

'Now Tupac Yupanqui was a mighty king and a proud man. He would not believe that there was anywhere the children of Inti could not go, so he embarked upon a secret expedition with three trusted companions, to see this cursed place for himself.

'For days, they struggled through the thick jungle following trails that only ever led in one direction. Superstition took hold, for they trod the path of dead men. Finally, they came upon the boggy mountains, shrouded in thick rolling mists. The air was hot and the stench of death and decay clung to every leaf.

'For the first time in his life, Tupac Yupanqui felt fear. He called to the men, but none replied.

'The king panicked; the silence was overwhelming. He hacked at the undergrowth, trying to retrace his steps and miraculously staggered from the fog. A long vine oozing a milky sap was wound around the blade of his sword and he snatched at it, enraged.

'The minute Tupac touched the vine, numbness shot through his fingers, up his arms and into his body. The king lost control of his muscles and slumped to the ground, paralysed. Unable to move even his eyelids, he lay in a heap for hours, the oozing vine resting in his hand.

'But fate, it would seem, was not done with Tupac Yupanqui, for that night the heavens opened and Apotequil, the god of lightning, threw mighty bolts across the skies. So heavy was the rain that the area where the king lay soon became a muddy stream, which grew in force until the earth gave way and Tupac Yupanqui found himself rocketing down the hillside, back through the gates of Ukhu Pacha! He was buffeted from pillar to post, banging against trees and rocks. The king was moments from death, the dreaded apparition of Zupay surely waiting in the shadows to claim him.

'His body spun when he hit another tree. His arm bore the brunt of the force, sending the treacherous vine hurtling from his grip. And there was darkness.

'Tupac Yupanqui woke to the glorious light of Inti caressing him. He opened his eyes and before him lay a valley. The most beautiful, fertile valley he had ever seen. Truly, this was the sacred hereafter.

'It was when Tupac Yupanqui tried to move that the king discovered he was not, in fact, dead. He realised that the vines were responsible for his paralysis. Armed with this knowledge, the king made his way back through the mist, using fire and long sticks to avoid the treacherous creepers.

'Returning to Cuzco in the dead of night, he kept his discovery secret. He built a temple in the mist and allowed the myth of Ukhu Pacha to prevail, naming the valley the *Garden of Inti*, a sacred place he vowed would remain untouched for all time.'

Joe was enthralled. 'That's some story!'

'Yeah,' Sam agreed. 'But I don't understand why the vines paralyse you?'

'Ah.' Miguel leant back, stretching. 'They're carnivorous. Distant cousins to *Dionaea muscipula*, the Venus Fly Trap. You see plants evolved photosynthesis to create sugar. However, they also need amino acids, vitamins and other nutrients. In boggy areas where the soil is acidic, as it is on the mountain, certain key minerals and nutrients are scarce. Most plants can't survive in such conditions but some like the Lanelia and the Venus Flytrap have evolved ways to compensate.

'As a body decomposes, digestive enzymes within the sap help the plant to obtain these vital nutrients. Unlike curare, which is a paralyzing poison used by the Macusi Indians, Lanelia only inhibits voluntary muscle control. Arrows or darts that are dipped in curare cause asphyxiation, as the respiratory muscles are unable to contract. It's a quick and painless death. Lanelia paralysis, however, is a slow, agonising death, for the victim dies from dehydration.'

Veronique looked aghast. 'You mean all those people who went into the fog never returned because they became wrapped up in those horrid vines and died of thirst?'

'Afraid so.' Miguel said.

Sam watched Veronique push away her plate, appetite gone.

'Clever,' Fedor nodded approvingly.

'Oh, you would think it's cool, wouldn't you.' *Nikki the Indignant.*

Fedor shrugged.

'Try not to get too bent out of shape over the Lanelia,' Jen Si suggested. 'You're going to spend quite a lot of time working with them.'

'You think I'm going anywhere near that graveyard; you've got another thing coming!'

'Peace, *chica*.' Orma patted the girl's arm. 'The Lanelia only secrete their toxin in warm conditions and when there are no nutrients. The Lanelia we work with are kept in cool greenhouses and fertile soil, they're perfectly safe.'

'Well, I think that's enough for tonight.' Jen Si stood up. 'Plenty of food for thought and you've got an early start tomorrow.'

Fedor eased his aching body out of the chair and followed his friends into the tree top village, the walkways and canopy alive with thousands of twinkling fairy lights.

Chapter 16

RODENTS THAT BURROW

The next day, Jenny found her students in a clearing outside the inner circle of the valley, where a patchwork of neatly cropped fields and orchards flourished in the glorious Peruvian sunshine.

'Right.' Jen Si mopped his brow, the early morning equatorial heat taking its toll on the Tibetan. 'Line-of-sight-transport. LOST Folding!'

His students groaned.

'None of that, if you please,' the monk waved them to silence. 'This is easy, but we'll start small – that patch of grass, there.' He pointed five metres in front of them. 'Fold to it!'

By lunchtime, they were popping in and out of thin air at every corner of the field in a frenzied game of tag.

'Gotcha!' Veronique crowed, when she Folded behind Fedor, smacked his buttocks and disappeared, leaving him gawping at the violation to his personal space.

'Crazy *devotchka*,' he muttered, then spotted Joe on the other end of the field and created a Fold. Sam was proving an impossible target, for he did not stay in one place for more than a few seconds. He loved this new skill!

'That looks like progress,' Jenny commended their teacher. Lifting her body up on her arms, she sat on the fence beside the monk.

'Indeed. They learned fast – once they forgot everything they thought they knew. They'll be tired soon enough though. I don't think they realise how much bending the natural order will take out of them.'

'It looks like a very useful talent,' Jenny admitted, more than a little jealous.

'You've never had to catch a bus…' Jen Si said, making light of her envy.

Jenny could not help but smile. The monk was always one step ahead. 'Yes, I suppose there's a lot to be said for Speedlifts,' she agreed.

'Miguel said to bring them to the greenhouses after lunch.' She poked a laden rucksack with her toe. 'This should keep the wolves from the door for now.'

Jen Si surveyed the generous feast. 'Well, that's Fedor taken care of, but what about the rest of us?'

As the group lay in the midday sunshine, digesting their packed lunch, a stranger approached them.

'Dallas,' Jen Si smiled a greeting, 'what brings you to the Valley?'

'Why, I'm here to save these poor young souls from you, of course.'

The teenagers sat up. Joe threw his hands heavenward. 'There is a God!'

'Goddess,' Veronique corrected.

Dallas laughed. 'I've been called a few choice things in my time, but never that!' She removed her glasses and cap, freeing her dark hair. She had an athletic build and Sam reckoned could probably take them all on without breaking a sweat. She wore khaki combat trousers, climbing boots and a green vest top. Across her back, was a light hydration backpack.

'Everyone, this is Dallas Kim, Paladin for The Quiet Elves.'

'A female Paladin,' Veronique marvelled.

Dallas nodded. 'There aren't many of us. Not everyone wants to be saddled with looking after a bunch of smelly boys but I'm blessed with a few good ones. So, how's the training going?'

'Good,' Veronique said, 'I don't think any of us thought we'd be spending the summer here, but it's certainly interesting.'

Dallas smiled. 'Interesting is a good description. What's been the highlight so far?'

'The Mods are pretty cool.' Joe admitted.

'Yes,' Veronique agreed, 'we met Pip from Pandora's Box and she showed us the Bird Bone Mod. That was amazing!'

'And there was the Gec-' Joe was cut short when Fedor's foot found his ankle and reminded him Selina's demonstration had been a secret.

Veronique saw the monk raise an eyebrow and quickly continued the discussion. 'Do you use many Mods, Dallas?'

'Sure. They're an important part of Cadre life, but we do have other tricks up our sleeves.'

Sam's ear pricked. 'Oh, such as?'

'Gophers.'

Joe frowned. 'Not the most reliable of rodents.'

Dallas laughed. 'No!' She shrugged off her backpack and pulled out a canvas bag. 'This is a Gopher.'

Sam frowned. 'There's an animal in there?'

Fedor snorted.

Dallas knelt to open the bag. 'A Gopher is a helper, as in *go for this, go for that*.' She took out two small silver rings and handed them to Veronique. 'Put one on the index finger of each hand, darling.' Dallas then handed her a pair of glasses, which Veronique put on, confused.

'Ready?' Dallas asked.

'Er, I guess…'

The final item in the bag was a ball of grey plastic. Dallas flipped it at Fedor. 'You look like you've got a good arm on you. Throw that as far as you can.'

Fedor got up and casually tossed the plastic ball into the distance.

As it soared into the air, the glasses on Veronique's face sprang to life, as did the rings on her fingers. A screen appeared before her eyes and she could see the ground rushing toward her. She gasped and flinched, the rings vibrating when the ball hit the ground.

The boys looked at each other, then at Dallas and Veronique.

'Right,' Dallas said. 'Let's have some fun. Clap your hands.'

Veronique could only see a blur of grass but, when she brought her palms together, the rings vibrated and she could suddenly make out herself and her friends from the other side of the field.

'Oh my God, I can see us!'

Sam looked over to where the ball had vanished and, sure enough, a small grey head and two large eyes poked above the grass.

'Wow!' he exclaimed. 'It's a robot!'

Dallas raised her eyebrow, 'It's a lot more than just a robot,' she assured him. 'The Gopher is a Clone Drone. The rings allow it to mimic your movements, the glasses support a full panoramic camera, and voice-controls access a host of other features. Try turning your head.'

Veronique turned her head and, as she moved, the camera moved with her.

'Yup, the head's moving!' Joe reported.

Sam noticed Dallas lean over and whisper in Veronique's ear.

Veronique nodded. 'Gopher,' she commanded, 'Adaptive camouflage!' The grey head shimmered and disappeared.

'No *way!*' Sam's jaw dropped.

'Right, let's try moving her,' Dallas said. 'There are gyroscopic sensors in the glasses and rings. Your head controls her head and your arms control the movement. Rotating the rings allows you to switch between controlling the arms and legs but that takes some practice, so we'll just do legs for now. Move your hand left.'

The Gopher stepped sideways.

'Now bend your elbows as if you were going to run,' Dallas instructed, 'and move your arms forward and backward slowly. She should start walking forward. Left arm is left leg, right arm, right leg.'

Veronique watched as the Gopher approached her friends.

'There,' Fedor pointed. 'Look at the ripple in the grass. It's there but we can't see it. That's amazing.'

Veronique began pumping her arms back and forth faster and Sam saw the ripple suddenly speed up, as the Gopher raced toward them.

'Look out,' Joe rolled away. 'She's not even got her licence!'

Veronique stopped it just short of the group. 'Gopher, deactivate Active Camouflage,' she cried.

The air around the Gopher shimmered and before them stood a small, humanoid drone. Its legs and arms were short but functional. It had three chubby fingers and the feet were split into two toes. It had two eyes and no mouth

Joe sat up, adjusting his glasses to inspect the device. 'What else can it do?'

Dallas shrugged. 'Pretty much everything you can, sweetie. It takes a while to learn all the arm and leg movements but, once you've got the hang of it, you can make a Gopher walk, crawl, run, jump, climb and swim. They're not designed for any form of combat, but they can fetch and carry – and they make excellent spies! If at any time you think it's in danger, you simply tell it to burrow.'

Veronique took her cue. 'Gopher, burrow.'

Sam marvelled as the drone immediately collapsed in on itself, leaving an innocuous grey ball in the grass.

Dallas tapped it. 'The outer shell is harder than diamond, you could drive a tank over it and not leave a mark.'

'Can it fly?' Sam asked.

'No, that would eat up the battery. There's Piggyback though, which is an expansion pack for flight. That has its own power supply and is quite bulky.' Dallas paused and appeared to be listening to someone. 'Yes, I was just coming to that. Kika says you can also transfer your A.I. into it, when you need an expert for your second pair of hands!'

Sam smiled. 'That's so cool. I know what I want for Christmas!'

Joe looked at the curled-up drone. Meeting the Paladin had made him worry about the mysterious CruciBowl, which loomed closer with every day. Or their possible failure before they even reached that stage. 'I wish I could do that,' he said quietly.

'Disappear?' Dallas smiled.

'Well, yes, that too. But the indestructible shell looks pretty handy.'

'You want ArmaArmour then – the Armadillo Mod. But have you seen the Chameleon Mod?' Dallas asked.

Joe's eyes widened. 'No…'

'Well, technically it's the gene from a Cuttle Fish, but Cuttle Mod doesn't quite have the same ring to it.'

'Er, we're trying not to focus too much on *that* side of things right now,' Jen Si said, then caught the forlorn looks and quickly added, 'but maybe a quick demonstration wouldn't hurt.'

'*Oui*!' Veronique clapped her hands together.

Ten minutes later, the little group were gathered near the edge of the jungle.

'Okay,' Dallas handed Fedor her backpack. 'So, my clothes are already pretty good for blending into the jungle, but with this baby, you can take things to the next level.'

She studied the bark of a nearby tree and put her back to it, arms at her sides. At first, it seemed nothing was happening. Then, to Sam's amazement, the skin on her arms and neck began to mottle. The change was subtle at first, gentle hues and delicate textures that gradually took on more complex detail, spreading up her arms, then appearing at her neck. Soon Dallas' skin had taken on the intricate pattern of the tree.

'Amazing,' Veronique reached out to touch her arm. 'Does it hurt?'

'Not at all. It tingles, a bit like water running over your skin.'

Joe pointed to another species of tree beside Sam. 'Ooo, do this one next.'

Jen Si sighed. This could take a while.

Chapter 17

After the Paladin's visit, Jenny had led the teenagers back to the canopy highway.

Sam opted to bring up the rear, putting as much distance as possible between himself and Jenny's retreating form. Better to remove the temptation, he thought

'Do you think about girls all the time?' he'd asked Fedor over lunch, whilst Joe grilled Jenny about water purification.

Veronique had rolled her eyes when the inquisition had begun, but was now eying her drink, surreptitiously waiting for an answer.

Fedor shrugged, chewing noisily. 'I guess. Sometimes. There aren't any near our house.'

'Not all the time though?' Sam pressed him.

Fedor glanced at Veronique long enough for Sam to catch it. He chuckled. 'Oh ho!'

Fedor's eyes snapped back, glaring at him. 'What?'

'You like the Parrot!'

He crammed another triangle into his mouth. 'Rubbish!'

'I just saw you look at her!' Sam laughed. 'Good call. Out of our league though.'

Fedor swore, looking away. Veronique blushed slightly.

'Oh, well,' Sam watched Joe toss his water into the grass, 'at least I'm not the only one!'

Jenny led them through the heart of the jungle.

Workers in harnesses glided around them on ropes and pulleys, flying between avenues of trees and tending the species that could only survive high in the canopy. Rows of planters were nestled in the top branches, some hosting colourful flowers and fruits, many brimming with herbs and shrubs. Other beds were anchored between the trees at lower levels, offering better conditions for the species that would wilt under the equatorial sun.

The Garden teemed with all kinds of life. Noisy birds and colourful insects scurried between the plants, thieving monkeys chased by angry robotic gardeners.

'Incredible,' Veronique breathed. 'How do they keep it running so smoothly?'

'A lot of experience,' Jenny supplied. 'The Ortega and Cuzco families have lived here for centuries and, with the help of a little technology,' she pointed to a robot shooing away insects whilst checking the moisture and nutrient levels of a nearby plant, 'they have been able to dramatically increase the capacity of the Garden and quadruple the seed stocks.'

As they walked, Sam noticed that one of the droids seemed to be following them. Sidling closer, it waved a telescopic arm. '*Psst*!'.

Sam looked ahead but no one else had noticed the peculiar little machine hailing him. He slowed down.

'A mutual friend sends you a message.' The robot made a show of probing another nearby plant, snipping at the leaves whilst trying not to look at Sam.

'I'm sorry, are you talking to me?'

'Do you see anyone else nearby, biped?' It moved along the line of trees next to the walkway.

Sam slowed his pace. 'Biped?'

'You have two feet, don't you?'

The boy looked down. 'Last time I checked.'

'Zip it. Our *friend*, the one who likes *filing* things,' it flashed its eyes, 'has some news for you. She said it would be music to your ears.'

Sam's eyes widened. 'Oh!'

'Finally! Goodbye.' Its message delivered, the robot banked away towards another poor tray of unsuspecting shrubbery.

Flic had figured out the riddle of the flute.

'Helloooo?!' Joe trilled from the end of the bridge.

'Sorry. Coming!'

The greenhouses were modern glass structures with air-conditioning and sprinkler systems, well shaded and much cooler than the rest of the jungle.

Miguel was waiting for them. 'Welcome to the Lanelia Houses,' he said. 'Or the Fridge, as we used to call it as kids.'

'Brilliant.' Veronique muttered.

Miguel noticed her sour look. 'Still feeling a little apprehensive?'

'She's always like this,' Joe quipped. 'There's no pleasing some people.'

Veronique ignored him. 'If, by apprehensive, you mean loathe to asphyxiate in the arms of a grotesque meat-eating monster plant, then yes.' Suffocating was her greatest fear.

Miguel laughed. 'Okay, okay, let's dispel that myth right now. As Orma said last night, Lanelia can only "sweat" when the temperature is above 20°C. The greenhouses are climate controlled at 12.5°C. Secondly, they only produce SNS-C when the soil is low in nitrogen and other key nutrients. Otherwise, they happily photosynthesise away as normal. The soil we use is the most fertile, nutrient rich variety you could imagine. So, there are not one, but two safety measures in place.'

'What's SNS-C?' Joe piped up.

'It's the name we've given to the active compound responsible for the paralysis – Somatic Nervous System Curare. The somatic nervous system handles voluntary muscle control in the body, and it's the communication of this system with the brain that SNS-C somehow targets and inhibits.'

'Somehow!' Joe scoffed. 'You don't sound very sure?'

'I'm no neurologist,' Miguel shrugged. 'I'm sure they could explain it better.'

The air in the Fridge was cool and refreshing and Sam enjoyed the relief it gave from the close heat of the jungle. He fanned his sweat sodden shirt, looking around at the greenhouses' curious residents.

Lanelia was a strange and colourful vine. It's weaving fronds were dark green and purple and covered in thousands of tiny perforations. Large fan-shaped leaves resembling Swiss cheese hung from the thicker vines, but the flowers were the focal point of the plant. Each petal was a mesmerising kaleidoscope of red, orange and yellow swirls, surrounding a curved blue carpel and long, elegant stamens. The sepals wrapped around the base of the flower creating an irresistible invitation.

'And therein lies the danger.' Miguel pushed his arm through the vines to reach the bloom. 'The flower is an alluring princess in an impenetrable fortress.' The second his fingers touched the pollen-laden anthers, the petals snapped shut.

'Fascinating.' Joe reached over and strummed the petals of the closest flower, which did nothing until he worried the middle. 'Just like the Venus Fly Trap.'

'Exactly.' Miguel admired his pets. 'A sophisticated and evolved predator.'

'How are they pollinated then?'

'Ants.'

'Clever.'

'Was this the flower your wife was wearing at dinner?' Veronique asked.

The curator nodded. 'Go on,' he assured her. 'It's perfectly safe.'

Grimacing, she pressed her fingers together, sliding her hand through the damp, fleshy vines. Goose pimples sprang up the moment they made contact.

'Urgh,' she shuddered, snatching the arm back.

Fedor sighed. 'Oh please.' He pushed his arm through the masses of vines and plucked a flower before Miguel could object, tossing the impromptu corsage at her.

Veronique caught the flower. 'Thanks.' She looked at him with surprise. Fedor grunted in response and turned away.

Miguel looked pained. 'Please don't do that. They don't respond well to stress.' To illustrate his point, the entire bouquet Fedor had violated snapped shut and a milky latex began to ooze from the vine.

'Let's leave this one be.' Miguel steered them away from the angry plant. 'Regardless of the conditions, doing *that* will most certainly make it mad.'

He herded the group over to a work-bench. A young Lanelia with no flowers and a few spindly vines waited for them in a terracotta tub.

'Now, you're no doubt wondering why we're so focused on Lanelia.' Miguel pulled the small vine closer.

'Anaesthetic?' Joe guessed.

Miguel nodded. 'It was, but that was many years ago and medicine has moved on. Our interest in Lanelia, or more to the point, with SNS-C, is now the development of non-lethal weapons.'

Joe smacked his forehead. 'Of course.'

Sam saw Veronique staring at the flower in her hands, only half listening. He wondered what distracted her.

'How?' she asked, looking up.

Miguel handed each of them a clear plastic pellet.

Sam rolled the malleable sphere between his fingertips. 'Looks like a paintball.'

Don't squeeze it too hard,' Miguel warned him, 'they're designed to break on impact.'

'It's a bullet?' Fedor asked, examining his capsule.

The curator grinned like a schoolboy, holding up a marker pen.

Joe fidgeted. 'Mightier than the sword.'

Their host winked at the boy, then turned the pen around so that the clip of the cap rested under his thumb. He aimed the shaft at the wall and looked at the teenagers. 'Ready?'

They nodded.

Miguel pressed the clip into the lid and there was a pop. A pellet shot out and splattered onto the glass, leaving a sticky blob.

He walked over and collected the contents on a piece of card. 'Active SNS-C. Outside the capsule, the mixture begins to oxidise and loses its effect after about thirty minutes. But within those thirty minutes it can inflict total paralysis.'

The boys crowded over the piece of card, gawping at the remains of the pellet. Veronique looked over their shoulders. 'For how long does the target stay down?'

The boys looked at her, surprised.

'From the time the SNS-C is no longer active, usually about two hours. So, maximum would be two and a half hours.

'Er, I wouldn't do that...' he cautioned, noticing Joe's finger edging toward the mixture.

'You wouldn't stop him if you'd known him longer,' Fedor said. 'Two and a half hours of peace.'

'Oi!'

'I'll give you my supper, if you can hold your tongue for five minutes.'

'Done!'

'This ought to be interesting,' Sam chuckled, sitting back and toying with his pellet. He heard Veronique sigh.

'So,' Miguel continued, 'as you can see, it's a very simple and effective means to subdue a potential attacker, guard, angry teacher...'

They all laughed.

'SNS-C can be also used in more surreptitious ways: to guard something, or coat an object you know your target is going to touch. Provided it's touched within thirty minutes of application.'

'What about metered doses?' Joe asked.

'I win,' Fedor grunted.

'What? Oh, that doesn't count!'

'Rules seemed pretty clear to me...'

Joe swore.

'None of that,' Jenny chided. 'We're in polite company.'

Joe swore again, in Italian.

'And I do speak Italian,' Miguel laughed. 'Anyway, metered doses? Yes, larger SNS-C projectile weapons can be fitted with modified darts. The shaft of the dart is equipped with tiny vials of SNS-C which are drawn out as each application dries, sustaining paralysis over twenty-four hours.'

Sam grimaced. 'That's a long time to go without a loo break!'

Veronique and Jenny wrinkled their noses and sighed.

'What? I'm just saying!'

Miguel removed the card from the table and produced a box of latex medical gloves. 'Ready to harvest some SNS-C?'

Over the next few hours, the head curator showed them how to use boiling water to raise the ambient temperature of the plant. Wearing gloves, Sam scraped the milky fluid from the pores. For once, the rest of the group were silent as they practiced.

When they'd finished the task to his satisfaction, Miguel produced a bag of marker pens. 'Each marker can hold five pellets. To activate you unscrew the chamber here, remove the felt tip and add the pellets. The shaft is equipped with a tiny compressed gas cylinder, good for twenty shots. Its range is accurate to five metres. Past ten, the capsule won't have the force behind it to burst.'

To illustrate his point, this time he fired at the far wall. The capsule lost altitude after about seven metres, bouncing off with an embarrassed ping.

'These,' he pulled four clear plastic bags filled with red pellets from the drawer, 'are practice pellets. I can't trust you with the real thing just yet. These little babies are filled with syrup and food dye – harmless.'

When Jen Si opened the door to collect his pupils for supper, he found everything in the room, the walls, floor, ceiling, furniture, and students, riddled with sticky red spots.

Fedor and Sam peeked at their teacher from behind the upturned sofa, eyes wide, markers held to their chests. Veronique and Joe, who had been peppering them with a volley of pellets from behind the bathroom door, stopped mid-fire, mouths hanging open.

'Well, there goes our deposit,' Jen Si sighed.

The next week passed in a sweltering blur. The monk had designed a diabolical obstacle course for them to complete that wound around the inner valley following the ring of abandoned lookout posts. The platforms' rope ladders had long since rotted away, but each post was within sight of its immediate neighbours making them ideal Folding targets.

This time there were no accommodating nets suspended below the treetop limpets, and the teenager's first few laps had several close calls. The course ended at the waterfall, where they swam and relaxed over lunch.

Their days were filled with challenges and excitement, but the threat of failure and its consequences was never far from their minds. He might not wish to, but Sam felt himself getting attached to his new friends. He wasn't alone in taking this risk, and it bonded them. He had to admit it was nice to really feel part of something.

Their afternoons were spent either in the greenhouses with Miguel or suspended from rope harnesses with Orma learning about the wide variety of plants in the Garden. Their uses were mainly medicinal, though some held more sinister secrets.

From these deadly toxins they manufactured salves that induced loss of balance, powders to cause temporary blindness and liquids that set nerves aflame. Sam and his friends picked, plucked, cured and concocted a multitude of potions and remedies, creating a complete apothecary.

One of their creations, a nasty itching compound they smuggled from the classroom, became a weapon of war between the teenagers as they found more innovative places to smear it in their game; socks, underwear, pillows and bedclothes, door handles, toilet seats and even deodorant sticks. Their cunning was driven to new heights by each prank.

It was not until Jenny became an unwitting casualty that the pastime was brought to an abrupt halt. It was safe to say she would never ask any of them for a tissue ever again.

'It's your fault!' Veronique chided Fedor.

'Pff,' he dismissed the admonishment, kicking his sandals off.

Joe and Sam had gone to help Orma carry seeds pods back to the Seed Store.

'Don't walk away from me!'

But Fedor had already taken his shirt off and was heading for the bathroom. He felt the familiar 'splat' of a marker pellet on his back and turned to give the girl a withering look.

Shock, however, replaced the look as a cold numbness spread across his skin. He slumped to the floor.

'I said, *don't* walk away from me!' Veronique grunted, rolling him over. *Nikki, the Huntress!*

'You all forgot about the pellets Miguel passed round, didn't you?' she gloated, poking him with her pedicured toes. 'I've been saving it for the right occasion…' she grinned, putting her foot on his chest.

Fedor could do nothing but glare when she slid her foot over his chin, took his nose between her big and second toes and gave it a tweak.

'You know, I've always been a believer,' she brandished the tainted tissues, 'that the punishment should fit the crime. I wonder if you can still feel your skin when you're paralysed? Let's find out!' She pulled one out with a grin. 'Now, where shall I start?'

An hour later, Sam and Joe burst through the door. 'We're back!'

'In here,' Veronique called from the bathroom.

'Okay.' Sam rolled his eyes. 'Just leave us some hot water!' He looked around. 'Where's the bottomless pit?'

'Hungry. 'Going out.' She mimicked Fedor's voice in reply.

'Of course he was!' Joe laughed.

Veronique emerged, ensconced in towels. 'All yours,' she called, disappearing into her room and closing the door.

'So, how are we doing?' she asked her victim.

Fedor still lay on the floor, his skin an angry red colour.

'Cat got your tongue? Well, I need to get ready and as I can't trust you not to peek…' She dumped her wet hair towel on Fedor's head, humming to herself.

'Hurry up!' Sam kicked her door a short time later, 'we're starving and Joe said there's not nearly enough make-up in there to make you pretty!'

'OMG!' Joe's eyes widened. 'I did not say that!'

Veronique knelt to retrieve the towel. 'We're off to supper now, *môn cheri*,' she whispered, 'but feel free to join us when you can.'

Then, she leant forward and kissed his frozen lips. '*À bientôt*,' she smiled, just as surprised as he by the action.

The anger faded from the boy's eyes.

Chapter 18

'Stop messing around.' Sam tried not to sigh when Joe materialised on the rickety lookout post. 'We're never going to finish at this rate!'

'I'm not!' The boy slumped against the tree. 'I'm exhausted! Didn't sleep a wink – *he* fidgeted all night. Huffing, puffing and scratching!'

'Yeah,' Sam turned to Fedor, 'what was up with you? First you were late to supper, then all the thrashing about in your sleep. Is it hygiene issues?'

Fedor scowled, ignoring the smirk tugging the corners of Veronique's mouth. 'You should know,' he lied, 'one of you put blasted itching cream on the soap!'

Sam burst out laughing. 'What? Well, it wasn't me! Brilliant though, wish I'd thought of it.'

Joe looked worried, 'It certainly wasn't me! So, don't get any funny ideas!'

Veronique did her best to look disinterested. 'Ugh, boys – do you ever grow up?' She disappeared before anyone could see the mischievous glint in her eyes.

Nikki, the Victorious!

'Right,' Sam chuckled. 'Let's crack on.'

As the morning progressed, Joe watched his friends vanish and disappear all over the valley.

He squinted at his current destination. The sun hit his glasses and obscured his view, but he was impatient not to fall behind the others, so he formed the image as best he could and created the Fold.

He landed on the platform and sighed, looking ahead for the next one.

It was not there. He turned to look for the platform he had just left but couldn't see that, either. 'Oh, ffs,' Joe indulged in a long and colourful tirade.

He walked around the tree and was both surprised and relieved to find a rope bridge. He must have Folded to the wrong place. A thought occurred to him, *Why would a rope bridge lead to a platform that didn't go anywhere?* He walked around the tree again. Nothing. *Maybe it was unfinished?* But neither the platform nor bridge looked new.

He leant against the trunk, and to his surprise a knot in the bark gave way, sinking into the tree. Joe heard a faint 'click' and was amazed to see a segment of wood swing open.

He crept forward and peered through the crack. The air smelt artificial, conditioned. He deployed an exploratory finger and encountered cool metal. Joe took a deep breath then slipped through the mysterious portal.

'He can't be that far behind.' Sam tried to dismiss Veronique's concerns whilst they sat in the shade waiting for Joe.

'What if he's fallen and is tangled in the branches, or worse yet, on the ground with broken bones? Who knows what creatures could be crawling all over him, biting him?'

'Okay, okay.' Sam stood. 'We'll go look for him. How many platforms back was it?'

'Three?' She sounded unsure.

'Four,' Fedor said.

'Come on then.' Sam tried not to imagine the worst and Folded.

'This is it,' Veronique said when they'd retraced their jumps to the fourth platform. 'I peeled this bark while Fedor was whining about the soap.'

'I was not whining!'

'Were too.'

'Was no—'

'Enough!' Sam was starting to worry. He'd expected to find Joe here, bleating about being tired. 'He's not here and he's not over there on the fifth.'

'Which just leaves down there.' Veronique pointed to the dark jungle floor.

Sam barked a laugh. 'You want to go down there?'

'No.' Her eyes were hard. 'But he's our friend. And he didn't let us down in that stupid cave, did he?'

Sam felt ashamed. 'No. He didn't.'

Fedor was looking over the edge. 'Here.' He stepped back and raised his knee to his chest, then brought his foot down, shattering one of the aging floorboards near the trunk.

'Woah!' Sam leapt back and grabbed the branch above him as Fedor broke another plank.

'What the hell are you doing?'

'There are two ways down.' He exposed the branch below. 'Falling is one, this is the other.' He slid his legs through the hole. 'So, are you falling or climbing?'

Veronique was also clinging to the tree for dear life. 'Climbing sounds good!'

Nikki, the Koala!

Veronique slipped twice.

She abandoned her sandals to gain better purchase on the lichen-encrusted limbs. The sunlight faded with every branch and by the time they dropped onto the spongy jungle floor, the landscape resembled an alien planet.

Sam felt uneasy but hated the idea of Joe being alone or hurt down here. How could he let this happen? *This is all my fault. If only I hadn't been so hard on him...*

'*JOE!*' Veronique called, cupping her hands. '*JOOOE!*'

'Split up?' Fedor suggested, though he did not look pleased at the prospect.

'It'd make sense,' Sam agreed, 'but then we run the risk of getting lost altogether.'

'We could Fold back to Ortega's deck? I'm pretty sure I remember it well enough.'

Sam nodded. 'True. Veronique, do you remember it?'

'I think so, but why don't we just do that now, and get help?'

Sam shook his head. 'And then how do we get back here? Besides, this could just be another evil test. If he's hurt, we may not have the time – even with Jenny's Tracker Node things.

'I'll go this way. Fedor, you look over there. V, you carry on that way. If you find him, scream your head off. If you get into trouble... well, same goes. Okay?'

They nodded.

'Good luck!' Sam tried to sound reassuring 'And pray we don't find anything but Joe,' he muttered pushing a large, damp leaf aside.

The door clicked closed behind Joe.

There was a faint hum and a line of electric lights along the wall pinged to life, bathing him in an eerie blue glow. He stood on a small metal landing of a spiral staircase winding down into the hollow of the tree.

Down he went. The air conditioning, refreshing at first, became uncomfortably cold and Joe hugged his arms to his chest. The staircase ended at a chamber with a circular carving in the floor.

'Ł ô ç ħ æ ġ ü ħ æ ɔ ġ ʋ ř ô ü ç ô?' a mechanical voice asked.

Joe jumped, his heart leaping into his throat.

'Ł ô ç ħ æ ġ ü ħ æ ɔ ġ ʋ ř ô ü ç ô?'

He could see no speaker. Nor was there a console. Joe combed every inch of the room, squinting in the inky blue gloom, whilst the voice kept repeating the same question over and over.

'Is this what being around me is like?' he muttered sourly.

Joe walked back up the staircase to get a clearer look at the pattern on the floor, hoping he'd recognise something to give him a clue, but both the markings and their arrangement were entirely foreign.

We're in South America. It must respond to either Spanish or Portuguese?

'Hola?'

Nothing.

Stupid! Hello is not the answer to a question. It sounds like it's asking a question...

He tried again. '*Lo siento, no entiendo. ¿Otra vez, por favor?*'

'*Destinacion, por favor?*' the voice replied.

Joe was exultant when the computer asked him for his destination. He tried the Spanish for 'options'.

It worked and the voice began rattling off a list of words, too fast for Joe to process, and so he latched onto the first one he recognised.

'*Mineria*,' he repeated the word, wondering what on earth they could be mining, then stumbled as the circular carving suddenly slid into the floor, carrying him with it. Joe looked up to see another stone disc sliding into place above him.

The same blue lights illuminated the lift shaft, becoming a single, cerulean blur as his descent quickened.

Suddenly, the bedrock and lights were gone and Joe felt as if he had been dropped into a void. His heart pounded against his chest. Sweat ran into his eyes. He waited for the disc to cast him into the darkness.

Eventually, once his eyes grew accustomed to the weak light, he was able to make out walls – not near, like the bedrock, but in the distance. They looked like they were perforated by giant circular passages, the scale of which made him shudder. Edging closer to the rim of the lift, Joe was dealt a nauseating bout of vertigo.

Far below him, awash with artificial light, was an entire city.

'*JOE!*' Sam called; he was well beyond worried, guilt was ravaging him now.

He could hear Veronique and Fedor's calls growing fainter with every step. So far, all he had found were colourful frogs, fat spiders, and a millipede sporting a ridiculous number of legs. There were also several foul-smelling flowers that resembled Lanelia far too closely for his liking.

It was not surprising that he did not notice the long, sinuous coils of the anaconda as it unwound itself from the branch above his head.

It lowered its triangular head toward the boy. Unblinking eyes regarded its prey, forked tongue flickering.

It struck Sam high on the thigh and he gasped, looking down in confusion. Then let out a scream as he saw the gaping jaws of a giant snake attached to his leg. He continued screaming as the rest of the snake coiled itself around him.

'Sam?' Fedor turned. He retraced his steps, following the meticulous line of broken stems and branches.

'*Sam*!'

'Fedor?' He heard Veronique nearby. 'What's wrong, was that Sam?'

'I think so.'

The screaming started.

Fedor sprang forward. 'This way!'

Sam clawed at the serpent's face, as its coils squeezed tighter.

'*Aargh!*' he screamed, waves of pain rushing through his body. He beat at the giant flat head, trying to push his fingers into eyes that were now firmly shut.

Fedor burst from the jungle and stopped dead in his tracks.

'What's going o—' Veronique's question died on her lips. '*DO SOMETHING!*' She pushed Fedor towards the intertwined bodies.

Fedor looked around, found a dead branch and lifted it in both hands. 'HIT IT!'

The knot of coils appeared to have no end, nor weakness. '*WHERE?*'

'Who cares! Just hit it!'

Fedor swung the branch with all his might.

Sam screamed again as the snake sank its fangs further into his thigh. 'Don't!' he managed to breathe. The coils had almost reached his chest.

'We have to do *something*!' Fedor look around, helpless. He spied a short, sharp stick and picked it up, sinking it into the snake. Again, the serpent bored into Sam and thrashed its tail.

'Fedor!' Veronique shouted. 'Look!'

Sam was vaguely aware of his friend dropping the weapon. Their voices became distant and his vision began to swim. The pressure around his torso had reached bone-crushing intensity and he could no longer breathe.

Too late, he thought about the flute in his pocket. He would not have had the breath to blow it, were it already glued to his lips. This was it. He'd failed. Everyone.

There was a cracking noise and vicious pain. Darkness crept into the corner of his vision, the world becoming a quiet, agonising blur.

Sam's last conscious thought was of his beloved Sophie.

We'll be together soon...

The disc settled on the cavern floor without so much as a bump.

Still seated cross-legged and wide-eyed in the centre, Joe looked around, a bout of nervous laughter brewing in his chest.

The cavern was lit by an eerie radiance, and the size of it was wondrous enough, but the city sprawled across its base was the true marvel.

A giant pyramid adorned with massive sculptures stood at the far end of a wide avenue flanked by symmetrical rows of dwellings. Other roads ran across the area in front of the pyramid in a neat grid.

Joe heard a dim roar drift across the silent suburbs to his right, and could see a long shimmering waterfall plummeting into a lake feeding the series of aqueducts that wound through the sleeping city.

But the city's architecture and sophistication didn't make sense to him. Its sculpted facades, contoured columns and tiled roofs were Greco Roman, while the temples and statues appeared to be Inca or Mayan. The pyramid was a mix of both Egyptian and Aztec design. Lamp posts lined the empty cobbled avenues...

And why was it so quiet? Joe's mind buzzed with questions as he observed the metropolis. Market squares, hungry for busy crowds and traders' stalls, stood empty; fountains and bathing pools, amphitheatres and temples, all silent stages. How did it come to be buried or built beneath a hidden valley, in the Amazon?

'It's unbelievable,' he breathed.

'Isn't it just?' came an unexpected reply.

Joe almost jumped out of his skin when a dark wraith of a man melted from the doorway of the nearest building and approached him.

'Who the hell are you?' cried the startled youngster, edging away.

'I might ask you the same question,' the stranger replied, 'but I know who you are, Giuseppe, last of your line. What I will ask is how you found your way here?'

Joe could now make out the man's features in the dim light. He was tall and lean, and moved with unnerving grace. His eyes held the boy in a hard relentless gaze.

'It was quite by accident, I assure you,' Joe laughed nervously. 'My friends and I— This tree, you see— I leant against it. And, there was this doorway with a staircase. Then a strange room that wouldn't shut up . . .'

The man drew closer.

Joe's laughter died and he retreated. 'Who are you? Where am I?'

The man paused. 'You have entered *Udias El'suma Natro*, The City of Eternal Night. Who I am is not important and this place does not exist. But don't worry, for soon you will remember nothing.'

Now within reach of the boy, the man suddenly struck Joe's temple with enough force to knock him out. Joe's eyes glazed over and rolled back.

'Oh, come on,' Baid muttered in disgust, as he caught the boy in his arms, noticing a nasty swelling already forming on his temple as he slung him over his shoulder. 'I barely touched you.'

Gazing out over the city whose existence he had helped protect for thousands of years, he patted his inert cargo. 'Some secrets must remain hidden, no matter the cost. Even if this one, technically, belongs to you.'

Sam awoke from a nightmare. Everything was quiet. Peaceful. He sighed and began to roll over, relishing the prospect of a long lie in, so was not at all ready for the hot pain that exploded through his leg in waves of agony.

He cried out and he felt a firm hand on his shoulder, easing him down. 'Gently, Sam,' a voice soothed him, 'you're safe now.'

His head flopped back onto his sweat-drenched pillow.

Cold, reptilian eyes. Endless suffocating coils tightening around him...

'Oh my God!'

'Easy, Sam.' The voice belonged to the monk. 'The snake's gone. You're safe.'

He was on a bed in a tidy room with white walls and a bright ceiling. A robot hovered at the monk's shoulder.

'You're in Medical. Luckily, Miguel's team had the facilities for me to treat you.'

The robot made a small sound and the monk rolled his eyes. 'Sorry, where *we* could treat you.'

Sam swallowed. His throat was dry and raw.

Jen Si lifted a mug of ice chips. 'Suck these.'

'What happened?' Sam asked after a few fitful attempts to speak. 'How long have I—?'

'Three days.' The monk shifted in his seat. 'Fedor and Veronique saved you. Were it not for their quick thinking...' His face was pale and drawn. 'Eight of your ribs were shattered and several had punctured your lungs. Florence,' he indicated the attentive medical robot, 'used Nanites to rebuild the bone and tissue. It was the only way to save you. It was touch and go, but you should be back to full strength in no time.'

Sam examined his strapped chest. His thigh was also heavily bandaged. 'How did they kill the snake?'

'They didn't.'

Sam looked up.

'I'll let Fedor explain. I wouldn't want to steal his thunder. Now that you're awake and Joe has been discharged, I could do with some rest myself.'

Sam felt embarrassed. He had forgotten all about his friend. 'Joe's safe? Where was he? What happened?'

'He fell. Or so we think. Miguel had the Garden robots scour the jungle after his Tracker Nodes failed to pinpoint him. They found him unconscious in the branches below a lookout post with a nasty bump on the head. He can't remember how he got there, but it seems obvious. He was firing a never-ending barrage of questions at me this morning, so he's clearly himself again.'

Sam managed a weak smile. 'I'm glad he's safe. I never should've let him go last. I've let everyone down...'

Jen Si shook his head. 'Rubbish. It wasn't your fault. Joe needs to find strength in himself, not others. We've all seen how much you try to look after him. After all of them, but you can't always protect everyone. You shouldn't put that responsibility on yourself.'

Sam grunted, staring at the ceiling. 'Where are they now?'

'Joe and Veronique have gone home. We brought the course break forward. Fedor asked to stay and I thought you could use the company.'

There was a tap at the door.

'Speak of the devil.'

The tall boy poked his head around it.

'Awake?'

'Yes,' the monk said, 'come on in.'

'Slacker,' Fedor greeted him, closing the door.

Sam smiled weakly. 'Dustbin.'

Jen Si rose and stretched. 'I'll leave you to catch up. Ten minutes, Fedor. He needs his rest.'

'Okay.'

Sam turned to regard his friend. 'Thank you.'

'We're even now,' Fedor shrugged. 'Besides, the parrot saved you, I just helped.'

'Really? How?'

He used a heavy Russian accent. 'Well, we heard you screaming like leetle gurl... Veronique spotted some Lanelia and we managed to sedate your playmate and pull you apart.'

Fedor's mask was slipping. The country bumpkin, 'all brawn, no brain' facade he tried so hard to maintain, was all for show. Now, however, was not the time to tug at it.

Sam drew a deep breath, but the pain in his chest caused him to cough in gurgled agony.

Florence buzzed over. 'That's enough! You, out! And you,' she glared down at her charge, 'it's time for your medication.'

'Okay, okay,' Sam winced, closing his eyes.

Fedor rose and made his way to the door, admiring a brightly coloured pot plant. 'Don't spend all weekend lazing around,' he called over his shoulder. But Sam was already asleep.

From a workshop hidden deep within a secluded corner of the Gardens, Eugene Nomeholt listened to the exchange with great interest, courtesy of the brightly coloured pot plant near the door.

Microflowers were, without doubt, one of his finest creations. Organic CarboSilicone flora able to relay sights and sounds, indistinguishable from normal blooms, had revolutionised covert surveillance. Easily hidden, and needing no electricity or mechanics, his creations could interface with the Earth Song network from anywhere in the world.

He was proud of all of his work. The infamous Sleeping Beauty Rose. His Tengar sterility constructs. Eugene had weaponised Lanelia and created Paralysis pollen. The plant kingdom offered a wealth of unimaginable diversity that, in the right hands – hands with green fingers – could yield any number of amazing hybrids.

Eugene loved his work, but he hated the moniker it had earned him. Gene Gnome.

He knew where it had originated: Creed. *Dominic* Creed; the loud, brash American geneticist who thought his clumsy, barbaric animal Mods were superior, pushing true delicate genius into the shade.

Eugene had tried the Firefly Fingers Mod. Once. It was clearly a poor plagiarism of his Firefly Fern. Though he hated to admit that Creed's Eagle Eyes seemed to be a stroke of genius. As was his success in isolating the hibernation gene from the Woolly Bear caterpillar, finally making Suspended Animation possible. Not to mention his use of shark DNA to create Passive Electrolocation, a sixth sense for detecting objects without sight or sound.

Still, the man wasn't civil. There was no need for name-calling.

The centrifuge beside Eugene whirred to a halt with a click, ending his period of reflection.

Swivelling round on his stool, feet far from the floor, he ceased his eavesdropping, and left the patient to his recuperation. Pushing his octagonal glasses up, Eugene returned to the task at hand.

Chapter 19

Part III

'It's not enough that we do our best; sometimes we have to do what's required.'

Sir Winston Churchill

'Quiet!' Mikael snapped. 'I should never have let you come, *Kuritsa*!'
Sasha fumed. Puffing away a stray lock of sooty hair, she stood motionless; fists clenched fighting the traitorous tears welling up in her large brown eyes.

A lone cricket chirped.

Mikael sighed. He sometimes forgot his sister was only eight. Not a grown up, like he was. He would be eleven on his next name day. Then everyone would take notice of him.

'You sure he's back?' his sibling hissed when Mikael took pity and beckoned her over to where he crouched behind a moss-encrusted wall.

'Yes, I overheard Papa say *"That fool, Ivan, has returned"*.'

'From the lands to the South?'

'Yes.'

'Where the dark-skinned men and horses with bumpy backs live?'

Mikael nodded again. He pointed between the trees to the orange glow from a ramshackle cottage on the outskirts of their village. 'Follow me and keep quiet!'

Sasha nodded, lips a firm bud.

Dodging chickens and keeping low whilst they scurried across the yard.

The sun slid behind the mountains. Crouched below the window of the cottage, the siblings grinned at each other, hands over mouths to muffle their excitement.

All the children in the village had heard tales of Ivan: Ivan the Wild, Ivan the Foolish, Ivan the Wanderer, the list of less than flattering names went on. None of them, however, had ever laid eyes on him. He was a figure of mystery and his voyages to exotic lands were the subject of fervent fireside speculation. Just think of the tale they would have, were they to actually *see* him!

'This is *it*?' a woman asked from within the hut.

'Yes,' came the sulky reply.

The children stole a peek over the sill, eyes wide in anticipation. Ivan the Adventurer looked the part with his mane of long, dark hair and wild blue eyes. His scarred arms were hairy and muscular and his mismatched clothes were well past travel-worn.

'After all these years... The winters I've endured alone. The crops I've sown and harvested alone. You come back from your fool's errand with this...this tatty old...?'

'Scroll,' he muttered. 'Careful!' Ivan moved his wife's hand away. 'This tatty old scroll will change our lives, Anya.' He caressed the swell of her scruffy dress. 'And our children's.'

His wife snorted. 'It's a wonder I'm with child, especially yours!' She began scrubbing at the day's dirt. 'You're a fool. Hard work is the only thing that'll change our lives and you've neither the backbone nor stomach for it.'

The cottage fell into a sullen silence.

'Did you hear something?' Ivan hurried to the door, his hand straying to the hilt of the chipped blade hanging beside it. He peered between the warped wooden slats.

'Hear what?' Anya wiped her jaw. 'Why are you so jumpy?' There was a thoughtful pause and then she threw the cloth into the bowl. 'You stole it, didn't you?'

Ivan did not reply.

His wife swore. '*Durak*! You are an idiot! Where did it come from, who does it belong to?'

'No one.' He rounded on her. 'It belongs to none but he who holds it, and I hold it now. The power will be mine to control!'

'Power?' came the incredulous shriek.

Mikael and Sasha gawped, snickering. 'Look!' The little girl pointed to a hellish figure moving toward the hut. 'He has horns!'

Mikael squinted. 'No, they're swords across his back.'

From the shadows a figure approached the small cottage, treading lightly. Then another man slid from the gloom, and a third. The chickens and crickets were silent. Mikael felt a cold sweat grip him 'We need to get away from here.'

Sasha looked confused.

'Now.' He shoved his sister away from the window. The command was punctuated by a hiss and heavy thud, something splintering the wooden sill. They both let out cries.

It was an arrow, followed in quick succession by a second, then a third. The last sailed through the window of the cottage and, with a sickening thud, found its mark. They did not see the fabled Ivan slump to the floor, his adventures brought to an untimely end.

'Sasha, *run*!' Mikael shouted, shielding her slight frame with his own. Tears blurring her vision, the girl stumbled and tripped over the rough ground.

A dark-skinned man with intricately scarred cheeks stepped into the hovel, casting a demonic silhouette in the doorway. He crossed the room, heading straight for the table.

The beautifully carved wooden spindles of the parchment had once been gilded masterpieces. Now, only the faintest flecks of gold remained and the settings mourned the loss of countless precious stones. But its veneer was of no importance, the words inside – the secret – held an incalculable value.

The scarred man paid no heed to the body on the floor and ignored the woman with her arms wrapped protectively around her stomach. Picking up the scroll, the man left.

Outside, the figures surrounding the cottage withdrew, melting into the night.

'*MAMA*!' Sasha burst through the door. '*PAPA*!'

'Sasha?' Her grandmother struggled upright. The old gypsy coughed, a dry, hacking sound that kept them awake at night. 'What is it?'

'It's Mikael,' she wept. 'He fell, back there, I...I can't find him.'

The woman pushed herself up. Clawing the lantern from the table, she wrestled a thick cloak across her bony shoulders and fought another coughing fit. 'Show me.'

Fortified by the warm light and the presence of a grown up, Sasha hurried between the trees, back towards Ivan's tumbledown house.

'Over there.' The little girl pointed. 'There was a man with horns an-'

The flickering glow from the lantern found a small, crumpled figure on the path.

'No!' Their grandmother sank to her knees. She set down the lantern, hands shaking. 'No, no, no! Don't look, sweetheart. Go and find your Papa, quickly. Take the lantern. Go!'

Eyes wide, mouth slack, the child nodded and scurried back into the night.

Coughing violently, the old woman reached forward, gnarled hands caressing the sandy curls she had loved since the first day she'd seen them. She cradled Mikael's limp head in her lap, unable to look at the hateful outline of that feathered shaft.

Screams from the cottage carried through the darkness. 'Ivan! *IVAN!*'

Anya stood over her husband, stomach cramping. The baby was coming. The door creaked and she threw herself back. The old gypsy from the village shuffled in.

'He did this,' she pointed to the body beside the pregnant woman. Her worn face was tear stained. 'He brought this evil to our homes.'

Anya drew back, as the woman lifted her crooked fingers.

'You will pay, Ivan *Durak* – Ivan, the Foolish,' she promised, stepping over him. 'The sins of the father will follow your seed through the ages. I *curse* you!' Her hand moved toward Anya's stomach. 'They will know no rest. There shall be no respite. They will be branded the heralds of disaster. Cursed. Shunned. Scorned! Persecuted for all time!'

'No,' Anya pleaded, shying away, as her waters broke. 'My baby is innocent!'

The gypsy stepped forward and drew a tiny knife. 'Mikael was innocent!' Slicing her palm, she spat on the wound. Mixing hate and blood, she bound an ancient curse. 'No peace,' she crept forward. 'No rest.' In her other hand, she grasped a lock of sandy hair. 'No solace shall they find.'

Anya tried to slap the hand away, but clasping Mikael's hair in her blood-soaked palm, the old woman drew it over the woman's heaving stomach.

'His sin will mark them. Through this life and the next! There shall be no penance.' As her voice grew louder a fetid wind burst through the open door and banged the shutters, racing around the pair, soaking up the warmth and light.

'All shall rue this day!'

TODAY...

Ivan woke with a start. Troy, his floating robotic nuisance, nicknamed *Popov* after the famous clown, was peeking from between the heavy curtains, throwing a sliver of sunlight across his pillow and eyes with razor-like precision.

Ivan moaned, rolling over and pulling the covers over his head.

Troy jumped and let the curtain fall, releasing a cloud of dust. 'Sorry.' The robot's nimbus bleached to sombre mustard. 'I thought I heard something.'

'You heard Anatoly, you fool. He lives here too, remember?'

Troy said nothing, used to his morning disposition.

'Urgh!' Ivan groaned, flinging the covers back. He was awake now. 'Curse you, Popov! Make yourself useful and get me coffee!'

Troy bobbed and fled the room.

As usual, Ivan was tired. Bone tired. He had been in bed for ten hours but it felt like his head had just hit the pillow. He inspected his hands, as he had every morning since he was twelve. They were covered in ink again, despite being clean when he'd gone to bed. 'Busy night?' He asked his fingers. 'What marvels await me this morning, I wonder?' He noticed a dark welt on his wrist. 'That's new. Thought that stupid robot was meant to stop me killing myself?'

A laboured hum heralded Troy's return, struggling under the weight of a full cup. As his model was not designed for heavy lifting, Ivan's brother, Anatoly, had redesigned the tiny pincer arms after Ivan's demands had damaged them.

'Your coffee, Sir.' Troy murmured, sloshing the brimming cup.

'And this?' Ivan demanded, showing the robot the welt.

Troy's nimbus darkened. 'You fell, sir. Tripped on the carpet—'

Ivan cut off further explanation with a curt wave of his hand.

'What use are you? Get out of my sight.'

Troy's grill dipped and he spluttered from the room.

Ignoring the ink stained sheets, Ivan swung his legs and sat on the edge of his bed. His big toe was also bruised and the nail looked chipped. '*Tupoy* Popov!'

His study was opposite his bedroom for a very good reason. Ivan was a sleepwalker. Every night, a part of his mind came to life, rousing him from his bed to the drawing table in the next room. Every morning Ivan awoke to a new creation. It was like being possessed by Da Vinci's ghost.

It was a curse. Quite literally. A very old, very powerful curse, manifesting in each first-born son of his family, each called Ivan in morbid memory of the first, Ivan the Foolish.

He was Ivan the Eighteenth.

'What do we have this morning, Popov?' he asked, shuffling into the study.

Troy was examining a detailed schematic on the desk. The flash from his camera pinged periodically, photographing the large page in sections.

Ivan found himself marvelling at the grace and precision of the new design. Its neat, clipped lines, precise curves and perfect angles. Annotated and to scale. During the day, he didn't have the level of artistic ability of primordial ooze. But at night he was cursed with refinement and genius. Sentenced to an existence of exhaustion and isolation.

'Looks complicated.'

'It is,' the robot's tone was clipped.

'What's wrong?'

'You've designed an Antimatter bomb, Ivan.'

Ivan noticed his slippers did not match. 'Is that bad?'

'It's not good.'

Ivan took another noisy sip, leaning forward to peer at the innocuous drawing. 'How bad?'

'In the wrong hands, it's end-of-the-world bad.'

Ivan the Eighteenth choked on his coffee.

RUSSIA, 1506 AD

Sam's eyes shot open, blood pumping, as though it were Christmas morning. Gingerly, he took a breath. No pain. *Strange.*

He wiggled a toe. No pain. 'Hmm.'

He raised his head off the pillow; still no pain.

Sam sat upright and swung his legs off the bed. And still there was no pain. 'Curious.'

There was no bandage around his thigh, nor strapping at his chest. 'Oh God, how long was I out?'

Voices drifted through the door, rapidly getting louder. Then it burst open. Jen Si strode in, face crimson, followed closely by Florence. They both stopped and stared at Sam.

The monk closed his eyes and sighed. 'What have you done?'

'Nothing, I've literally just—' he pointed to the fresh indent in his pillow. 'No, not you. Her!'

Florence's nimbus became an indignant orange. 'I did what I had to. The boy was dying.'

'What?' Sam's eyes widened.

Jen Si started pacing. 'You took a turn for the worse during the night and Florence unilaterally decided to treat you with a highly experimental artificial blood called Femtoglobin, designed to repair tissue damage at a cellular level.'

'It was the only thing that could have saved him,' Florence stated.

Jen Si turned on her, 'It may well have been, but you should've spoken to someone first. Did you inject him with the inhibitor too?'

Florence's nimbus turned pink.

'You didn't read that far on the patent, did you? So his blood stream is swarming with Femtoglobin!'

Sam look at his arms. Everything looked normal. 'And that's bad, why?'

Jen Si stopped pacing. 'It's bad because now we've no idea what effect it will have on you. Femtoglobin is composed of living, albeit synthetic, micro-organisms. They're designed to perform a function within the body then breakdown and be absorbed.'

'So, what's the problem?'

'The inhibitor stops them replicating. You've missed the window to take it.'

Sam blanched. 'Come again?' He gulped. 'Will they stop?'

The monk shrugged. 'No idea. It's so experimental, Florence shouldn't even know of its existence, let alone be able to synthesise and administer it.'

There was a pause. Sam felt uneasy. Jen Si wasn't simply angry at the robot's insurrection, he looked worried. 'There's something else, isn't there?'

'We don't know how they'll effect you, Sam. The micro-organisms are always injected fully-fed and with the inhibitor, they degrade before they start to seek more energy. Yours continue to multiply inside of you and are going to get hungry.'

As if on cue, Sam felt a wave of dizziness and spread his arms to steady himself.

'It's started. Sam, lie back.'

'Florence, assuming total saturation of the bloodstream, calculate how much energy would they need per hour and convert it to calories.'

Florence was silent for a few seconds. 'Two thousand.'

Jen Si let out an explosive breath. 'That's a day's worth of food!'

Sam's mind felt like jelly. 'What happens if they don't get food? Any chance they could grab a takeaway?'

'They require ATP, so will begin catabolism.' Florence responded.

'Wha—?'

'Adenosine Triphosphate: they take energy from food. But if there's none available, they will digest muscle, fat and tissue.'

'You mean they will…' Sam gulped, '…eat me?'

Jen Si gave the robot a murderous glare. 'That's not going to happen.'

'Navitium?'

The monk looked fit to burst. 'Where are you getting your information? These are all highly classified—'

'I am required to treat and heal. I have access to all areas of the Cube.'

'What's Navitium?' Sam slurred. The room was whirling.

'It's a compound that yields large quantities of energy, and the formula is *also* classified.' He turned back to Florence. 'How many millilitres for two thousand calories?'

'Ninety-seven.'

'In theory.'

Sam groaned.

'We're running out of time. Do you have everything you need to synthesise it here?

'Yes.'

'Why am I not surprised? Do it. I'll try to get some food down him in the meantime. But we need to have a long chat after this, Florence.' The monk regarded the robot darkly.

'I don't report to you.' Florence left the room via a portal in the ceiling.

'Sam,' Jen Si prodded the sleepy boy, 'I'll be right back.'

'Okay, Mum,' Sam's eyelids were fluttering. 'Waffles or pancakes for breaky, pwease.' He licked his lips weakly and patted Jen Si's hand.

The monk rolled his eyes and stood up. It was going to be one of those days!

Jenny looked from the monk, to Sam, to Florence and then swore. Then she swore again.

Fedor who, had been sitting silently at the back of the room since they'd arrived, let out a low whistle.

Sam was propped up in the bed, the picture of health. Any signs of his recent brush with death vanished.

'And a transfusion won't work? We can't get them out?'

'Nope. For Femtoglobin to be a universal donor, it's designed to mimic hematopoietic stem cells. The prolonged exposure has resulted in the Femtoglobin impregnating his bone marrow and infecting his myeloid tissue. Even if we could purge his blood and lymphatic system, his body will now continue to synthesise it.'

'A bone marrow transfer?'

The monk shuddered. 'You could never replace it well enough. They're permanent and Sam will need to consume two thousand calories an hour just to keep them from breaking his body down for fuel.'

'And that's where the Navitium comes in?'

'Correct. Though I'm not sure it was intended for continual use. It's designed to be an extreme booster for some Mods, highly strenuous physical exertion or jump-starting starved systems.'

'What happens when he's sleeping?'

At this point, Sam noticed Jen Si began to look uncertain. 'Well, the body's metabolism naturally slows during rest, so we're hoping the Femtoglobin will follow suit. They are designed to repair cellular damage and, in theory, excluding the normal oxidative stress caused by free radical damage, they shouldn't have much to do during a sleep cycle. Hopefully, they will operate at almost the same energy level as normal blood cells.'

A thought occurred to Fedor. 'So, Sam will never get sick?'

'I suppose not. Well, not for very long at any rate.'

'Will he age?'

They all turned to look at him.

The boy shrugged. 'Ruben said Baid didn't age because he had an antibody that hunted free radicals. You just said Sam's Femtoglobin will act on free radical damage. If it's such a powerful healer, then he will never be affected by a natural build-up of free radicals and, therefore, should not age. Is this correct?'

Jen Si had underestimated this boy; his quiet nature hid a keen mind.

Florence broke the silence. 'He is correct.'

Sam looked horrified. 'You mean I'm going to stay fifteen forever?'

Jen Si shook his head. 'That's development, not aging. It's unlikely you'll age much past the point of physical maturity. This is very worrying.'

'Cooool!' the boys breathed in unison.

'No, it's not cool! How on earth are we going to explain this to his parents? To Mr D'Angelo...' Jenny's face drained of colour. 'I'm so fired!'

'Let's worry about that later,' the monk said. 'For now, we need to concern ourselves with keeping him supplied with Navitium.'

'I can help,' Florence interjected.

'I think we've had enough of your 'help', thank you, Florence.'

Uninhibited by emotion, Florence ignored the jibe. 'Navitium is usually administered in liquid form. In gaseous form, one could achieve the same result with a much smaller quantity.'

'Go on.'

'An inhaler. One dose could yield the hourly requirement.'

'Like an asthma pump?' Sam ventured.

'How long will it take you to have a prototype ready?' Jenny asked.

'I have sent the plans to Engineering. We will have a prototype ready within the hour.'

'Shouldn't you have waited for us to discuss it first?'

'It was the only logical course of action. Further discussion would be a delay.'

Sam heard Jen Si mutter something unflattering under his breath but was more concerned about being eaten alive by blood parasites, how his parents would take it, and if this meant they'd failed the course. He decided to focus on one thing at a time. 'How long would this inhaler last?'

'Based on sixteen doses a day, one week,' Florence calculated.

'That's not too bad,' Fedor said. 'Just make sure you always have a spare. Maybe get one of those bottomless bags?'

Jenny blinked. 'Fedor, you're a genius! Florence, could we modify the inhaler so that the gas canister is linked to the Quartermaster's Stores?'

'It is possible,' the robot admitted.

'Fine.' Jenny sat up. 'Get some ideas over to Engineering. We'll start Sam on the prototype and five spare inhalers, so that each of us can carry one.'

Sam suddenly felt restless. 'Can we please get out of here? I've not seen blue sky in, like, forever!'

'Let's wait for the inhaler,' Jen Si said. 'Then you can take it – and your new passengers – for a test drive.'

Seconds after the first puff, Sam felt ready to wrestle a Russian – and as luck would have it, he knew just where to find one. He thanked his cyber nurse who, when she was sure the others were out of earshot, gave Sam the same cryptic message the gardening robot had. Sam suspected Flic might also be the mystery benefactor behind Florence's timely patent knowledge.

The first thing Sam did after being discharged from his sick bed was Fold to the Ortegas' sundeck in the Garden.

Fedor was leaning against the gazebo. 'How do you feel?'

Sam put on his best Russian accent. 'Strong, like bull'.

Fedor shook his head. 'Brain like bull, more like...'

'Race you to the waterfall?' Sam challenged.

'Keep an eye out for snakes,' Fedor winked and vanished.

They spent the rest of the afternoon lying in the sun, talking and staring up at the cloudless sky.

'Could I try it?' Fedor asked when Sam took his hourly puff. Sam tossed the inhaler over.

'Woah!' Fedor's body sprung to life. 'Imagine a dose of that before a fight!' He rolled over and started performing fingertip press-ups.

'Well, it just stops me from being eaten,' Sam replied sourly.

'Yeah but remember the upside.' Fedor flipped to his feet with chemically enhanced speed. 'No sickness, no aging and I bet you heal super quickly.'

'You think so?'

'Only one way to find out.' Fedor walked over to the water and found a sharp sliver of rock.

Sam raised an eyebrow. 'You're kidding? I still feel pain!'

'Don't be such a wimp, just a small cut, no need to be dramatic.'

Sam pressed it to his fingertip.

'Go on,' Fedor chided. 'Are all English boys such babies?'

'A baby? And I'm not English.' But the chastisement did the trick, bright red blood seeping from the laceration.

Fedor sat down next to him, both boys transfixed by Sam's finger.

Nothing happened.

'Great.' Sam shook his head. 'Now it won't stop bleeding and I'll probably get sepsis.' He waggled his finger in the water and then wiped it dry on his shorts.

Fedor grabbed his hand. 'Look!'

The wound was gone.

Sam snatched his hand back, raising the finger to his nose. Not a scratch.

Fedor let out a whistle. 'Woah!'

'Not sure it's worth being chained to an inhaler for the rest of your life, though.'

'A very long life.' Fedor pulled his shirt on.

Sam made a face. He wasn't as excited as his friend. A long, lonely life plagued by bad memories was not something he felt any enthusiasm for. He slid an arm through the sleeve of his own shirt, hiding the scars that were a constant reminder of how alone he was already. There was only one advantage to all of this: next time he was attacked, he'd not be so easy to beat.

'Come on, Wonder Boy, I'm starving.' It had been an hour since Fedor had eaten.

'You know,' Sam pursed his lips, 'I think your nickname should be Pit.'

Fedor gave a rare smile. 'As in Brad?'

'As in bottomless.'

'How do you boys feel about a little detour?' Jenny asked, over dinner.

'Eh?' Sam looked up from his *Lomo saltado*, a delicious local beef dish.

'Well, Jen Si has been summoned by the Council to discuss Sam's accident and I've been instructed to retrieve an important schematic from a contact in Russia.'

Fedor's ears pricked. 'Whereabouts?'

'I'm not at liberty to say. But, if you boys don't feel like joining me, I'm sure Miguel would appreciate the extra hands for harvesting?'

Sam nearly choked. 'We don't need to know where. We'd love to come.'

Fedor tore at a loaf of bread. 'Can we ask who the contact is?'

'It's a "they", actually. Brothers Ivan and Anatoly.' Jenny topped up her wine. 'Ivan was the youngest chess Grand Master and has at least five games going at any time. At night, however, he's a Dreamer, and will sketch incredible inventions in his sleep. He's never interested in any of them, preferring online gaming and being a bit of a lump, but his brother Anatoly, makes up for his disinterest. He holds doctorates in Engineering, Biochemistry, Genetics and Quantum Mechanics, and is what you might call a tinkerer. Anatoly leaps on whatever Ivan dreams up. Together, they are the perfect inventor – and possibly the most dangerous.'

Sam's eyes brightened. 'Why?'

'Genius rarely asks if something *should* be done, its only focus is what *can* be done. Ivan's not conscious when he concocts his designs and Anatoly never considers the potential impact of what Ivan dreams up. He's consumed by the challenge of trying to build it, which is not so good when it's a weapon or harmful biological agent.'

'Femtoglobin?' Fedor guessed.

She nodded. 'Yes, you have them to thank for that. This time it's a device of some kind – something that shouldn't fall into the wrong hands. I went to school with Anatoly, so we have a rapport of sorts. That always helps when you have to confiscate someone's toys.'

'Sounds fun.' Sam wanted to go, but there was something else weighing on his mind. 'What about our next test?' he decided to force the monster out of the cupboard. 'Things haven't exactly gone according to plan recently,' he rubbed his ribs, 'but I'm pretty sure we need to come away from the jungle having achieved something?'

'You've done it.' Jenny assured him, 'Trust me! The benchmark to pass this section of the training was being able to harvest then use one of the compounds Miguel and Orma have shown you – and Fedor certainly did that!'

The boys were relieved and pleasantly surprised.

'Ah, well, every cloud,' Sam took another mouthful. 'Let's go and visit Mother Russia then!'

Joe awoke with a start. He was drenched in sweat, sitting upright in his bed, panting. It took him a while to realise he was home. In his own bed, with his things around him. Safe. Finally.

He flopped back into the clammy sheets and his hand drifted to the lump on his head. It had almost gone. Thankfully, his mother hadn't noticed, so he felt no need to tell her everything that had happened so far, certainly not falling out of a fifty-foot tree.

He closed his eyes. Why did he keep waking up so scared and breathless? He remembered pieces of his dream, but not why they should have this effect. A rabbit. A long, dark passageway. Tumbling through darkness toward something

'Argh!' He rolled onto his side, and glanced at his clock.

02:37

'Ugh!' He squeezed his eyes shut. *Just breathe...* In and out. In and out... He drifted off again.

He was still falling. In the dim light he could almost make out shapes below him...blocks, a pattern, something...what was it?

Sleep claimed him, a heavy and dreamless slumber.

Veronique could not sleep. The sounds of Parisian nightlife called to her; its music, voices and laughter rising from the streets below. She so wanted to answer the call, to socialise and dazzle, leaving a trail of broken hearts in her wake. It was summer and the city was alive, brimming with excitement and promising adventure.

But *adventure* had taken on new meaning, no longer constrained by the boundaries of cosy cafes, moonlight boulevards and the words of charming strangers; adventure was now tainted by dark caverns, treacherous waters and hot, deadly jungles.

She shuddered, recalling the image of Fedor lifting Sam's broken body, his jaw slack, lips bloody, his limbs dangling from a chest that seemed impossibly thin.

It was no wonder she could not sleep. The amusements of the streets below seemed a distant, childish delight. Idle prattle and the senseless laughter of fools who knew nothing of the world being destroyed around them.

In her lap she held her Tarot cards. With trembling fingers, she reached toward the top card, but stopped. For the first time, Veronique felt scared that the cards might hold the truth. That they were no longer a childish flight of fancy.

'*You follow the cards.*' She could still hear the gypsy's voice. '*Do not follow too closely, for the hand that holds them is not always your own.*'

She now feared what might lie beneath.

Nikki, the Coward.

Jen Si waited outside the Council chambers.

He was not usually nervous. He had been through the thick oak doors in the statue's neck many times, though they seldom led to the same place. The first time they had opened on a sun-bathed clearing in a forest of ancient oaks, the Council seated around a gigantic stone table. It had been many years before he had appeared before them again, gathered on the deck of a large Chinese junk moored in the placid waters of a remote archipelago. He idly wondered where they would lead today; a castle tower perched on a misty mountain, or perhaps a vaulted stone chamber far below the forgotten city…

A guard interrupted his reverie. 'You may go in.'

As usual, Baid was present, though this time he was dressed in a tailored charcoal suit and crimson silk shirt. He returned the monk's greeting with the faintest nod, then turned and led him down a narrow corridor lined with wooden torches.

'I don't believe I've been here before.'

'No.'

'Where are we?'

The ancient warrior snorted but did not reply, and Jen Si felt the sting of chastisement. He'd known Baid all his life and sometimes forgot how transient others must seem to the Sumerian, but the monk was a legend in his own right and was used to being treated as such. His genetic memory gave him the skill and knowledge of countless ancestors, everyone respected him. Except Baid.

'Stop.'

The passage was a dead end. The monk looked over Baid's shoulder, wondering if they were lost. 'Wher—' he muttered before he could catch himself, provoking a growl of irritation.

'Never mind.'

Careful not to sully his suit, Baid placed his right hand on one of the stones lining the near side of the passage. With his left, he found a slightly higher spot on the opposite wall, placed his feet on two flagstones, and began pressing the four stones in sequence. Jen Si heard the familiar grating of blocks moving, as the flagstones of the passage behind them descended, one by one, into the floor, becoming a staircase.

'Left foot, right foot…' Baid instructed.

A short descent brought them into a long, well-lit chamber. Large statues of warriors in strange armour lined the avenue, their gauntleted hands clasped at their sides. Sharp, angular helmets hid their features but, as Baid slipped past and took the lead, Jen Si could not help but feel there was something very alien beneath the visors. Picking up the pace, he followed his ancient companion toward a round studded metal door and the Council beyond.

Chapter 20

'I win!' Sam whooped in amazement as the basketball rattled off the backboard and sank through the hoop.

Fedor, flushed and sweating, muttered something unflattering in Russian and slapped the ball away. The partisan crowd on the bench chuckled.

'Well done, Sam.' Anatoly stood up, handing him the Navitium pump.

Their host was tall and lean with a shaven head and dark beard speckled with grey. His hands were calloused and his coarse, hairy arms thick with muscle. 'Ivan used to give me a half decent game, before his backside got too big to leave the sofa.'

Ivan was the antithesis of his brother, short, overweight and boasting a full head of dark, greasy hair. Lounging on the bench, between the towels and bottles of water, he favoured Anatoly with a retort so colourful even Fedor raised an eyebrow.

'It's a very good thing you don't speak the mother tongue, Sam.' Anatoly ignored the profanity. 'You'd think very little of our upbringing. Fedor, I trust we'll not catch you repeating those words? Good. Let's see what food my porcine brother has left us. You boys must be starved.'

'I could eat.' Fedor almost looked happy.

Hidden away in the foothills of the Urals, Ivan and Anatoly were kings of their castle. They lived in a veritable rabbit warren of ancient halls, stone chambers and turrets, which the brothers had filled with every imaginable toy, gadget and invention.

They had taken the boys on a tour through vaulted ballrooms, a chapel, and numerous stately dining rooms before reaching the basketball court, go-kart track, SNS-C paintball course, arcade, pool and dojo – and they had only covered the east wing so far!

The castle courtyard housed a collection of scramblers, quad bikes and ATVs. There was even a helicopter and a fighter jet, just to round off things.

'Ah, the MIG.' Anatoly chuckled, noticing Sam's gobsmacked expression. 'A Soviet era icon I retrofitted to take off and land without a runway. Goes through fuel like a pig does truffles. I'm working on an alternative formula but need to refine the mix. The first batch of IG60 blew out the starboard engine – sent it clean through Ivan's favourite Hoverbike. He was not pleased.'

'*Hoverbike*!' Sam's eyes widened.

Anatoly grinned. 'Oooh, yes.' He pointed to a cluster of peculiar bikes below them. 'We have quite a few. All built on Ivan's Anti-Gravity engine. You see it—'

'Oooh, no.' Jenny cut him off and ushered her wards away before Anatoly suggested a race (for money, of course). 'Sam's not yet recovered from his last "adventure". Maybe next time.'

Veronique and Joe arrived that evening, escorted by a very sombre monk.

The teenager's excited reunion was held over a dinner of pizzas cooked by the culinary-adventurous Anatoly. He and Ivan listened intently as the youngsters recounted their adventures in the jungle.

'Vodka?' Anatoly plopped the bottle on the table, belching into his fist. The look he received from Jenny could have turned Medusa to stone.

'Oh, come on, don't give me that, they are not babies! Movie, anyone?' He changed the subject, removing the bottle and disappointing the teenagers,

They waddled into the cinema room and flopped onto the sofa with a contented sigh, asleep before the opening credits left the screen.

Jen Si, Jenny and the brothers covered them with blankets and left, Anatoly gently closing the door behind them. Turning, he cuffed his brother on the back of the head.

'*Hey*! What's that for?' Ivan protested.

'Call it a pre-emptive strike; I doubt they're here because of anything *I* dreamt up.'

'Ah.' His brother rubbed his head.

'Well, for once, that's not entirely true,' Jenny said.

Anatoly raised his bushy brows. 'Come again?'

'Femtoglobin.'

Anatoly raised his hands and Ivan instinctively ducked. 'I've not synthesised *any* Femtoglobin.'

'No,' Jen Si said. 'But you did type up a rather comprehensive methodology that a well-meaning EMT robot followed and administered to young Sam.'

'The one with the asthma pump?'

'What's an EMT?' Ivan chipped in.

'Emergency Medical Technician,' Jenny whispered.

'Ah.'

'He's not asthmatic,' the monk's tone was serious, his grilling from the Council still raw. 'The EMT failed to administer the inhibitor.'

'But then they'd replicate exponentially and the energy requirement would far exceed...' Anatoly's jaw clenched and he paled. 'How's he still alive?'

'Navitium. From the gas inhaler which, as you noticed, he's now chained to.'

The inventor slumped back and stared at the ceiling.

'So, it's not my fault you're here?' Ivan gloated.

Jenny shot him a look. 'You're on my list, too.'

'The Antimatter device.' he guessed. 'You've got a big, fat mouth, Popov!' Ivan glared at Troy. The robot's nimbus faded until he was barely visible in the dim room.

Jenny cut him off. 'And you wonder why we keep such a close eye on you two.'

Anatoly shrugged, grinding his teeth. Her visits were a nice distraction, but he could do without the lectures on his brother's curse and his own lack of ethics. Progress did not care about right or wrong, only possible and not possible. Evolution was unstoppable and it was not limited to organic life.

If only she knew just how many of Ivan's nocturnal flights of fancies went undetected, replaced, or altered by Anatoly before dawn, and spirited away to a hidden workshop far beneath the castle. It was just a pity he had not beaten their little robotic spy to the study on this occasion.

'Anatoly?' They were all staring at him.

He waved his hands. 'The plans are safe. You can have them. I'm more concerned by the boy.'

'You mean intrigued.' Jenny's expression was sour.

He shrugged. 'Semantics. Can I examine him or not?'

'He's not a lab rat. Sam's been through enough,' said Jen Si.

'I can probably fix it.' From anyone else, the statement would have been arrogant but from Anatoly, it was simply a fact. If anyone could cure Sam, it would be him.

'You can take blood,' the monk relented, 'but in the morning and only after we have the plans and any copies of the Antimatter device.'

'Fine,' he hissed. 'Troy can show you where they are. He seems to know the place better than we do.'

'*All* the copies.' Jenny's tone was firm as the inventor stalked from the room without another word.

Anatoly blinked. His mouth was dry. He lay in bed, staring at the canopy of the four-poster bed, wondering what had woken him. It would not be Ivan. Their rooms were far enough apart for his brother's sleep walking not to disturb him and the guest rooms were nowhere near his corner of the castle.

He glanced at the faded green hands of the clock. It was a little after 1am, hours before the alarm that allowed him time to steal into his brother's study before their interfering robotic nanny. He muttered a string of curses and tried to roll over but the bedclothes were caught on something. He wrenched at the duvet, kicking it like a petulant child. His feet struck something solid, something that should not be there.

Anatoly fumbled for the lamp. Light spilt across the room, over the boxes, tools and half-finished gadgets that littered his chamber.

At the foot of his bed sat a man with scarred cheeks, his hands folded in his lap.

'Baid!' Anatoly gasped. 'You scared the life out of me! What the hell are you doing?'

The intruder raised a solitary eyebrow but said nothing.

Anatoly took several deep breaths, heart thumping. He reached for the glass beside the clock, without taking his eyes off his guest, and drew a noisy sip.

Baid simply watched.

'I suppose asking how you got in here would be futile?' Nothing usually came within ten kilometres of the forgotten palace without him knowing.

'Yes.'

'What do you want?'

Baid raised a gloved hand, offering the contents of his closed fist. Anatoly reached out and his visitor dropped a small purple crystal, the size of a vitamin tablet, into his palm. The second it touched his skin, it burst to life in a spreading kaleidoscope of neon-purple tendrils. Anatoly felt a surge of electricity shoot up his arm, numbing it. He dropped it onto the covers.

'*Woah*!' He flexed his fingers, trying to rid them of the anaesthetising sensation. 'What was that?'

Baid shook his head. 'Tomorrow, when you examine the boy, implant this crystal near the femoral artery. He will not need stitches; there will be no scar. The wound will heal before the blood dries. Do not let it come into contact with any metals or sunlight. Handle it only with gloves and plastic instruments. Do nothing else with it. If you do, I will know. Do you understand?'

It was the most Anatoly had ever heard from the man, and that alone was enough to frighten him to agree. He nodded.

Baid wrapped a piece of black cloth around the shard. 'Tell them you've slowed the Femtoglobin and he won't need the pump anymore.'

Anatoly opened the drawer beside his bed. When he then turned back to Baid, the man was gone. He gulped, searching the gloom. Nothing.

'Remember,' came a voice from the shadows. 'I'll be watching…'

Baid opened the study door and slipped through. On the other side, Gabriel Laurent, Head of the Council, was sitting legs crossed in his favourite chair, a cloud of bluish smoke blossoming from his pipe.

'Done?'

Baid closed the door and nodded, taking a seat beside the Far Sight window. They watched as the three figures slept. The first, and by far the largest, lay spread eagled on top of the covers. Head back, jaw open, almost certainly snoring. Loudly. The second, much smaller, was wrapped head to toe in his covers, legs pulled into the foetal position. Only his nose was visible. The third lay on his back, an arm draped over his eyes, chest rising and falling rapidly.

It was this boy who held the old man's attention. 'The Russian understands what to do?'

Baid nodded. 'And he's curious.'

'I'm relying on your ominous reputation to quell that. It's been known to accomplish far greater things.'

Baid snorted in reply.

They watched the sleeping boy for several more minutes.

'I don't think this is a good idea—'

Gabriel slammed his fist down against the arm of his chair. 'I don't care what you think! If I want to know, I'll bloody well ask!'

Baid pursed his lips. He was not used to being spoken to in such a way. No one dared.

Gabriel's gaze bored into him, daring the dark-skinned immortal to speak. Baid might have been untouchable to Mother Nature and the steely hands of Father Time, but no one was impervious to the power Gabriel could wield. The tension between the two men was taut. Aphrodite, Gabriel's C.A, fluttered nervously in the corner of the room until a tap at the door broke the silence.

A massive head appeared. 'Uh, everything all right, Sir?'

'Perfectly fine.' Gabriel answered the guard, but his attention did not waver from Baid.

'All I'm saying,' Baid continued when the door closed, 'is that I don't think it wise to let it out of our sight. Let alone implant it in the leg of some boy.'

'Well, luckily for you, it's not your decision to make.'

'You are both my responsibility.'

Gabriel smiled. 'Then I guess you're now fully invested in the wellbeing of young Samuel Van Sandt.'

Baid blinked. He'd been checkmated.

Gabriel lowered his eyes, struck a match and raised it to the pipe. Gripping the worn stem, his attention returned to the screen.

Sam was going to need all the help he could get and guardians came no better than Baid.

Sam fidgeted as he waited on the medical table. He did not like the open backed gown, or the bright sterile environment. Everything in the room gleamed. From the countertop, medical apparatus emitted the occasional 'beep'.

'Right.' Anatoly snapped on a latex glove and guided Sam's head back to the pillow. 'Let Anatoly have a look at these little beasties of yours.'

'Er, did Anatoly just refer to himself in the third person?'

'Did he? Hazard of spending too much time by yourself.' He shrugged. 'Now, a slight prick...'

Sam opened his mouth to protest, but the room began to swim and the ring of bright lights swirled and blurred into darkness.

'Sam?' Anatoly said.

No reply. The boy's pulse was stable, his breathing slow and steady. The sedative had been risky. Given the Femtoglobin, the anaesthetic could wear off at once, so he had quadrupled the dose.

Anatoly picked up an alcoholic swab, exposing Sam's thigh. There was no room for error and no time for caution; he must be quick and precise. Half an inch too deep and he could sever the femoral artery.

He paused and looked again at the neatly addressed envelope on the counter. He had read the contents a hundred times since it had arrived, addressed to him at the University.

"Sam will be the perfect candidate. A faster healer, there will be no scar. No one would ever know..."

Anatoly was renowned for his stubborn and rebellious nature, and the person behind the letter clearly knew his ego could not resist such a temptation. But how had he known this opportunity would present itself?

Anatoly swore and set down the swab, retrieving a small blue vial from the safe. EverMod: His finest creation. No one else knew of its existence, except the author of that letter. He was being led. Played.

"If this works, you can change everything…"

Flicking the ampule, he picked up a syringe and taking the mysterious stranger's advice, prepared to make history.

'Sam?'

Sam's eyes fluttered open. Someone was patting his cheek.

'Huh?'

Anatoly hid the smelling salts. 'Hey, come on now, that was only a tiny needle!'

Sam raised his hand to shield his eyes and shuffled up onto his elbow. 'What happened?'

'You fainted,' Anatoly scoffed, sealing a blood vial and placing it into a rack. It was not Sam's blood, just a prop. Baid had been right, the cut had faded by the time he wiped the wound. 'I thought you Africans were made of stronger stuff. Just wait till I tell Fedor!'

'Fainted?'

'Like leettle gurl!'

Sam swore. 'Please don't tell Fedor!'

Anatoly made a face. 'Well, I guess I could let it slide – just this once.'

'That would be great!'

'Right,' the scientist waved toward the door, 'Anatoly has tests to run. Why don't you ask Ivan to show you the Hoverbike track?'

Sam's face lit up. Shrugging on his shirt, he left.

Outside, he checked the corridor to make sure he was alone and felt in his pocket for the Stepping Stone. Hoverbikes sounded appealing, but first he had to make an overdue visit.

'Chess?' Joe blurted, twisting to insert himself into the conversation.

Veronique sighed, rolling her eyes at Jenny, but saying nothing. She flicked over the card at the top of the deck. The Fool taunted her. *How apt.*

Ivan nodded at Joe's question. 'You play?'

'Best in my school! Are you any good?' The gauntlet was down.

'I've played once or twice,' Ivan lied. 'Can you explain the rules as we go?'

Joe nodded. 'Definitely.'

'No playing for money,' Jenny warned them.

Joe looked confused. 'But I haven't got any?'

'I wasn't talking to you.'

'Okay, okay!' Ivan threw up his hands. 'What's the point in having guests, if you can't have a little fun?' He stomped toward the door. 'You coming, Popov Junior?'

Joe hopped to his feet. 'Who you calling a clown?'

Ivan was impressed. 'Not just a pretty face, eh?'

Fedor watched Joe leave with the large Dreamer.

And then, there were three...

Anatoly had purloined Sam before breakfast for tests, and Jen Si had gone off with the robot, so Fedor now sat listening to Veronique and Jenny.

See all, hear all, say nothing. His father's advice came to mind. Fedor shook his head. The man was a mediocre role model, but his endless stream of clichés did hold some value. The girls were curled up on the sofa, poring over Veronique's Tarot cards.

For some reason, he felt restless today. Stretching, he eased out of the sofa and left the room, wandering into a long passage adorned with tapestries, mismatched suits of armour and flaking portraits. Fedor paused to stare into the faded eyes of the long dead aristocrats.

'Shoddy décor, wouldn't you say?' a voice whispered over his shoulder.

Fedor jumped and instantly spun around.

'Now *that's* how a trained fighter reacts, people. See how he gave himself distance whilst achieving perfect positioning of the feet and arms?'

Fedor was faced with three strangers wearing matching black outfits, masks and goggles. Their suits were laced with a network of thin neon wires that appeared to be cooling the air around them, creating a fog. Strapped across their chests were flat palm-sized panels that pulsed faintly.

The owner of the voice was tall and lean. He, mirrored Fedor and eased into a combat stance, though he kept his hands – and whatever they held – behind him. To his left, stood a thickset figure lacking the loose, easy stance of a fighter. *Built for strength, not speed.* Fedor assessed him. *Not an immediate threat.*

To the man's right, a slim girl watched Fedor calmly, a bulky black bag on her back. *What does she have in there?*

'Who are you?' he asked.

'Who is anyone, really?' the man quipped. 'We're just fellow art lovers! Here to admire the tapestries. A wonderful collection, if a tad dated. Must run though, *tempus fugit!*'

The man's left hand shot forward, a blue tipped staff in his hands. It was hissing ominously and set to deliver an unpleasant surprise.

Fedor managed to avoid the attack by sliding to the side and delivering a double-handed blow to the man's chest, but the minute his fists came into contact with the man's suit, he felt a numbing sensation shoot up his arms and into his legs, causing him to buckle.

The impact still drove the man back and sent the charged staff slamming into the girl on his right. She screamed, the wires of her suit lighting up as the charge diffused across her body. The panel on her chest fizzed and popped.

His attacker recovered and pushed Fedor back with a rough kick to the chest. Still numb, Fedor was unable to block the thrust and fell, his head glancing off the wall.

The stocky figure fixed Fedor with a murderous glare. His shoulders bunched, fingers curling and knuckles cracking.

'No time for that.' The lean man stopped him. 'We've got what we came for. Let's go.' He helped the girl up and favoured Fedor with a mocking little bow. 'Until next time.' He pressed the device on his chest, turned and vanished.

The girl, still groggy, smacked the panel on her chest, but this time nothing happened. She looked down and smashed her hand repeatedly against the panel, but it was dead.

At that moment, a piercing siren wailed out from the depths of the castle and an angry voice crackled over a loudspeaker.

'What'd it say?' she asked, panicking.

Her partner shrugged, looking up and down the corridor.

Fedor chuckled, leaning against the wall. 'It's Russian. And it means *INTRUDER!*'

The trespassers exchanged mirrored looks of horror.
'*RUN!*'

Chapter 21

The siren blared and the chess rivals looked up for a moment, confused. The game was going well, neither side with a clear advantage and Ivan (though he hated to admit it) was forced to abandon three of the online games he had started on the sly, when a pawn made an unexpected departure from the field of play.

How intriguing!

The next thought was far less congenial, for a disgusted bishop followed suit moments later. Ivan was getting a run for his money.

Not that they were playing for money, of course. They were not allowed to!

Suffice it to say, neither would be answering the Castle's distress call.

The Hanged Man lay on the table. Jenny and Veronique both looked down at the card.

Jenny made a face. 'Oh, dear, that can't be good.'

'I wouldn't worry, it's very subjective. They can rarely be taken at face val—'

She was cut off by the long wail of the alarm.

Anatoly sighed when Sam left. Leaning back on the counter, he took a deep breath. No more Baid. Soon, no more visitors. Soon things would return to normal and he could return to his own skulduggery.

He couldn't have been more wrong.

The lights dimmed and the emergency light above the door flared to life, shattering his hopes.

Anatoly swore, at length. 'What now!' Pulling off his surgical gloves, he yanked the door open and stuck his head out. 'Sam?'

Sam, however, was nowhere to be seen.

Veronique put her hands to her ears. 'What is it? What do we do?'

'Stay here,' Jenny shouted. 'I'll find Anatoly. It must be a false alarm.' She paused. 'But, just in case it isn't – don't move!'

Veronique turned to bellow at Fedor, but he was not there 'Wha—?

'Sneaky sod; Never about when you need him.' She noticed one of the doors was ajar. Collecting her cards she got up to investigate, damned if Fedor was going to have all the fun.

The siren was less oppressive in the corridor and she looked left then right. 'Nikki Livingstone, I presume?' She flipped a card, hoping for an omen. The figure on the tarot was facing left. 'Left, it is!'

Rounding a corner, taking a wide berth to avoid a hideous suit of armour, Veronique slammed head first into a large, dark wall. Or rather, the large, dark wall slammed into her. The intrepid Dr Livingstone was flung backwards, the wind driven from her sails, gasping as tarot cards rained down around her. She watched the wall turn into a large man dressed all in black. He stumbled briefly, then carried on without so much as glancing at her. He was dragging something behind him – a girl, also dressed in black and carrying a large bag. She looked down Veronique as they passed in a cloud of mist.

Someone shouted and Veronique felt hands pulling at her. Another large boy was trying to drag her to her feet. This one looked more familiar and her lips curved. 'Dr Livingstone, I presume,' she cooed.

'*What?*' Fedor screwed up his face.

'The jungle,' she pointed, hands rolling on wilted wrists. 'I'm an explorer…'

'He's knocked out what little sense you had!'

Veronique's eyes started to roll back in her head.

'Oh no, no, no! You can't go to sleep, get up!' He shook his concussed friend.

'Huh?'

'Up, you crazy mare!' Fedor pulled the rag doll to her feet and guided her arm over his shoulder. 'Come on, this could be another bloody test and we're not failing it!'

Veronique squinted and smiled. 'You're quite pretty, for a boy.'

'Oh, good god.' Fedor groaned.

'Do we need to do anything about tha—?' Joe stopped when Ivan moved his remaining bishop, lining up to attack the white knight.

'Uh?'

'The bell…thingy?' Joe pushed his glasses up, brow furrowed.

Ivan dismissed the military-grade siren. 'Probably just the Dominos drone.'

'You get pizza deliveries out here?' Joe's finger hovered over his knight.

'Touch move!'

'I didn't touch it!'

Ivan leant closer. 'I'm just saying.'

'Ssh! I thought you said you'd played before?'

Ivan spluttered, trying to form words, a suitable riposte, but then Joe moved his knight and all thought of a retort died.

Veronique staggered beside Fedor. *Nikki, the Wounded.*

'Not so fast,' she whined, legs crossing.

'But they're getting away!'

'Who cares? Her stupor was beginning to pass, leaving one thing in its place: Pain.

'I care, as should you. Ivan and Anatoly opened their home to us and now someone is robbing them. Trying to stop them is the least we can do!'

'Oh, don't be so dramatic! How do you know they were robbing them?'

'Dressed in black. Wearing masks. Carrying a heavy bag and running from an alarm.'

'Well, when you put it that way...'

The corridor opened onto a courtyard filled with motorised toys. The thieves were seated astride a Hoverbike.

'They'll never get it started.' Veronique leaned against the wall, thankful for the brief respite.

There was a rumble when the Anti-Gravity engine roared to life. Fedor shot Veronique a dark look.

'Oh, shut up! How are they going to get out – through the wall?'

'Come on!'

Joe gave a 'Ha!', lifting Ivan's castle, 'TTFN!'

Ivan fumed, scouring the squares feverishly.

'Try this!' he countered, moving a pawn toward Joe's queen.

A loud groan sounded above the din of the revving bike. 'They've found a way to open the gate!' Fedor let loose a blistering batch of expletives.

'Oh, stop it!' Veronique hobbled to the nearest bike.

It was a lean machine, painted red and black with sleek curves and a powerful engine. In the place of wheels, two skis sat between the forks of the shock absorbers, lightly resting on the ground.

'Now what?' Fedor sulked, hands on hips.

'We follow them.'

'How? I don't know how to ride one of these things!'

'You think they did? Didn't stop them trying. What's wrong, you scared?'

'No!'

'Then what?'

Fedor faltered. 'I don't want you to get hurt.'

At that precise moment in time, every part of Veronique's body hurt. 'Touching,' she swung her leg over the bike, 'now get on or stay behind!'

Fedor did not move.

'Get ON!'

'Have you ever ridden a motorbike before?'

'Of course!' *How different can it be from a Vespa?* 'Front brakes.' She gave him a crash course in the mechanics. 'Accelerator. Back breaks. Gears.' She flicked the pedal down, then lifted it back up until it slid into neutral. 'Aaaand,' she finally found the red switch, 'power!' The bike shuddered, rising off the ground. A holographic display flickered between the handlebars. There was a bird's eye view of the terrain and a flashing green blip.

'There!' Fedor's arm shot over her shoulder. 'That must be them!'

'Right.' Veronique cranked the accelerator. The engine roared. *Nikki, the Hoverbike racer!* She grinned. 'Let's go!'

The bike leapt forward, as smooth as a marble on glass.

'WOAH!' Fedor was flung back. Gripping the seat with his knees, he wrapped his arms around Veronique's waist. The bike sped out of the open gate, onto a dirty track and up into the mountains.

'Nooo!' Joe threw his head back and beat the air when his second bishop was marched from the board.

Ivan rolled the piece between forefinger and thumb.

Joe gave him a sour look. 'At least yours won't feel so left out! They've been off for quite some time now.'

Ivan's eyes narrowed. 'How's your queen doing, she seems hard pressed?'

'At least, I know how to use mine! Yours is cowering like a frightened maid. Do you need me to explain how she can move?'

Ivan muttered something rude in Russian.

Joe mimicked him in gobbledy gook.

'You're a childish little man,' Ivan said.

'TFS! You're down another rook BTW.' Joe snatched the piece off the board.

An agonised scream echoed around the castle.

Anatoly sat at the monitors in the security room trying to figure out just what the hell was going on. He turned off the alarm, which had been triggered by an energy signature in the north wing. Thermal and motion sensors found nothing. He switched to the standard CCTV and then located three intruders wearing what appeared to be Cold Suits.

No matter how smart you think you are, there's always some Mudak with a better plan...

Anatoly despised being outsmarted. Cold Suits were thermal cloaking devices, supposedly made from similar Nanothread to Inertia Dampening Armour. Neither motion nor heat sensors would detect them for the outer body temperature would be below the range of any surveillance system. The theory was sound, but he had never seen one assembled.

Very clever.

Had it not been for the discharge of a weapon, they would have gone undetected.

Well done, Fedor!

Anatoly located his brother and the Italian boy in the Den, still playing chess.

Typical!

Jenny was roaming the halls, no doubt looking for him. The monk appeared unconscious in the study and neither Sam nor their useless robot nanny were anywhere to be seen. The outer gate had been opened, his brother's Hoverbike was missing and now Fedor and the French girl appeared to be... Anatoly swore. 'And there it goes!' He lifted his hands in despair as the pair sped out of the courtyard on his favourite toy.

'I *hate* visitors!'

Nikki, the Racer, had the hang of it. Almost. The road zigzagged up the mountain, but her suicidal driving had closed the gap between them and the intruders, their dust hadn't yet settled on the track ahead. Fedor, legs cramping, scoured the area for signs of the other bike.

The higher they climbed, the cooler the air became and it was not long before they rode into the cloud level. The track crested a rise and flattened out. Not thirty metres in the distance, they saw the other Hoverbike fleeing down a grassy bank.

'Hang on.' Veronique leant forward, cranking the accelerator and grinning as the track entered the tree line and wound between and around the gnarled trunks.

The trees eventually thinned out and the terrain turned from ragged tufts to shale. The sun dipped behind the mountains and a thick fog began to roll in. They had lost sight of their quarry, but tracked them on the bike's panel.

'Nearly there,' Fedor shouted.

Veronique realised the green dot was no longer moving. The stationary bike suddenly appeared out of the gloom, wedged between two boulders.

'We're going to hit it!'

The front ski struck and they shot upward. Fedor's weight, his arms wrapped around her waist, saved Veronique, for it dragged them both from the handlebars. The bike looped into the air and came down with a crunch on top of a pile of rocks.

Still in his arms, Veronique heard the air rush from Fedor's lungs as they hit the ground and tumbled away from the two bikes.

He groaned, releasing her. Every bone in her body was aching.

Nikki, the Racer was officially retired. 'You okay?' she managed.

Nothing.

'Fedor?' She forced herself up. He was lying on his back, arms wrapped around his chest, his face screwed up.

'Oh no, not your ribs again?'

He nodded, his breath hissing between gritted teeth.

She looked around. Silence, save for the whistle of the wind. Then she heard voices, floating through the gloom.

'Fedor.' She wriggled closer. 'Can you stand? I can hear them, they're getting away.'

He opened his eyes and struggled up, one arm clutching his ribs. 'Which way?'

'Over there.'

He bent down to pick up a nasty-looking stick.

'Check!' Ivan hissed.

Joe moved his king.

'Check!'

Joe swore.

Ivan tutted. 'Ready to give up? Feel free to knock your king over at any time.'

Joe offered a pawn and Ivan took the bait, his queen swooping across the board.

Joe tried to hide his smile, when Ivan dangled the piece in front of him. *In three moves, you're mine!*

Fedor stumbled over the loose ground, fog and gloom hemming them in. Behind him, Veronique followed, eyes glued to the floor, hand knotted in his. Again, the voices carried over the wind to them, closer now, more urgent.

Veronique tripped, sending a shower of shale skittering down the ravine and Fedor closed his eyes. There was no chance they had not heard that.

'Sorry!' she whispered.

'It's okay,' he lied, through gritted teeth.

They caught another snippet of clipped conversation in earnest, frightened tones.

'We're close.' Fedor tightened his grip on the club, pushing Veronique back.

There was a flurry of words, a heated exchange; they could not be more than a few feet away. Drawing his arm back, he stepped around the boulder, ready to strike.

'Checkmate!' Joe pounced.

'No!'

The boy sat back in his chair and folded his hands behind his head as Ivan's eyes raced across the board.

'Don't beat yourself up.' Joe was magnanimous for once. 'You did say you'd only played a few times. I've been playing for years. You could be quite good with a bit of practice.'

Ivan felt his chest tighten and a sharp pain in his left arm.

Fedor prepared to deliver swift vengeance, but there was no one there, just a ledge and a drop into darkness. He thought he could make out a faint red line in the air, but it soon vanished.

He let the club fall. After five long seconds, he heard it clatter off the rocks. If they'd gone that way, they weren't alive anymore.

'Where are they?' Veronique tried to look past him.

'Gone.' He said nothing about the mysterious red line. Probably just spots in his vision from the latest in a long line of blows to the chest.

'Gone?' she scoffed. 'Where?'

The boy shrugged. 'I don't know, but there's no point hanging about here, it's getting dark and we don't want to get lost up here.'

They made their way back down the mountain. It was not long before a cold fog crept in, stealing every bit of warmth from their bodies.

'I can't go on.' Veronique stumbled. Adrenaline had carried her this far, but the day's events were catching up. Shaking, her limbs had turned to jelly.

Fedor stopped. 'Over there,' he said, pointing to an outcrop of rock. They huddled under the ledge, squinting out into the gloom.

'Are we lost?' Veronique dreaded the answer.

'Yup.'

'You think they'll find us?'

'We're tagged, remember that injection?'

'Didn't help Joe in the jungle...' Veronique's teeth clattered and she clamped her mouth shut.

Fedor glanced at the girl out of the corner of his eye. Her golden hair was plastered against her skull, her face drawn and pale. Veronique's thin arms were drawn around her knees and she was shaking, even though her fists gripped them tightly, trying to mask it.

He lifted his arm and wrapped it around her. She burrowed into him and moments later, her deep, even breathing signalled she was fast asleep.

Fedor bent to kiss the top of her head, then he, too, closed his eyes.

Chapter 22

S am found himself amid the familiar shelves of Theoretical Genetics, oblivious to the events about to unfold half a world away. Thankfully, the lights were dim and the passage quiet.

'Flic?' he ventured. 'FLIC! Nothing. He dared not wander around the archives by himself, so sat down.

The Navitium inhaler dug into his leg and he fished it out, trying to remember when he had last used it. His hands were steady as stone. No tremor. This was all so weird. His body was no longer his own, he now shared it with a billion tiny invaders. But, if they helped him do more, be more and most importantly make sure he did not fail this apprenticeship…well then maybe they weren't so bad. Pity they couldn't help him with the nightmares and cold sweats.

He heard a familiar hum. 'Flic?'

The engine halted and moments later the robot appeared. 'Sam! Where have you been? How are you feeling? Did the Navitium work?'

'Russia! With Ivan and Anatoly.'

Flic's nimbus dulled. 'Oh. Them. Don't pick up any bad habits. I've heard nothing good about that pair. Come to the office, it's still early and no one's about.'

Sam wondered if Flic had changed anything since Felicity Farnsworth had left The Royal Society, for the office was filled with priceless clutter. The walls were covered with mismatched photos and yellowed newspaper cuttings. Laboratory notes from some of the greatest discoveries in history were strewn about, forgotten.

Flic caught his gaze. 'That,' she pointed to a helix above him, 'is one of Watson and Crick's first diagrams of DNA. And over here,' she buzzed across to an elongated frame that held several pages of smudged Chinese writing, 'is Wu's methodology for perpetual motion. There are even some of Christopher Wren's Hidden Invention plans somewhere…'

'It's incredible... There are so many secrets and so much history locked away down here... Do you ever wonder whether the world would be a better place if it knew what was truly possible?'

She mulled it over. 'Humanity is not inherently good, nor logical, Sam. In fact, you're the only species that acts against its own self-interest. Until that changes, there will always be a need for us to exist.'

'I guess. Just seems a bit…extreme.'

'Extreme? The atom bomb was extreme. Agent Orange is extreme. No, Sam, we're not being extreme, we're simply realists.'

She was probably right. Anything new and exciting would be exploited. He could see how people were programmed to be greedy and dissatisfied.

The robot buzzed around the office, agitated, then settled at Sam's eye level. 'Now, your flute. It's a rather unique find. Let's just say it's not from around here.'

'From London?'

'From Earth.'

Sam gawped. 'Come again?'

'It's made of bone; at least I think it is. I ran loads of tests and its composition is organic but the DNA is unlike anything we have on record, and what's more, it seems to be made from several elements that don't exist in our periodic table.'

'Could you dumb that down please?'

'DNA is the code of instructions that controls how cells differentiate into tissues, organs, and limbs. It's arranged into pairs called chromosomes. The more chromosomes an organism has, the more complex the species is. Humans have twenty-three pairs of chromosomes. That piece of bone has forty-six.'

Sam blinked. He really needed to start paying more attention at school!

'What's even more fascinating are the elements that make up the bone. In humans, it's mainly calcium, phosphorous, sodium and some other minerals – that piece of bone has all of those, plus four more that do not exist in any scientific record. Which leads me to believe,' Flic put on her best Cowboy lilt, 'that it ain't from around these here parts, partner!'

'Woah!'

'Quite.' The robot agreed and continued her report. 'I then ran simulations of the chords and put the note you showed me through a synthesiser; neither test produced results. Therefore its effect must be connected to the way the bone material resonates with its shape. Consequently, all I have been able to create is a list of notes for you to try. But I must stress, Sam, I have no idea what they will do. Remember, the human body does not respond well to low level frequencies and the result could be irreparable soft tissue damage.'

Sam nodded. 'I'll be careful, I promise.' He put the paper into his pocket. 'Any luck with the rune?'

If a robot was capable of gloating, Flic would have oozed smug. 'Oh, yes. But it's bizarre. The rune is extremely old. Does the name *Hveðrungr* mean anything to you?'

Sam shook his head.

'How about Loki?'

Sam knew that name; Their Rhodesian Ridgeback in Africa had been named Loki, because he was always up to no good. 'The Norse god of mischief?'

'That's the one. They are the same.'

Sam gulped, and then a thought occurred to him. 'That couldn't have been his tomb...'

'The tomb is new information,' she flashed annoyance, 'but if you believe Norse legends, Loki is not dead, but chained, awaiting Ragnarok.'

Sam let out a low whistle. 'Wow, Flic, this is surreal. Alien bones, chained Gods, the end of the world… Are you sure?'

'I can only provide you with information. The flute is made of bone and unlike anything we have on record. The rune you drew is that of Hveðrungr, the Norse God Loki. Make of that what you will.'

Sam took a deep breath, letting it all sink in. 'Well, I'd better be getting back before anyone notices I'm gone, but you've done an amazing job, Flic; thank you sooo much!'

'You're welcome. Just remember what I said about that flute. Keep it safe and be careful.'

Sam nodded and put his hand into his pocket, feeling for the Krusa. 'I will!'

He stepped back into the castle bedroom, thankful to find neither Joe nor Fedor.

Sam put the flute and the list of chords under his pillow just before Jenny burst into the room, making him jump.

A look of relief and anger crossed her face when she saw him. 'Sam! Where've you been, didn't you hear the alarm?'

'I've been asleep. No breakfast, then all the poking and prodding. Just passed out.'

'Come with me. Jen Si's been attacked. Fedor and Veronique are missing!'

Sam's heart sank. 'What? How?' *The minute I turn my back!*

'Hurry up. I'll tell you on the way.'

Anatoly handed the monk a glass of water, while Ivan fetched a bag of frozen peas.

'I thought monks didn't feel pain?'

'I don't think being shot in the back with a Pulse weapon at close range was taken into consideration by whomever made that assertion,' Jen Si moaned. 'I've never felt anything like it. Every part of me feels bruised.'

'Pulse weapons are nasty, though I still don't understand how the first shot didn't set off the alarm. I must check the sensors in the study.' Anatoly chewed his lip then shook his head. 'It was one of Ivan's gifts, but you already knew that, didn't you?'

'You think we like watching over you? What would happen if one of Ivan's creations fell into the wrong hands? Those people today weren't after your silverware! We promised to look after your family hundreds of years ago. We found you this castle and we fund your extravagant lifestyle; neither is cheap. It's not just *your* curse anymore!'

The brothers had the good grace to look embarrassed.

'We protect *you* from being shot in the back over a piece of paper and prevent *him* being chained to a drawing board in some dungeon for the rest of his miserable life. For make no mistake, that's all they want.' He shook his head. 'But if you think we're here just to spoil your fun, confiscate your toys, deprive you of glory... Poor you...' He closed his eyes and turned the bag of peas over.

There was a moment of silence before Anatoly broke it, extending an olive branch. 'Well, it doesn't look like they took anything. Nothing missing from the study or library – the Antimatter plans are on the floor where you dropped them.'

'The only thing I can't find is Popov,' Ivan laughed. 'He's probably hiding under my bed.'

Jen Si's face drained of what little colour it had. 'Find him! Find him now!'

'The robot? What about the kids up on the mountain?'

At that moment, Jenny and Sam hurried into the room.

'*The robot*!' Jen Si roared. 'They don't need any plans if they have the robot – they have your entire library and study in one! Ours too, given my recent run of luck! You take care of your business, and we'll take care of ours. Just find that bloody robot, *now*!'

Fedor's chin drooped again and he woke with a start. He was cold and sore, damaged ribs jarring with every breath. He peered into the gloom. No light, no sound. It seemed no one was coming to save them. He tried to relieve his cramp without waking Veronique.

He peered down at the girl still curled up beside him, head buried in his chest, arms wrapped around him. He had still not forgiven her for humiliating him with the Lanelia pellet but at least no one else knew about it.

She stirred, eyes fluttering open. 'Where?' Then she groaned. 'We're still here.'

'Yep.'

Veronique tried to burrow further under his arm. 'I'm so cold.'

There was a crunch of feet, followed by cursing as someone lost their footing. Moments later, a bright light shone into their eyes.

'Oooh,' a familiar voice cooed, 'very cosy! Is this a private sleepover or can anyone join? Come on, scooch up – room for a little one?'

Fedor had never thought he'd be so glad to hear Joe's voice.

Anatoly tended to Fedor's ribs.

'Just badly bruised. A good night's sleep and a few doses of the monk's mysterious tonic should see you right.

'You might want to self-medicate with the old tonic, too,' he gave Jen Si a pointed look. 'You're no picture of health, either.'

'I'll take it under advice. Where are we with the robot?'

There was still no sign of Troy.

'Gone. I've checked the security system and Ivan has walked our meagre dwelling from top to bottom. Nothing.'

'I was afraid of that,' Jen Si said. 'I think you better brace yourself for some more visitors.'

Anatoly groaned.

'Go on.' Joe sat on the edge of Fedor's bed, legs jiggling. 'Tell us everything!'

'Can't it wait?' Fedor wanted to rest, not answer hundreds of questions. 'Besides,' he said, tilting his head to the adjacent bed, 'Veronique did the hard work, it's her story to tell.'

'Oh, thanks!'

'Really?' Joe's attention switched to Veronique. 'The dashing heroine, was it?'

'Ha, ha.'

'Mad woman, more like,' Fedor said managing a weak smile.

'At least I had the guts to try!'

'Woah, *devotchka*!' Fedor patted her hand. 'I'm just teasing, you were brilliant.'

'Really?' she asked.

He nodded.

'Okaaay.' Sam felt a tad uncomfortable. 'Is someone going to spill the beans or do the married couple want some privacy?'

'What?'

'Huh?' Fedor snatched his hand back and Veronique looked away.

Joe and Sam laughed.

After a late breakfast they retired to the lounge and Sam flopped into the deep cushioned sofa with a grateful sigh.

'So, the good news,' Anatoly said, 'is that I managed to slow the metabolic rate of Sam's Femtoglobin. I take it you've not needed the inhaler since yesterday?'

'Nope.'

Joe patted him on the back. 'That's good news!'

'What about the other…side effects?' Fedor asked, trying to shift his weight so that the ache in his ribs was bearable.

Sam noticed Anatoly's puzzled look. 'Oh, nothing,' he jumped in, not wishing to go down the whole 'can't bleed, won't age' road.

Fedor shrugged, confused.

'Tribes?' Joe asked, taking out the board. 'Not you,' he snubbed Ivan, when the man sat up, eyes bright. 'Your game language is not fit for civilised company.'

'Aw! I'll be good. We can even play for money if you like?'

'Still here,' Jenny called, not looking up from her magazine.

'Only joking,' Ivan laughed nervously, mouthing to Joe *'I'm not.'*

When Jen Si entered the room, flanked by two hulking shadows, the group huddled around the Tribes board did not notice. Ivan's promise to keep the game clean had lasted all of five minutes and Veronique had joined Jenny on the other side of the room after his first foul-mouthed tirade.

'Well, well, well, ain't this cosy?'

Sam recognised the tone and looked up. Greeves loomed over them.

'Little Van Sandt! Trouble sticks to you lot like glue, doesn't it?' His piggy eyes landed on Joe. 'And a royal, too. The little Lord himself! I'm surprised you can stand to be in the same room as a Van Sandt, given the family history.'

Joe looked at Sam, who raised his eyebrows and shrugged. 'What are you talking about? Who are you?' His eyes flicked back to the board when he caught Ivan's nimble fingers moving. 'Oi you, none of that!' Ivan muttered something unintelligible but withdrew the offending hand.

Greeves smiled cruelly. 'Someone who knew your father...'

The board was instantly forgotten and Joe looked up.

'My father?'

'That's enough!' Jen Si snapped before Greeves could do any more damage. 'Find that robot before the Council knows it's missing, or *your* father will be mourning a son!'

Greeves glared down at the monk. 'Which one had contact with them?'

Fedor got up. 'Me.'

Greeves looked Fedor up and down with a sneer. 'Let them get away, big boy like you?'

'If they got away,' his companion spoke for the first time, 'it won't be because my brother let them.' He inclined his head. 'Fedor.'

'Karl.'

Neither broke the faintest smile.

Sam listened, as Karl spoke to his brother in Russian, ignoring Greeves. Fedor gave short, factual answers to which his brother reacted with curt nods.

The Russian guard then turned to his companion. 'There were three of them. Probably Harbinger. One was armed with a Pulse rod by the sound of it, and another was carrying a bag. The one with the Pulse rod activated a Turner, the other two fled into the mountains. My brother and his companion lost their trail over a cliff, so I think it's safe to assume they found another way to Turn and are in possession of the robot. We must ensure all its connections to the Cube are severed and set up Ping traps in case they try to use its CPU to access the network.'

'You can access the Cube from my lab,' Anatoly offered.

'Thank you.' Karl spoke briefly to his brother then nodded to the rest of the group. 'Thank you for your time.'

Without allowing Greeves the opportunity to dip his poisoned spoon back into the pot, they left. The guard still managed one last sneer.

'What an utter bastard.' Sam spat.

'Tell me about it,' Joe agreed. 'And what the hell was he going on about? What family history?'

Sam shrugged. 'It's probably nothing. I think he just likes to put his boot in. He was awful to my Dad when I first met him. Why did he call you a royal?'

Joe shrugged evasively.

'If you really want to rile him,' Ivan did not look up from the board, 'just call him Purple Pirate – he hates that!'

'Why?'

'His nose – didn't you see it? Looks a like a ripe turnip.'

They all laughed.

Sam turned to Fedor. 'Dude, your brother is *huge*!'

'Did you hear what they said?' Joe asked. 'Harbinger! It could be the people Selina said were after the Dark Mods—'

'Right.' Jenny cut in, Veronique in tow. 'I think we've outstayed our welcome, boys. Time to pack.'

'Aw?' They were all disappointed by the news, and none more so than Ivan, – until Joe plopped a cunning tribesman on the board in front of him and converted a horde of his tribe. Ivan swore, flipped the board over and stormed out.

'And not a moment too soon.' Jenny concluded, as tribesmen flew far and wide.

Ivan handed Joe a black plastic tube the size of a torch. 'Here.'

The boy looked up. He sat on a stool at the kitchen table savouring a glass of warm milk. He was packed and ready to leave. 'Um, thank you?'

'Open it.'

Joe turned the tube over in his hands, tapping carefully then sniffing it.

'It's not ticking!' Ivan sighed, shifting his weight. 'Here.' He snatched the gift back and pulled it apart. The cover slid off, revealing a short cylinder with four spindly arms. Ivan pressed a button on the base and placed it on the countertop with the four arms pointing upward. They immediately sprang to life, opening like a flower until they were horizontal with the table, forming a cross shape above the base. The arms then began to extend until they had each doubled in size. Hundreds of tiny LED lights began to glow around the tube.

'Ready?' Ivan grinned, seeing the sheer bewilderment in Joe's face.

The boy hunched closer to the table, brow creased. 'What is it?'

'This is *my* only invention. Well, my only idea – Anatoly made it. It's not something I dreamt up, it's all me. I call it *iTribes*'.

A well-timed burst of music came from the base of the peculiar contraption and the hundreds of tiny LED bulbs erupted into life.

Joe squinted, and to his amazement a three-dimensional board appeared.

'It's a 3D, holographic Tribes board.' Ivan beamed taking a seat opposite Joe. 'Fully interactive with over one hundred animated and customisable tribes. There are fifty battlegrounds complete with active scenery, character fatalities, Kamikaze moves and even an online mode. It's going to revolutionise strategy gaming!'

'Oh…My…*God*!' Joe could not remember being this excited in his entire life.

'I know!' Ivan jiggled.

'Background music, sound effects when they fight, Tribal chants and war cries during the game, volcanoes, earthquakes, pirates, booby trapped squares! Not only do you have your opponent to worry about, but the landscape too, adding a whole new dimension to the peril. It's so life-like, you feel like you're there. The board's sensors detect and respond to movement, so you can pick and move pieces as though they were real.'

'*Sssht*!' Joe held up his hands. 'Enough chatter!' He pointed to the board with both hands. 'Let's play!'

Ivan roared with laughter. 'I thought you'd never ask!'

Three hotly waged wars later Joe's Warrior Trolls had decimated Ivan's Amazonians on a volcanic island, lava having reduced half the board to magma-encrusted statues within minutes of the opening war cries.

Ivan's Flying Monkeys had then narrowly defeated Joe's Medieval Knights on a treacherous iceberg whilst Orcas and killer penguins leapt from the frozen depths to drag unsuspecting tribesmen to their doom.

There were even pitiful bubbles, from the hapless souls who were pulled beneath the waves!

The best-of-three marathon ended with a feverish encounter over the scorching dunes of Egypt, Ivan's Masai Warriors taking on Joe's Navaho Indians, whilst giant scorpions, moaning mummies and blinding sandstorms added agonising complexity to an already fearsome battle.

'Yes!' Joe flopped back in his chair and turned to Ivan, 'Wow – you've broken the mould. This is next level gaming. I'm very jealous.'

'You don't have to be,' the man smiled. 'It's yours.'

Joe's eyes widened.

'How else are we meant to continue these delightful little contests when you're on the other side of the world? It's not every day one comes across such a worthy adversary.'

'I can't…' Joe lamented. 'It's too much.'

'Nonsense. Anatoly will whip me up a new one in no time and then we can use the Virtual Reality headsets.'

Joe extended his hand through the hologram. 'It's incredible, thank you!'

Ivan shook it warmly. 'Don't thank me yet – you'll be pulling your hair out, when I whip your skinny ass from one side of the world to the other!' he laughed.

* * *

Ms Keller tapped her perfect nails against the glass. 'Hellooo?' she cooed.

On the other side, the shutters on a pair of robotic eyes flickered. Troy looked around, his nimbus a confused purple.

'Ah, you're awake.' Ms Keller smiled disingenuously, taking her seat. Crossing her legs and arranging the pencil skirt over her knees, she tapped the tall glass box with the tip of her stiletto, picking at a thread in her fishnet stockings, while the little robot took in its surroundings.

'Apologies for the theatrics,' she lied. 'But we were not expecting you to have guests at the castle. We'd hoped to breeze in and out, without so much as a whisper, but best laid plans and all that.'

'I'm of no use to you.' Troy realised there was only one fate ahead of him and there was no point in stalling it; he was suspended by two Perspex bars and his levitation motor had been cut. Several wires were now connected to his auxiliary communications ports.

'I have no access to data files, only my logic chip and basic short-term memory reside locally. None of these retain useful information.'

'No access at all, you say? How does that work?' Ms Keller was intrigued. 'Are you telling me you remember nothing?'

'No.' Troy saw no reason for subterfuge. 'I remember everything, however the detail is absent.'

'I see. Very clever. Well, it's a good thing we're not after any of your data then, isn't it?'

Troy was confused. 'You don't want the plans?'

Ms Keller enjoyed prey struggling in her net, particularly the moment when they realised they did not, in fact, possess the upper hand. 'The plans sound most intriguing, but no, it's your master I want'

'Ivan?' That name, at least, was still in his short-term memory.

Ms Keller smiled. 'No, Archimedes, your real master.' Oh, yes,' she chuckled, ruby red lips inches from the glass. 'We know who you are Archimedes, and you're going to help us find what we're looking for.'

The robot's face would have paled were he human. Archimedes felt a jolt of electricity as the wires in his communications port sprang to life, viral code oozing into him like hot lava. 'No,' he managed, before his CPU was overrun. Then his Heads-Up-Display flickered and died.

Chapter 23

Veronique was in heaven.

The battered group had been allowed to recuperate on the sun-drenched shores of Fiji, with little more to do than swim, eat and sleep, and it was just perfect. She rolled over, the warm afternoon rays caressing her back, the soothing sound of waves lapping the shore. Eyes closed, she dozed.

Joe, on the other hand, was bored. He was not a sun worshipper or even beach lover and was beginning to feel claustrophobic holed up beneath the thatched pagoda. But he was at least surrounded by a mountain of fresh books, although his request for reading material on Harbinger Robotics and Dark Mods had been studiously ignored. Neither Jen Si nor Jenny could be drawn into conversation about them.

He looked over the hefty tome he was absorbing, snatching his third glance in as many minutes at Veronique's bikini clad form. Her skin had tanned in the unrelenting Pacific sun and she positively gleamed. There were definitely some benefits to his current situation. He returned to the exquisitely detailed account of 'Medieval Siege Engines and other Weapons of War' with a contented sigh.

Fedor's ribs were on the mend at last. He had begun stretching and strengthening the area as soon as the strappings were removed, using a blend of isometric and improvised exercises. From his position near the tree line, where he hung from a branch, he could not help emulating Joe's admiration of Veronique in her bathing suit. They'd not spent much time together since their adventure on the mountain but he found himself thinking about her more and more.

She turned over, eyes opening for an instant and fluttering in his direction. He quickly looked away. *No good will come of this.*

Closing his eyes, Fedor took a deep breath and continued his exercises, determined not to return home in worse shape than he had left

Sam felt sunburned. Years of living in an English climate had lulled him into a false sense of security regarding its bite, for he had failed to take Jenny's miracle sunscreen pill when returning from his brief visit home.

His family had been ecstatic to see him, even Chloe had fussed more than usual. For the first time since Sophie's death, *Arthur's Rest* had felt like home again.

His mother had given him the envelope found behind the dresser, but he'd put it away and forgotten about it before he left again.

Lying under an umbrella, sandwiched between a snoring Jenny and a drooling Veronique, Sam waded through *The Art of War*.

'You coming in?' Fedor asked him.

Sam noticed Veronique open an eye, following the progress of the boy's bare chest and broad shoulders toward the waves.

'Going to order off the menu?' Sam could not help himself.

Her eye slammed shut and his comment was rebuffed by indignant silence. Sam smirked, dumping a handful of sand into the small of her back as he got to his feet and raced for the water, a string of foul language hot on his heels.

A loud bang shook the air, making Joe jump. Jenny snorted awake and lifted the rim of her hat. 'Huh? Did someone call me?' The group in the water stopped playing and looked around.

The next bang was louder and followed by the sound of splitting wood. It was coming from the trees. Jenny sat up and the others came over.

'What is that?' Veronique asked, wrapping herself in a towel.

'I'm not sure.' Jenny slipped on her sandals. 'Let's go have a look.'

Another boom. The palm trees shook.

'Look out for falling coconuts,' Joe advised, peering heavenward. 'They kill more people than sharks.'

Fedor raised an eyebrow, but nonetheless proceeded with caution.

They could hear a buzzing now, like the low hum of electricity. Sam thought he could make out a shimmering blue light.

'Get behind me,' Jenny ordered. She took another step and pushed back the vegetation to expose a small clearing. Broken palms and piles of coconuts lay scattered between smouldering tree stumps. In the centre of the carnage stood a large man, stripped to his waist and sweating profusely. His fists were clenched and the muscles on his chest and shoulders were bulging. His arms shimmered and crackled with electricity.

'Jonathan!' Jenny gasped.

The man, who was clearly not expecting visitors, let out an undignified shriek. 'MacLeod!' He gasped, 'What on earth are you doing here?'

'I could ask you the same thing! And what the hell are those?'

Jonathan lifted his arms and beamed at his charged palms. 'Ah, these babies are my pride and joy. Electric Eel Mod. Cool, huh? We'll see who gets the last laugh at CruciBowl this year!'

Jenny sighed and rolled her eyes.

Jonathan Schultz, Tec to his friends, was a bit of a monster.

'He could eat me in one gulp,' Joe whispered to Sam, who nodded in awe. They were sitting around the fire on the beach. The sea and sky were a mixture of reds and purples and a gentle breeze rippled through the remaining palm trees.

Tec was a Juggernaut. Like the teenagers, he and his cadre, The Madrigals, had come to Fiji for a few days' rest. Jenny had left her team in his care while she visited their island.

'A match at the CruciBowl, eh?' he said, when Veronique told him how their summer was going to end – if all went smoothly. 'That ought to be fun. I've got a big grudge match of my own coming up then, too.'

'Could you tell us more about the competition?' Joe asked. 'What is it?'

'It's held during The Inventors Fair, in an old volcano called the Crucible, a bit of a savage place, I won't lie. But the contest allows the Cadres to blow off a little steam, test ourselves against other teams and show off our new Mods.'

Joe nodded towards the trees. 'Hence the lumberjacking?'

Tec chuckled. 'Yup. That's one potent Mod. Takes up a lot of juice though. I'm wrecked! But I needed to see what I could do with it.'

'You have a grudge match?' Fedor reminded him, curious.

'Well, there 'some bad blood between us and a cadre called The Tinkers. Goes right back to our Induction, and then last year, Tiny Tim, their Juggernaut, used the Ultimate Insult on me during a Cathedral match, which was the last straw, so I'm out for some payback.'

'The Ultimate insult?'

'Cathedral match?' Veronique and Joe spoke at once.

Sam laughed. 'Sorry, we have enquiring minds.'

'No stress,' Tec rolled his neck and shoulders. 'The Ultimate Insult is a pulse grenade that messes with your nervous system. You lose control of your upper body and it makes you run around like a headless chicken.

'The Cathedral is one of the arenas we use for Quest matches. It's a big old church, loads of stairs and places to hide. But I don't want to spoil the surprise. If you've never been to CruciBowl before, you're in for a wild ride!'

'I wonder why they call him Tec?' Joe murmured to Sam.

'Feel free to ask,' Sam said, 'but you'd better be quick, I think he's nearly asleep.'

Sure enough, Tec, who had been leaning further and further back as they lounged around the fire, was now completely horizontal. His giant head flopped on to Fedor's thigh and he began to snore loudly.

'Aw,' Sam smiled and winked. 'How cute. you've made a friend.'

Veronique giggled and Fedor rolled his eyes, giving Sam the finger.

'Well now,' Sam feigned indignation. 'There's no need to be rude!'

Their holiday was over all too soon. The five intrepid explorers now stood at the base of another mountain, backpacks hooked under thumbs, to take the weight off their sun-kissed shoulders.

'That's a lot of steps!' Joe whimpered, his pack all the heavier for the final armful of books he had rammed in.

Cut into the hillside by hands long since returned to the earth, Sam followed the line of worn stone steps that rose out of sight. 'Always with the steps – can't we just *whoosh*,' he made a disappearing motion with his hand, 'to the top?'

Jenny stopped. 'No. Master Ono doesn't permit any *whooshing*.'

'Are you coming?' Sam asked, noticing Jenny's pack was missing.

'Nope, this is as far as I go. Master Ono disowned me when the Council approved my recommendation to teach Krav Maga.'

'Good style,' Fedor nodded. 'Nearly as good as Sambo.'

'Nevertheless,' Jenny continued, 'you're on your own from here. Try not to rile him, he's an evil old bastard when he wants to be. Jen Si will check in on you in a few days, try to not get into too much trouble before then.'

'I'll keep an eye on them,' Veronique offered.

'Some more than others.' Sam grinned.

Veronique glared back.

'Right!' Jenny gave Joe's bulging backpack a shove toward the steps before the bickering broke out. 'Remember to be polite and do as you're told – Master Ono is the best martial arts teacher there is and you're very lucky to be studying under him, even if it is only for a few weeks.'

'Bye, Mum!' Sam waved, falling in behind Joe. 'Do you really need all those books?' He watched the smaller boy wobble slightly on the steps under the weight of his pack. 'It's too much, you know; you look a bit like a turtle. Come on, Donatello, pick up the pace!' Joe swore back at him, which made Sam chuckle more.

A tiring hour or two later, the steps ended in a small, sun-soaked escarpment.

'My legs will never work again,' Joe moaned, collapsing on the ground.

'Pity the same can't be said about your mouth,' Fedor muttered.

'Nice!'

They lay in silence for several minutes. Sam folded his arms over his eyes, listening to the birds and the gentle wash of the wind.

'*Nani ga hoshii desu ka*?' a voice barked.

Fedor shrugged off his backpack and was on his feet in seconds.

A group of boys, around their age and dressed in dojo attire, stood on the path ahead of them, the tips of their long fighting sticks resting on the ground. They uttered another challenge in Japanese.

'What did they say?' Veronique asked Joe.

'Don't look at me,' he shrugged. 'All I caught was '*baka*' and '*gaijin*'.'

'And they mean?'

'Um, stupid and foreigner.'

Sam laughed, rising to his feet. *Seems as good a time as any, to test the old super blood.*

'Hi!' he gave the welcome party a wave. 'I'm Sam and these are my band mates, Veronique, Fedor and Turtle.'

'*Samuel!*' Veronique chided.

'Sorry, Joe! I meant Joe.' His friend was shooting daggers at him. 'we're looking for Master Ono?'

The boys exchanged a flurry of sharp words.

'Anything that time?' Sam looked at Joe.

The boy decided not to translate the less than friendly exchange. 'Nothing nice.'

'I see.'

'What do you want with Master Ono?' the leader demanded.

'Well, now,' Sam was battling to remain cordial, 'that would be between him and us.'

The boy laughed and moved forward. 'Well, now, it's between you...' he spread his hands, '...and us.'

'Careful.' Sam's hand slid into his pocket, fingers brushing the smooth surface of the bone flute. 'We have a particularly nasty Russian and are not afraid to use him.'

Fedor stepped forward, snapping his head and neck from side to side. Sam watched as he raised one hand and crooked his fingers in a beckoning motion.

The Japanese boy raised a scornful eyebrow. 'Do you always make someone else to fight your battles?'

'Battles?' Sam smiled broadly. 'Trust me, this is no battle. I just know how cranky my friend gets without a little exercise. I'm doing us all a favour in the long run.'

'He's right.' Joe nodded, safely behind Sam. 'Very crabby. But just to make things fair, shouldn't we wait till more of your friends arrive? There's only four of you...'

'Oh, and no one you're terribly fond of,' Veronique added, scrunching up her nose. 'He does get a little carried away,' she finished, in a perfect copy of the Japanese boy's accent.

Fedor was getting impatient. 'You're boring me. Talk or fight?'

The boy nodded, smiling. 'Oh, I choose fight.' He eased into his stance, inclining his head toward Fedor with the faintest of bows.

Fedor returned the bow, sliding onto the balls of his feet; knuckles rising to either side of his temple, he lowered his head. 'I was hoping you'd say that...'

'*Enough!*' a woman barked, striding into the clearing. 'Hirohito, is this how we welcome guests?' She slapped the youngster across the back of the head. 'Get back to the house now, all of you – and pray I don't tell your grandfather about this! He'll have you practising Horse Stance in front of the White Wall for days!'

The boys exchanged worried glances before melting back, eyes downcast, bowing. Only Hirohito did not move, his face red.

'*Hiro*!' the woman said. 'Home – *now*!'

'Next time, it'll be just you and me, *gaijin*. No *daiki* in the way.' The boy glared at Fedor, then turned to leave.

Sam blew Hiro a kiss. 'Wear something pretty!'

The boy hissed and started forward, but the woman's arm shot out. 'Enough, I said – and that goes for you, too!'

Sam's face was granite. 'I don't like my friends being threatened.'

'It's no threat, *gaijin*,' Hiro hissed as he backed away. 'It's a promise.'

The woman launched into Japanese, waving her arm and spitting like a cobra. She then took a deep breath and favoured them with a strained smile. 'I must apologise for my son. He is most protective of our home. The woman beamed. '*Konnichiwa.* I'm Yuki, Master Ono's daughter.'

'I'm Joe.' Joe staggered past Sam and almost tripped when attempting a formal bow. '*Konnichiwa.*'

'*Bon jour*,' Veronique smiled, bowing. 'I'm Veronique – you've met Sam,' she pointed, 'and that's Fedor.'

Yuki bowed to each in turn. 'Please, come this way. Let's get you settled before you meet my father.'

'What's a *Daiki*?' Fedor asked Joe, as they followed the woman toward the homestead.

'Um, I think it means "big tree"?'

'Ah! Well, I've been called far worse.'

'Hard to imagine.' Joe laughed.

The family home of the Ono clan was magnificent. The house, *Dojo*, stables and yard had nestled in the sprawling grounds for over a thousand years. Though parts of it had been rebuilt over the centuries, many of its original features had been preserved. Stately trees dotted the lawns and willows draped delicate limbs into pretty streams. The outer wall and sturdy gate were high and foreboding, however, once inside the perimeter, the graceful landscaping and intricate gardens exuded tranquillity and understated grandeur.

They reached the main house by crossing an elegant arched bridge. Bamboo chimes and ornate cages teeming with coloured songbirds swung from the eaves.

Sharp shouts from the training ground and the clash of wooden swords were the only disturbances to an otherwise peaceful afternoon.

'This way.' Yuki showed them to a long, narrow building next to the main house. 'This is where you will be staying.' Taking off her shoes at the door and sliding her feet into a pair of slippers she motioned for them to do the same.

The corridor was lined with *shoji* – sliding walls made from wood and paper. Yuki slid open the first, offering the room to Veronique. 'The bathroom is at the end of the hall. You'll find *karategi*-' she stopped, noticing the confused looks. '*Karategi*, or 'gi' are training clothes. I've placed some in your rooms. Please change and meet me outside.' Bowing, she shuffled back down the corridor, leaving the boys to find their rooms alone.

'My door has no lock!'

Sam watched Veronique rattle the flimsy portal. 'Well, you'd better hope no one gets confused, then.' Fedor said nothing and disappeared into his room, undressing as he went.

Joe poked the screen, chewing his lip. 'Hardly secure, or fireproof.'

'Come on then.' Sam stripped off. 'I've always wanted to meet Mister Miyagi!'

Master Ono was as far from the movie stereotype Kung Fu master as one could be. Long of limb, broad-shouldered with jet-black hair and a neat moustache, the Grand Master sat before a squat table, hands hidden in his sleeves.

'Grandfather?' Sam whispered to Veronique, when they followed Yuki onto a wide veranda. 'He looks younger than my dad!'

Veronique said nothing, for a steely pair of eyes had shot in their direction.

Yuki bowed then spoke briefly to her father in Japanese. He grunted and nodded toward the door. Bowing again, she took her leave.

'Why are you here?' Master Ono's voice was deep and calm.

The group exchanged sidelong looks.

'We are here to learn, Master,' Fedor answered, emulating Yuki's humble manner. He even looked at the floor when he spoke.

If Master Ono was pleased with the response, he did not show it. 'And what is it you are here to learn?'

'How to listen and obey, Master.' The responses rolled off the boy's tongue.

'Do you always speak for them?' His stern gaze flickered over the rest of the group.

'No, Master.'

'Good, then let them answer. What makes a good fighter?'

A dozen flippant responses sprang to Sam's mind, but Joe picked up the conch before he could put his foot into his mouth.

'A calm mind?' The boy fidgeted with his glasses, daring to look up for a moment. He'd read well over a dozen books and manuals on the martial arts. 'Mind over matter' was a recurring theme through the dogma, regardless of the author or origin.

Master Ono nodded again.

'You,' he pointed at Sam, 'what's the best form of defence?'

Sam made a concerted effort not to look at the man. He should've spent more time studying and less admiring Veronique's bikini. 'Well, I'm sure there's a better way to put it,' his eyes found an odd shaped floorboard, 'but not being in the way tends to work for me.'

Master Ono actually smiled. It was not the laconic, worn response he usually got. The sandy-haired boy was battling to suppress a confident demeanour. Jaw clenched, fingers curling and unfurling, he clearly fought to keep his gaze lowered.

'And you,' he shifted his attention to Veronique, 'when is the best time to fight?'

Nikki, the Ninja knows the answer to this one. She smiled inwardly, her alter ego suiting up. 'The moment before your enemy knows they're going to attack…. Master,' she added, after a pause.

Bugger! Sam kicked himself. *Knew I'd forgotten something!*

Master Ono motioned to the cushions around the table. 'Please, sit.'

Yuki returned with tea, setting it down before her father.

'What are your names?' their host enquired, lifting the lid of the pot and peering inside. Drawing his long sleeve back with a practised motion, the Master lifted the teapot and poured the green liquid into their cups. 'Please, drink.'

Sam burnt his tongue. Fedor did the same. Veronique displayed perfect form. Shoulders straight, back arched and arms tucked at her sides, she allowed the infusion to trickle down her throat.

Nikki, the Geisha!

'*Bugei Juhappan*,' Master Ono gazed into the steam, 'is the Japanese term that refers to the eighteen skills studied by *Bushi* – the warrior. It takes a lifetime to understand and master these skills, so what they expect me to teach you in two weeks, I'm not entirely sure. That said, a house is only as good as its foundation, so that's where we'll start. Tomorrow, my daughter will begin your training. If I do not like what I see, you will be asked to leave. Is that clear?'

They nodded.

'Good. Now tell me a little about yourselves.'

Master Ono proved to be a lively conversationalist, though Sam saw his face darken when he heard about Hiro's welcome, and he reiterated his daughter's apology for the lack of civility. Mention of Jenny did little to endear themselves to him either, and Fedor swiftly offered a diversion from Joe's question by asking about the use of pressure points in modern tournament fighting.

'It's funny you should mention that.' Master Ono stretched. 'It's a subject we'll focus on during your time here. The study of pressure points forms the basis for much of the Three Rules.'

'What are they?' Sam asked.

Joe squirmed because he already knew and was trying not to share too much.

Master Ono tried to conceal his smile and held up a finger. 'Can't see, cannot fight. Can't stand, cannot fight. Can't breathe,' he tapped his chest, 'cannot fight. There are many ways to use all or some of them. The easiest is, don't be seen. You seldom have to fight someone who doesn't know you are there.'

'I like the sound of that one,' Joe agreed.

'You would.' Fedor winked. 'Pity you can't find a real turtle shell to hide in.'

'Hey! I'm not a muscle-bound behemoth like you, so excuse me if I seek a less confrontational route to achieve my goal.'

Master Ono nodded. 'Exactly. Embrace your strengths. Outwit your opponent. And if you must fight, then do so as swiftly as possible. And, as an old friend loved to tell me, never leave an enemy at your back. Speed, agility and strength are just as important as stealth, guile and cunning.'

Joe felt confident for the first time since leaving Lake Como. He might not be big or fast, but just one afternoon with Master Ono had made him realise that courage and intelligence could be just as useful.

They finished their meal and retired to recharge for the next day.

Alone in his room, Sam was feeling homesick. The brief trip home had made him realise just how much he missed his family and how many questions he had for his parents.

What was their link to The Order?

Why had they kept it a secret from him?

Why did Greeves hate his father and what 'family history' did they share with Joe's?

Did they know anything about Harbinger Robotics? Or worse, had Harbinger had something to do with Sophie's death?!

Time had been short and he was still processing most of it. There was also so much he was dying to tell them, about the Krusa, the flute, his accident and the Femtoglobin, but Mr D'Angelo had advised against telling them anything and that had made Sam feel even more isolated. It had felt more like a warning than any advice.

There was something very 'off' about D'Angelo. Sam didn't trust him, and would certainly not be telling *him* about the flute. That was one secret best kept to himself and his friends for now. He had to remain focused on making sure he did not fail them or this training. He felt more and more responsible for them every day.

Fedor finished his shower with a blast of icy water. Wrapping a towel around his waist, he picked up his clothes as Veronique rounded the corner and walked into him with a solid *thump.*

'*Merde!*' she swore, nose and lips crushed against his damp chest.

Fedor struggled to keep his makeshift loincloth in place and Veronique stepped back only slightly, looking at the boy with an amused smile.

'Sorry,' he muttered. Their eyes met and he was not sure why she had not yet moved.

'Why?' Her voice was soft.

'I was just heading…back to the…' The words became a tangled mess, his mouth dry and useless. Veronique's proximity was very distracting, he could smell her freshly-washed hair, fruity and inviting, her face cream smelt of oatmeal and her lips... Fedor's breathing became more laboured and his head began bending toward hers. Veronique's chin inclined ever so slightly, lids dropping, as she stretched toward him.

Then Fedor felt a stab of panic and began to back away, but her arms snaked around him, one at his waist, the other around his neck, her fingers locking into his hair.

'Oh no,' she breathed, bringing up her lips to meet his. 'You're not getting away this time!'

With a triumphant sigh, *Nikki, the Temptress* claimed her prize.

Chapter 24

There was good news and bad news the next morning.

The good news was that their first exercises were familiar. Yuki followed the same Tai Chi drills they'd been taught by the monks. The bad news was that Hiro and his buddies were to be their classmates. Sam and Fedor glowered at the group when they entered and took up positions at the front of the class.

Once they were warmed up, Yuki guided them through some new moves. As they practised in groups, the Japanese boys whispered amongst themselves, snatching snickering glances over their shoulders, as Sam, Veronique and Joe wobbled around.

Master Ono sat on the balcony, cup in hand, watching them, and a sharp word brought their mockery to a swift end.

Yuki followed the group's every move with a practised eye, her skilled hands repositioning limbs and movements as they tried to repeat the simple Kata she demonstrated.

Sam heard another command issued from above the training ground and Yuki bowed, disappearing into the house.

'What did he say?' Sam whispered to Joe, who shrugged, trying not to lose his balance.

'He said you have flat feet,' Hiro hissed. 'You stamp more than a bull.'

'Well, at least we don't eat our pets,' Sam threw the first offensive thing that came to mind at him, conscious of the watchful eyes above them.

'*What*?' Hiro was outraged, as Sam intended.

'I think you're confusing your racial stereotypes,' Joe whispered.

Sam glanced up very briefly and Joe backed off, realising what his friend was trying to do. It was a cunning move, but could succeed in separating them from the hostile group of boys.

'How *do* you prepare Chihuahua – shall I ask your mum?' Sam asked sweetly

Hiro whirled, screaming in Japanese.

'*HIROHITO!*' Master Ono roared, rising to his feet, tea flying over the railing.

Hiro paled. He saw the smirk spread across Sam's face and realised that he had taken the outrageous bait. Clenching his jaw, he looked up as a blistering tirade of abuse rained down upon him. The chastisement continued for a full minute, ending with Master Ono pointing toward a white wall. Hiro bowed and followed his instruction. Facing the wall, he freed the fabric of his Gi and settled into an uncomfortable looking squat, his thighs parallel to the ground, fists drawn into his sides.

'Horse stance,' Fedor said. 'Very hard to maintain. Tough punishment.'

'Good.' Sam said, without remorse.

'Continue!' Master Ono barked.

Yuki returned with a bowl of uncooked rice and a roll of tape.

'FFS, this doesn't look good.' Joe cocked an eyebrow. She tore off long strips of tape and laid them on the ground, pouring the hard rice on to the sticky surface.

Fedor winced. 'Rice sandals.'

'Please, be seated,' Yuki said to the back row. The front line grinned, continuing to weave through the Kata.

'Speed and balance are very important,' she explained, crouching down in front of Sam and sticking a long strip of tape to the side of his ankle. 'To achieve this, fighters must be light on their feet.' She ran the tape down the side of his leg and under his foot, so that the hard grains of rice were taped to his heel. She added several more. 'This will help you stay on the balls of your feet, which is how a fighter must always stand.' She wound the roll around his ankle several times. 'Please, stand.'

Sam winced when his heel touched the ground and the rice dug into his soft skin.

'You see?' Yuki slid her hand under the space Sam had created between his heel and the ground. 'This is a good fighting stance. You will wear the Rice Sandals day and night until Master Ono decides you no longer need them.'

That evening, Joe was so exhausted, he did not even want to read.

Veronique had retired to the bath, a phial of Lazarus root in her hand, grumbling whenever her raw heels caught the floor. Orma had extolled the virtue of the powder for relaxing and rejuvenating tired and aching muscles – at this rate, there would be none left by the weekend!

'Oh, my God!' Sam groaned, flopping onto his bed. 'That was hard work!'

'Meh.' Joe whimpered through the flimsy screen.

'I wonder if Hiro's attitude will improve tomorrow, or if he'll even be with us,' Sam tried to cheer himself up. 'No wonder Jenny told us not to upset the Old Man – he's evil!'

'He demands discipline.' Fedor's voice drifted through the other screen. 'Without it, a fighter is nothing more than a drone, repeating engrained drills.'

'Speaking of deeply engrained,' Sam picked at the tape that had melted into a solid sticky mass during the heat of the day, 'these things are just plain nasty!'

'*Meheh!*' Joe agreed, too tired to even speak.

'They do the trick though,' Sam conceded. 'I guess we can be thankful it was rice and not tacks – though I wouldn't put that past him.'

A small sob escaped from his neighbour.

'Cheer up, Fedor,' Sam said.

'That wasn't me, fool.'

Sam attempted to lighten the mood. 'Come on, Turtle, let's get you into a nice warm bath. If you ask politely, maybe Fedor will wash your back and give you a massage.'

The scathing reply from their burly neighbour said otherwise.

Sam winced. 'Or not!'

Veronique lay in the bath, her tape-bound feet peeking out of the steaming water. She regarded them mournfully, they were in desperate need of a pedicure. '*Nikki, the Tortured*,' she moaned, shifting her aching body to stir up the bath salts.

She closed her eyes and her mind drifted back to the kiss. The corners of her mouth curled at the memory...

At dawn, Master Ono and Yuki were nowhere to be seen. Neither were Hiro nor his friends.

Joe could not help but pump his fists. 'Yes!'

The reprieve, however, was short-lived, for Sam noticed a man sat upon a statue in the training yard, waiting for them patiently.

'Hello,' he said, 'your hosts are on a family outing today. Mountain Day, I think they said. I'm Harper, but everyone calls me Ghost.'

Ghost was indeed an apt description of the man, for his skin was very pale, to the point of translucence. As was his white blonde hair and almost colourless eyes.

'Fedor?' he guessed, 'Sam?'

The boys nodded.

'Which would make you Veronique and Joe.'

'It's hard to tell them apart,' Sam admitted, 'even we get it wrong every now and then.'

Veronique's eyes narrowed, whilst Joe feigned a curtsy.

'So,' Ghost vaulted from his perch, 'today we're going to have some fun and games with gadgets.' He picked up a bundle from beside the statue and drew out two plastic sticks with handles. 'These are Rigor Mortis fighting sticks. Blunt, no edge, relatively harmless and much more forgiving than their Kali counterparts. But when they are switched on, any part of the body that the active surface touches, gets a shock and stiffens up. They're a supremely effective, non-lethal weapon.' He peered into the bag. 'I also have some Sai – the three-pronged Okinawa sort. Tonfa – police batons. Bōjutsu – the traditional long staff, and of course everyone's favourite – the sword!' He paused. 'Actually, the rapier requires quite a bit more training, so let's go with either sticks or Sai for today.'

The group descended on the weapons cache.

'They're very light,' Veronique waggled a pair of plastic Sai, 'how do they turn on?'

With a flick of his wrist, Ghost twirled his rapier to point the hilt at them. 'The sword and bō grips are split in two. Simply place one hand on the top half and the other hand on the bottom, then twist in the opposite direction, like so.'

Sam's eye widened when the sword sprang to life and the plastic blade began to glow menacingly.

'With double-handle weapons, such as fighting sticks, Sai or tonfa – simply tap the base of the handles together twice.'

'Cool!' They manhandled their respective weapons until they ignited.

'Just please *don't* touch the surface once it's lit,' Ghost reiterated.

Veronique stepped away from Joe who was madly whirling his newly acquired neon arsenal.

'Look out,' Sam laughed, 'it's Dork Maul!'

Joe parried an imaginary attack, 'how do I look?'

'Like a danger to yourself and everyone around you,' Fedor grunted.

'Must you always tease him?' Veronique huffed. She was so tired of the boys making fun of Joe.

All three of them looked surprised. 'We're not being mean,' Sam said. 'It's just what guys do. Repressed affection.'

'Rubbish.'

Fedor nodded. 'It's true. We're not that big on cuddles or feelings. This is much easier.'

'Really?' Veronique looked unconvinced. 'And you're okay with this?' she turned to Joe.

'God, yes. It's a million times better than being ignored or bullied, trust me. I know they're not being serious, and if they step over the line, I still have the itching powder for my revenge...' he grinned. 'Besides, I'd rather be called turtle than a little cabbage.' Joe raised his eyebrows at Veronique. He was perfectly capable of sticking up for himself.

'Hmm,' she muttered, a little embarrassed.

'Right,' Ghost intervened, turning off the weapons with a master remote. 'If we're done with the group therapy session, let's get on with some basic drills. Then it's on to the maiming and shaming – the CruciBowl ain't far off!'

By noon, they were a sweaty mess.

Ghost, Sam noticed, remained daisy fresh, despite working at twice the rate they were.

'You're. Just. Not. Human!' Joe wheezed, hands on his knees.

Even Fedor seemed to be feeling the effects of the pace the man set.

It was a good thing the weapons were light, for every muscle in Sam's tired body felt useless.

'Arm up. Elbow in. Bend your knees. Lighter feet. Looser wrists. Use both hands!' The pale blur weaved between them, delivering a continual stream of guidance.

'Right,' Ghost glided to a halt, 'let's have some lunch, then we'll turn 'em on and see what you've learned!'

Joe slumped onto the steps. 'I don't think I could keep anything down now.'

Sam saw Fedor brighten immediately. 'More for me!' He placed his hands on his hips and stretched. 'That was great, thank you.'

'You're very welcome,' Ghost said, sitting beside Joe, 'it's a nice change of pace to do some coaching.'

'You're not a teacher?' Veronique asked.

Ghost shook his head. 'God no, I'm the Charlatan in Caleb Roth's team.' The name was clearly meant to mean something but he was met with blank looks. 'The Silent Knight? Winner of last year's CruciBowl?'

'Sorry,' Sam apologized, 'I've no idea who you're talking about.'

'Ah, I did wonder why no one asked for an autograph,' Ghost said. 'My book's been number one in the college library for sixty weeks.'

'Book?' Joe's tired eyes lit up.

Ghost nodded. 'Yup. *The Silent Knight and the Forbidden Inventions*, it's quite the rousing tale, even if I do say so myself.'

Veronique was fascinated. 'So, you're an author and a Charlatan?'

He nodded. 'That I am.'

'You're very... unique. Do you find it hard to blend in?'

Sam choked. 'V!'

'That's okay,' Ghost laughed, 'it's a fair question; it's true, I do have to work harder than most to keep a low profile, but I have a few Mods that help level the playing field.'

Joe's ears pricked. 'Ooo! Such as?'

'Well, there's my Mimic Mod, extracted from the Mimic Octopus. It allows me to change my skin and hair colour in a matter of seconds.'

Veronique was delighted. 'You're kidding! Oh my God, I'd *love* that. Can you show us it, please?'

Ghost laughed. 'Not today, unfortunately, I didn't bring anything like that with me. Today is all about the bigger stuff!'

Sam noticed that both Joe and Veronique were disappointed by this news but soon perked up when lunch was accompanied by Ghost's very animated account of The Silent Knight tackling a mad inventor with a black hole bomb...

'Right,' Ghost dabbed his mouth, 'show time. Let's have Sam versus Joe and Fedor can try to keep up with Veronique. Now remember, the stick will give you quite a kick when it makes contact. The numbing feeling will be followed by localised paralysis. It can't affect anything vital, so don't panic if you catch it in the chest or face, but it'll hurt. The rest, well, you'll pick it up as we go. *En Garde!*'

'*Magnifique!*' Veronique declared, finding some space and beckoning to Fedor. 'Let's see what you've got, muscles.'

Fedor burped, bumping the handles of his fighting sticks together. 'Just indigestion, at this rate...'

Unsurprisingly, the first time the Rigor Mortis weapons made contact resulted in a fair bit of yelping.

Sam made short work of Joe, who was only too happy to be removed from the combat.

The battle between Fedor and Veronique was more fiercely contested for neither was going to give up easily. Fedor was no slouch, and had the advantage with longer reach, but Veronique was nimbler, darting around him like a viper. In the end, she was victorious, rolling under his guard and managing to catch both legs with her glowing Sai, bringing him to a staggering halt.

'Very nice indeed,' Ghost congratulated her, 'you're a natural. Have you given any thought to where you'd see yourself in a Cadre?'

'Charlatan,' she replied without hesitation.

'Good choice! Right, swap partners. You and Sam can crack on straight away.' He turned to Fedor and Joe. As for the wooden soldiers here,' he raised an eyebrow, 'you'll need to up your game!'

Joe gave a whimper. 'Would it be considered poor form to fall on my sword?'

Fedor just muttered as he tried to rub the feeling back into his legs.

By the time sun slipped behind the mountain, they were all utterly exhausted.

'Same time tomorrow?' Ghost asked, wrapping up his plastic arsenal.

Joe's face fell. 'You what? I'm broken!'

Ghost laughed. 'I'm kidding. It was a one-night-only gig, but great to meet you guys, you've done really well today. Keep up with the drills I've shown you and good luck with old Iron Ono. He's meaner than a Siberian winter, but there isn't a finer teacher. I'll keep an eye out for you at the CruciBowl.'

Joe sighed and gave a fake smile. 'Can't wait.'

Joe looked at the strips of weighted cloth with horror.

'Speed,' Yuki stood before them, the rising sun at her back, 'is essential for both defence and offence. The quicker you react, the less likely you are to be hit. The quicker you strike, the more likely you are to survive. These,' she indicated the series of coarse straps stuffed with flat bars of iron, 'will improve your speed.' She motioned to Sam to lift an arm and attached a weight to his left wrist and then the right. She repeated the process around each ankle. Sam lifted his arms. It was not unbearably heavy, but after a few hours of drills, it would feel as though a small car were attached to every limb.

Veronique sighed. *First the rice, and now this; Nikki, the Ninja, wants to go home.*

Fedor chanced a glance at Veronique. He'd not been able to stop thinking about that surprising kiss, but she had barely spoken to or looked at him since. He was more confused than ever. *Are all girls like her?* He wondered as Yuki reached him, interrupting his thoughts.

'Good.' Their instructor stepped back. 'Move about, let's make sure they're not going to fly off. Now pair up.' She beckoned to Hiro and his friends.

Hiro headed straight for Sam. Eyes locked, the boys stood facing each other in silence.

'The Kata we've practised is a combination of basic blocks. Today we're going to put them into practice. We'll start with the head block, like so...' Yuki made a wide sweeping motion with her arm, ending above her head. 'Now you try. Good. This time, your partner will *slowly* aim a strike at your face. Meet their arm with yours, and then guide it up and away. Don't worry about moving your feet or body. For now, just concentrate on your form. Begin!'

Hiro's fist shot toward Sam and glanced off his temple.

'You call that slow?' Sam glared, head throbbing.

'You call that fast?' Hiro scoffed, returning to his stance.

'*HEY!*' Fedor roared and Sam turned to see Joe stagger back, hands held to his nose.

It seemed they had all received the same vicious greeting from the Japanese boys, but Joe had not dodged the blow. He sobbed as thick drops of blood oozed between his fingers. His partner sneered, and Fedor advanced.

'Enough!' Master Ono bellowed, but the command fell upon deaf ears.

Sam had not seen Fedor hit anyone before and was amazed at the speed and purpose with which he moved. He was on the boy in two steps, curled fists raised, chin tucked into his chest.

Fedor easily avoided a punch and delivered a blistering uppercut. His eyes rolled back when Fedor's meaty fist made contact, unconscious before his toes left the ground.

Rising slowly into the air, the boy arched backwards before crumpling onto the stone tiles with a sickening thud.

The grim Russian spun around to face the remaining boys, expecting them to attack.

But they didn't.

Yuki rushed over to Joe's partner, giving Fedor a wide berth. Hiro and his friends stood watching the large boy with their mouths open.,.

'Fedor!' Veronique broke the silence, looking up whilst she tilted Joe's head back. 'What have you done?'

Sam watched Fedor blink and focus, the red mist passing.

Master Ono left the house, feet moving silently as he hurried across the courtyard.

'Is he alright?' he asked, not taking his eyes from Fedor who had now begun to back away from everyone.

'He's fine,' Yuki said. 'Just knocked out.'

'Good.' Master Ono pursed his lips. 'At least the lesson he learned today will not be his last. You,' he snapped his gaze back to Fedor, 'come with me.'

Fedor stopped moving and lowered his hands. 'You okay?' he asked, looking down at Joe.

'I think so,' he managed, blinking away tears.

'Good.' Fedor turned to face Yuki. 'I'm sorry,' he said, giving a curt bow before following Master Ono into the house.

'You're leaving?' Joe squeaked.

'Yup.' Fedor was ramming clothes into the backpack. 'Apparently, I'm too unpredictable. Jen Si will be here to collect me in the morning.'

'That's not fair!' Sam sat on the edge of the bed. 'You were only defending your friend.'

'I was,' Fedor agreed. 'But I shouldn't have over-reacted. I should've had more self-control. I *have* more self-control.'

'Hey, come on, this isn't you.' Sam patted his back. 'What's going on?

Fedor shied away. 'Something is messing with my mind and I need to straightened it out. Maybe being away from all *this* is what I need.'

Sam saw anger flash across Veronique's face. Eyes glistening, she turned and stormed out.

'Ah,' Sam said softly. 'I see.'

Joe looked up. 'What?'

'Nothing.'

'Well, if Fedor's going, so am I!' Joe insisted, reaching for his bag.

'No, you're bloody not!' Fedor rounded on him. 'You need to suck it up and learn from this – I'm not always going to be around to protect you! You can't fail at this, Joe. Never mind Hiro, or Harbinger getting the better of us, you know what happens to *all* our families if we fail at this. You can't whimper and cry, you have to grow a pair!'

Joe stared, mouth opening and closing, tears welling up. Head down, Sam watched him get up and follow Veronique out of the room.

'Nice going,' Sam said, trying not to think about the fact that his friend was leaving, and they may well now fail regardless of his speech. 'That's two of them you've made cry.'

'We can make it three for three.' Fedor snarled. 'Besides, no one made you Paladin, so stop acting like it. I don't answer to any of you!'

Sam did not move. 'It's a lot easier to hurt people than it is to be nice to them, isn't it?'

Fedor kicked his bag savagely. 'Just get out and leave me alone. I never wanted this, anyway.'

Sam walked to the door. 'I don't pay much attention at school, but I did hear one quote that stuck with me. *"It's not enough that we do our best; sometimes we have to do what's required"*. None of us asked for this, Fedor, least of all Joe, and we're very aware of what will happen if we fail, but we've proved that together, we're strong enough to do what is required. On our own,' he paused, 'well, we'd all probably just die in some stupid cave.'

Fedor said nothing. Back turned, head bent, he clenched and unclenched his fists.

Sam nodded sadly and left.

Chapter 25

S am squared up to Hiro. 'How's your friend?'
'Sore.'

'Fedor overreacted. We're all a little protective of Turtle.'

Hiro aimed a more manageable blow at Sam's head. 'Turtle?'

Sam explained and was surprised to see his opponent nearly crack a smile.

'Why all the talking?' Master Ono cuffed Sam as he inspected their form. 'Yesterday I could barely keep you from each other's throats.' Master Ono had decided to take a more hands-on approach to the schooling of his oddball class. 'Fast lips where there should be fast hands, Hirohito – quicker!'

Hiro shrugged and delivered Sam a blistering blow.

'Good.' The sensei moved on to where Joe and his new partner were engaged in a more tentative exchange. 'And just what in the eight hells are you two doing? This isn't ballet!'

Nikki, the Nimble Ninja! Veronique danced around her opponent, dodging and deflecting punches and kicks.

In the days following Fedor's departure the mismatched group had found an uneasy equilibrium under the watchful eye of Master Ono. More complexity had crept into their routines until they glided between the different forms. Even Joe.

Sam knew Fedor's parting words had stung him deeply, for a new Giuseppe – determined and focused – had emerged to tackle the martial arts.

After the first week, they moved onto training with basic weapons, the long staff and Bokken – a wooden practice sword –leaving bumps and bruises on every inch of their bodies.

Master Ono used many techniques to speed up the development of his pupils. Rice Sandals, weighted Training Belts, blindfolds, earplugs and the various other techniques were gruelling and took their toll, but the teenagers soon felt stronger, their speed and stamina building.

The remaining Thieves grew closer, capitalising upon the skills each possessed to become stronger as a unit. Sam was always first to step up and take the hardest knocks, knowing full well that the pain would pass and his super-charged blood would tackle any damage.

Veronique, light and nimble, had perfect co-ordination from years of dancing and a knack for remembering the intricate Kata. At night, after her Lazarus-infused bath, she rehearsed the movements with her not-so-gifted classmates, until it became second nature to them, too.

Joe brought his big brain (and even bigger book collection) to bear on their advancement, schooling his friends on the theory behind the Three Rules, and how to use pressure points to defend and attack an opponent. When the time came to try these things on the practice field, they suffered only minor discomfort.

Joe also briefed them on the other disciplines of the *Bugei Juhappan*, talking late into the night about the secret arts of spying, strategy and tactics – and with practical experience, it all began to fall into place. No one would have admitted it, but the shock of Fedor's departure had brought the three of them closer together.

The Russian's comment about being their self-appointed Paladin had hurt Sam. He had no delusions of grandeur, just an over-eager desire to protect the people he cared about, which was hardly surprising given what had happened to Sophie. He did his best to keep them safe and focused. If he did end up becoming a Paladin, he would make sure he was worthy of the title – he would *not* lose anyone else.

Their new skills were soon put to the test. The next morning, Master Ono led all the teenagers to the practice yard and allowed them to fall into their natural teams.

'This is your final lesson,' he said, standing in front of the teenagers. 'Or rather, your final test. It's called "Capture the Flag". Are you familiar with it?'

Joe and Veronique shook their heads. Hiro and his friends smiled.

'One team will guard a flag; the other team will try to take it.

'Hiro, your team will guard the flag,' he pointed to a small terrace at the far end of the garden. Then he turned to Sam and his friends. 'I want you three to try and take it.

'The test is over when you have succeeded, surrendered, or when the time is up. You have one hour. Good luck.'

Hiro and his posse wasted no time. Picking up their wooden swords, they trotted over to the Dojo to talk tactics.

'You'll no longer be needing these.' Yuki fetched a pair of scissors and cut away their Rice Sandals.

'I'll give you half an hour to walk the grounds and discuss your strategy, then please meet me back here. Remember, the objective is to use everything Master Ono has taught you and any other skills you have. You must apply yourselves completely – skill alone will not yield victory.'

Sam climbed the stairs to the stone terrace where the flag flapped in the breeze. A small wall surrounded the sun-soaked spot, which had a clear view of the entire picturesque estate. There was one way up and one way down.

'Talk about easy to defend,' Joe moaned. 'That staircase is only wide enough for one at a time, they'll see us coming a mile away!'

Sam nodded, chewing his lip.

'Then we make them come to us?' Veronique said.

'But, why would they? All they have to do, is sit up here and wait it out for an hour, then they win.'

Joe thought about it. 'Where's the honour in that? We must ensure the bait is just too tempting to pass up,'

Sam and Veronique leaned in closer.

They met Yuki back at the practice grounds as promised.

'This test will mark either a pass or fail for the martial arts part of your training,' she said. 'Ready?'

They nodded.

'This way.' Yuki walked across the bridge and into the gardens, leaving them behind a sheltered tool shed on the opposite side of the grounds. The cover was a pleasing counterpoint to Hiro's elevated advantage.

'Right,' Sam looked at his friends. 'Everyone know what to do?'

They nodded again.

'Excellent.' He pulled the Krusa from under his *gi*. They were *not* getting sent home today. 'Ok, let's even the odds.'

Hiro crouched behind the wall. Beside him, Kaede, with black eyes and broken nose, flicked the handle of his sword impatiently. Natsuo hid behind a statue near the far wall of the garden, and Setsuna was crouched under a thick hedge on the other side. To reach the flag, the *baka gaijins* would need to come between the two boys, allowing Hiro and Kaede to slip behind them and prevent any retreat.

Sam Folded. Red tiles crunched under his feet, as he stepped onto a carefully selected dip in the roof. Hidden from the terrace, the position gave him a complete view of the garden. Hiro, and the boy Fedor had beaten up, were hiding behind the wall.

Sam waited, watching as Hiro glanced left and right. Following his line of sight, Sam found the remaining two defenders.

Joe fidgeted, willing Sam to reappear.

'Calm down,' Veronique chided. 'You're getting yourself all worked up.'

'Easy for you to say, Crouching Tigress – you're a whizz with a sword.'

'And you're a whizz with your wits, so keep them about you!'

A smug Sam reappeared. 'They've taken up flanking positions on each wall and are waiting for us to cross the bridge.

'V, you follow the east wall, there's one by the statue with the big hat. I'll take the other side. Turtle, you've got the bridge – we're counting on you!'

Turtle sighed.

Why did this name have to catch on?

Hiro stole another glance around the wall. *Where were they?* Time was ticking away.

Then he caught sight of movement. The small foreigner with glasses was trying to dash from tree to tree without being seen. This was going to be easier than he thought!

Nudging Kaede, he pointed to where the fool wiggled along the ground on his elbows. Upon reaching the bridge the boy struggled to his feet, sword in hand, and dashed across. He tripped halfway and fell, his weapon clattering across the slats and into the water.

'What a moron,' Kaede guffawed.

They watched the boy, now on his stomach, reach down and scoop the water noisily, trying to coax the sword nearer. 'This is too good to pass up!' Kaede hurried down the steps.

'*Wait!*' Hiro hissed. 'It could be a trap.' But Kaede had already reached the grass and was heading for the bridge, sword drawn.

'I wouldn't worry about that, it's not like you knew which end to hold, anyway,' Kaede padded onto the bridge.

The small boy jumped and then let out a weird laugh. He drew a bamboo cane from his Gi and took up a clumsy stance.

Kaede laughed. 'What's that? You think you're going to beat me with a plant stake?' He moved forward. 'Yield now and I won't have to hurt you again – this is the only chance you'll get.'

The boy glanced about, the tip of his makeshift sword shaking.

'I'm going to enjoy this,' Kaede smiled. His sword lashed out, catching his opponent high on the thigh. The boy yelped and staggered back. Kaede pressed him, this time feinting and delivering a sharp kick to the stomach.

Joe doubled over, air and nervous laughter rushing from his lungs. *Well, this is going well!*

'Give up!' came the demand.

Grow a pair! Fedor's words stung him anew, and Joe rallied his composure.

Struggling to his feet, his face pale, the boy suddenly shot forward.

Kaede swatted the hissing cane away, snapping it completely with the boy's second swipe, but not before he felt it sting his hand.

'You see-' he began to sneer, then his eyes widened and his sword slipped from his grasp. A numbing sensation slithered up his arm. Kaede slumped to his knees before falling on his side.

'Can't stand,' Joe gasped. 'Can't fight.'

Turning, he staggered back into the safety of the trees.

Hiro watched with amazement as Kaede lay motionless on the bridge. *What the hell just happened?* 'GET UP!' he roared in Japanese over the wall, caution forgotten.

Kaede, stiff as a board, ignored the instruction.

Brilliant! Nikki, the Ninja beamed when Joe's Lanelia-tipped cane found its mark. *Now it's my turn.*

On the balls of her feet, she edged toward the statue, hearing shouting from the terrace as she moved closer to her mark.

Then she stepped on the stick.

Veronique looked up to see her quarry dash from behind the statue, sword raised. She caught his first thrust awkwardly and barely had time to meet the second, a stinging backhand that sent light spots bursting across her vision.

Smarting, she made two quick ballet leaps back.

Natsuo watched the girl. She was the quickest of the three and good with a sword. Still, she was no match for him. He was Samurai. His family had been Samurai for countless generations, as far back as their bloodline could be traced.

Edging forward, Natsuo circled her.

The girl, moving in time, never took her eyes from him, either.

The boy lunged at her.

Veronique waited just out of his reach. Bending her knees, she let her guard down, inviting him to come closer.

He took the bait.

With a quick flick, she tossed her sword at him, which was the last thing he was expecting and his charge faltered. Natsuo was forced to take his eye from her to catch the projectile.

Nikki, the Nimble Ninja rolled under his guard, casting a fistful of Devil's Dust in his eyes – another botanical souvenir from their time in the jungle.

'Can't see, can't fight!' she cried triumphantly.

Natsuo lifted his hands to his eyes, coughing. Blinking, he stepped back, waving his sword around blindly.

Nikki, the Ninja slipped behind him and waited until he staggered into her; then she struck with kicks to his legs and finger-strikes on the pressure points under his armpits.

He dropped to his knees with a cry.

Placing her feet into the backs of his knees, Veronique pinned him to the ground and slid her arm around his neck, locking in the choke hold. 'Can't breathe, can't fight!' was the last thing Natsuo heard.

Hiro watched in disbelief as the girl lowered his friend to the floor and slipped back into the bushes.

Setsuna, looked toward the mount for support. Hiro waved at him frantically, beckoning him, and the boy eased out of the bush.

'Going somewhere?'

Setsuna whirled around when Sam spoke, sword flashing in a blistering arc.

Sam stepped back, the tip inches from his face. 'Phoof! That was close!'

Setsuna was an excellent swordsman, there was no way Sam could beat him, but he had no real intention of trying; he only needed to distract the boy. He lashed out and his blow was turned aside with ease.

Setsuna closed in, confident that the first victory of the day would be his. There was a faint 'whoosh' and something heavy suddenly landed on his back. He looked down to see a thin pair of arms and legs wrapped around him.

'Gotcha!' Hands covered Setsuna's eyes. He cursed and tried to free himself. Joe held on tight as the boy thrashed about.

'Now you really do look like a turtle,' Sam laughed, grabbing their opponent's weapon.

'Very funny,' Joe muttered between gritted teeth. 'Hurry up and help me!'

Sam dropped both swords. Fists curled, he delivered a sharp double-handed strike to their opponent's exposed solar plexus.

Setsuna could do nothing. He tensed, but the strike pushed the air from his lungs. Collapsing to his knees, he managed to gasp '*Akirameru*! I give up!'

'Woo *hoo*!' Joe leapt free. He bent down and smiled triumphantly at the boy.

'Can't breathe – can't fight!'

Hiro screamed.

Sam picked up his sword and rested on it as though it were a walking stick. 'Give up?' he shouted up at the boy.

The silence was deafening.

'Here I am.' Sam spread his arms. 'It's just you and me. Isn't that what you wanted?'

Hiro glared down at his enemy, a light breeze whipping the flag. All he had to do was hold his ground and the victory would be his.

'This is probably the last chance you'll get,' Sam continued. 'We're leaving tomorrow and you've not redeemed your honour, have you? What about your grandfather's honour, Hirohito? It must have hurt when they replaced him? How many times can your family lose face?'

Hiro's face went from white to red. He drew his sword, taking the stairs two at a time.

Sam swallowed. Super blood or not, he was playing a dangerous game, for he knew he could not beat Hiro. *I really hope this heals quickly.*

Veronique suddenly appeared on the unguarded terrace and snatched the red cloth just before a gong sounded from the veranda.

But none of this had registered in Hiro's mind as he drew back his sword.

The fool didn't even try to defend himself.

The ground flew under the young Samurai's feet as he launched himself at Sam, intent on restoring his family honour.

But as his blade cut through clean air, Hiro lost his balance. Rolling over as he hit the ground, he leaped to his feet, cursing, eyes ablaze. This time he would not miss.

But the garden around him was empty.

'Up here!'

Hiro looked up to see the three outsiders waving at him and holding the flag.

His jaw clenched, Hiro closed his eyes and bowed his head with shame. Defeat was the most bitter of tastes.

Chapter 26

Fedor opened his eyes to see Jen Si.

'How do you feel?' the monk asked him.

Fedor pondered the question. 'Lighter.' It was the best way he could describe the tranquillity he felt. The heavy knot in his chest, the tightness in his neck and shoulders was gone.

The monk smiled. 'A good description. You've done well' He praised the boy for his transformation. When Fedor had arrived from Japan, a seething ball of rage, Jen Si hadn't been sure they'd untangle him...

Fedor flung his backpack into the corner of his room at the monastery and slammed the door behind him.

Humiliated, frustrated and confused he prowled its corners, restless. He was disappointed with himself, and he wanted to blame her. It was the easiest thing to do. Veronique was messing with his head, clouding his judgement; it was her fault he couldn't sleep, and that his every thought invariably led to her. He had not asked for this distraction; he had not invited it. He felt vulnerable, and that made him angry. He didn't really understand how he felt.

Fedor hissed, balling his fists again.

There was a tap at the door.

'What?' he barked in Russian, then again, in English.

'May I come in?' asked the monk.

Fedor sighed, his head flopping back. 'If you must.'

Jen Si let himself in. 'Would you like to talk?'

'No.'

'I see. Do you mind if I talk?'

'It's your house.'

'You know, I've tried telling the others that for years, but no one will listen.'

Fedor's pacing faltered and he glared at the monk. 'What good does talking do?'

'Feelings are often easier to deal with when you put them into words. It can help get to the bottom of what's really bothering you.'

'What makes you think something's bothering me?'

'Do you usually batter people? Even someone hurting your friend?'

'I don't have any friends.'

'I know three people who would be very disappointed to hear you say that.'

Fedor said nothing.

'I was in love once,' the monk said, over the sound of marching feet.

'What's love got to do with anything?'

'You're not born a monk. It would be easier if you were. You cannot fully appreciate a thing until you understand how much it means to you.'

'What are you going on about?'

'How would your father react to what you did today? Would he be proud? Smile and pat you on the back?'

Fedor spun around. 'Leave him out of this!'

'I thought he'd taught you greater restraint, and not how to be a thug, ruled only by his emotions. It's certainly not what your brothers appear to have learnt but then I guess every barrel has a bad apple.'

Fedor lashed out.

Had Jen Si's provocation not been deliberate, he would have been hard pressed to avoid the blow. Stepping to the side, he moved just enough to allow the boy's fist to whistle past his cheek. There was a nasty crunch as knuckle met stone and Jen Si felt a stab of guilt, hearing the bones crack.

'Argh!' Fedor clasped his hand to his chest. He looked down at his mashed knuckles, the blood welling over his fingers and swore, long and colourfully, hopping from one foot to the other.

Jen Si stood watching, a creased brow his only show of concern. 'Anger rarely brings reward.'

'Save me the lecture, monk,' Fedor hissed between gritted teeth. 'You were trying to provoke me!'

'I was. All it took was a mention of love and your father, and look at the result. Who are you? The boy I know is calm and composed. What happened to change all that?'

Fedor said nothing, trying to staunch the bleeding.

'I can think of a possibility.'

The boy shot him a dark look.

'You're in love.'

'Love doesn't do this!' Fedor waved his mangled hand, fat drops of blood splattering onto the floor.

Jen Si laughed, a genuine, heartfelt sound. 'Oh, it can do that and far worse when it's not understood. It's the most powerful force in the universe and one you must learn to find harmony with. The minute you let it, or any other emotion, rule you... well, it's a slippery slope.

'Now, come on.' He stepped forward and put his arm around the boy, leading him from the bedroom. 'Let's see what we can do about fixing that hand.'

That night, wrapped in furs and standing on the frosty ground outside the monastery, Fedor stared into the clear night. He had never seen the sky so dark, nor the stars so bright.

'They represent endless possibility.' Jen Si's breath made a heavy cloud. He wore the same sandals and robes as he did inside. 'So many worlds, so many stars and here we are, the most insignificant of creatures, on a tiny planet among hundreds of millions of other celestial bodies . . . the thought is very humbling.

'Yet I still believe I can do anything I put my mind to. The universe allows me to exist, to choose my path. Harmony or discord, it does not judge. The only thing I have control over in this wide universe is…Do you know?'

Fedor shrugged.

'Myself. No matter what anyone else does, what they give or take from you, the only thing you can truly be master of, is yourself.'

'I don't feel like the master of anything right now,' the boy grunted.

'Well, realising that is the first step. Awareness. Take off your coat.'

Fedor raised an eyebrow. 'Are you serious?'

'Very.'

'It's freezing!'

Jen Si shrugged. 'Do you want to take control of your life?'

'Isn't that what I would be doing by keeping the jacket,' Fedor muttered, easing his sore hand out of the sleeve. The boy gasped as goose pimples erupted across his skin when it met the chill.

'Can you feel the coolness of the air on your skin?' the monk asked, closing his eyes and tilting his head back.

'Coolness? I could snap my arm hairs off one by one.'

'Close your eyes.'

'What if my eyelashes freeze shut?'

'Then you won't be able to find your way back inside and will probably fall off the cliff.'

Fedor did as he was told, teeth rattling.

'Concentrate on your core, the deepest part of your chest; Listen to your heart beating, feel the heat and warmth and focus on that. The cold you're feeling is only your mind telling you what your body is experiencing. I want you to learn to ignore those messages. Concentrate on convincing your body that it's not cold.'

Yeah, right, thought the boy. On the plus side, Fedor's fist was now so cold he could barely feel it.

'I can hear your teeth chattering from here.'

'Okay, okay,' he muttered, taking a lungful of icy air and exhaling slowly. He felt the steady rise and fall of his chest, and as he focused all his senses inward, Fedor's body began to relax until he could hear his own pulse.

'Good.'

The words seemed far away. Fedor burrowed deeper, allowing the outside world to fall further and further behind. He felt a flutter of warmth with each heartbeat; faint at first, then stronger, like the sun coming out from behind a cloud, spreading warmth across his skin. Nothing else existed but that feeling. Even the rise and fall of his chest grew quiet as the pulsing waves of energy wrapped him in a cocoon of blissful solitude. Time lost all meaning.

A painful noise battered against the walls of his sanctuary. He became aware of movement, a rocking motion.

'Fedor!' Jen Si was shaking him. 'There we go.' The monk's face relaxed as Fedor blinked. The sun had stolen a march on the horizon.

How long had they been out here?

'Look at me.' Jen Si forced him to focus. 'Deep breaths. There we go. Good.'

Fedor looked down, his arms were still folded beneath his chest, but he was no longer shivering. His teeth were clenched, but not chattering.

'How long?'

'All night. I'm truly amazed.'

'Wow.' Fedor shook his numb arm. 'All night, really?'

Jen Si nodded.

'Wow.' was all he could manage.

'Tell me about your father.'

They were seated in the monk's study. Every day Jen Si had pushed him to take further control of his body and mind. He had used bowls of steaming water, fasting, and nights without sleep. Jen Si pressed Fedor to ignore all stimulus against which his body would normally protest.

It was not surprising to find that food was his ultimate weakness. Dips in his blood sugar levels were not something he could overcome with ease.

They talked during the evenings, covering casual topics at first: Fedor's training, school, his dogs, the bear. Then, the more sensitive topics had come up: His parents, his brothers, his friends.

Fedor found the chats surprisingly cathartic. And though he hated to admit it, he felt a lot better for opening up.

He came to realise he loved the company of his dogs because they made no demands on him. He loved fighting because it made him feel in control and that, the more he put into it, the better he got, which was a tangible reward for his efforts. He admitted his feelings for his brothers, their sibling rivalry and the pressure to suppress his intelligence for fear it would prevent him from becoming what his father wanted him to be: The perfect fighter.

'Where to start?'

'What do you feel when you think of him?'

'Fear. Anger. Rejection. Disappointment. Frustration. More anger.'

'Why is that, do you think?'

'He's always wanted me to be more than I am. Whenever I did what he wanted, it wasn't enough; it could've been better. Then he would move on to the next task, the next demand. I've never succeeded at anything in his eyes.'

'What do you think, do you always fail?'

'No.'

'Then what does it matter what he thinks?'

'I want to make him proud.'

'Why? Have you ever not tried your hardest?'

Fedor had to think about that. 'No. But that's what he told us to do: We must make him proud and not let him down.'

'Then he's the one with the problem, not you. If you feel you've done your best and couldn't try any harder, that's all that matters. There's no reason for this guilt and anxiety.'

'I guess not.'

'Remember what I told you about anger?'

'It rarely brings reward.'

'You mentioned it twice when I asked how he makes you feel.'

'Did I?'

'Yes. You don't take failure well and you don't like being out of control, both of which your father makes you feel. You need to stop feeling like a failure, because you're not.'

'Hmm. Easier said than done.'

'Easier than spending a night in the snow?'

'Much!'

They both laughed.

'There's one subject we've yet to discuss.'

'Oh yes, and what's that?'

'Veronique.'

Fedor had to stop himself flinching when the monk said her name out loud. His walls went up and he clenched his fist sending a tingling reminder of his cut up his arm. It was all but healed, but was a token of the turmoil Fedor had been in.

'What about her?'

Jen Si smiled. 'You tell me. Her name clearly makes you feel something.'

Fedor tried not to clench his jaw as well. He found it hard to describe the intensity and relentlessness of his feelings. She was always in his thoughts. 'Confusion,' he admitted. 'Frustration. Rejection.'

'Anything good?'

Fedor snorted. 'Not now, but when she is around…' He shrugged. 'Then yes, I have good feelings.'

'How does she feel about you?'

Fedor laughed. 'NO idea!'

'Have you asked her?'

A few unintelligible splutters burst from the boy in protest.

'When it comes to a love of this nature there isn't much I can tell you from experience. The one thing I do know is that communication is key. Talk to the girl. We regret the things we never had the courage to try. Those thoughts will haunt you.'

It didn't sound easy to Fedor, but it did make sense.

'I'm not saying you'll ever truly understand her,' The monk winked, 'for no man is blessed with such insight, but you can reveal your feelings. And in return… well, at least you'll be less confused.'

They both smiled.

'Thank you,' Fedor nodded. 'For everything. I didn't realise quite how messed up I'd become.'

'Bottling emotions only creates a volcano.'

'The boy I beat up, is he okay?'

'He's fine. Black eyes, an off-centre nose, but nothing permanent.'

'I'm glad. And I'm sorry for what I did.'

'I know you are.'

'Should I tell him?'

Jen Si chewed it over. 'Best leave it for now. If your paths ever cross again, I'm sure the apology won't go amiss.'

'Okay.'

'How about a little exercise?'

The boy's face brightened, he had enjoyed training with the monks. They were fierce warriors and skilled in ways he envied. 'Weapons training with Ling Pi?'

Jen Si bobbed his head. 'Not quite what I had in mind.'

Fedor winced. A week in the cold monastery had not prepared his body for the sweltering Mediterranean sun.

'Welcome to Greece.' Jen Si waved his arm at the rocks, dust and the odd ragged shrub. It was hot and dry, with no trace of clouds for a reprieve.

Fedor lifted his hand to shield his eyes. 'What are we doing here?' They stood amongst the ruins of an ancient temple nestled at the base of a small mountain.

'Exercise!'

'It's quite a hike back to the monastery.'

'Ah, no. That would be a tad excessive! But I didn't want you to feel you'd missed out with the others being in Japan, so thought you might enjoy this. Besides, we can't have you failing martial arts training and letting the others down, can we?'

Fedor did not have time to answer, for the monk set off toward the summit at a brisk pace.

Icarus Bayne sighed and prised a speck of dirt from beneath his fingernail. His half-sister could be very trying at times.

'You know what I want, Teddy.' The beautiful woman glared at him from across the table.

'Don't call me that.' Icarus Bayne's real name was Theodore. Teddy, when he was younger.

She grinned. 'What's wrong, Teddy Bear?' Ms Keller never used the unfortunate moniker he had been given after surviving a fall from a five-storey building.

Theodore 'Icarus' Bayne raised one hand without looking up from the other, and unfurled a single digit.

'Charming.'

'Hmm.'

'How hard can it be?' Ms Keller uncrossed and crossed her long legs. Her brother's laconic manner always frustrated her.

He shrugged. 'If you think it's that easy, you do it.' The silence that followed was delicious. He relished the rare moments when he managed to put his cocky sibling in her place and would pay a king's ransom for more of them.

'Fine. I will.'

He looked up and was met by cold eyes.

'Don't be stupid, Danni, you know that's not what I meant.'

She shrugged. 'Nevertheless, the idea has merit. I can't say I'd be happy to sit idly by and leave it to someone else anyway. Not after all we've been through.'

Theodore began to panic. His little sister was not without means. He'd seen men twice his size reduced to blubbering wrecks by her slender hands, but what she suggested was the single most daring feat in the history of the Harbingers.

'Danni—'

'My mind's made up. How long until the Turner's ready?'

He knew her look well enough not to argue. She was serious and no amount of arguing would change her mind.

'Well, we've never used a Turner like this before. The standard Harbinger model uses a proprietary system to map and record a location. Accounting for celestial motion, it creates a Landmark to which you can return. We've never tried to fool it into going somewhere it's never been before. We think we've been able to use the robot's four-dimensional global positioning system to extract what we hope are compatible co-ordinates, to create a fake Landmark. I'm going to send a probe through first to—'

'No. Too risky. If they detect it, we lose the element of surprise. We'll only have one crack at this.'

'Then why don't we just let Zip wiggle her fingers and open a "rift" thingy,' he made a wild gesture. 'And just…'

'Ha! Trust me, I already floated that idea.'

'Shut down?'

'Like a knock-off theme park full of Disney characters.'

Theodore grimaced. 'It's dangerous. We could materialise in a wall, mid-air, above a staircase or in a cupboard. Remember, our little friend flew everywhere. We've assumed average hover height and estimated floor levels, but make no mistake, Danni, this is still very, *very* risky…'

'Nothing ventured—'

'Nothing lost!'

'Ha, ha. Or gained.'

Theodore had the bit between his teeth. 'This could go a lot smoother if we were allowed to take Whisper or Remora with us.'

'We're not allowed to use Zip and Aura has deserted us. Do you really think we'll be given access to *any* of the remaining Symbionts?'

Fine! Then I'm going through first. You're an evil harpy, but you're not trained for this.'

'Neither are your two sidekicks.'

'They learn on the job, you know that.'

'I think this would fall rather spectacularly outside any known job description. Besides, we both know what happened *your* first day on the job, Icarus.'

He shrugged. 'They can stay behind, if you like?'

Ms Keller considered it.

'No.' She pursed her perfectly painted lips. 'In for a penny.'

'Let's just hope it's not a pound of flesh. Is this scroll worth the risk?'

'It's the key to finding The Book, my dear Teddy, and make no mistake, there is nothing I… we… shouldn't risk for it.'

'Except a Symbiont.' Teddy rubbed his face. 'When do we leave?'

'Soon,' Ms Keller smiled, as he finally capitulated. 'Our unwilling accomplice has set events in motion that will give us a unique window.'

Her brother stretched and rose from the chair with feline grace. 'We'd better get you some Cold Suit gloves then.'

Chapter 27

'Pankration?' Sam looked at his friend blankly and Fedor nodded.

'It's a Greek martial art,' Joe supplied from behind his book.

He was the happiest he had been in months, for they were now ensconced in the recesses of Ruben's library. The diminutive curator had left them alone after a warm welcome and much fussing over their loaned books, and gone off in search of refreshments.

Joe couldn't resist offering more information. 'It's supposedly the oldest mixed martial art, and is a vicious combination of boxing and wrestling taught to the Spartans. No rules, and its intention was to kill. It was very tough, or so I've read!' he added with a wink, popping his nose over the book.

Fedor rolled his aching shoulders and Veronique groaned. 'Just what he needed, more ways to fight! Never mind giving a monkey a machine gun, they're arming an ape with a nuke!'

He had endured workouts in the relentless Greek sun, been pushed from sunrise to sunset by a man as hard and unyielding as the landscape he survived in. Every inch of his body had been battered, bruised and burned as he'd practiced the brutal Spartan arts.

'So, Jen Si wasn't kidding when he offered you some "exercise"?' Sam laughed.

'A bare-faced lie,' the bronzed boy said.

'Well, since they've let you come back, and we won our task, we must have passed this stage!' Sam was relieved. They all were.

Their reunion with Fedor had been awkward at first. During their time apart, Sam, Joe and Veronique had grown much closer.

'I'm sorry,' their comrade had said.

Their protests had fallen upon deaf ears, for Fedor, enabled by his new communication skills, had spent a good ten minutes exorcising his demons. When he'd finished there was an awkward silence.

'Well,' Sam picked up the conch, 'on behalf of the group, I'd just like to say thanks for sharing.'

'Wow' came Joe's rejoinder. 'You literally *can't* stop talking!'

'And you've picked up some nice colour,' Veronique commented with barely veiled admiration on Fedor's sun-kissed skin, then noticed the pink scar on his hand. 'And that?'

He looked down and scowled, flexing his stiff fingers. 'A little reminder of the last time I'll ever lose my temper. But enough about me, I want to hear all about your training.'

He clapped when they reached the conclusion of their Capture the Flag tale. 'I would've loved to have seen his face!'

'I'll take it to my grave,' Joe said. 'Which hopefully, is still a fair way off!'

They all laughed.

'Looks like you made a good Paladin after all,' Fedor smiled at Sam. 'I'm sorry about what I said; it wasn't fair. You're always the first to step up and that takes courage.'

Sam blushed. 'Stop.'

'It's true,' Joe agreed. 'I certainly look to you when the proverbial poo heads for the fan and I think the others do too?'

Veronique nodded. 'Oui. Just don't get a big head.'

'Speaking of which,' Sam muttered quietly, inclining his head toward a new arrival in the library.

The lean frame of Mr D'Angelo was cresting the top of the stairs. 'Well, I see we're all still in one piece.'

Sam heard Joe whisper '*Barely,*' before putting on a fake smile for the man, while the others murmured similar disingenuous pleasantries.

'I've followed your progress with keen enthusiasm and I must say, you've exceeded your potential. You passed the course with flying colours.' As he listed a few of his personal highlights from their escapades around the globe, Jen Si and Jenny joined them.

'Which brings us to the climax of this little adventure, the CruciBowl!'

The teenagers could not help wriggling in their seats.

'As you may know, we hold an annual gathering on Valsieve island for the entire Order to enjoy. It's quite an event and includes The Inventors Fair and the annual Cadre tournament – fondly known as CruciBowl.'

Sam's excitement was building. 'We've heard it's savage!'

Salvador smiled, feeling his prey tugging the bait. 'Indeed! Valsieve is a dormant volcano that was crafted into a gigantic coliseum just for the event.'

An *Oooh* rippled around the room.

'The weeks leading up to the tournament still fill me with excitement, even after all these years. I'll never forget my first match – Titans vs. The Two Steps...'

'What kind of competition is it?' Veronique's interest came more from cautiousness than enthusiasm. She didn't relish the promise of carnage and chaos.

'It's the best kind,' Salvador's eyes gleamed. 'Cadres compete in Quest matches, pitting their physical and mental skills against one another in an arena like no other.'

'Sounds fun,' Sam said.

Fedor shook his head. 'It's not. My brothers have told me about Quest matches. No field is ever the same. They use one-way portals, Holobotics, SATs... All sorts of nasty surprises, not to mention the other Cadres all armed and angry!'

'Are Mods allowed?' Joe asked, closing his tome with a musty clap.

'SATs? Holobotics?' Sam looked bewildered. 'What are you lot prattling on about now? Does this adventure have a glossary? How come I don't know any of this?'

Veronique pulled a tongue. 'We're special.'

He glared back at her.

'Suspended Animation Traps – SATs,' Joe supplied an explanation, 'are very high tech. They transform any object into a trap, harmless until you touch it and *BAM* – you're caught! Frozen. Some are portals, so not only do they paralyse you, they also transport you someplace else.'

And what about the other thing? Holo…'

Mr D'Angelo raised his hand.

'All your questions will be answered in good time. Tomorrow you leave for Valsieve.'

Somewhere in the Pacific Ocean near the Equator and most definitely off the beaten track, lay the mysterious island of Valsieve.

Far from any shipping lanes and flight paths, and (thanks to contacts at the highest level of global government) hidden from satellite surveillance, the island was the one place where The Few were able to fully exploit and enjoy their technology without fear.

It boasted miles of unspoilt, golden sand, swaying palms and cool salty waters. Neat stone paths cleaved its dense jungle, running between rows of incredible tree houses. It was also home to chattering parrots, wide-eyed monkeys, snakes, lizards and all types of insects; and, at its heart, crowned with a ringlet of fluffy white clouds, was the volcano.

'I thought we were done with tree houses?' Veronique moaned when their khaki clad guide closed the door, leaving them in a particularly palatial high-rise dwelling. 'I bet there's no bath, no mirrors and dare I even mention a hair dryer?'

Fedor sighed, dropped his bag and stalked over to the bathroom. Inside were polished tiles and gleaming taps. Full-length mirrors covered one wall and a bewildering array of towels, scrubs and lotions adorned the other. There was a wet room larger than his mother's kitchen and a bath that was arguably seaworthy.

'No, you're right.' His face was deadpan. 'There's just a hole in the floor, a rusty bucket and a greenish flannel. I'll go first.'

'Oh, no, you don't!' she shrieked and barged past him.

Skidding to a halt on the buffed flooring, she gazed with awe at the gorgeous bathroom. 'Why you—'

Fedor closed the door in her face and held the handle with both hands, while Joe and Sam snickered.

The path ahead forked again.

'I don't think I'm ready to be lost in another jungle just yet.' Sam's hands strayed to his recently repaired rib cage.

Getting lost had been a recurring theme since they'd left their plush accommodation to explore the island the next morning.

'We're not lost.' Joe pointed at the manicured path. 'We're just not sure exactly where we are….'

'I told you to bring the map,' Veronique chided. 'But, noooo – you didn't want us to look like tourists. News flash – everyone here is a tourist!'

'Well, not everyone.' Two children appeared from behind a creeper clad tree. They were both lean and tanned with straight dark hair and violet coloured eyes, mirror images of each other, except that one was a boy and the other, a girl.

It was the girl who had spoken and she smiled as she approached them, her bare feet and ankles wet from the undergrowth. The boy hesitated before following her.

'Your pretty friend is right, you should've brought your map. These paths are a maze.'

'Err, who are you,' Joe peered into the jungle, 'and where did you come from?'

The girl pointed back to the tree. 'Over there. Weren't you watching?'

'No, I mean what were you doing in there?' he nodded toward the dense greenery.

'Following you, of course. Casius reckoned you'd just keep going, but I knew you'd stop eventually.'

Sam looked at the boy. 'You're Casius?'

'I am. And you're Sam.'

Sam's eyes narrowed. 'How—'

'Relax,' the girl waved her hands, 'old man D'Angelo sent us, but we got sidetracked at The Inventors Fair. The Magnetic Ink stall do the most amazing tattoos. I sooo badly want a Cadre sigil, but I just can't decide which. Anyway, you'd already left by the time we arrived.'

'I'm Camiel. And before you ask, yes, we're twins.'

'Wonderful!' Joe clapped his hands. 'Do you have any sort of connection? Finish each other's sentences, know where the other one is at all times. . . Oooh...do you know what the other is thinking?'

Sam felt a sharp pang. The bond he'd lost when Sophie died had left an empty space inside him forever.

'She said we're twins, not circus freaks,' Casius grated, lips pursing.

Joe paled, his eager mind yet again triumphing over his underdeveloped tact.

'*Enchantées.*' Veronique extended her hand between the two boys.

Camiel replied in French, bobbing a curtsey.

'Oh my!' Veronique clapped her other hand over the girl's. 'That was just perfect!'

'Sorry,' Joe extended his hand to Casius, 'I've no filter.'

'Don't worry about it,' said Casius.

'You live on this island?' Fedor entered the conversation in his usual calm tone.

'We do,' Camiel nodded. 'Born and raised.'

Casius snorted and his sister shot him a dark look.

'Er, are we missing something?' Sam asked.

'No,' the girl forced a smile.

'Is the jungle not dangerous?' Veronique asked. 'We were warned to stay on the paths.'

'Oh, it is,' Casius puffed his chest, 'but we've been swinging from these vines since before we could walk, though the old jaguar still takes a half-hearted swipe at us every now and then.' He proudly turned over his forearm to show them four long white scars stretching from elbow to wrist.

'Any snakes?' Sam paled.

'Loads!' the boy nodded. 'You like them?'

'I'm kinda off the big ones at the moment.'

'It's not the big ones you need to worry about.' Casius waved his hand. 'It's the Two Steps you have to look out for.'

'Two Steps?'

'Yup. It's so poisonous, you can only take two steps,' he made a tree chopping motion, 'and game over!'

'Casius, stop it!' his sister chided. 'Don't listen to him, Sam, snakes are more scared of you than you are of them.'

Sam's heart was pounding. 'Don't bet on it!'

'So, do you live near the volcano?' Joe asked.

'Not exactly; we live on the other side of the island.'

'I didn't know there was another side to the island.' Sam noticed the look Casius gave his sister.

'It's not common knowledge,' she admitted, ignoring him.

'Camiel!' the boy hissed.

'What?' She rounded on him, annoyed. 'I'm tired of being alone, I want to talk to people other than you!'

There was an uncomfortable silence as the twins glared at each other.

'Here.' Casius reached into his pocket and pulled out a worn map. Flipping it open, he tore his eyes away from his sister and stabbed his finger at a crossroads near the centrefold. 'We're here. Follow the road to the east and you will reach the main complex in about fifteen minutes.' Thrusting the map into Sam's hands, he grabbed his sister by the elbow and led her back into the jungle. She squealed in protest and tried to pull away.

'Should we...?' Joe looked at the others.

'No,' Fedor shook his head. 'It's not our place. Besides, I get the feeling they're not being completely straight with us.'

Sam nodded. 'Strange pair.'

'Well,' Veronique liberated the map from Sam with a quick flick and turned it over, 'at least we've got one of these now and if you don't mind, I'll look after it.' She turned and pointed to the right-hand fork.

'This way, boys!'

Nikki Livingstone had returned!

Chapter 28

The Inventors Fair was an eclectic mix of old world charm and modern flair. Carnival stalls and marquees of all shapes, sizes and colours were crammed into a bustling market at the base of the volcano. It had the noise and vibrancy of the most spectacular Mardi Gras.

People of all ages jostled from one attraction to the next, all breathless children once more. The air was alive with bangs and pops, mechanical roars competed with the whine of electric engines. There were clouds of sweet, coloured smoke, shrieks of laughter and cries of amazement all around the youngsters. The Inventors Fair was everything Sam imagined and more.

And, at the centre of the maelstrom, facing off across the courtyard and rising high above the crowd, stood two mighty statues, their lances down and visors lowered, preparing to charge.

'Who are those for?' Sam asked when Jenny pointed out two grandiose marquees below the statues.

'Dominic Creed and Eugene Nomeholt. Two very gifted, very different geneticists, and the main attractions for the last ten years.'

'LOL! Sergeant Splice and the Gene Gnome,' Joe grinned. 'That's what they supposedly call each other.'

'I don't think either of them like those names,' Jenny chided.

Sam sighed. 'At the risk of repeating myself…'

'Well,' Jenny supplied, 'Dominic Creed was Head of Genetic Research for the American military, but combining genius and warfare is never going to produce good things, so we recruited him. Splicing is the process by which genes are joined together and since he was a military man...' The boys smiled at her.

'Eugene is…vertically challenged, his surname is Nomeholt. Nome. Gnome. You see where this is going?'

'Gene Gnome,' Sam chuckled to Fedor. 'I like it.'

Veronique and Jenny both sighed.

'Anyway,' Jenny continued, 'Eugene has green fingers. He loves plants and all his research to this date has been centred on flora, whilst Dominic's is focused solely on animals. Naturally, they both believe their field superior...'

'So, they hate each other?' Sam concluded.

'Well, hate is probably a bit strong but there is certainly a healthy rivalry. Each year their stalls get bigger and their inventions more spectacular. Creed created the Stingray Slap, as well as Eagle Eye, Firefly Fingers, Spider-Silk Skin and many more Mods. Whilst Eugene created the Microflowers, plants with organic cameras and microphones, the Sleeping Beauty Rose, Paralysis Pollen – the list is almost endless.

'Why don't you lot explore? Try to stay out of trouble and I'll see you at the entrance to the Crucible arena in a few hours. You don't need any money, everything's free here.' That bit of news was greeted by four wide grins. 'The first match is at noon.'

They chose to start on the outer fringes of the square, where new inventors vied to make a name for themselves and where the crowds were less dense.

'We need to get some Dragon's Breath before we try any Mods.' Joe pointed to a holographic dragon rising in front of a stall, roaring and spitting flames at unsuspecting passers-by. 'Jenny said that even the simplest Mods use up energy, so Dragon's Breath is a must. Apparently, it's pure power!'

The shelves of the stall were lined with dozens of miniature dragons with long spiky tails and shimmering eyes. Sam watched a boy grab a bright green dragon-can from the shelf and break the seal on the drink by pulling its ear. The mouth opened with a hiss of smoky carbonated gas and the drink roared to life.

'Woah...' Fedor looked surprised.

'What flavour are you going for?' Joe asked the others, his fingers drumming against his chin. He picked up a purple dragon with a spindly head and psychedelic eyes.

'Spicy Cinnamon.' Fedor coughed in surprise, when the red can he had chosen erupted in his mouth.

'I forgot to mention that Jenny said the mouth of the can is always filled with Crackling Candy.' Joe apologised.

'Mmm, Preppy Peach.' Veronique smacked her lips, her eyes watering.

Sam grabbed a sinuous jade dragon from the shelf. Snapping its ear, he put the hissing beast to his lips. The rush of energy was instantaneous, the fizzy liquid and popping candy collided in his mouth and raced down his throat as a sweet, bubbly lava. Gasping, he swore. 'That's intense!'

'The next sip is better,' Joe promised. 'Once the Crackling Candy has gone, it's a much smoother ride.'

'Remember, kids, just the one,' an attendant warned them. 'You won't sleep for a week otherwise.' Just to make sure they listened, he gave them each a glowing stamp on their wrists that changed colour when they moved.

'How long will the effect last for?' Joe asked the man, wiping his mouth.

'Depends how many Mods you try, but I'd say three hours at most, maybe four.' The attendant winked at them and Sam saw his pupils were bright yellow. 'Feisty Feline mod! Freaky, aren't they?'

'Magnificent.' Veronique moved closer. 'Where did you get it?'

'Vincent the Viking over near the Nevamelt hut. You can see in the dark with these. I've heard his Serpent Eyes are pretty wicked too, but no one has been brave enough yet to try Demon's Stare!'

'OMG!' Joe barely contained an excited shimmy.

Sam was not convinced. 'You wanna try Demon's Stare?'

'No! They have Nevamelt here!' The boy's mouth was watering. 'Please, please, please can we go there?'

Joe's endless whining drove them out of every tent en route to the Nevamelt stall, giving them little time to marvel at the endless supply of wonders within. Sam had to practically drag Fedor from the Rigor Mortis stall, where he was marvelling over the splendid array of limb-stiffening weaponry available.

'I really want those knuckle dusters,' he grinned at Sam, smacking his fist into his palm.

'Okay, are you lot stalking me?' Sam heard a familiar voice ask. The tall frame of Anatoly emerged from a nearby marquee.

'*Privyet*,' he greeted Fedor, giving a warm smile to the others.

Joe looked around excitedly. 'Where's Ivan?'

'Somewhere over there,' he waved toward the other side of the square 'in the Tribes tent. He's desperately trying to find someone who hasn't heard his reputation. To swindle them, of course!'

Joe's eyes widened and he lifted a foot in the direction Anatoly was pointing. A firm hand brought him back to earth with a dejected plonk.

'Oh, no, you don't.' Sam shook his head. 'One degenerate gambler in the extended family is enough.'

'But—'

'No.'

'I—'

'Still no.'

'FML!' Joe folded his arms, pouting.

Anatoly laughed. 'Cheer up; I've brought you a present. I was going to give it to you later, just before your match, but it might be better to do so now, because *technically* neither you nor I should have anything like it.' He glanced about. 'Over there.' They slipped between two tents.

Sam watched the eccentric inventor rifle through his backpack.

'Aha!' He finally drew out a sturdy black fabric sleeve, slightly longer than his hand and very similar to a Spartan vambrace. The sleeve had two clips on the side, both facing in the same direction. The first clip was near the top of the sleeve and the second was at the bottom. Dividing the two, three quarters of the way down, was a thick metal band. A blue LED light twinkled on either side of it.

Anatoly looked at their confused faces. 'Ready?' he asked.

Four nods.

'Okay, then.' He held up the cylinder and turned it on its side, showing it to each in turn. It was hollow. 'Looks ordinary enough, yes?'

Sam nodded.

Anatoly grabbed the sleeve on either side of the metal band and gave it a firm tug. The sleeve split in two, creating a long piece and a slightly shorter piece, both with a clip. The blue lights on the now separated pieces turned red. He put the long piece into his pocket, anchoring to the fabric with the clip. He handed the shorter end to Joe.

The boy held it at arm's length. Anatoly secured the clip. There was a click and the red light on the piece Joe was holding turned green. The inventor then slid his hand into his pocket, and into the metal sleeve.

Four wiggling fingers appeared from the end Joe was holding.

'Holy s—!' he clamped his hand over his mouth, dropping the bodiless digits.

Sam glanced over his shoulder, but no one had registered the startled cry.

Veronique picked up the vambrace, careful to avoid the ghostly fingers. 'Amazing!' she breathed.

'Isn't it? Anatoly beamed. 'I'm calling it the Bottomless Pocket!'

'So, it's like a Rummager?' Sam asked, as they crowded round Veronique to peer at the curious contraption.

'Yup. Same principle as Mandle's original patent, with a few modifications and one major advantage—.'

'You can change where you put the other end!' Joe cut him off. 'Bottomless bags are all linked to shelves in the Quartermaster's Stores, but this...! Fedor, just think – you could link yours to your mother's kitchen and never go hungry again!'

Sam laughed.

'Exactly!' Anatoly clapped the boy on the back. 'And, in the spirit of the proverbial cooking show, here's one I made earlier.' He rotated his hips and they noticed a clip peeking from his other pocket.

'Oh, go on!' Joe was jiggling with excitement. Even Veronique and Fedor were staring intently in anticipation.

Anatoly stole a quick look behind his audience, then pressed the clip and reached into his other pocket. He couldn't help indulging a little in theatrics; he seldom had the opportunity to show anyone his creations, and he enjoyed the looks on their faces... 'Ready?'

Sam nodded.

'You sure?'

'Argh!' Joe protested. 'You're as bad as your brother!'

'I am *not*!'

'C'mon,' Sam chivvied. 'Show us!'

'Okay, okay!' Anatoly's pocket bulged as he withdrew his hand, a tightly woven cylindrical object in his grasp. The bulge continued to change shape, becoming more angular as he pulled it through.

'It's a sword!' Joe exclaimed, seeing the hilt of a katana followed by a length of sharp, shiny steel. Anatoly's arm bent awkwardly, trying to work the long weapon from his pocket.

He raised it aloft. 'Ta-da!'

Sam laughed. 'By the power of Greyskull!'

They whooped and clapped in amazement, and Anatoly passed the sword round.

'You like?'

Joe beamed. 'We LOVE!'

'Absolutely awesome!' Sam agreed. Fedor and Veronique nodded, too.

'But how does it work?' Joe snatched the smaller sleeve from Veronique.

Anatoly tried to guide the point of the sword back into his pocket without opening a vein or being arrested! 'The mechanics are all in the metal band,' he supplied. 'It was no mean feat to create a working portal in something that size. The blue light shows the sleeves are joined but inactive. Red means they are separated, but still not functional.

'You activate the portal by pressing the clip, like so,' he gave the clip on his other pocket another prod, 'and the green light appears when the sleeves are paired.'

'Brilliant!'

'I'm very glad you like it.' Anatoly beamed, pulling the larger piece from his pocket and slotting it back into the part Joe was holding. 'As this one's yours.' The lights turned blue.

'Noooo!' the boy's jaw dropped. 'Really?'

The inventor nodded, fishing in his backpack. 'And these,' he handed a cylinder each to Sam and Fedor, 'are yours. Just don't lose them, please. And I'd prefer you to keep them from Jenny as long as is humanly possible, for I will no doubt get a spectacular roasting for this; but what's life without a few beatings!'

'Hmm,' muttered Joe, his attention consumed by the generous gift.

Sam, however, was aware of Veronique's disappointment. But Anatoly had caught the look too. 'Fear not, fair maiden!' he said, pulling a red velvet sleeve with more ornate metal clips from the depths of his bag. 'You get an extra special one!'

Veronique clapped her hands. '*Magnifique!*' She gave her benefactor an emphatic kiss on the cheek, drawing a dark look from the younger Russian and a blush from the elder.

'You're all most welcome and I do hope they'll come in handy later. Now, I've made them fingerprint specific, so first we need to programme them…'

The group bent their heads to discuss and examine their new toys. Anatoly could not help smiling, as the teenagers plotted how to hide their various new Rigor Mortis weapons.

Maybe having visitors wasn't that bad, after all. Anatoly had decided he liked the kids, and had made another decision, too. 'Sam, wait.' he held the boy back when they had said their farewells. 'I… I've done something I probably shouldn't have. Jenny and her bloody lectures on ethics!'

Sam's brow furrowed. 'Okay…'

Anatoly handed him a small grey screen. 'This is for you. It's an eBook.'

'You're right, you shouldn't have,' the boy grinned.

'Very funny; now pay attention. This is the user guide for my greatest invention – the EverMod. It will also tell you how to use every transient and permanent Mod available, including the Activation and Deactivation sequences to control them – something no one else has.'

Sam frowned. 'That's great, Anatoly, but I'm not sure why I'd—'

'Just keep it safe. And secret. You'll know why soon enough, now go.' He placed a firm hand on the boy's shoulder. 'And good luck.'

Sam watched the man disappear between the tents. He looked down at the blank screen – another mystery with no apparent answer. 'Just what I need, *more* secrets to keep.'

'Whose bright idea was it to mix ice cream with Dragon's Breath?' Sam said, casting his Nevamelt into the bin with a sigh.

Anatoly had gone in search of Ivan, and the teenagers had commenced an ice cream hunt.

Veronique looked queasy, her apple pie flavoured delight landing next to Sam's.

'Oh, buck up,' Joe chastised the pair, giving his Tiramisu cone another lick.

'Hey, isn't that the stall the weird kids mentioned?' Fedor pointed to a sign.

'*Magnetinc*...? Oh, I get it,' Joe managed around a mouthful. 'Magnetic ink. Shall we have a look?'

Fedor marched toward the tent and the others followed.

Magnetinc was a tattoo parlour, though it was unlike any tattoo parlour that Sam could imagine. The walls were not lined with pages of the designs it offered, there were no chairs, or well-inked artists craning over buzzing pens. Instead, standing on bright podiums circling the tent were underwear-clad models, one male and one female.

Fedor was puzzled. 'I don't get it.'

'Hi guys! Are you after a Cadre sigil?' the woman asked from her perch.

'Er, no.' Joe said. 'A friend told us about Magnetic ink, but we're not quite sure what it is.'

The woman beckoned them to the holographic monitor beside her. 'No problem. The easiest way is to show you. Pick a picture.'

Joe bustled over and began swiping through the images.

'That one,' Fedor suggested over his shoulder. It was a Celtic wolf design, harsh black lines and savage curves.

She pointed a pen with a blue LED tip at the picture and clicked it. The blue light flashed for a few seconds then turned green.

'Ready?' she asked.

They nodded.

Sam watched the model turn to expose her slender shoulder and press the tip of the pen to her skin. Beneath the surface, millions of tiny shapes began to move, as though a hand was sketching the design from within. The lines became more defined and the swirling strokes created patterns, until their shivering stopped, leaving the dark imprint of a wolf on her skin.

'Oh, my God,' Joe gasped, 'it's used for tattoos!'

'Sigils mainly. But not just tattoos,' the girl smiled at Veronique, 'make up, too.'

'Does it hurt?' Sam asked.

'Not at all. One injection of the Magnetinc Femtobots and that's it. They're subcutaneous and stay in a neutral tone until activated. Then they move to the place you've chosen and form the pattern the pen transmits. Simple. It feels a little strange at first, sorta like water flowing under your skin.'

Fedor had always wanted a tattoo. 'How long do they last?'

'The bots are CarboSilicone, so they're designed to degrade after a few years. You get about a thousand patterns from one shot. Bigger patterns may take a few more injections.

'And if you don't want it anymore?' Veronique loved having options.

'Just touch the pen to the pattern with no design loaded,' the model pressed the blue nib against her shoulder, 'and the bots reset.' Sure enough, the dark lines began to fade and, after a few moments, her shoulder was once more blemish free.

'Amazing!' Joe clapped. 'Just brilliant.'

'Want to give it a go?' the model pointed to a man with a hypodermic gun.

Sam saw Joe wince. 'Needles?'

The model laughed. 'Honey, you should try the conventional method. Trust me, this is a kiss on the lips in comparison.'

The boy's eyes brightened. *Well, if you're offering...*

A figure caught Sam's eye. 'Hey,' he prodded Fedor, 'isn't that...?'

'Camiel.' Veronique had seen her, too.

Fedor scanned the crowd. 'Can't see the brother.'

'Shall we go over?' Joe would encourage any course of action that would lead them away from sharp objects. 'Be rude not to.'

Sam was still curious about the barefoot girl. 'Yes, let's.'

'Hi!' Veronique tapped Camiel on the shoulder as the girl was admiring the male model who had angel wings spreading across his back.

She jumped. 'Er, hi!' She looked about quickly.

'We didn't expect to see you again so soon,' Veronique said. 'What happened earlier?'

Camiel regained her composure. 'Oh, nothing, my brother's just intensely private. He has trust issues.'

'Is he here now?'

'No, he wanted to try and get good seats for the first Quest match, so I left him to it.'

The wings on the model were now fully formed, his entire back covered with life-like feathers. Camiel cast them a mischievous smile. 'Wanna see something cool?' Without waiting for an answer, she lifted her hand in the direction of the model and made the faintest of gestures.

It would have gone unnoticed in the busy room had they not been watching her. At first nothing happened, then Sam saw the model's skin begin to ripple and, one by one, the feathers dropped away and disappeared until all that was left of the majestic tattoo were gaunt skeletal wings.

People began to gasp, and Camiel drank in their reaction. She turned to the female model stood beside him and moved her hand again. The beautiful red rose tattoo she was showing a young couple began to sprout thick green tendrils with barbed thorns and rotting petals. Sam watched as the vines spread up her arms and across her body, wrapping themselves around the woman's neck and face.

She screamed and leapt off her podium, racing over to the man in the lab coat.

This time Sam heard Camiel laugh.

'How the—?' he looked around. The pandemonium was spreading. Everywhere in the tent, those injected with Magnetinc gasped in horror as their skin morphed and erupted into gruesome designs.

'Camiel!' Veronique hissed. 'Are you doing this?'

'Huh?'

'Stop it!'

Camiel turned her wide violet eyes on them. 'But look at them, these sheep; so eager to accept something into their body without knowing what it is or how to control it. They are learning an important lesson.'

'That's enough.' Fedor grabbed the small girl and lifted her till their faces were level. 'If you're doing this, stop it. Can't you see these people are terrified?'

She hung in his grip, staring back at him calmly. 'Do you think you scare me?' she said meeting his stony gaze. 'Put me down before *you* find out what fear really is.'

'*CAMIEL!*' Casius burst past Sam and Joe, his face puce. 'What have you done?

'Quick,' he thrust his chin toward the door, 'take her outside, I'll fix this mess. As always.' His last words were barely audible.

Fedor started to protest, but Casius was already weaving through the frantic crowd, moving his hands back and forth in the same way his sister had.

With rogue siblings of his own, Sam knew an impending disaster when he saw one. 'Let's get out of here.'

When they had left the stall Camiel shook herself free of Fedor's grasp. 'I don't know what all the fuss is about,' she eyed them accusingly. 'You people come here and swan about like nothing is wrong. This island is just one big amusement park to you. It's not, you know – far from it! You didn't even know there was another side to the island until we told you. Well, it's a dark and nasty place. Just ask your precious Mr D'Angelo,' she spat the name. 'He's the worst of the lot! Ask him about The Freezer – ask him about our father!' The girl was sobbing now, her arms stiff at her sides, fists clenched.

'That's enough!' Casius pushed past, folding his sister in his arms. 'Come on,' he brushed her hair tenderly. 'We need to get out of here before someone sees us. Forget about them, they can't help us – no one can. It's just you and me, Cam, like it's always been; and that's all we need.'

'Wait.' Sam stepped forward. 'Don't leave again. Tell us what's going on; we might be able to help you. We're just a little out of our depth here, that was a lot to take in. How did she...? How did you...?' He waved toward the now vacant stall.

'OMG! It's the CarboSilicone, isn't it?' Joe whispered, after a long silence. 'That's the only explanation. You can control it!'

Casius pushed Camiel away from his chest; her eyes were squeezed shut. 'See what you've done?' Sam heard him hiss. 'I *told* you this was a bad idea. They're just like the others. We're a threat to all of them.'

'We're not—' Sam stepped forward but Casius rounded on him, his palm stopping inches from Sam's chest. He made a strange gesture.

Sam looked down at the hand, then up at the boy, puzzled.

'You've no implants.' Casius stepped back. 'You should have implants. How can you not— Who are you?'

Camiel opened her eyes now, sniffing. She, too, raised her hand and made a swirling motion, her jaw dropping when whatever she thought would happen, didn't.

'I'm right, aren't' I?' Joe clapped his hands together. 'You can control CarboSilicone, but not us, because we're implant free!'

Casius took another step back. 'You're not a Cadre?'

The four teenagers looked at each other and smiled. 'Oh, we are,' Sam confirmed. 'But we're the next generation.'

'Currently in Beta testing,' Joe added.

'We need to get out of here, now!' Casius pushed his sister toward a gap in the tents. 'Forget these fools.'

'Hold on a minute.' Sam Folded in front of them, blocking their way. The twins skidded to a halt, eyes wide.

'Where—?' Casius turned to the spot Sam had occupied moments ago. 'How?'

Sam folded his arms. 'You're not the only one with tricks up your sleeve.'

'Please,' Casius's tone became earnest, 'you must let us go. If they find us here, they'll lock us up, too.'

'Who?' Veronique demanded. 'Who'll lock you up? What's this Freezer? Why do you hate Mr D'Angelo – what has he done to your father?'

'It's a prison,' Camiel whispered. 'For Harbingers. For anyone who disobeys The Few or does anything that may expose the Order. It's for those who won't conform, and won't be tamed.'

'A prison?' Joe looked shocked. 'Here? On the island?'

The twins nodded. 'Yes. A Suspended Animation prison, that's why it's called The Freezer and that's where our father is.'

The others looked equally shocked. 'What about your mother?' Veronique asked gently.

'We never had one.' Casius took a deep breath. 'That's why our father was imprisoned. He created us. We're the first, and probably the last, full CarboSilicone constructs.'

Sam looked blank.

Casius sighed. 'We were grown in a lab.'

Chapter 29

A colossal clap of thunder rang out across the square, shaking every tent, pole and person.

Sam looked toward the Crucible arena; above it a pair of huge holographic figures were locked in battle. A burst of energy shot from the hand of one of the gladiators and the air shook once more.

They were gone just as suddenly, leaving an excited buzz of voices in their wake, as people began moving toward the entrance to the volcano. The CruciBowl was about to begin!

Sam turned back to the twins, but they had vanished.

'Brilliant!' He threw up his arms in disgust.

'Oh.' Joe and Veronique looked around.

Fedor shook his head. 'They're gone – and we've got far more important things to worry about.'

'FML. The match,' Joe paled. 'I'd almost forgotten about it.'

'But didn't you hear what they just said?' Sam was upset that the mysterious pair had disappeared. Again. 'There's a prison somewhere on this island where they store people like…. like frozen food! And what did Casius mean when he said they were grown in a lab?'

'Load of rubbish, they're not all there,' Fedor said. 'The screen's on, but the battery's fried.'

Veronique nodded. 'It does sound a little far-fetched to me, too.'

'But you saw what she did in there!' Sam pointed.

They nodded.

'There's definitely something very strange about them,' Joe said, 'but I don't think we're going to get any answers right now and, as our giant companion has so painfully pointed out, we're about to be thrown to the lions. A prospect, for the record, I'm less than thrilled about!'

An hour later, the strange siblings were the furthest thing from Sam's mind. Standing high above the shimmering floor of the dormant volcano, The Stone Thieves leant against a railing, drinking in the vista of the packed coliseum.

Levi Orbs raced around the arena, feeding large Holoscreens above each of the stands. Sam studied other excited faces in the audience, altered by Mods or emblazoned with the colours of their favourite cadre, beaming when the cameras passed, or waving and whooping wildly. Their rich banners, gigantic Holographic mascots and happy chatter brought the stadium to life.

'There's someone I want you to meet,' Jenny shouted over the noise.

Sam reluctantly joined the others in Mr D'Angelo's private box, where he found Jen Si talking to a tall man he didn't recognise.

'Gentlemen,' Jenny interrupted them.

The stranger had a firm, weather-beaten face, dark eyes, short hair and day-old stubble. Sam noticed him sizing them up. Everything about the man, from the way he moved to the clothes he wore, seemed methodical. Efficient.

'This is Caleb Roth, winner of last year's CruciBowl.

'Caleb, meet Sam, Fedor, Veronique and Turt...' she caught herself, 'Giuseppe.'

The man smiled when he caught the evil look Joe was giving Jenny. 'My pleasure.'

'Your cadre is The Silent Knight?' Sam saw Joe try not to wince, when the man shook his hand.

'It is and speak of the Devil...' he glanced over to three people who had just stepped into view at the rear of the room. Well, two people and a mountain.

'Basher!' Jenny greeted the largest man Sam had ever seen.

'It's the little Scot!' he grinned at her, his voice rich and smooth. 'And who are these poor wee souls?' he asked, looking down at the gawping faces. 'Your latest victims?' He lowered his voice, 'Whatever she tells you, always do the opposite – you'll live longer!'

'Very funny.

'Basher is just jealous that I broke two of his field records.'

'Pah!' The Māori giant grunted, pretending to look over the gathering. He stretched, releasing a series of cracks from his spine that sounded more like small arms fire to Sam than the movement of muscle and fibre.

Jenny turned to a pale man who stood beside the sulky giant. 'You already know Harper.'

Ghost winked. 'Hello, again. I hope you've been practising?'

'And I'm Polly,' the final member of the team stepped forward and introduced herself. 'Though, that's a nickname, too.'

'Why do they call you Polly?' Sam asked.

'Because she can recite anything she's ever seen or heard, like a parrot.' Basher tousled the woman's dyed hair. 'Not because her hairdresser thinks she's a Macaw.'

Polly's hair was an eclectic mixture of red, blue and green streaks, swept up in a ponytail.

'Another eidetic memory!' Joe marvelled. 'How wonderful.'

'Indeed.' Polly said. 'A gift and a curse.'

'How so?' Fedor asked.

'Well,' Sam noticed Polly's voice had taken on a more sombre tone. 'There are some things you'd rather forget.'

'Tell me about it,' Joe muttered.

'Aha, fabulous, you've all met!' Mr D'Angelo made a timely appearance, striding over to clap Basher and Caleb on the back. 'Now don't be too alarmed,' he said, with his arms spread between the solid men. 'It's just going to be an exhibition match and besides, you'll have IDA...'

Sam saw Jenny wince. 'Er, we were still getting to that.'

Joe turned whiter than Ghost. 'You're kidding? Them! You're expecting us to fight *THEM*?'

Basher looked down at Mr D'Angelo. 'Wait. What?'

'Now, now, let's all calm down,' the silver-tongued man began.

'IDA?' Sam whispered to Fedor, when everyone began speaking at once.

'Inertia Dampening Armour. Supposedly takes the sting out of big hits.'

'Hits that big?' Basher had shrugged off Mr D'Angelo's arm and was pointing at Joe.

'Think it's too late to try jumping into our new Bottomless pockets?' Sam lamented.

Fedor pursed his lips. 'Probably, but I like where your head's at.' He glared at Mr D'Angelo. 'It's almost as if he *wants* us to fail and get kicked out of The Order.'

The Quartermaster's Store was in the competitors' section of the arena.

'So, this is where every Rummager goes?' Sam craned his neck over the counter, peering into the cavernous recesses of the storeroom, which appeared to lead off for miles in every direction. An army of 3D printers whirred away under the close supervision of technicians with clipboards and safety glasses.

'I can't believe we're missing the Opening Ceremony,' Veronique pouted.

From within the muffled recesses of the volcano, Sam could hear distant cheers and rapturous applause, as the annual CruciBowl was ushered into existence with what he could only imagine would be unparalleled pageantry.

'Really?' Joe glared at her. 'You think that's the thing we should be upset about?' He turned to Jenny. 'And when can I have my Krusa back?'

'When I can be sure you're not going to vanish, never to be seen or heard from again.'

'Give it to him,' Veronique pleaded. 'Or here, you can have mine, just promise you'll use it straight away.'

Sam laughed, as she pretended to pat herself down.

'Ha. Ha. Ha.' The boy's voice held no mirth whatsoever.

Fedor slapped him on the back. 'Suck it up. Besides, you're small. I doubt Basher will even notice you out there. If he does, maybe you could dazzle him with some fun facts about seahorses.'

'I hate you all,' Joe muttered, a traitorous tear forming.

'Right then, who's next?' The Quartermaster appeared, bushy moustache bristling with crumbs. 'Oh,' he looked at the four youngsters, 'I think you're in the wrong place. This is not the Curio Centre; you want to go back down that hall and turn ri—'

Jenny cut him off. 'We're here for a fitting.'

The man looked even more perplexed. 'But they're just children.' He looked at Fedor and his brow knotted. 'Well, those three are. My, my, you are a beefy specimen, aren't you? Eat a lot of red meat, do we?'

Sam saw Fedor raise one eyebrow but he said nothing.

'Salvador sent us,' Jenny said.

The man's moustache swished from side to side. 'For a fitting, you say?' He looked over the unlikely quartet. 'Well, ours is not to reason why. 'Felix!'

A racing green robot with brushed aluminium trim whirred over. 'Sir?'

'Three, err four,' he looked at Fedor again, 'for IDA, please.'

'What about Rigor Mortis sticks?' Joe demanded. 'Ghost taught us how to use them and we've done the drills. Seems only fair we have some.'

Jenny shrugged. 'Sure. Four sets of those, too.'

'Sai for me, please,' Veronique quickly amended the order.

'Coming right up.' The man turned away and then stopped, looking back at them. 'Better add some extra padding to that one's IDA.' He cocked his head in Joe's direction. 'I think the big one's stealing his food.'

Felix floated over the counter. 'Stand apart, please. And spread your arms and legs.' A series of green beams erupted from the metal body as it scanned up and down, then from left to right. 'Names?'

Jenny supplied the information.

'The bracelets will be ready in one hour. Will you be requiring any Mod pens or assigned shelves?'

Jenny shook her head. 'Could you send it all up to Mr D'Angelo's suite, please?'

'Certainly.' Sam watched Felix whirr over the counter and out of sight.

'So, that's it.' Joe looked forlorn. 'We're really going to do this?'

Were he to be honest, Sam was not relishing the thought of squaring up against Caleb Roth and his Cadre one bit. Nor could he imagine were Veronique or Fedor. But if Joe also saw how petrified they were of what lay ahead, the boy would go to pieces.

'Look, we're a team and whatever happens, we'll face it as a team. What doesn't kill you...'

Joe snorted, thinking back over the summer. 'Invariably scars, breaks bones and leaves psychological trauma. How are your ribs anyway?'

'*Mon dieu*!' Veronique threw her hands up. 'Never mind half full, your glass has dropped, broken and shattered into a thousand tiny pieces! All of which are now buried in your feet, fingers and eyes. Find a corner and hide, then. Live to run away another day. Or, trust in us and yourself. Either way, we must do this, so try to accept it and let's go see what all the fuss is about. *Oui*?'

'*Oui*,' Joe groaned, stomping after Jenny, equally heavy of heart and foot.

'Maybe we could pop back out to Sgt what's-his-name's tent,' Sam said to Fedor. 'See if he has a turtle Mod and hook him up with a real shell!'

Fedor snorted. 'Actually, ArmaArmour – the Armadillo Armour Mod Dallas mentioned – might not be a bad call. Karl tried it once and said absolutely *nothing* gets through that stuff!'

Back on the balcony, the roar of the crowd filling every corner and crevice of Valsieve's volcano, Sam gawped in amazement as the CruciBowl begun.

Ruben and his colossal guardian, Allegarus, had been waiting in the box when they returned.

'Are you joining us to watch the matches?' Joe had taken a real shine to the librarian over the summer and was glad of his company.

'I'd every intention of doing so,' Ruben peered through the glass, 'but I didn't quite fully appreciate the enormity of all this. So, no, we'll be heading back. I just wanted to wish you good luck!'

Allegarus had not been impressed by this development.

Despite Mr D'Angelo's most earnest diplomatic charm, they were unable to sway the curator and, wishing them well, he had left.

Sam watched the shimmering floor of the arena begin to ripple and swirl, as billions upon billions of microscopic Holobotic robots assembled to form the field for the first Quest match.

'Every single Holobot,' Jenny shouted, 'is capable of not only connecting to other Holobots but also of emitting light. This means that when they are joined together, they are able to form physical holograms.'

Sam frowned. 'You mean you can touch them?'

'Touch them, walk on them, jump on them – hide under them,' she winked at Joe. 'They look like the real thing, but don't feel the same.'

'So, they can be grass, or a wall, but would still be metal?'

'Exactly. Cold, hard metal.'

Sam imagined slamming into a wall of tiny metal robots at speed.

Fedor was on the same page. 'IDA to the rescue!'

'They are programmed to respond to certain movement,' Jenny said. 'So, there's some give. The water works in the same way.'

Beneath them, the volcano was a hive of inorganic activity, waves and columns of Holobotic robots forming complex shapes and structures.

'That looks like a tree.' Veronique pointed to the far corner of the arena.

'OMG,' Joe perked up, 'so does that.'

'It's like a deranged Lava lamp,' Sam said.

'There,' Veronique indicated another pocket of activity. 'That could be a wing.'

'A plane?' Sam heard Fedor venture.

'Oooh, it's the jungle crash site!' Jenny said. 'Tough one to start with.'

'Who's up first?' Joe squinted up at the closest Holoscreen and Sam followed his gaze. A pair of three-dimensional dials were whirring around, the sigils of the Cadres an unrecognisable blur. Gradually they slowed, before clicking to a stop.

'The Quiet Elves vs. Pandora's Box? What strange names.'

Jenny winced. 'Don't let anyone hear you say that. Fans are very protective of their Cadres – and wear their sigils proudly. Most have Magnetinc tattoos of them. They can't all be as cool as The Stone Thieves!'

'True story.' Sam agreed. 'Same type of sigils Pip told us about?'

Joe nodded. 'Yup. Usually a crest or coat of arms. Jenny, is there a programme with a list of the Cadres and their sigils?'

She handed him a glossy pamphlet. 'Back page. There's also bios and stats on all the teams. Should keep you quiet for a minute. Maybe two.'

They crowded around Joe, pouring over the profiles.

'There's Pip,' Veronique pointed excitedly. 'And Selina. I can't wait to see what Mods they're going to be using.'

'Not sure Gecko Fingers would be much use today,' Fedor said, 'unless you're trying to climb out in a hurry.' He elbowed Joe and winked.

'God, don't forget Tec,' Sam added. 'If he uses that Electric Eel thing, it could get really messy.'

'Ooo, Fire Lords,' Joe's eyes widened. 'They sound scary. There's Dallas. I'm looking forward to seeing her again, too.'

Veronique snorted. 'You just want a go with her Gopher!'

'I might do,' he tried to sound casual.

'And Ghost,' Fedor flirted with the fringes of excitement, 'bet he's lethal with that Rigor Mortis rapier of his.'

Joe's mood soured instantly. 'Well, we're probably going to find that out the hard way. I might just run straight at him, get it over with!'

Sam was glad when Veronique tried to distract him. 'Hey, I wonder if the Stone Thieves had a sigil? We could get a Magnetinc tattoo and our parents would never know!'

Fedor and Sam beamed, nodding.

'Better yet,' she continued, 'I bet you could get Anatoly to create iTribes for all the Cadres and I may even do the voice-overs if you ask nicely.'

'There'll be holographic Top Trumps on sale after the tournament,' Jenny added from the periphery. 'They're pretty cool, I used to collect them.'

'Geek,' Sam coughed into his hand and everyone laughed at Jenny's indignant pout.

* * *

Icarus Bayne was getting impatient. 'It's not a fashion show! Just put the gloves on and clap your hands together and the suit will activate.'

The wet-look material of Mrs Keller's suit came to life and flowed down her arms and over her body. His sister admired herself in the mirror. She had never worn a Cold Suit before and, if she had to be honest, the sleek, black outfit looked delicious on her.

Icarus Bayne sighed the long-suffering sigh of a man who wished he was alone. 'I'm going without you.'

She wound her silky mane into a ponytail and the hood of the suit formed around it, the goggles snapping into place.

He turned to his two wards stood waiting patiently. 'Ready?'

The boy and the girl nodded.

'Right. Let's go see a man about a scroll.'

* * *

The CruciBowl final had been spectacular. [*]

The boys were slapping each other excitedly, jumping and cheering. Even Veronique had to admit the finale had made her grip the rail as she watched.

The sun had long since slipped from the sky and the coliseum was bathed in a floodlit glow. With a puff of smoke, the final Holobot disappeared

When everyone had made their way back to the box, Jenny held out Joe's Krusa. 'You'll be needing this.'

The boy took it, his smile fading. The door closed, the levity of the tournament remaining outside. On the table lay their IDA bracelets and a bundle of Rigor Mortis weapons.

Sam looked at them, heart pounding. It all came down to this. The fate of their families now rested with them. With him.

Don't let me down, super blood.

Mr D'Angelo was oblivious to their sombre mood. 'Jen Si will show you down to the competitors' area where you can suit up, calm your nerves and get ready to show everyone just what The Stone Thieves are made of!' He did manage to detect the colour draining from Joe's face and added a final assurance. 'Not literally, of course!'

The wall suddenly shimmered and a huge man stumbled into the room. Allegarus Nazareth's face was badly swollen and bruised, his hair slick with blood and sweat. His legs gave way and he fell over the refreshments table with a tremendous crash.

Jen Si pushed Joe aside and bent over the fallen man. 'He... he's dead.'

'That's impossible,' Sam blurted. 'He was just here. How could he be...? Who could possibly—'

Joe's eyes widened. 'Ruben!' he gasped.

Krusa in one hand, IDA bracelet in the other, the boy vanished before the librarian's name had left his lips.

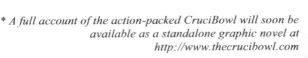

[*] A full account of the action-packed CruciBowl will soon be available as a standalone graphic novel at http://www.thecrucibowl.com

Chapter 30

There are usually a handful of defining moments in a person's life, and the scene that met Joe in the Library would be one of his.

He Folded to the top of the spiral staircase, immediately aware that the air felt wrong; that the silence was oppressive. He sniffed, catching the caustic odour of burnt machinery, then heard a faint pop and fizzing sound.

Joe looked down. At the foot of the stairs lay the smouldering remains of an electronic assistant. Next to them, stood a lean woman, surrounded by fog and covered head to toe in a dark, shiny suit complete with black goggles. In her hand, she held a scroll. Behind her, the rows of meticulously arranged bookshelves had been obliterated, as if a giant hand had swept them aside like dominoes. Clouds of scorched pages and black ash hung in the air.

None of this mattered for Joe's gaze was pinned to the ground in front of the woman where a small, broken body lay motionless.

'Ruben! No!' The words escaped his lips without thought as shock and anger shot through him. 'I'll kill you!'

The woman's head snapped up. A charged staff glowed in her other hand. A man appeared from the wreckage, alerted by Joe's cry. He shouted to the woman as two more figures stumbled from the wreckage.

Four on one. Great.

Joe caught a flicker of movement and was relieved to see Sam, Fedor, Jen Si and Veronique step into view near the Library's entrance, improving his odds of survival.

'Look out!' he shouted tos them.

The man near the bookcases hurled a glowing orb at the newcomers. It let out a high-pitched whine as it rose toward the ceiling, pulsing furiously before erupting in a blast of blinding light and emitting a noise so piercing that everyone without a black suit fell to the floor in agony.

The move was the only thing that saved Joe from the woman's missile, which missed him by inches. Clasping his hands to his ears, he retched, choking back rising waves of nausea.

The sound weapon landed within Fedor's reach and instinctively he lashed out.

'Don't—' the monk tried to warn him.

The boy brought his fist down with a force that would have shattered most devices, but this particular weapon had defences. As he struck, it discharged its battery in one almighty blast, sending Fedor flying across the room. But his swift action did bring the blinding light and debilitating sound to an end.

Sam, would not have considered the calm monk to be a man of action, but he now saw another side of their mentor. Jen Si was on his feet at once.

He pointed towards the woman near the stairs. 'Sam, Veronique – help Joe and get that scroll!' His feet hardly seemed to touch the floor, as he then made for the masked man.

Sam struggled onto one elbow and tried not to be sick. 'V, you okay?'

'Not really.'

'Fair enough.' Sam blinked, trying to clear his vision.

'Where's Fedor?'

He could hear the concern in her voice. 'There's nothing we can do for him right now.' Sam glanced toward the door. 'This lot's had the better of us once already. It's not going to happen again.' He eyed the woman climbing the staircase toward Joe. 'Time to try something new!'

Sam placed his hands over his shoulders and flipped onto his feet. Giving his destination a final glance, he leapt as high as he could, raising his knees to his chest, and disappeared.

Veronique swivelled her head toward Joe and saw Sam rematerialize in mid-air at the top of the staircase, just as the woman reached it. She whooped when he drove both legs into the woman's chest, sending them flying back down the stairs. Then Veronique Folded across the library and caught him.

Grabbing the woman's wrist, she then prepared to deliver a kick to her exposed armpit. Instead, she cried out and withdrew her hand in agony.

'It's not called a Cold Suit for nothing, my dear,' the woman sneered as she staggered to her feet. She still held the scroll, but her staff had been lost in the fall.

'Veronique!' a panicked voice called from above. Joe, IDA bracelet in hand, vaulted over the side of the balcony and vanished.

Sam and Veronique waited for agonising seconds, expecting him to repeat Sam's feat and reappear above the woman, crushing her into the ground. Reappear he did, however slightly to the left of his target, so he crashed into a pile of books.

'It looked so easy,' he groaned, rolling over in agony.

'Beginner's luck,' Sam shrugged, leaping toward the woman, Veronique just a heartbeat behind him.

Jen Si fed the flame and banished his emotion. He was calm, focused…and deadly.

His feet left the ground and he Folded, reappearing beside the man, throwing out his leg to catch his opponent's knee. If they wished to fight dirty, he would oblige.

The sound of the impact was unpleasant, but pity was also fodder for the flame. The man fell hard and cried out. Jen Si Folded again, reappearing in front of him and delivering a sharp blow to his temple. The man slumped; arms raised to protect himself.

Jen Si continued to Fold and attack. He made no quips. It was a short and brutal fight, embarrassingly one-sided. It could hardly be otherwise when one adversary had the knowledge and skill of countless generations.

Jen Si did not fight often, but when he had to, he was without equal. Gadgets may have levelled the playing field, but he gave his opponent no chance to use them.

Eventually the man slumped forward, unconscious.

Jen Si looked up, just in time to see Sam appear above the staircase.

Who taught him that? He smiled at the boy proudly. But the moment of pride cost him dearly. He failed to hear the staff and the blow caught him unaware, a blast of energy knocking him clean off his feet.

'Uncle?' A figure bent over his unconscious adversary.

Jen Si lay shaking on the ground nearby, waiting for the convulsions to pass and praying he did not meet his end before they did. Emotion. Would he ever learn?

Icarus Bayne drifted in tranquillity. Floating on a silent sea, happy and carefree. He did not remember how he got here, but that didn't matter now, for he felt warm and safe. He might even go so far as to say, content.

Something battered on the silence; a voice hammering at the edges of his restful state. *Typical!* Then he felt movement, and with it something else... Pain.

His boat tipped, rocked and capsized, casting him into violent waters. The calm washed away, and light, noise and agony replaced it.

'Uncle!' The cry seized his senses as hard as the hands that shook him. 'Please, wake up! You need to move. We must help Mother!'

Sam and Veronique drove the woman backward with a barrage of well-placed kicks. Punching was out of the question as Veronique's forearm was still numb and there had yet to be any opportunity to find a weapon in the graveyard of bookshelves.

Their opponent was meeting their assault with precision and experience. She was no simple thief, however she would not be able to overpower the two of them in the debris, so her strategy appeared to be that of defence.

Joe found his feet and followed them into the bowels of the archive, hungry for blood. He kept trying to squeeze past, to find a way around his friends, but the terrain of broken wood and slippery piles of books was proving difficult to navigate, so he fell back, looking for another way.

It was only then that he caught a movement nearby and realised why the woman was so happy to defend herself against the two inexperienced fighters.

She was leading them into a trap.

Ms Keller had to concede these kids were good. She deflected one kick and barely dodged the next, deliberately giving more ground.

Their unexpected battle with that monster of a guard had taken every trick, gadget and ounce of cunning the four of them could muster, laying waste to the library in the process. She shuddered to think of the history and knowledge that had been lost.

Ms Keller did not want to make her retreat look too easy and she lashed out, catching the girl with the heel of her boot.

Fedor's eyes fluttered, his vision was blurry and his ears rang. He swore. The pain was everywhere.

Couldn't have picked up the IDA bracelet first...

He swore again. It didn't help the pain, but it did make him feel a bit better.

He coughed up a mouthful of blood, certain he felt more than one tooth move. He was lying face down in a pile of wreckage but could not recall how he had got there or why every inch of him was on fire. The ringing in his ears was unbearable and he wiggled his jaw to try and make them pop.

More pain.

He tested his extremities, flexing arms and legs, then wiggling fingers and toes. All protested but reluctantly complied. He moved his hips and his ribs, which, it had to be said, had taken an undue amount of punishment of late. Thankfully, they did not appear broken either. Taking a breath, he braced himself and prepared to move. It was just another day in his summer from hell.

Joe bit his lip. *Now what?* Did he try to warn Sam and Veronique, or would that distract them and give the woman the opening for which she was looking? Or worse, would it cause this mystery person to act in haste and bring more destruction raining down upon them?

His eyes flickered between the fight and the stocky figure trying to stay out of their peripheral vision. The man's hands were low and Joe could not see if he was holding anything. Safe to say that, if he were, it wasn't flowers or half time refreshments!

Joe dropped back. He looked around for a memorable spot and saw Ruben's Hologlobe, far from home, lying on its side amongst the rubble. *Sad, but that'll do.*

With that landmark firmly set in his mind, he vanished.

Icarus Bayne had felt better, much better, in fact.

He struggled to his feet with the aid of his earnest niece; only to falter the moment he placed his weight on the damaged knee. He swore.

'That's no help,' came her frustrated remonstration.

Icarus looked over at the monk, who lay twitching a few metres away. *What a demon! Didn't see that coming...*

He pointed to a long piece of broken bookshelf nearby. 'Grab that.'

The girl bent down and helped him onto the makeshift crutch.

'Now give me the staff,' Bayne held out his hand, not taking his eyes off the monk.

'We don't have time for that, we need to find Mum. He's not going anywhere.'

'What's the golden rule?'

The girl sighed. 'Now? Really?'

'Yes.'

'Never leave an enemy behind you.'

'Exactly. Look at the state of me. Does he look like an enemy you'd like to face? I'm certainly not itching for a second round. Either you finish him, or I will.'

There was a savage crunch, as the staff was smashed in half.

'Hi, there.' Fedor swung a chunk of bookshelf across his shoulders and rested both hands on the cudgel. He smiled at the faceless girl whom he now assumed was the same one he had chased up the mountain a few weeks ago. 'Sooo, how've you been?'

Joe materialised on the spiral staircase.

Trying not to look at Ruben's broken body, he searched for the woman's staff. He leant over the balcony, scanning the wreckage. *Please, please, please...* 'Yes!' He spied the short staff in the mess below and rushed down, taking the steps two at a time. Beside it, lay his IDA bracelet. *Fortune does favour the brave!*

He snatched it up, then bent to retrieve the weapon, and stopped. What if it was coded to its owner and set to deliver a shock – or worse? His outstretched fingers waggled, impatient; his mind was racing.

Tick tock. Tick tock.

Joe swore. He looked at the IDA bracelet.

That might work!

Joe put the bracelet on and gave the small blue button a push. Nanothread erupted from the band, it covered his fingers and then surged up his arm and over his shoulders. It rippled over his shoes and up the back of his neck, stopping at the base of his skull. Joe turned his arms over, examining the shimmering grey and purple armour that now covered his body. He did not see the large red 'L' across his back. *This is more like it!*

He turned his wrist and patted the handle of the staff with the back of his armoured hand. Nothing.

Joe heaved a sigh of relief and grabbed it, giving the device a terse examination. He flicked a switch at his thumb and the tip sprang to life, crackling ominously.

The boy grinned.

He found a pocket in the armour and stuffed the device in, then grabbed his Krusa. 'My turn.'

Fedor regarded the girl. Neither she nor the injured man moved a muscle.

The man looked down at the mass of sparks, pops and shattered circuitry. 'Well, that wasn't very nice. Those aren't cheap, you know! Where shall we send the bill?' His laconic voice told Fedor that he had mocked him at the castle, too.

The man turned to the girl. 'Anything else up your sleeve, my dear? I'm afraid I'm all out.'

The girl took a step back, reaching behind her.

Fedor moved at once, swinging the club off his shoulder and placing himself between Jen Si and the pair in the black suits.

His opponent drew out a long coil of black rubber, and turning her body sideways, settled into a fighting stance. She unfurled the silver-tipped whip with a shake, swirling the fog around her.

Fedor heard a click as she pressed a button in the handle and the tip crackled, bouncing off the floor like an electric jumping bean.

Fedor swore.

'Now, now,' the man chided. 'That's no way to speak to a lady.'

Joe took in the scene. Sam and Veronique had backed the woman into a corner and were pressing her hard. They were exactly where she wanted them, completely oblivious to the figure moving in from the side, who now raised a strange pistol and prepared to fire.

'Hey!' Joe called nervously.

The figure halted and spun, swinging the gun in Joe's direction.

'You dropped something!' Joe tossed him a hollow object.

The tip of their pistol dipped as the figure looked up and instinctively caught the hollow ring, oblivious to the small green LED blinking on its side.

'Jesus, what are you wearing and what the hell is thi—'

Joe flicked the switch on the staff and shoved the charged end into his pocket. It leapt from the Bottomless pocket-ring in his opponent's hand and, hissing ferociously, took him squarely between the eyes.

'Ha! Anatoly, you're a genius!' the boy laughed.

The victory, however, was short lived. Falling back, their body convulsing, his foe gave the trigger of the pistol several involuntary tugs.

Even with his armour, the first blast knocked Joe off his feet, sending him crashing into the Hologlobe. His laughter died.

Other shots were fired, scattering books and broken shelves alike. The final blast headed straight for Sam and Veronique.

'Look out!' Sam tried to push the girl away and took the majority of the force in the chest.

No one was any the wiser when Anatoly's secret gift kicked in. It reacted instantly. Switching to Defence mode, EverMod activated the ArmaArmour gene. Armadillo scales instantly spread beneath Sam's shirt and diffused the blast before it could do any real damage.

There was a ripple of purple neon energy as his crystal infused Femtoglobin responded, then the Mod disappeared.

Fedor ducked and rushed forward. The whip whistled over his head. He could feel the air prickling and knew that if the buzzing tip found its mark, he was in trouble.

But the girl was now too close to use it and she spun, aiming a perfect roundhouse kick at his lowered head. Fedor gave ground, allowing her to retreat and recoil the whip.

He Folded, coming up behind her, but instead of smashing the base of his makeshift club into the back of her head, as he should have, the boy drove his foot into the back of her legs.

She rolled forwards, using the momentum to her advantage, and was up again, her whip spinning round.

'No good deed...' he muttered, as the hissing rubber snake shot towards him.

This time Fedor raised his cudgel and allowed her whip to wrap around it. The tip stopped inches from his face, its bright blue charge blurring his vision. Before the girl could uncoil it, Fedor leapt backwards and Folded behind the only pair of shelves left standing.

There was a loud thump and the shelves rocked as something hit them – hard. He let go of the club and peered around the corner. On the other side, the girl, still clinging to the whip, lay unconscious.

'Sorry about that.'

Ms Keller stood in stunned silence. Quite literally. Around her, four teenagers lay unconscious.

She zipped the scroll into a special pocket in her Cold Suit and picked her way through the rubble to the stocky youth who lay convulsing on the floor. Bending down, she retrieved the offending pistol. She selected the 'Unresponsive' setting on his Turner and the panel changed from blue to purple. It emitted several warning beeps before both the device and boy wearing it disappeared.

Inspecting the pistol, she gave the other three bodies a thoughtful glance.

Jen Si felt the convulsions growing weaker.

He managed to swivel his head to where Fedor had Folded and dragged the girl into the bookcase. It was a brilliant move and the monk felt another swell of pride.

Then he saw a woman slip from the wreckage, pistol in hand. He opened his mouth to warn the boy, but the only sound he could manage was a gurgling groan and he closed his eyes, unable to watch. The stun gun's discharge was followed by a crash, as Fedor was hurled across the room for the second time in ten minutes.

'And who do we have here?' the woman asked.

'Well, I may be wrong, but I think this may be *the* fabled monk. Took me apart in seconds. Truly awesome.'

The woman bent down to peer at Jen Si. 'How remarkable,' she purred. 'We can't kill you then, can we? This is simply too good an opportunity to pass up. I have just the opening for a man of your stature. My exhibit will finally have a star attraction.'

Chapter 31

Four bruised and battered teenagers sat in the lounge where, only a few short months ago, their incredible adventure had begun.

Sam could never have imagined it would end like this.

'I can't believe they're gone,' Veronique sniffed, her red-rimmed eyes fresh with tears. Fedor cradled her hand in his.

Joe stared at the floor. He had no tears. He should have, he usually cried at anything. But he felt too broken.

'The intruders used the CruciBowl as a distraction,' Mr D'Angelo said. 'They must've known everyone would be there. Ruben should have been, too. Their intent was theft, not murder.'

Joe swore. 'You mean it was Harbinger. Stop treating us like kids – you opened this can of worms. Their intention doesn't matter. All that matters is what they did.'

Sam noticed that this time Salvador had no glib answer. 'We think they – Harbinger – used the stolen Cybernetic Assistant to programme a Turner with the co-ordinates to the Library. There's no other explanation.'

'But why would Troy have the co-ordinates to the Library?' Jenny asked.

D'Angelo explained to the teenagers that Troy was, in fact, Archimedes, the CA programmed to help Ruben catalogue the Old Library. He had been re-assigned to Ivan when it became clear that the Order needed someone with considerable experience to differentiate between his harmful and benign nocturnal ramblings.

'Do we know what they took?' Jenny was solemn.

Mr D'Angelo shook his head. 'No, and I'm afraid, given the extent of the damage to the library, there's no way to tell. Not in the short term, at least.'

'What'll happen now?' Joe's thirst for vengeance was raw.

'Baid will find them.' Salvador's tone was cold. 'Rescue the monk and reclaim what is ours. Ruben will have justice.'

They sat in silence for a few moments before Joe asked another question. 'And his library?'

Mr D'Angelo looked at the ruined chamber. 'It'll close.' He shrugged. 'There's no one left with his knowledge or passion to sort this mess out.'

Joe looked up with renewed purpose. 'I'll do it!'

Salvador suppressed his laugh when he saw the boy was serious. 'Perhaps in a few years, when you finish school,' he tried to sound diplomatic, 'we could consider it. For now, we'll clean things up as best we can—'

'I've finished school.'

'You what?' Sam gawped.

'I graduated this year,' he shrugged, 'I was pushed up a year, several, in fact. The curriculum was easy and the teachers got tired of me correcting them.'

'We know how they feel,' Fedor winked.

'Well,' Mr D'Angelo took a breath, letting the idea settle, 'if you've finished school then, technically, you should be starting your Induction-'

'For which I am too young and, quite frankly, not cut out for.'

'This could be a good stop gap?' Jenny suggested. Sam was glad when she lent more weight to the cause.

'Let me think on it, I'm not saying no but, I'm not saying yes – yet, either.' Mr D'Angelo silenced further debate with a wave of his hand. 'For now, we have more sombre matters to attend to.'

Ruben's funeral was held in Venice.

The days since the attack on the Old Library were the hardest of the summer. The loss of Jen Si was felt keenly. Harbinger had struck at the heart of The Few and no one felt safe.

Security was present everywhere, but it did little to fill the gaping hole the monk had left, or dull the painful memory of Ruben's passing.

Jenny did her best to help them try and make sense of it all, as did their parents, but everything was different now. Their own near-death experiences had made the importance of their training and the danger Harbinger posed, suddenly very real.

Casius and Camiel. The Freezer. Dark Mods and the host of other mysteries that had surfaced over the summer, no longer seemed so important and were quietly shipped to the back of Sam's mind.

Ruben's body was laid to rest at sunset in an unmarked family crypt, joining a long line of lauded ancestors. The canals were illuminated by hundreds of small floating candles.

His eulogy had been poignant and the size of the congregation bore testament to how many lives, this larger-than-life character had touched, despite his seclusion. There was not a dry eye when they said their goodbyes, pushing the small glowing vessels out into the fading light across the water.

'Think they'll let you do it?' Sam asked, whilst he, Fedor and Joe watched Veronique and Jenny light their candles. 'The library?'

Joe shrugged. 'IDK. Hope so. I think he'd want me to.'

Sam nodded. 'There's nobody better.'

Joe blushed and his friend slapped him on the back.

'Come on,' Fedor suggested, 'let's get something to eat.'

Despite the sombre mood, Sam laughed for the first time in a week. 'I see some things will never change.'

The next day the teenagers and Jenny were summoned to Mr D'Angelo's office.

'Suffice to say, we're all deeply saddened and concerned by recent events,' he began. 'Jen Si's absence is felt by all of us, but we must focus on the here and now, as he would have us. You've all shown considerable promise over the summer and, despite the Council being unable to gauge the fruits of your labour first-hand, the programme has been deemed a success. For now.'

'So, we've passed?' Sam felt his chest tighten. With everything that had happened, it had seemed inappropriate to mention the sword still dangling above their heads, but it had weighed heavily on all their minds.

Mr D'Angelo gazed at the frosty tip of Mount Kilimanjaro through his Far Sight window for what felt like an eternity. 'You have, but we will need you to return next year, to continue your training.'

Sam saw Joe blanch. 'You can't be serious – after everything that's happened? I'm not cut out for this – none of us are!'

'I'm very serious, and you need to give yourselves more credit. We need to make radical changes now more than ever,' Salvador patted the boy on the shoulder and walked over to the cabinet beside his desk. Ever the master of misdirection, he picked up a box and offered it to them, 'In the interim, however, I think you'll be needing this.'

'Go on,' Veronique prompted, when Joe didn't move, 'open it!'

Joe, still baffled by what he had heard or how they could possibly be considering doing this all again, took the box and put it down on the desk.

'Here.' Veronique swatted away his idle hands. Inside, was a shiny new CA,

Joe stared at it. 'I don't understand,' he said, looking up.

Sam watched Mr D'Angelo smile his most fabulous fake smile. 'Well, if you're going to sort out that tip of a library, you're going to need some help and I'm afraid I simply can't spare anyone else.'

Joe's eyes widened. The distraction had worked. 'Really? You're going to let me do it?'

'On one condition,' Mr D'Angelo applied the golden handcuff, 'next summer, you join your friends again.'

'But Ruben? Jen Si?'

'Are things you cannot do anything about. We'll handle that. This, however, is how you can help. Will you join The Few?'

There was a long pause. 'Yes.'

Mr D'Angelo smiled.

Fedor pursed his lips. 'Does he get to name it?' He pointed to the box.

Mr D'Angelo shrugged, but nodded. 'Sure.'

'Can I make a suggestion?'

Joe looked dubious. 'Go on…'

'Turtle!'

The mood instantly lightened. Nothing would undo recent events, but at some point, they would have to move on.

'Turtle, it is!' Joe managed a smile.

'One final piece of housekeeping,' Mr D'Angelo pointed to the table beside the box, 'I'll need your Krusa back. For now.'

This request was met with general dejection, but they all surrendered the relics reluctantly.

It was then that Veronique noticed something strange. Having never seen all four carvings in the same place before, their size and shapes appeared to have no meaning, but when the pieces lay beside one another…

Moving them around, the Krusa's pattern began to make sense. She made a few more adjustments.

'Ooo,' Joe peered over her shoulder. 'I didn't know they did that. Look, it forms a circle, but there's one missing. And there's an inscription on the side. *El'var Duresdai—*'

Mr D'Angelo's hand swooped in and swept up the stones. 'That's enough of that. I've got the only dodecahedron Rubik cube in existence around here somewhere, if it's a puzzle you're after.'

'But—' Joe pointed.

'But nothing; don't you have a CA to commission? That library's not going to sort itself out, young man.'

'Now scoot, all of you.' He ushered the four teenagers toward the door.

'I wonder what it means?' Joe pondered out loud when they reached the door.

'What?' Veronique asked.

'The inscription on the Krusa: *El'var Duresdai.*'

Persephone, hovering nearby, overheard the seemingly innocent question.

'It means The Hall of a Thousand Worlds,' she translated.

'*Out*!' Mr D'Angelo fumed, glaring at the robot.

The door closed with a bang.

'There's definitely something about the Krusa he doesn't want us to know.' Veronique said.

'Add that to about a thousand other mysteries and unanswered questions,' Sam sighed. 'And yet he expects us to come back...'

'All right,' Jenny shook her head, 'that's enough negativity and conspiracy for one day. We can't do anything about what happened to Ruben, but we can try and prevent it from happening again.

'And stop fretting about Jen Si, if anyone can take care of himself, it's him – trust me. Now back to the library; then it's home for you lot and a *long* overdue holiday for me!'

The final goodbyes were hard.

Sam had not realised how bad the prospect of not seeing his friends for a year would seem, but neither did he relish the idea of returning

'I could create a group chat for us?' he suggested, looking forward to the thought of finally getting his phone back.

'Yes!' Veronique agreed. 'Though chatting and you...' she gave Fedor a meaningful dig in the ribs.

'I don't have a phone, otherwise I'd give it a go,' he grunted. 'Besides, it's Turtle and Turtle Junior who are the least likely to keep in touch.'

'YCMU!' the pair declared in unison.

'Barely an hour together and they couldn't be more alike!' Sam laughed.

Joe and the freshly hatched Turtle, resplendent in his new shiny green paint job, exchanged a startled look.

Sam surveyed the library. 'You've certainly got your work cut out for you.'

Veronique turned to Jenny. 'You'll keep us posted about Jen Si, and let us know when they find him?'

Jenny nodded. 'Oh, and that reminds me, I have presents for you.' She fished in her pocket and pulled out four badges. 'Took some doing, but Nessie found it. It's your sigil: the Stone Thieves.'

'Oh, wow!' Veronique examined the ornate emblem. 'Are those—?'

'The Krusa!' Joe cut her off. 'Yes! Wait, does that mean the first Cadre *stole* the Krusa? But from whom?'

Jenny smiled mysteriously. 'Come back next year and maybe I'll tell you. Now, hugs, kisses and handshakes – I'm late for a date in Cabo.'

'But—' Joe protested.

'No more questions!'

Chapter 32

Sam flopped on his bed, tired enough to sleep for a month. He couldn't begin to process the events of the summer, let alone contemplate returning next year. It had been an incredible journey, both physically and emotionally, and despite the way it had ended, he felt stronger for surviving it.

There were many things that still worried him, but he now felt like he belonged to something. He was actually one of The Few, he'd joined The Honourable Order of Inventors and was part of a Cadre, with a real purpose. And, he and his family had escaped banishment. Well, so far, at any rate.

For the first time since losing Sophie, Sam didn't feel quite so alone. He rubbed his scar and wondered what she would have made of all this. Would they have done it together if she were here?

A sliver of white caught the corner of his eye. Lids drooping, he raised his head off the pillow and saw the travel-worn envelope gathering dust on his bedside table. 'Who the hell would be *writing* to me?' he mumbled, reaching out for it.

Rolling onto his back, Sam examined the neatly addressed envelope before breaking the seal.

"My Dear Sam,

It feels so strange writing to you after all this time. There are so many things I want to say. Things that, with the benefit of hindsight, I now understand were never your fault, but none of that would make sense to you now.

In a few days' time, we're going to begin the most fantastic adventure – the first of so many – but before then, I need to tell you something very important and our futures depend on you believing me.

He is alive!"

'What the—?' Sam stopped and picked up the envelope. The postmark was months old. He swore and continued reading…

* * *

Danica Keller took a sip of red wine, then switched off the light and closed the door on her exhibit, leaving Jen Si in the dark with the others.

Back in her office, she settled into an armchair, her gaze falling on the scroll on the table. The back of her stiletto slipped from her heel and she rolled a stiff ankle.

'Your health, Mr D'Angelo!' she raised her glass and toasted her absent and unwilling accomplice. Her final piece on the board had toppled the proverbial king, for he had skilfully managed to create a big enough distraction to allow them to slip in and get what they needed – almost, without incident. A father would do anything to keep his family safe, betray even his friends. *Family was a weakness*, she thought of her brother, then looked at the picture of her green-eyed daughter on the table.

Danica set down her empty glass. Her attention returned to the scroll. Leaning forward, she picked at the ancient seal and carefully unfurled the brittle manuscript.

She was only one step away from finding Herredrion's bloody book.

The moon had long slipped from the heavens and the rosy tinge of dawn caressed the horizon before she had finished her study. Bleary-eyed and stiff-backed, Danica sat straight in her chair. Her mind was raw and the wine bottle was empty.

Rubbing her eyes, she padded around the study, rolling her neck and shoulders. She shook herself, wiggled her fingers and cleared her throat.

It took two full minutes of tongue-twisting to work through the Sumerian dialect. Her rendition was far from flawless, but as the last word left her lips, Danica felt a surge of pride. Then she waited in silence.

Nothing.

She looked around the room, not sure what exactly to expect, but aware that something should have happened.

Still nothing.

The shrill ring of her mobile phone broke the silence.

Danica swore. A bitter surge of disappointment welled up in her, as she fumbled in her bag.

It was a withheld number.

With a final, cathartic curse, she lifted the phone to her ear and barked at the caller. 'Yes?'

'Not the reception I was expecting,' a gravelly voice chastised her.

'You'll have to live with the disappointment. What do you want?'

'Is that your first question?'

Danica opened her mouth, ready to spit acid, then caught sight of the scroll and stopped herself.

'That's right,' the voice confirmed her unspoken thought.

'This isn't what I was expecting.'

'What did you expect? A lamp? A puff of blue smoke?' the voice laughed, but there was no humour in the hollow sound. 'One must move with the times, Danica.' The emphasis on her name made her skin crawl.

'So how does this work? Do I get three—?'

'Wishes? No. This is no fairy tale. You get answers and only one is free.'

'Just one?'

'Only one is free.'

'One will be enough.'

'We shall see. What is your question?'

'How specific do I need to be?'

'There will be no tricks. Ask.'

'Where is Herredrion's Book?'

It all came down to this one question.

'The Book resides with its master.' The voice was factual and firm.

Danica swore. 'What kind of flaky answer is that?'

'It is the answer to your question.' The response was unemotional.

Danica stood up, livid. She could not believe this! After all this time and effort all she had uncovered was this pathetic ambiguity.

She paced the room, mulling it over. *Its master must be Herredrion. And if the Book is with him, then it must be buried, so,* 'where is Herredrion's grave?' she whispered.

'Is that your next question?'

Danica had not realised she'd spoken aloud. 'I thought I only got one question?'

'Only one comes without a price.'

She had come too far to fail now. The bit was between her teeth. Besides, whatever the price, Harbinger was far from without means.

'Name your price.'

The was another long silence.

'Well?' she demanded.

The response was unexpected.

'*What?*' she breathed, incredulous.

The voice repeated its terms.

'How long?'

Her eyes widened. 'That's a heavy price.'

'Then be satisfied with the answer you have.'

Danica's mind raced. 'Fine.' The word tumbled out.

'You accept my price?'

'Yes.'

'Then we have an accord. Ask your question.'

'Where is Herredrion buried?'

Again, there was agonising silence before the information came. 'Herredrion is not buried.'

'*WHAT?*' Danica hurled the phone into the folds of the heavy curtains and screamed. Stalking across the carpet, she whipped the drapes back and forth until she found the handset.

'No chance!' she muttered, picking it up and holding it to her ear without noticing that the screen was dead.

'No way!' she spat into the handset. 'You tricked me.'

'I did no such thing. You have the answer to your question. You will pay my price.'

'You tricked me. Your answer is too vague. For all I know, he was cremated or exposed and eaten by worms. It's too insubstantial, so I do not agree to your terms!'

Silence.

'I will give you one more question,' the voice offered. 'But only if you abide by the terms we agreed.'

'You want the same again?' she scoffed.

'The price remains the same, however you shall be granted two questions, not one.'

Every ounce of her common sense told her to hang up. But she was so close. 'I want a proper answer.' She could not believe the words were coming from her mouth. 'I'm going to ask a long, complicated question and I want a long, complicated answer. Do you understand me?'

'I do.'

Danica took a breath. She would not be beaten by this trickster; she would follow it logically. 'You said the book is with its master. Herredrion is master of the book, so therefore it is with him. Yet you also said he is not buried. If his physical remains are not located anywhere, then how can that be true, how can it be with its master – where is the *bloody book*?'

There was no silence this time. The answer came instantly. It did not, however, come from her phone, but as a whisper from a malevolent presence behind her.

'It's simple, *Danica*.' The Djinn's breath was as cold as it was foul. 'Herredrion is not dead.'

As the sun set, two men sat in the ruins of a long-forgotten city.

'Well?'

'They all survived,' Baid reported.

'I should hope so,' the man beside him snorted. 'They're the grandchildren of the Council and the future leaders of this merry little enterprise. Though, that may well change when Giuseppe finds out that Jasper is the reason his father's dead,' he paused.

'We may have underestimated D'Angelo's ambition. If the children had failed, their entire families would have been expelled, including their grandparents. No more Council and a tempting power vacuum...

'But you know I wasn't referring to our new Stone Thieves.'

Baid ignored the hint. 'I still don't understand why you wanted the Antheridium crystal placed in the Van Sandt boy'

'You don't understand why I'd want to create someone who doesn't age? Someone with super healing abilities that may finally be capable of removing the cerebral block?'

Baid's eyes widened. 'Oh.'

The man smiled. 'Oh, indeed.

'Now, back to my original question.'

'I wasn't able to stop Harbinger.' The words were bile in his mouth. Baid seldom failed, and wasn't used to reporting it. 'Project Apostle was a success.'

'So, they've created a synthetic atom?' his companion tried not to sound impressed.

'Yes. The Adam atom.'

A faint smile creased the man's face. 'Cute.' He drummed his fingers. 'And the gypsy? Sorry, she prefers "Madame Carla", doesn't she?'

'Vanished. Both her and Aura. They don't have them. The Door is secure though, Harbinger didn't use it.'

'I'll bet Lilliantha really hates that two of her precious Symbionts jumped ship.'

The man chewed his lip briefly. 'And the Antimatter device?'

Baid suppressed a sigh, finding the inquisition tiresome. 'The plans are safe, but I don't understand why we can't destroy them.'

The man shrugged. 'You never know when they may come in handy.'

Baid raised an eyebrow. 'When would a doomsday device ever come in handy?'

'There are more things in heaven and earth—'

'Please don't quote Shakespeare at me.' Baid protested. 'You know full well how much I disliked that pompous little toad.'

'Yes,' Baid's companion chuckled at the memory, 'he did promise to "eviscerate you in fiction", didn't he? And what of the scroll, does Keller have it?'

This was relentless and Baid had been dreading it. He tried not to clench his fist. 'Despite your best efforts to hide it and suppress all knowledge of its existence...' the man continued.

A long silence followed before he nodded.

'Excellent!'

Baid looked up. 'I don't understand. I've spent hundreds of years and killed countless people to stop anyone getting their hands on that damned scroll, and you think this is excellent?'

The man spread his hands. 'What's the easiest way to destroy thine enemy, Al'Ubaid?'

Baid shrugged. He hated that name.

'Give them the means to destroy themselves.'

Baid shook his head. 'You mean this was all a ruse? You intended for them to steal the scroll all along?'

'Yes. The forbidden is most tempting, is it not?'

'For nine *hundred* years?' Even by his standards, that was a long time.

'Time is of no importance, my young friend.' Herredrion's eyes glinted in the ruddy twilight. 'The result is all that matters. So, unless someone got their grubby hands on the plans for Wren's blasted Time Box – wherever the hell he hid them – and built it, everything will finally unfold according to plan...'

Epilogue

THE STORY WILL CONTINUE
IN BOOK TWO OF
THE FABULOUS ARRANGEMENT
OF ATOMS

"THE TRICKY DEVILS AND THE
ADAM ATOM"

ACKNOWLEDGEMENTS

Many wonderful people made this book possible. The QR code below will take you to an online acknowledgement which allows me to credit and provide links to the fabulous artists who have contributed their time and patience to bringing my world to life.

Acknowledgements

Printed in Poland
by Amazon Fulfillment
Poland Sp. z o.o., Wrocław
07 April 2023

872b30df-a253-4053-a98c-bcc3089d5db1R01